THE
MISSING SHADE
OF BLUE

Jennie Erdal

ABACUS

First published in Great Britain in 2012 by Little, Brown
This paperback edition published in 2013 by Abacus

A CIP catalogue record for this book
is available from the British Library.

ISBN 978-0-349-00026-8

Typeset in Perpetua by M Rules
Printed and bound in Great Britain by
Clays Ltd, St Ives plc

Papers used by Abacus are from well-managed forests
and other responsible sources.

MIX
Paper from
responsible sources
FSC® C104740

Abacus
An imprint of
Little, Brown Book Group
100 Victoria Embankment
London EC4Y 0DY

An Hachette UK Company
www.hachette.co.uk

www.littlebrown.co.uk

In memory of Wilkie Crawford, 2006–2007
And for his parents

Suppose therefore a person to have enjoyed his sight for thirty years, and to have become perfectly well acquainted with colours of all kinds, excepting one particular shade of blue, for instance, which it never has been his fortune to meet with. Let all the different shades of that colour, except that single one, be placed before him, descending gradually from the deepest to the lightest; it is plain, that he will perceive a blank, where that shade is wanting, and will be sensible, that there is a greater distance in that place betwixt the contiguous colours, than in any other. Now I ask, whether it is possible for him, from his own imagination, to supply this deficiency, and raise up to himself the idea of that particular shade, though it had never been conveyed to him by his senses?

David Hume, *A Treatise of Human Nature*

And the abyss? The abyss?
The abyss you can't miss:
It's right where you are —
A step down the stair.

Theodore Roethke, 'The Abyss'

I

At the start, there was nothing to indicate that I would become involved in their lives as I did, so deeply, so irrevocably. Up till then I had lacked the talent for friendship. Later I would sometimes wonder what it was about the Sandersons that made the difference, what it was that sucked me in and held me there, even through the difficult times.

The friendship itself was unlooked for. The reason I had gone to Edinburgh was to work. And the reason behind that – behind everything, more or less – was my father. I knew that as long as I drew breath I would feel bound up with him.

One way and another most of my life has been spent in books, reading other people's stories, living vicariously through characters that don't exist. Fiction feels safe – you know where you are with it. In a black-and-white film, for example, you can rely on the shape of things: there is the shrill ring of a telephone, or a knock at the door, and you can happily sink back into your seat knowing that the story has *begun*. That's the way it is with films. Books too. Every beginning an artifice. But that thing we call real life is actually a continuum, awkward and unedited. And with your own story it's hard to know where to start, or even what to tell.

*

When Sanderson first mentioned to me that his wife was seeing someone, we were driving through the Scottish Borders on our way once more to spend the day fishing. It was a Saturday morning, the first in October, and the journey to the river was already quite familiar. The bracken on the hills had turned brown, and I remember thinking as we whooshed past that the berries in the hedgerows looked like splatters of blood. I had been in Edinburgh for just over a month, but already it felt as if Sanderson was an old friend. Whenever I thought of this, it seemed like a small miracle. Sanderson had his eyes fixed on the road ahead. He hardly spoke at all when he was fishing, but a good deal of what he thought about the world, or chose to reveal about himself, was discharged at the wheel of his elderly Renault.

To begin with, I misunderstood what he meant by 'seeing someone'. Not because I am French, or because the phrase was new to me, but because I took the context to be medical rather than extramarital. Sanderson had once or twice hinted that his wife's mental state was not entirely sound. And just the day before, my own suspicions had also been aroused. 'Seeing someone' made me think at first that his wife must have been persuaded to seek professional help for her problems. With Sanderson it was unusual to take something the wrong way. He was generally quite precise, and his meaning seldom in doubt – partly because he used his whole body to communicate. But when he said: 'My wife is seeing someone, Eddie,' he was rigid in his seat and his poor disfigured hands were firmly attached to the steering wheel. Also, there was no intimation – as there might have been if he had prefaced the words with an *I suspect* or even an *I believe* – of the significance of the sentence, or indeed the pain and loss of self that were to come.

'Seeing someone?' I repeated. 'You mean a doctor?'

'No, Eddie, no,' said Sanderson, making a strange sound halfway between chuckling and gagging. 'Another man, that's who.' After which for a minute or so there was silence, which

I didn't try to fill, sensing that he would say more when he was ready.

When I look back, this seems to mark the beginning, though in time I came to understand that there must have been other beginnings before this one.

2

I arrived in Edinburgh on the last day of August. Everyone has heard unfavourable accounts of summer in Scotland, but it was easy to doubt them that day. The heat I had left behind in Paris was the kind that choked you and made you feel only half alive, but on that Monday in August the city that was to be my temporary home stretched out gloriously beneath a vast blue sky. When I got off the airport bus in the centre of town, there was a fresh breeze that stroked the skin and filled me with a sense of possibility. It was one of those rare moments when the outer physical world seemed perfectly in tune with the inner self. Edinburgh was conspicuously a city *en fête*: the streets were filled with jugglers and men on stilts, and every surface seemed to have a poster on it, each promising a different cultural thrill – Japanese drumming, comic opera, Russian ballet, reduced Shakespeare (whatever that was). Already it felt good to be there.

I was to spend six months in Scotland, working on eighteenth-century manuscripts held in the National Library. A publisher in Paris had recently signed me up to do a French edition of the essays of David Hume. The idea of going to Edinburgh to work on Hume had been forming in my mind for years, and now that it was finally happening, I felt quite light-headed with anticipation. I would be able to consult the original manuscripts in the library where David Hume himself had once been the curator, and in fanciful moments I liked to think that Hume's spirit would infuse the project. The decision to go to Edinburgh also contained an element of personal pilgrimage. Quite apart from being the city in which Hume had lived and died, it was also where my own father had studied.

The preceding months had been taken up with sorting out the practicalities: establishing that the National Library in Edinburgh would make Hume's manuscripts available to me, applying to various cultural foundations for extra funding, writing to Edinburgh University to request an honorary fellowship in the philosophy department – this way I would have access to libraries and staff facilities. Everything had fallen into place quickly and smoothly. It remained only to let out my apartment in Paris and fix up accommodation in Edinburgh. Here again the university helped out, putting me in touch with an academic called Martin Blandford, with whom I was lucky enough to do a straight swap. He wanted to spend his sabbatical leave at the Sorbonne writing a book on Jean-Paul Sartre. The neatness of this arrangement – Sartre in exchange for Hume – was a delight, there being no doubt in my mind as to who had got the better deal.

Martin Blandford's place in Edinburgh turned out to be in a charming little terrace, horseshoe-shaped, just off Calton Hill to the east of the city centre. The taxi driver had said: 'Ah, that'll be a mews cottage,' and in my mental lexicon I saw it as 'muse cottage' – surely just the thing for a literary adventure. Later, when I came to know the city, I discovered lots of mews, built in the early nineteenth century to complement the grand houses nearby. The ground floors had been used for stabling horses, with the grooms and coachmen sleeping upstairs. As far as I knew there was no equivalent of a mews cottage in Paris – at least none that I'd seen. Which made me wonder where all the French horses and coachmen had spent their nights.

My mews – my *muse* – suited me perfectly, beyond anything I could have imagined in the middle of a city. Like a doll's house, it was one of a set of about a dozen, in a cobbled courtyard with a raised pear-shaped garden full of trees and shrubs in the centre. A secluded little hideaway, like a miniature village, that seemed to have no obvious connection with the rest of the city, it could have been a child's drawing of a street, quaint and lop-sided with the perspective all askew. The little house itself was covered in ivy, and to the right of the door was a built-in garage (the old stable), painted blue. Inside, there was a hallway with a narrow table, with the rest of the ground floor given over to an open-plan kitchen and dining room. Off the kitchen there was a small utility room with a washing machine and dryer, and, bizarrely, a bicycle hanging from a hook on the ceiling. Another door, presumably connecting with the garage, was firmly locked. Upstairs there was a sitting room, a double bedroom and a small study with a table and two empty bookcases – ideal for my purpose. In the corner of the sitting room a colourful batik cloth was draped over something large and square. I half expected to discover a sleeping bird in a cage, but no, it was a television set, hidden from view like piano legs in Victorian England. The room was sparsely furnished, and the walls were bare, apart from a solitary painting. It seemed to have been arranged for someone who might be passing through rather than staying for half a year. Blandford had been very consider-ate. Everything smelled fresh and clean, and there were even cut flowers in a tall vase on the hall table. There was a softness to the colours, a palette that people sometimes call feminine. Almost certainly gay, I decided, though it was quite possible that Blandford would be making the same assumption about me, based on my own carefully arranged apartment in Paris. In truth I knew nothing of Blandford's circumstances, but everything pointed to his living alone and liking order: no domestic clut-ter, no children's toys, no evidence of the messiness of ordinary living, no ghastly ornaments or *objets*, just here and there one or two tasteful ceramic bowls, and a single black-and-white photograph of a wedding couple, presumably his parents. Apart from the photograph and a few reference books on a shelf, the rooms were quite impersonal. I liked that. Personal could be so distracting, even disturbing. My preference was for something like a motel room, a place it would be easy to move into, and just as easy to disappear from overnight without leaving any mark. I looked round at my new surroundings and could hardly believe my luck. This was a place that held out the possibility of contentment.

On the table next to the flowers, Blandford had left a note.

Dear Edgar,

Welcome to Edinburgh. I trust you will find everything in order here. There is a spare set of keys at No 16 in case you lock yourself out, and a set of explanatory 'House Notes' in the drawer of the hall table. You are welcome to use my bicycle – it's hanging in the utility room. The garage contains my own personal effects and is therefore locked. Mrs Bannerman (cleaner) comes every Tuesday at 8.30 am for two hours. You don't have to be here – she has her own key – but you should leave £15 in cash on the hall table each week.

With best wishes for a productive few months.

Yours sincerely,

Martin Blandford

PS I've left an invitation that might interest you. Please feel free to go in my place.

The invitation – for later that day as it happened – was to a lecture entitled 'The Humanity of Hume', followed by a reception. I had planned to unpack and settle into my new lodgings, but this sounded too interesting to miss. The unpacking could wait.

With hindsight, this was perhaps the first of several decisions that were out of character. Edinburgh was already having a liberating effect.

The lecture was to take place in the David Hume Tower – evidently Hume was something of an industry in these parts. The printed card had the letters SUPA at the top, and in brackets underneath *Scottish Universities Philosophical Association*. Oddly enough, there was another card just next to it with a similar acronym in bold – a notification from SEPA, the Scottish Environmental Protection Agency, advising that a test of the water supply would be carried out during the following week. SUPA and SEPA – I spoke the strange new words aloud, trying them out for size.

3

I had imagined that a building bearing the name David Hume Tower would be an elegant eighteenth-century affair, with an ornate roof and a grand entrance, something like the Château de Bagatelle in Paris. But no, it was a huge block of concrete, whose ugliness made me gasp. Of course, there are tower blocks like it in any metropolis, even in complacently beautiful cities like Munich, but generally they are hidden away on the outskirts, housing the disadvantaged high above ground level and protecting the civic conscience. By contrast, the David Hume Tower seemed like a terrible blemish in the heart of Edinburgh, and brazen with it.

The lecture theatre was full. Noisy chatter suddenly gave way to an expectant hush as two characters appeared on stage and took up their positions side by side in throne-like chairs. One was the guest lecturer, a man called Whitebrook, Professor of Philosophy at the University of Cambridge. The other, dressed in colourful robes, was a grand-looking specimen who got to his feet and proceeded to list in a dreary monotone the achievements of the visiting speaker: long distinguished career, international reputation, impressive list of publications, and so on. After a polite ripple of applause Professor Whitebrook stood up and moved to the lectern, taking a few moments for the careful placement of his spectacles, which were attached to a lanyard round his neck. He cut an impressive figure: tall, boyish-looking despite a thick crust of white hair, his face like geometry, all regular lines and angles, and under his voluminous gown an ivory waistcoat and yellow bow tie.

He began his lecture by placing Hume in the context of eighteenth-century Scotland, a time of Calvinist faith and other brands of revealed religion, he explained, going on to detail the strength of the attacks on the philosopher in his own lifetime. These attacks, said the professor, came mostly from prominent theologians, although later, when Hume began to question the basis of natural religion too, fellow philosophers joined battle. According to Whitebrook Hume had not set out with the intention of being an unbeliever. Rather he had followed the arguments for religion and found them wanting. He was a man primarily interested in explaining our place in the world so that we might live better lives; and the art of living well, he soon discovered, did not sit happily with clinging on to illusions. In Hume's view the world was painfully disturbed by what he called *superstition* and *enthusiasms*, and he set about trying to dispel them with characteristic elegance and humour. The religious arguments given such prominence over the centuries had been dismantled one by one, to the fury of their adherents. 'And their fury was heightened,' said Whitebrook, 'by the fact that Hume seemed to be laughing at them, albeit in his good-natured way. It did not seem to have occurred to them that the reason he was laughing at the arguments was that they were inherently risible.'

Whitebrook spoke with an air of innate authority, his tone beautifully modulated, his delivery perfectly timed. His voice was rich and creamy, with a crust to it, like a perfect crème brûlée. From his body movements I fancied I could visualise the full range of punctuation of his text: a slight lift of the eyebrows for a comma, higher still for a semi-colon, and a bowing of the head for anything more substantial, like a full stop or a colon. Every so often he gave a furtive look to the side of the stage, as if expecting someone to appear from the wings, and when he raised his arms to make a point, the folds of his gown rose with him, giving him the appearance of a bird of prey about to swoop on its next meal. I pictured him as a peregrine falcon on account of his white breast (waistcoat) and yellow beak (bow tie), together with the mass of black plumage (academic gown).

It is fatal to have these thoughts in lectures. Once you allow them even a tiny space in your mind, they can quickly get out of control. You start – as I did then – seeing everyone around you as a different kind of bird, and before you know it several minutes of fanciful frivolity have passed, during which you haven't taken in a word of the lecture. As soon as I got back to concentrating on Whitebrook, however, the rewards were huge. He spoke with such good sense and clarity that it was almost as if some of David Hume's own qualities had rubbed off on him. The dangers involved in criticising religion in the eighteenth century were very great, he told his audience, so much so that Hume had been forced to use sophisticated rhetorical devices to disguise his most extreme scepticism. Textual examples of these were beamed up on overhead slides, each one neatly decoded by the professor, who paused every now and then to salute Hume's courage and ingenuity. This great man, he said, had ascribed the origin of religious belief to 'the incessant hopes and fears, which actuate the human mind'. Whitebrook paused for a moment, and after removing his spectacles and fixing his gaze at the back of the hall, he ended with a sombre reminder that although God had been pronounced dead many times in the intervening two hundred and fifty years or so, these hopes and fears were still alive and more pernicious than ever.

The reception afterwards was held in a smallish room off the lecture theatre with no natural light. Inside there were about thirty or forty people, most of whom I judged to be academics.

Clutching a glass of red wine (cool and rather too acidic), I hung back near the doorway, anticipating a need to escape. Large groups of people make me uneasy, unless they happen to be on the streets of Paris or on the metro or at the market, where there is rarely any obligation to interact. (I put this down to being an only child – a convenient explanation for almost every-thing problematic in adult life.) The company in the room divided into listeners and talkers – the ratio was probably about five to one. It was noticeable that the talkers seemed to be enjoying themselves more than the listeners. I could make out only the odd word, usually when it was italicised, as in derision or disbelief perhaps, but it was impossible to make sense of the connecting passages. Loud babble in English sounds very dif-ferent from loud babble in French. In French, you can still tell it's a language, that people are communicating in meaningful sentences and using the full tonal range. But here on the ground floor of the tower block, the homogenised sound being bounced off the low ceiling seemed more animal than human, like cattle being crammed in a truck on their way to the slaughterhouse.

After a short while, someone whose name I failed to catch tapped me on the arm and ushered me into a small circle of about six people, all men, philosophy teachers at the university. As a student I had come across only individual philosophers, and never socially. Was there perhaps a collective noun for philoso-phers? I made a mental note to look it up. During my abiding love affair with the English language I had once become side-tracked into the fascinating array of collective nouns – *a pontificality of prelates*, *a chaos of children*, and so on. Based on the group of people before me, I decided it would have to be *a pom-posity of philosophers*. They competed openly with one another, keen to talk, loath to listen. Another distinctive feature was their curious eagerness, the moment I was introduced, to demon-strate a familiarity with French. Before long the air was thick with *de rigueurs* and *billets-doux* and even *bien-pensants*. This surely couldn't be normal. At least, it was hard to imagine that this was how they usually spoke amongst themselves. One man with a lofty look kept saying *au contraire* every few seconds, just dropping those two words into the conversation, ostensibly in response to whatever had just been said, but inanely all the same. Another – again I think he meant well – offered to put me in touch with some French people he knew. I thanked him warmly, desperate not to commit myself to anything. You can never be too careful in this sort of situation. Yet another, a round-faced man with a bulbous nose, raised his glass to the assembled company and exclaimed: '*Après moi le déluge!*' What on earth was wrong with everyone? The most charitable diagnosis was nervousness, or muddled kindness perhaps, but as soon as it was decent to do so, I gave a must-get-away smile and made for the exit.

Which was where I met Sanderson, who was also on the point of leaving. He was a man of about sixty, I guessed, slightly dishevelled, with a large head and a solid face that looked as if it could have been cut from lumps of iron and hammered into shape by a blacksmith. His hair, thinning and slightly wild, hinted at W. B. Yeats in later life, and beneath his eyes there were pockets of rust that suggested bloodhound. He held out his hand – the skin was broken and flaking – and introduced himself. His handshake felt damp – not sweaty, but curiously oily. *Harry Sanderson*, he said, which made my spirits dive, Harry being one of the hardest names for a Frenchman to pronounce, even a Frenchman who feels quite at home in English. Everything about it is difficult – the aspirated aitch, the rolled 'r', the deceptive brevity and simplicity. Harry is the sort of name that squirms around in a French mouth and can end up sounding like the clearing of phlegm.

'Edgar Logan,' I said, shaking his hand and thinking how much more considerate my own name was for him.

'Ah, the man who's exporting Hume across the Channel,' he said.

It could have been an unfriendly remark, but the inflection was warm and open. Even so it's always unsettling to learn that you exist in the mind of strangers, especially if you're used to anonymity. Noticing my surprise, he explained that he taught philosophy at the university and had seen my application for honorary membership of the department.

'Does everyone call you Edgar?' he asked. His voice was Scottish, fresh and crisp with a touch of gravel. It reminded me of my father's.

'Yes, except for my father. He always called me Eddie.'

'Well,' he said, taking a pipe from his pocket and tapping it against his shoe, 'if you don't mind I'll call you Eddie too.'

'Fine,' I said, seeing the chance of making a deal. 'You call me Eddie – I'll call you Sanderson. I'm not sure I can manage Harry.'

And so began a conversation that would continue for several months and change us both.

4

As we walked across George Square, Sanderson stopped, turned round and nodded towards the building we had just left. 'What do you think of our monument to Scotland's greatest philosopher?' He was filling a pipe, tamping down the tobacco with his thumb.

'Well, it was a bit of a shock.' I smiled, not wishing to offend someone I had only just met.

'Don't hold back,' he said. 'It's one of the finest examples of architectural megalomania around. Cultural vandalism, Sixties-style. We lead the world in it.'

He turned out of the wind to light up, a lengthy process involving several matches and expletives, during which he asked through teeth that gripped his pipe what I thought of the lecture and if I had enjoyed the reception. It was so unusual for me to be asked my opinion about anything that if ever it happened my tongue would usually tie itself in knots. But I felt oddly relaxed with Sanderson, perhaps because he had not been part of the awkward group of academics. I told him how much I had enjoyed the lecture, how I was looking forward to the rest in the series, how I wished there had been lectures like it in my student days. As for the reception – well, I wasn't much good in company, especially a room full of philosophers.

'Ah, philosophers,' said Sanderson, looking into the middle distance. 'Well, they're all pretty much up themselves.'

'Up themselves?'

'You know, up their own arses. Their own fundaments.'

'Oh, I see,' I said, not seeing anything at all, except for a faint twinkle in his eye.

'It comes from all that navel-gazing.'

I waited for him to elaborate, but he didn't. We walked on in silence for a bit. Then, as if a new idea had just occurred to him, he said:

'An unhappy breed. Yes, that's what they are!'

'Is it perhaps the study of philosophy that makes them unhappy, do you think?' I surprised myself with this question.

'Well, that *is* an interesting point,' said Sanderson. His eyes were liquid black and swam brightly above the rust pools. 'Almost worthy of its own philosophical inquiry in fact. Does philosophy attract unhappy people, or is it that there is something in the nature of philosophical engagement that leads to unhappiness?'

It was a matter he had never considered, he said, despite the fact that he had just written a whole book on the subject of happiness.

'And believe me, there's nothing that saps the spirit quite so much as writing about happiness.'

It must be one of those chicken-and-egg questions, he said, the point being to work out which came first. Like, say, pondering the prevalence of sexual deviation amongst the clergy. Did the seminaries actually *produce* sexual deviants, or did they merely provide a protective environment for those whose deviant nature was already well formed? His manner was playful and self-mocking, but with a certain edge. I wondered what it betokened. My guess was that he was a man ill at ease with himself.

I asked him about his book on happiness and when it would be published, but all he would say was: 'Soon, much too soon.'

'You've finished it?'

'Yes, I've finished it, and it's finished me.' He gave a rueful laugh and said he thought that happiness as it was commonly understood had very little to do with philosophy. It was all psychology. 'And it's a psychological fact, albeit a kind of conundrum, that thinking too much about happiness and how it might be achieved can grind you down.'

At eight o'clock the light was still excellent. The sun had just gone down but it had left an afterglow the colour of champagne. We walked together through the Old Town, over George IV Bridge, and down the Mound. When you meet a sixty-something-year-old for the first time, it's hard not to think of the huge hinterland, the colossal number of events and experiences that have gone into the making of the man you see next to you, in which you played no part and of which you have no understanding. This was the thought that was uppermost in my mind as, during that first exchange, we did what people do when they first meet: get the usual stuff out of the way – inconsequential matters, the things strangers say to one another.

After which Sanderson talked a little about his colleagues, from whom he seemed keen to distance himself. He had grown rather tired of philosophy, he said, and one of the effects of this had been to create a gulf between him and his fellow philosophers. Quite simply, they didn't animate him any more. He spoke in generalities – vague disappointments, frustrations, resentments – and his sentences had a curious weightlessness. His criticisms, however, though not cruel or explicit, were cumulatively damning, his manner of speaking an odd mixture of rushes and hesitations. It made me think of a jerky driver, unsure of the gear shifts, modifying a decisive move with a softening adverb or a slight shilly-shally, as if questioning his own judgement at the same time as underscoring it. His speech patterns suggested a man weighed down by life and with no prospect of deliverance. What he talked about seemed to confirm this. He was out of kilter with the modern world, he said. It was full of catastrophe and calamity – nothing new in that, of course, but to have everything made into media events, turned into entertainment and eagerly consumed like packaged meals – well, that was more than he could bear. 'TV programmes full of weeping interviews, pouring out emotion everywhere you look. Makes me feel like a relic from a more rational age.' Every so often he gave a self-deprecating laugh, as if he had just been taken unawares by his own foolishness.

At the foot of the Mound we stopped for a moment or two before going our separate ways. Sanderson said he lived 'over there', pointing vaguely to the northwest. I myself was heading east to Calton Hill. We shook hands again and were exchanging the usual niceties, when Sanderson, still gripping my hand in his, suddenly said: 'You know, if you're not doing anything, you could come and have a bite to eat. Meet my wife. She'd like that. We don't see many people these days.'

5

The flat was on the top floor of a four-storey Georgian terraced house in a quiet street in the New Town. It had a grand entrance with iron railings, up four stone steps and through a huge wooden door with a brass knocker. Inside it wasn't quite so grand, but the stairway was attractively curved and the stone treads worn away in the middle by two centuries of human traffic. Sanderson went ahead, lumbering wearily up the stairs. From behind I noticed his dirty scuffed shoes, worn at the heel. A man with dirty shoes, my father believed, is a man who has lost self-respect.

Inside the flat there was a warm cheerful aroma, fresh bread and asparagus perhaps, plus something I couldn't quite identify – mint possibly. There was certainly no trace of the cooking smells that give Scotland a bad name – the long-boiled vegetables, the deep-fried everything.

Sanderson's wife – a younger woman than I was expecting – appeared in the hallway. Her face was open and alert, eyes set wide apart. There must have been twenty years or more between her and her husband. She had a natural elegance – nothing to do with clothes or cosmetics. When she saw me she tilted her head to one side, slightly quizzical and with a half-smile, leaving everything about her to be guessed at. Her white trousers floated as she walked, giving her an ethereal quality, beautiful and unsettling. Sanderson did the introductions.

'Cary?' I repeated, thinking immediately of Cary Grant in *North by Northwest*. I must have watched it ten times or more.

'Actually, it's C-A-R-R-I-E,' she said, spelling it out in a way that suggested she was used to being asked. 'It rhymes with Harry.' Her voice was soft and lilting.

'It's a lovely name,' I said.

Sanderson told her he had invited me for supper – was that OK? Yes, of course it was, she said. The food was in the oven and it would be ready any minute. And in fact Alice had phoned to ask if she could drop something off – she would also be staying to supper. Sanderson didn't seem surprised to hear this, yet he had told me just a few minutes before that they didn't see many people.

We were in the main room now – the drawing-room they called it – which ran the whole breadth of the building and took light from both sides through large bay windows with wooden shutters folded to the side.

'On a clear day,' Sanderson said, 'you can look north over the rooftops and out across the water to Fife, and on the other side, through the windows at the back, you can see Arthur's Seat in all its glory.' He explained that they had taken the flat mainly for the light.

'The north light is important for an artist,' he said, nodding towards Carrie as he opened a bottle of wine. 'My wife has her studio across the hallway.'

Over drinks we talked mainly about Carrie's work. The drawing-room was filled with large paintings, all hanging from the picture rail beneath an elaborate cornice, some of them in gilt-edged frames, others on unframed canvases stretched over wood. There were several full-size portraits, mainly female nudes in various attitudes. At the time I knew hardly anything about painting, but these pictures exerted a strange pull on me.

They were unusually vivid – it was possible to sense the blood beneath the skin, the heartbeat behind the ribcage. The adjective that came to mind was *truthful*, normally a word best avoided and certainly not one I had ever considered in the context of painting. Nearly every square centimetre of the surface was filled with naked, ample flesh, not in the least stylised, but raw and blemished and natural. With a different painter the effect might have been crude, but these paintings came over as bold and celebratory. I viewed each one in turn, wishing I could say something clever or knowledgeable, something sophisticated that would suggest being at home with pictures of naked women. Instead I said: 'These are *very* good,' which was meant to be admiring, but in my own ears sounded feeble and patronising.

In the corner by the door there was a painting that stood out from the others – a portrait of a man, just the head, not the body. The features struck me at first as exaggerated: the eyes and nose and lips, taken singly, were fantastic specimens, but together they looked like a mistake, a face put together in a hurry. And yet it was an *interesting* face, the different features not quite blending, but the overall effect captivating. It held me there in a kind of wonderment. Curiously, I had a faint sense of *déjà vu*: the longer I studied the face the more familiar it seemed. Suddenly Carrie was at my side.

'I can't help feeling I've seen this face before,' I said.

'You have,' she smiled. 'It's Harry. He was younger then, mind you.'

Of course!' A slow inexorable blush.

'I used to paint him a lot in our early years together, but he doesn't let me now.' She described how satisfying it had been to do Harry's portrait because of what she called the 'strong lineaments'. She said it was *a sort of Cubist face*. 'You know, like one of those Picasso self-portraits.' Sanderson sat in an armchair on the other side of the room and gave a loud artificial cough, pretending to be offended. Carrie laughed.

'No, no,' she protested, 'Cubist is *good*,' and at that moment I felt sure I could hear love in her laughter. 'Better than Dadaist, for example. A Dada face would be completely random – it would have to abandon any recognisable aesthetic form.'

'Well, thank you,' said Sanderson, pouring himself another drink. 'It's good to know one has contributed to modern art in some small way.'

At first sight – in ways to do with outward appearance and charm – they had looked an improbable couple. But this brief exchange between them seemed to open a small window onto their marriage, and those first impressions were of good-humoured ducking and weaving, the sort of teasing I imagined could come only from a rock-firm base. Through the window, I liked what I saw, though as always in my case it was not anything I identified with, nor anything that could ever have been reflected in my own being. To me, looking in, the shape and contours of their relationship seemed to fold and bend in all the right places. But what did I know? I was no expert in marital pairing.

The entryphone buzzer sounded, and Carrie told Alice to come straight up. It was obvious, even before she spoke, that Alice was American – something to do with a kind of undefiled look and the gleam of her perfectly straight teeth. It turned out that she and her husband were the owners of a small gallery in the New Town. Several of Carrie's paintings had sold recently, and she had come to deliver a cheque. There was something theatrical about Alice, not just the heavy make-up – so thickly applied that she might have undergone some sort of embalming process – or the dress that could easily have come from a costume play, but the way she stood quite far back from everyone as she spoke, like an actress delivering her lines from upstage. She was also someone who held your attention, though it was hard to pin-point anything that was obviously fascinating about her. She simply gave off an air of composure that made you want to look at her.

As we took our places at the kitchen table, brief biographies were exchanged and we learned a little about each other. Sanderson and his wife had lived in Edinburgh for the whole of their marriage. Carrie, originally from the Hebrides, had studied art history and moral philosophy at the university. Which was where she first met Sanderson, one of her philosophy lecturers, although years had passed before they had got together, she said. Before graduating she had transferred to the College of Art, specialising in drawing and painting, and now she taught there one day a week, the rest of her working time divided between private commissions and experimenting with different things 'just for my own amusement really'. Alice declared this to be modesty in the extreme – Carrie was 'a huge talent', she said.

Meanwhile I enthused about Edinburgh – my accommodation in particular, how quiet it was and yet how near to the city centre. My hosts were evidently acquainted with Martin Blandford (he was a colleague of Sanderson's), and they also appeared to know the cottage. Carrie praised its charm and mentioned that if ever Martin acquired anything new, something for the kitchen perhaps or even a book, he always removed an article of roughly the same size and took it immediately to a charity shop. In this way clutter was avoided. 'He has learned how to be disciplined,' she said, stopping abruptly, as if she'd heard herself say too much. At which point I thought I saw the corners of Sanderson's mouth tighten.

Tell me more about your book on happiness, I said, but he would disclose nothing of its contents, only how it had come about. He claimed he had been dragooned into it by his head of department. 'That's all anyone cares about nowadays – getting a book out. Doesn't matter *what* you publish, or whether it's any good.' Publications were the single thing that mattered when it came to rating a university department – such a mistake. Five Star was the best rating, he said, just like a hotel, and during the last Research Assessment Exercise – RAE it was called – their department had been given only a Four. And without a star –

something the new head was determined to improve on. Before long his colleagues were falling over each other in their haste to produce books. Not works of careful scholarship – no, no, that would have taken far too long – but new editions of this or that, or an introduction to a reprint, dressed up with a few learned notes – anything at all just as long as it was between hard covers. All in pursuit of a star, just like at primary school. And so they busied themselves with writing more and more about less and less, he said. 'Do you remember the fly on the axle wheel in *Aesop's Fables*?' He jabbed the air with his pipe. '*See what dust do I create! See what dust do I create!* Well, my colleagues are all pretty much flies on the axle.'

Meanwhile he himself, unwilling to join the unseemly rush to print, had done nothing. Everyone else was furiously scribbling, but he stayed aloof. Eventually, during a difficult exchange with the head of department, he was told he was at risk of being deemed what was termed *Research-Inactive*. 'What a load of bollocks, I told him. What about Socrates? Had he been Research-Inactive? Presumably yes, since he never wrote – far less published – a single word.'

But the head followed it up with a letter, explaining the implications of being *Research-Inactive*. 'RIA he called it.' Sanderson pulled a face. 'Can you believe it? Like the bloody IRA, and just as dangerous!' He hadn't wanted to write a book just for the sake of it, he said. Why would he, why would *anyone*? But with another RAE looming he had no choice. So, what to write? SUP – the Scottish University Press – had started a series called *Philosophical Reflections*, each title on a different theme, and designed to appeal to a popular as well as a specialised readership. (I made a mental note to add SUP to SEPA and SUPA.) The series already included volumes on Religion, Death, Liberty, Virtue, Aesthetics, and so on. By the time Sanderson put himself forward for the series they had only Truth, Lust and Happiness left. 'I tried to get Lust or Truth, of course, but some other buggers got there first, and I was stuck with Happiness.'

24

After this prolonged tirade, an odd mixture of self-doubt and self-importance, he fell silent for a while. Wondering what to make of it all, I stole a glance at Carrie and Alice. But they were impassive. No doubt they had heard it all before, perhaps many times. It occurred to me that if I had met Sanderson in a novel he might have been difficult to like – slightly repellent, even. He wasn't a naturally sympathetic character, and there was no obvious reason to care about him or what happened to him. And yet I did. There was a curious off-centre attraction to him. And while his flaws were there for all to see, shouting the odds and drawing attention to themselves, the real man was surely in a place of deep concealment – this at least was my sense. Or perhaps it was something to do with the fault lines in myself, and recognising them in someone else. Whatever the reason I found myself wanting to stick with him, if only to discover what had caused him to be this way.

Carrie had cooked vegetarian food – as splendid and colourful a meal as you could ever lay eyes on. But Sanderson, for whatever reason, seemed to feel the need to make fun of it. He made a big deal of sharpening a knife, his arm movements exaggerated like semaphore, as if preparing to carve a wild boar, then feigning a struggle as he sliced into a nut roast. More than once he tried to catch my eye, as if the performance were purely for my benefit. I wasn't sure about the etiquette of conniving with one host against another. Best to concentrate on the food. There were stuffed peppers and several bowls of exotic salads and vegetables, all magnificent feats of peeling and grating, chopping and stuffing, and all quite un-French. Sanderson passed round the plates and, just as we all began to eat, he explained that until three years ago Carrie had been enthusiastic about meat.

'In days gone by my dear wife even eschewed the neat sanitised packages in the supermarket in favour of the local butcher's bloody carcasses.'

I noticed that Sanderson tended to say 'my wife' or 'my dear wife' instead of using Carrie's name. And he used a particular tone, close to a sneer – quite removed from his earlier good will. There was no way of telling what it signified. The internal workings of a marriage are never shown to an outsider. You just have to wonder and guess.

'Then,' continued Sanderson, pausing for dramatic effect, 'with the suddenness and fervour of a Damascene conversion she switched to greens and pulses.'

He had been drinking his wine quickly, and he took another gulp now. 'I didn't mind in the least,' he continued, his tone suggesting it wasn't possible for a man to be more reasonable. 'I felt it might give her an interest in life, something to talk about.'

'Hmmmm,' said Alice on cue. 'These peppers are so-oh sweet! Did you roast them with brown sugar?'

'Actually no. A dash of lime juice in the stuffing seems to bring out their natural sweetness . . . '

'Have you noticed?' Sanderson turned again to me. 'Exchanges between women about food can go on indefinitely. When I first observed this, I used to think that they couldn't really be talking *just* about food, the ingredients of recipes, the preparation, the method, and so on. Their conversation must be in some way encoded, I thought, a strange language designed to exclude men, intelligible only to women. But no!' He repeated the No several times, seeming to get stuck on it until, like an actor suddenly remembering his lines, he declared: 'You see, there really is no subtext, no hidden message. They are, quite simply, talking about food. Now, that is the *real* mystery.'

'But men do it too,' I said. 'In France anyway . . . all the chefs are men . . . more like gods, some of them.' Was I making things better or worse? I had no idea.

After a constrained silence Alice announced to no one in particular: 'I'm not sure I would want to cook vegetarian the whole time, mind you. It must be quite a palaver, quite an effort.' Alice's stage presence had the effect of giving a kind of make-believe quality to the evening – the rest of us had been hired by a casting agency to act out a scene.

'But that's the point,' said Carrie. 'It *should* be an effort, the more effort the better. With a bit of imagination we can eat really well on things that can be grown. And then we wouldn't need to kill things in order to eat.'

'Pleading and reproaching at the same time,' said Sanderson. 'This is my wife's speciality.'

The smell of danger began to mingle with the other smells. For a few moments there was no sound apart from the munch of collective mastication. As we slowly tamed the roughage into something manageable, it struck me that the effort of eating must be on a par with the difficulty of preparation. The food was delicious, yet a mysterious law seemed to apply: the more you ate, the more seemed to be left on your plate. How could this be?

Sanderson picked up his glass of red wine and drained it. 'Well, if cooking is all about effort, what about *you* going to the trouble to produce, say, osso bucco for your carnivore friends?' He looked straight at Carrie. No answer.

He was not yet done. He went on to describe how the vegetarian ethic had seeped into other areas of his wife's life. There was reflexology, a whole lot of new-age nonsense, and a worrying flirtation with Buddhism.

'Oh Harry, you make perfectly harmless things sound wicked,' said Alice, coming to the rescue.

'Well, I feel queasy in the presence of religion. As you well know.'

'It's not a religion,' said Carrie. Her neck was blotchy now, a little pink doily at her throat.

'So what is it?'

'It's about accepting the fact' – she picked her words slowly – 'that there is suffering in the world, and finding ways of coping with it.'

'But that's surely what religions do.' He gave a fiendish laugh.

'They're *designed* to help us cope. That's the whole point of religion. To dress things up. To make death bearable.'

'Well, what's wrong with that?'

'Huh!' Sanderson spluttered. 'What's *wrong* with that? Where would you like me to begin?'

Carrie gave an uneasy laugh. 'Harry, *please*. Why do you have to do this?'

It wasn't a real question, but it was enough make him break step. I wondered how many of their conversations started out promisingly, and ended badly. In the few moments of silence that followed, Carrie folded and refolded her napkin. Then she smiled at him forgivingly – he might have been a naughty child – while he pulled a face that could have been read as remorse.

6

A week or more later, when Sanderson took me fishing for the first time, I had reason to recall this conversation. While we sat having a sandwich by the loch, he told me how his wife had taken up meditation, about a year ago, he supposed – 'quite without warning, and without, well, seeming to be the type'. At first he thought it might be a phase, but it had lasted longer than a phase and shown no sign of stopping. When he had tried to express interest, she was defensive, mistaking curiosity for criticism. One day she asked him to try it with her, and he did. But he found it too intimate, too unnatural. Bordering on the deviant almost, he told me.

'Deviant?'

'Well, you know, not natural. Not normal.'

He had felt embarrassed, he said, not just for himself, but also for her. The sort of embarrassment you felt when people you cared about suddenly started behaving oddly. When he couldn't manage staring at the wall, Carrie said he should try concentrating on an image – something really hard, something impossible. Like *what*, he asked. She had told him to think of a wine bottle – narrow neck, wider body. Imagine filling it with water and putting a small fish inside, she said. Then you turned the bottle on its side and it became a sort of goldfish bowl. *And then what?* He had found this very trying. You feed the fish and the fish grows bigger, she said, until one day it is too big to be able to swim out of the neck of the bottle. This is *my wife*, he had told himself. With whom I live. I must try to understand her. 'Don't you *see*?' she said, making him feel like an imbecile failing to grasp the simplest concept. 'That's what you have to concentrate on! *The impossibility of getting the fish out.* Except you mustn't hold on to the idea that it's impossible. You have to try and think of a way of doing it, without breaking the bottle. Do you see now?' But Sanderson didn't see.

'No, I don't bloody see,' he had told her. 'I don't see how you could ever do it without breaking the bottle. And I also don't see why it would be a tragedy to break the bottle, rescue the fish and put it in a bowl or a tank, or whatever. And I really don't see why anyone would waste time on thinking about this sort of thing. How could it possibly *help*? What good could possibly come of it?'

She had told him then that it was pointless talking to him further, and they had left it at that.

In truth, Sanderson confessed, he had no real objection to Carrie's new enthusiasms. He had even hoped that they might turn out to be good for her, and good for their marriage. But he no longer thought this possible. While it was true that in their early years together there had been a smooth and honeyed period during which there was a sense of deepening and ripening – like the getting of wisdom, he said – it had been followed by a much longer period in which the days and the disappointments piled up, and there was the ominous sense of one difficult thing finished and another about to begin. And now, since she had become so strange to him, the lentils and brown rice approach had seeped into all the little cracks of their relationship. There was no blood and guts any more, it was all husks and coarse pulses and flatulence.

With sex, he said, the problem went deeper. I wasn't sure I

wanted to hear this, but equally I wasn't sure how to prevent it, since he was clearly intent on telling me. In any case, part of me wanted him to continue so that I could get a sense of who this man was, and why he was troubled. 'You lose confidence over the years, Eddie,' he said, shoving a pipe cleaner up the spout of his pipe, and twisting it round and round. 'Either that, or something external, something not connected with the sex, gets in the way.' The pipe cleaner emerged, sludge-brown. His voice was gentle now, not straining for effect. He could, he said, just about recall a time when the world was purified and rendered new by marital sex. Now he felt like a dog eating grass to make itself sick. 'Can't quite help it, can't quite not help it.'

By the time Sanderson told me this, a picture was beginning to emerge of a man whose psyche was precariously balanced, like the inner workings of a carriage clock. Left to himself, undisturbed, I imagined he would have managed to keep the various parts in some kind of harmony. But circumstances – whatever they were – seemed to have pressed in on him and threatened the balance.

Back on that first evening, however, there was no clue as to what lay behind Sanderson's rage and gloom – only that they were sometimes hard to tell apart. His tone was by turns embattled and resigned, and what he said seemed to conceal as much as it revealed. Sometimes he spoke like the professional philosopher he was, dropping words like empirical or epistemological into the pot, stabbing the air with his pipe as he challenged the premises of this or the validity of that, and with a facial expression that seemed to say: This is going to hurt me more than you. At other times, his tone was soft, almost tender, and at these times he cradled his pipe in his hand as if it were a tiny bird with a broken wing.

He drank heavily throughout the evening, and perhaps this explained why he did most of the talking. It was doubtful that he was enjoying himself, but he seemed unable to stop. Sometimes he glanced at Carrie as though he held her personally responsible for his disaffection. I wondered what Alice thought of him, but it was impossible to tell. She met his eyes only momentarily before lowering her own and gazing into her wine glass, which she nursed in her lap. Like a trained actor, she never let her mask slip.

Carrie was even more enigmatic. Perhaps because she said less, she gave less away. Was she embarrassed by her husband or merely resigned to his melancholy – if that indeed was what it was? Apart from the tell-tale blotchiness on her neck, she appeared serene, though her eyes hinted at past troubles and made me wonder about the life now being lived. Much of the time she seemed to be examining her hands, as if waiting for them to tell her some-thing. At one point she announced in a stage whisper, as if divulging a family secret: 'Harry never passes up the chance of revisiting his prejudices. He likes to keep them in good repair.' And she gave him an indulgent look, which served to break the tension. At other times, after Sanderson had discharged another broadside against the university, or the state of the nation, or something in between, she would turn to Alice and say: 'He doesn't mean it, you know.' And then, smiling at me: 'He really can't help himself.' But these asides were social fillers rather than real disclosures. Whatever was really going on, the exchanges between Carrie and Sanderson jerked about like a hotel lift, soar-ing and plummeting, his sour rants taking the conversation down to the boilers and rats in the basement, her valiant efforts lifting it back to the gallery and ladies' powder room.

Hindsight puts its own distorting lens on past events, but looking back on that first evening there was the sense of a story unfolding. It was not fully realised, just something glimpsed out of the corner of my eye, and enough to give an intimation of vague calamities to come.

I walked back to Calton Hill with the varied noises of the city at night becoming more distant. By the time I turned off the main road all I could hear was the sound of my own footsteps. Despite the stillness inside the cottage, or perhaps because of it, I had trouble sleeping that night. My close reading of fiction had taught me that nearly all marriages occupied strange territory. But it was more vivid and startling to see it with your own eyes, even though they were the eyes of a tourist – sampling everything, understanding almost nothing. Different snippets of the evening's conversation, interspersed with those odd French phrases from the drinks reception, and tossed around by an avalanche of acronyms – SUPA and SEPA, RAE and the IRA – all combined to make a hideous jumble in my head. I tried to sleep, but Carrie's face – with its slightly pained expression – kept appearing on the skin of my eyelids. I thought of my small apartment in the heart of the fifth arrondissement on the Left Bank, and wondered if Martin Blandford also lay awake.

7

Dinner with strangers, an interesting prelude to my stay in Scotland – it might easily have ended there without further contact. But instead two things happened, the first of which I helped bring about, the second of which followed from the first.

In the afternoon following my evening with the Sandersons, I sat in the North Reading Room on the first floor of the National Library of Scotland, my notebook open in front of me, pen poised to make it look as if important scholarship was in progress. I had just completed the rather lengthy registration process, acquired my reader's ticket and ordered up my first manuscript. According to the person at the desk, it would take about thirty minutes to arrive. During the wait my thoughts turned to the strangeness of being there at all, working alongside other people, something I hadn't done for twenty years or more.

The day had started badly. After a fitful sleep I had woken with a thick head – the result of too much wine. It had taken all morning to unpack, to set up my workspace in the way that I liked, to make a list of provisions for the cottage and, crucially, to devise a detailed plan of action for the task ahead. The two most important elements in my working life at that time were routine and self-discipline – everything else was secondary. At home in Paris the pattern was to spend the mornings, the time between breakfast and lunch, reading over the previous day's efforts. This was a vital part of my kind of work, a way of getting into the right gear. People who live other kinds of lives often imagine that a translation can be picked up and laid down again, like a piece of knitting – a few rows here and there, a couple of plain and a couple of purl, and goodness, just look how much you've done. But it isn't like that at all. At least not for me. If you put your translation aside even for a short while, it takes time to feel your way back into it, like coming to believe again after a temporary loss of faith.

In Edinburgh my routine would have to be just as stringent, the main difference being that it would be divided between home and library. It was also part of my plan to include David Hume's daily practice of rising early and walking before breakfast round Salisbury Crags – six kilometres over hilly ground. I greatly admired Hume's self-discipline and his working methods. Throughout his life he had studied in libraries, not just in Edinburgh, but also in the magnificent surroundings of the Jesuit College libraries in Reims and La Flêche in Anjou. My own preference was always to work completely alone and in silence, but the books I needed to consult were part of the National Library's 'special collections', which could not be borrowed or taken out of the building. I would have to get used to working in company.

The North Reading Room was the designated space in the library for consulting rare books and manuscripts. Its name held out the possibility of the clear north light that Sanderson had spoken of, but in fact there were no windows and so no natural light at all. It was hard not to feel disappointed. Artificial light was enervating. A notice on the wall explained that light levels had to be kept low in order to prevent the ink from fading on old manuscripts. This might have been a small price to pay in exchange for richly panelled walls, reading alcoves, and an oak beam or two, such as I had come to love during my trip to Oxford a year or two before. But the North Reading Room was definitely more functional than inspirational. Tall bookcases lined the walls and in the middle sat eight large desks, each with a little heap of white cotton gloves – the sort a French sommelier might wear to handle a Château Latour. Beneath the bookcases ran deep shelves containing an assortment of what looked like bedding: pillows, sheets, beanbags and thick wedges of grey foam in different shapes and sizes, as though the room might at any moment convert to a dormitory for avid scholars. The bedding, however, as I knew perfectly well, was for the support of the ancient tomes that came up from the vaults, carried like frail elderly invalids before being placed on beds of foam with soft pillows to protect their aged backs and weakened spines.

The smell of old books is the same in any country – dust mingled with must, plus the unmistakable imprint of past lives. As a child in my parents' bookshop, and later as a student, I had often inhaled this distinctive mix. It was one that had tagged along into my first proper job – stacking shelves in one of the research libraries at the Sorbonne. The post had not been advertised, nor formally applied for; after I dropped out of university it was simply 'found' for me, a polite way of saying that strings were pulled. In a fit of naïve optimism, I had enrolled at the Sorbonne to prepare for my *agrégation*, hoping to please my father and dreaming of one day becoming a philosopher as he himself had been. The dream lasted barely two years, and my abrupt exit was ignominious as well as unsettling.

It was the spring of 1980, and Jean-Paul Sartre had just died. Sartre had fallen a little out of favour at that time, certainly in the narrow Parisian and political sense. His brand of existentialism was beginning to be seen as an expression of his own psychology, little more than his personal emblem of pessimism.

Dying can change everything, however, and when death came to Sartre, fifty thousand people, myself included, took to the streets of Paris. It was the done thing to be *engagé* – committed to a cause – and the crowd walked solemnly behind his coffin to the Montparnasse cemetery. There was a huge delegation from the Sorbonne, thousands of students who saw it as an opportunity for a demonstration, for holding banners proclaiming *LA CAUSE DE SARTRE* or *JEAN-PAUL: LA CONSCIENCE DU MONDE*. I have long forgotten what we thought we were demonstrating about or against, unless it was death itself, but what I do recall, with needle-sharp clarity, is the feeling of intoxication that came from being part of that slow, sombre mass of people following the cortège. Philosophers, not poets or politicians, were the true oracles: they alone were capable of dealing in truth, of revealing the mystery of life. We had lost a genius, a towering intellect, a man of courage and conviction. Without him, how could we go on? How would we manage to live? No one actually said this, but you could feel it in the air. Those who marched were proud to be French, we knew we were taking part in something important, something that the world would watch and be changed by. It was heady stuff and I was defenceless against it.

After the funeral came the numbness that can follow an event of great emotion – you think everything should be different in some way, in order to take proper account of what has happened, to mark it in history. Yet within minutes everything is exactly the same. As soon as Sartre was lowered into the ground, normal life resumed. The crowds dispersed and disappeared into the metro stations, the traffic started flowing again, and the road sweepers set about removing all trace of anything momentous ever having taken place. For several hours, feeling quietly desperate, I walked the streets.

At home that evening, with the taste of the graveyard still in my mouth, there were lamb cutlets for dinner. Lacking any appetite, I moved the food around on my plate. Surely my father would sense my distress, without my having to say anything. But when the funeral was reported on the radio news, he scoffed and called Sartre a poseur and a hypocrite. 'Quite honestly,' he said, 'that man never did a day's real work in his life.' Worse than that, he said, Sartre had done nothing for his country during the war, and had been quite content under Vichy, profiting from the regime like the worst collaborator. 'And as for his so-called philosophy – it's no more than a licence for moral dereliction.'

8

The day after the funeral, during a logic lecture on the principles of the syllogism, my head throbbing from baffling examples of deduction and induction, ambiguities and fallacies, all of them seemingly a variation on the manhood and mortality of Socrates —

> *tous les hommes sont mortels*
> *Socrate est un homme,*
> *donc Socrate est mortel*

— I suddenly heard a terrible shouting. Which turned out to be my own voice. I have only the faintest recollection of being restrained by university stewards, who pinned me to the ground and called the police. Even that recollection may have come from other people's memories, feeding into my own. There was no way of telling. Evidently, I had rushed towards the professor, still busy writing his premises on the whiteboard, and grabbed him by the throat, yelling all the while: 'There is no truth! There is no truth!' This at least was how my friend Antoine reported it to me many weeks after the event.

*

Memory is a slippery customer. You never know if you can trust it. The Swiss psychologist Jean Piaget, who died just a few months after Sartre, preserved one crystalline memory from early childhood: a dramatic rescue by his devoted nanny from an attempted kidnapping. Piaget could describe the attacker in detail, he remembered the nanny being scratched on her face as she fought to defend her charge from abduction, and he even had a clear image of the policeman who eventually came to the rescue with his baton. In later life, however, the nanny confessed that none of it had actually happened. She had invented the entire kidnapping story (the scratches had been self-inflicted) to attract sympathy and attention. Yet all the while this 'memory', in all its colourful precision, stayed rooted in Piaget's mind.

Whenever I call up my own memories I try to keep Piaget's experience to the fore. Maybe it didn't happen that way, I tell myself, or maybe it didn't happen at all. And even if it did, the link between past events and our memory of them is not mimetic. Memory cannot give us direct access to something *as it was* or *as it actually happened*. Everything is in some way revised or reshaped or reconstructed through the process of remembering it. How could it be otherwise? Even two witnesses of the same event – a road accident, let's say – trying honestly and unsparingly to capture the facts and tell the truth, even they will invariably come up with different stories. And in no time at all, and with no evil intent, the truth turns into a kind of fiction.

In hospital I was sedated. When the fog began to lift, the first thing I registered was that the room was painted a hideous shade of turquoise. Only later did I become aware of my father, who sat very still in a chair by the bed. His face was pale, the colour of candle wax, and in my confused state he seemed a ghostlike presence. He also looked too big for the space, as if the low ceiling and narrow walls might not be able to contain him. We looked at each other in silence for a while, and then the ghost spoke, asking in a voice so gentle I've remembered it always:

'Do you want to talk about it, Eddie?' Of course it was much too soon to know what 'it' was, or could possibly be, or have been.

Without answering I turned to gaze on my strange surroundings. A torn lampshade hung from the ceiling light, and the bedside cabinet was stained brown with cigarette burns. On the windowsill there was a container with a plastic plant that didn't resemble anything from the natural world. Even now I can still recall the grim detail of that room, such an unbeautiful place, impossible to believe it could have been designed with anyone's wellbeing in mind.

When the doctor arrived she referred to what had happened the day before, calling it *cet épisode*, as though it might have been part of a television drama. She asked me again and again to tell her what had led up to it. 'From the beginning, if you please, in your own words.' It sounded strange when she said 'in your own words', as if there could have been other words, belonging to someone else, that I might have spoken. And yet, when at last I did speak, the words did not in truth seem to be mine at all. They sounded as if they were coming from the next room, and winding down slowly like an old gramophone player. The doctor had an end-of-shift look, creases on her cheeks and a slight puffiness round the eyes that suggested broken nights. She gave the impression of wanting to be somewhere else, anywhere except there with me in that grim room. What could I tell her about what happened? That there had been a lecture on the syllogism? That all men were mortal, that Socrates was a man, and that Socrates was therefore mortal? I wanted to make her job easy, to compensate for her lack of sleep, but the right answers eluded me.

'Once more, as truthfully as you can,' she said.

There was no desire to be untruthful, but without a doubt I was an unreliable witness, with no means of judging the truthfulness or otherwise of what I said. My father had always maintained it was easy to get into a mess with truth, and hard to know what anyone meant by it. Something can have the look of truth, he would say, even the sound of truth, without actually being the truth.

It was a struggle to know what to say to the doctor. And any minute now she was bound to ask me about sex. I had read enough of Freud and psychoanalysis to know that all mental states could be traced back to it. But in fact she said nothing at all on the subject, for which I was thankful, not least because in spite of my deadened state, I had noticed the shape of her breasts beneath her white doctor's coat.

A week or two later my friend Antoine came to visit and asked me if I was having girl trouble. *Des problèmes de nanas*, he said.

'Girl trouble? What do you mean?'

'Well, you know, girls can lead to a whole lot of trouble,' he said. He was wearing an expensive jacket, which still had its new leather smell. 'They give off mixed signals, hard to interpret. That can get you all screwed up in the head.' *Ça te prend la tête* was how he put it. 'Maybe that's what's happened with you.' Antoine was the son of wealthy parents who had bought him his own apartment on the Left Bank. It was a difficult time in a man's life, he said, being at university. All that stimulation – intellectual, moral, sexual – it could be quite overwhelming. He continued in this vein for a while, and in the harsh light of the room his face took on a yellowish tinge, as if he'd been fed on corn.

'When you think about it, there is so much more to sexual need than sexual need,' he said, examining the flaking turquoise paint on the wall behind him and picking off bits with his gleaming white nails. 'Of course, that's a *post hoc* realisation. At the time, when you're caught up in the moment, sexual need is all that matters.'

He had got up from his chair now and was walking around, hands in pockets, his head nodding in agreement with himself, a hen pecking around in its own dirt.

'I mean, you share your ideals with a girl, and before you know it you're sharing bodies. One happens in a different moral space from the other. Afterwards what you feel is the loss of innocence and the impossibility of regaining it.'

After which he said an abrupt goodbye, promising to return the following week and expressing the hope for my swift recovery.

9

Illness takes us out of life and out of ourselves for a bit, allowing us to think. This is perhaps the whole point of it, my father said. I stayed in hospital for more than a month, eating bad food and protected from the world. In this sort of situation, removed from the ordinary structures of life, and living with people who are not entirely well, it is hard to claw your way back to something that might be called normality. Try to look upon it as an interlude, my father said, an opportunity to prepare yourself for the next thing. His visits were marked by a wonderful kindness. Meanwhile Dr Robel, who never lost her burned-out look, questioned me repeatedly: Did I ever hear voices? Did I think that others were talking about me behind my back? She explained that my mental state could make things seem more important than in fact they were – 'It can lead to exaggerated inferences about your environment.'

One day, when I was reading *Three Men in a Boat*, which my father had given me on his last but one visit, Dr Robel turned up in my room and, after a few preliminary remarks to the effect that I was making good progress, suddenly asked if I believed I possessed special powers. I considered the question, then said: 'No, not me. But my mother, when she was alive, had a special relationship with nature. She talked to her plants, trusted them with her secrets. And my father, well, he can peel a whole orange in a single unbroken strip.'

A few days later I was allowed to go home. Back to the real world – whatever anyone means by that. During my last meeting with the doctor she explained that I had experienced a psychotic episode. It was hard to predict the outcome, she said, but the chances were I would be all right. 'If you observe any worrying signs, come back and see us. But in all probability you will recover. We know less about those who do – they disappear and find a way of living without us.'

In due course a report was sent to my university tutor, a decent man who confessed in a touchingly tortuous way to having had 'difficulties' of his own at one time. He asked me to come to his office, and we sat facing one another, as if seeing each other for the first time. He handed me an envelope, which turned out to contain the psychiatric report. 'It's probably of more use to you than to us here,' he said, a hint of apology settling on the curve of his mouth. I couldn't help wondering about this kind man's difficulties, what they could have been, and if they were over.

The report was a fascinating document, marked CONFIDENTIAL, addressed *Aux personnes concernées*, typed on the headed notepaper of *Centre Hospitalier Sainte-Anne*, dated 10 June 1980, and signed by the consultant psychiatrist – the woman with the creased look. It was laid out as a sort of attestation (*Je soussignée certifie que . . .*), and began by describing the patient, Edgar Logan, as a twenty-year-old university student, who had been admitted 'in an agitated state', and whose manner had been 'threatening and aggressive', so much so that 'he was judged to be a danger to himself and others'. I read it so many times that soon I knew it off by heart. But no matter how hard I tried, it was impossible to identify myself as the subject. It might have been a work of fiction, part thriller, part mystery. It really had nothing to do with me. This is how it went on:

On arrival at hospital the patient had to be physically restrained. There were no accompanying relatives and the police had no further information on him. He was loquacious but not amenable to questioning. His speech was rapid and disorganised. He presented no obvious physical symptoms and there was no evidence of drug or alcohol abuse.

After treatment he became progressively calmer, and over the ensuing days he began to volunteer personal details. He described the incident in the lecture room as 'a one-off' ['exceptionnel'] and 'out-of-character' ['cela ne me ressemble pas'], arising from a sense of personal frustration with his own academic progress. There is no history of psychiatric illness in the immediate family and he has never been admitted to hospital previously. There is no evidence of suicidal tendencies.

M Logan was observed closely over a period of three weeks. During the third week medication was gradually withdrawn and there were no further signs of agitation or hypomania. It was not possible to establish with any degree of certainty the causative or precipitating trigger for his psychotic episode, but I am satisfied that the immediate crisis has subsided and that attendance at psychiatric day hospital is not indicated. It is impossible to say if this acute psychotic episode will be limited to a single occurrence. Should there be a recurrence, crisis intervention will be required.

In my opinion this young man might not be well adapted to cope with future difficulties or anxieties associated with academic life. Furthermore, he may be predisposed to neurotic illness or maladaptive responses to stressful situations. In the meantime, however, I am satisfied he has made a good recovery, which is likely to be sustained, and there is no ongoing treatment or follow-up.

Though many years have passed, I still carry that report in my wallet. Why do I hang on to it? I sometimes ask myself that question, but there is no single answer. In part I think I keep it as tangible evidence of something that once happened. The report deals in facts, unaltered by time, and therefore quite different from memory, which you can mould and shape into almost anything you like. However, it isn't entirely accurate: it states that there is no family history of psychiatric illness, and yet my mother was a victim for much of her life. And so it also is proof of something else: that medical reports, written by doctors trained to uncover the truth, can contain a lie at the centre. Crucially, however, it is a statement referring to then, more than twenty years before the now of this story. And to that extent I have come to see it as a protection against a recurrence. The report itself has become talismanic, impossible to destroy.

Even before leaving hospital I had begun to worry that my father would feel let down, disappointed in me. But if he did, he gave no sign. Nor did he have any truck with 'episodes'.

'It's best to call a spade a spade, Eddie,' he said. 'Everyone fights his own chaos. The struggle is usually very much the same – only the chaos is different.' People believed that philosophy ought to reduce the threat of mental disorder, but that wasn't necessarily true. Many philosophers had found this out for themselves, he said. Descartes, for example – 'regarded by many people as the father of philosophy, and not just in France' – had suffered a complete mental collapse as a young man. 'Right here in Paris,' he added, animated now, as if to suggest there might be something deranging in the Parisian air. And even David Hume – 'a beacon of sanity if ever there was one' – had experienced a nervous breakdown, at much the same age in fact, and brought on by an overdose of studying. In fact he became so caught up in philosophy that he began to fall apart. The symptoms were physical as well as mental – heart palpitations, excessive salivation and the like. His hands and feet had even broken out in scurvy spots – 'half crippled by them, he was' – and this in turn led to even more anxiety and terrible depression. It very nearly robbed him of his reason, said my father. Until he decided that philosophy was all very well but it was important to be still a man, which was how Hume put it. 'Take his advice, Eddie: *Reste un homme*.' Afterwards, Hume had gone on to do his finest work, he explained. 'But his early trouble was very real. In those days it was called the disease of the learnèd, so you're in very good company.'

From then on 'breakdown' was the no-nonsense name my father gave to what had happened. He was even surprisingly upbeat about it, declaring that there was a certain cachet to having had such a strong reaction to the Fallacy of the Undistributed Middle – the logical nicety that the professor had been trying to explain just before I attacked him. 'Much more distinguished than going to pieces over the Illicit Minor, don't you think?'

Finding absurdity in a situation was one of the ways my father engaged with the world. Yet he could be deadly serious too. Much of the time in his daily life he gave the impression of being filled with equivocation and doubt, but every so often he would fix me with his powder-blue eyes and say something about which you just knew he felt certain. Once when I referred to what had happened in the logic lecture as a 'moment of madness', he got up from his chair, put his hands deep in his pockets, bent his shoulders inwards slightly, and rocked back and forth on his heels. He was wearing his trademark trousers – durable herringbone tweed, generous cut, slightly baggy at the knee. A minute or two passed before he spoke. 'Don't dismiss those moments, Eddie. They are the precious vivid moments that confirm to us we're alive, that we're part of the messy unpredictable chaos that is the world.' He looked me straight in the eye. 'You had a breakdown, that's all. It can happen to anyone. You mustn't give yourself a hard time about it.'

And so it became my breakdown. By the time this conversation took place my mother had been dead for nearly a year. Since her death my father and I had spoken nothing but English with one another, except in the bookshop or when others were around and politeness dictated. In a curious way, this helped draw a line between my time in hospital and the start of my recovery. My father seemed to me a different person when he spoke English, and it was easy to pretend that I too was someone else – not the student who'd gone berserk over the syllogism and grabbed an innocent professor by the throat, but a normal healthy young man who still had his whole life ahead of him.

'Don't feel you have to go back to philosophy, Eddie,' my father said. 'You can live quite well without it.'

Whether or not this was true, my immediate choices were limited. My tutor's strong advice was to have a break from my studies and give myself a chance to 'feel well again'. It was at this point he found me a temporary position in the university library. My father said amiably that there was no shame in it, and that David Hume had worked as a librarian for longer than anything else. From then on my days were spent sorting books and placing them on the shelves. The simplicity of the job appealed, as well as the degree of order involved in classifying and cataloguing. There was a quiet rhythm to the work, and something calming in its repetitive nature. Special trolleys transported the books between the main desk and the stacks, and I took pride in loading my trolley so efficiently that it carried more books than anyone else's trolley. Such things can take on great importance in a job like that. Being in the presence of so many books – the sum of centuries of human endeavour – can do strange things to those who work amongst them. You brood over details: the evenness of a line of books on a shelf, the hum of the fluorescent lights, the iniquity of someone replacing a book in the wrong position. In a university library this is standard behaviour. As is a pervasive suspicion of your colleagues. There is talk of amorous trysts in Special Collections, fumblings between the stacks – even pilfering and large-scale theft. No one is above suspicion. There is mistrust in everyone's eyes. I discovered too that the stigma of madness is less acute in a library environment than in almost any other place of work. According to George Eliot, sane people do what their neighbours do, so that if there are any lunatics at large, they can immediately be spotted and avoided. But amongst library staff this principle is reversed: only the sane stand out. At the Sorbonne most people had a haunted look, plausible survivors of some terrible nameless disaster, and in addition to those who were clearly disturbed there was the usual quota of eccentrics and eggheads, obsessives and enthusiasts, cranks and misfits, all of them ill at ease with themselves or the world in some way or another. After a while it became clear that hardly anyone could be considered normal.

10

It was too early to judge whether the National Library in Edinburgh was on a par with the Sorbonne in this regard. I hadn't met enough people to conduct a controlled experiment, but already the librarian behind the desk looked like a promising candidate. A remarkably thin man, with the demeanour of someone who wanted to be even thinner, he moved tentatively around his workspace as if trying not to disturb the particles in the air. He coughed at regular intervals, the sort of cough that was not due to a cold or bronchial infection or too many cigarettes, but a desperately artificial hack that was almost certainly neurotic. Perhaps it was a way of affirming the importance of his position. I turned to look at him. He stopped coughing. I turned away, and he started again. Each bout of coughing followed a familiar metrical pattern. At first it seemed to be a perfect trochaic tetrameter, like Puck's lines in *A Midsummer Night's Dream* – *So awake when I am gone; For I must now to Oberon*, except that it lacked the last syllable, being one cough short. Then, as he obliged with another couplet, I realised with a sinking heart that this thin librarian was ruining my favourite Auden poem: *Lay your sleeping head, my love / Human on my faithless arm.*

At this point the door of the reading room opened and a porter in grey overalls wheeled in a trolley with the manuscripts

I had ordered. The man behind the desk, whose job it was to receive the books, called me over and began to speak, uncoughing now, quickly and conspiratorially. Each soft hurried clause began with an 'if' – *If you would care to check . . . if you'll bear with me for a moment . . . if you could just sign here* – before floating off into the fetid air of the overheated library.

Wearing the required white cotton gloves I picked up the bound manuscripts and placed them tenderly on the pillows on my table. Even so, the spines creaked and rasped – dry murmurs of pain that made me shudder.

To be able to read David Hume's work in his own hand was a moment I had long anticipated, but nothing could have prepared me for the thrill of seeing and holding the manuscript of his short autobiographical essay, *My Own Life*. The published version, which I had first read as a young man in my father's bookshop, runs to only a few printed pages, but the original is inscribed on three large sheets of yellowed parchment, folded in the centre to make six double sides, with the handwriting fine and neat, almost copperplate, becoming smaller and thinner towards the bottom of the page, and with only the occasional blotting. It is laid out like a letter: the date, 18th of April 1776, written top left, and the title *My Own Life* occupying the position of the address, as if this might be the actual place Hume is writing from – which, for a man on the point of death, shows a certain wit and stoicism. He begins by stating that his autobiography will be short, for 'it is difficult for a man to speak long of himself without Vanity', and after shining a light on his remarkable life, in prose infused with benevolence towards the human race, he ends on a note of apology: 'I cannot say, there is no Vanity in making this funeral Oration of myself; but I hope it is not a misplac'd one'.

I had come to David Hume already loving him – a feeling that could be traced back to the affection and near-reverence that my own father had expressed for Hume over the years. 'There is no finer philosopher,' he would say, 'and he was that rarest of creatures: a good man.'

I I

Is any decision truly spontaneous? Perhaps not. The subconscious is always at work, pulling the strings.

On leaving the library that day, my head still whirring from the thrill of handling Hume's papers, I collected my bike from the railings in Parliament Square. Just inside the Square a flower seller had laid out her stall, and on impulse – that's anyway how it seemed – I bought flowers for Carrie as a thank you for the previous evening. Doing something without prior planning normally made me anxious, yet choosing six enormous sunflowers for a woman barely known to me felt curiously exhilarating.

Carrie buzzed me in and appeared at the top of the stairs. She was wearing an artist's smock, slightly ragged and splashed with colour, the sleeves folded back to reveal strong muscled arms. Her face lit up when she saw the flowers. 'They've probably been flown in from France,' she said. 'Just like you!' She beckoned me indoors and went off to find a vase. She would let Harry know they had a visitor. 'But first come into the studio while I finish clearing up.'

Carrie's studio was a large light space. Wooden floorboards, flecked with paint, no curtains, large jars full of brushes, canvases stacked against the walls, curiosities suspended from the ceiling, a sink in the corner and next to it an old pine cupboard with a kettle on top and an elderly teapot with hairline cracks in its bulge. Lots of clutter and chaos – the sort of upheaval that usually made me nervous – and yet I felt completely at ease. Carrie took a large green jar from the cupboard and put the sunflowers straight in. They fell easily into a pleasing group as if responding to their tasteful setting and the artist's touch. On the easel was a large canvas glistening with wet paint. I wanted to say something intelligent about it, but there was no telling what it was meant to be. At that point the language to interpret a painting was simply not available to me. Later Carrie would tell me this was an advantage. My eyes were innocent like those of a child, though to me they were simply crude and ignorant.

I walked round the studio, taking it all in, hoping I wasn't intruding, conscious of how hateful it was if anyone entered my own place of work. 'I hope you don't mind the interruption,' I said. She replied with a smile and told me she had come to the end of her working day – it was rare for her to work beyond five or six in the evening. She was at her best mid-morning, she said, providing she could get herself into the right frame of mind. 'I'm not one of those people who can leap out of bed and take up my paintbrush.'

She asked me then about my own work, how my day was structured. As she spoke she took off her smock, and with a couple of graceful movements folded it and threw it in a corner. I described how my time in Edinburgh would be divided – mornings at home, afternoons in the library – and how important it was for me to have a fixed routine. I thought: how boring this must sound. But the questions kept coming, and she seemed interested and attentive. Sometimes you don't know the significance of a conversation till afterwards.

As she poured tea into two mugs she said that she knew practically nothing about translation, though she'd noticed that when people praised a translation they usually called it *faithful*. 'You know, like Greyfriars Bobby or something.' She laughed, and because she laughed I did too.

'Who is Greyfriars Bobby?'

She laughed again, this time at me, but I didn't mind. When she told me the story of the dog sitting by his master's grave for fourteen years until his own death, I said that the connection wasn't obvious – between a good translation and lying on a grave. 'Though maybe I should give it a try.' More laughter.

We talked easily and eagerly, and for me at any rate the experience was quite novel. I felt so relaxed that anyone looking on might have thought I was used to this sort of engagement. I told her the French had a maxim that compared translation to wives – either they were plain and faithful, or they were beautiful and treacherous. 'It sounds better in French because it rhymes: *Les traductions sont comme les femmes: quand elles sont belles, elles ne sont pas fidèles; et quand elles sont fidèles, elles ne sont pas belles.*'

She said she thought that was a very French notion – the idea that a wife couldn't be both beautiful and faithful. It occurred to me that I might have offended her, but her smile told me otherwise. I said that in translation you had to try to be faithful, yes, but no matter how hard you tried there would always be something lost. You just had to accept it, you were always aware of it, and sometimes it could even overwhelm you, though you tried not to let it. I stood up and went over to the easel. 'I suppose it's quite different with painting.' She didn't respond immediately, but I sensed her eyes on my back, and then she spoke.

'Actually, most of what I paint is about loss. It's been like that for a while now.'

I wanted to know more, but something made me hold back. That conversation would be for another day.

12

I knocked at the door of Sanderson's study and pushed it open.

'Do I disturb you?'

'No, come in.'

'I just called round to say thank you for yesterday.'

'Yes, I knew you were here. I could hear the two of you laughing.'

His tone was inscrutable. I closed the door behind me and approached the desk.

The room, narrow and tenebrous, smelled of stale pipe tobacco. Sanderson was hunched over his desk, an antique oak writing bureau that reminded me of my father's old escritoire in the bookshop. He didn't look up. He was attaching something – it looked like a small vice – onto the edge of the desk. His sleeves were rolled up, revealing inflamed patches of skin on his arms, thickened and raised, with silvery, fish-like scales.

The room was lightly furnished. Apart from the bureau, there was a filing cabinet with four drawers, an old leather armchair that seemed to have taken on Sanderson's shape and contours, a couple of wooden stools, a wicker tub chair, and on one wall a small bookcase with dog-eared volumes: *The Practical Angler*, *Nymphs and the Trout*, *Fly-Dressing Materials* and a score of similar books. Next to the bureau was a standard lamp in the modern style, all thin and bendy like a Giacometti figure. This was a very different space from Carrie's bright studio: no windows at all, just a small aperture high up on the back wall giving out onto the stairwell. It had a fortified feel, like an embrasure. No one could look in.

After a moment or two Sanderson got up, poured me a whisky and motioned to the armchair. I stayed standing by the desk. The angled top was folded down, displaying twelve small drawers, six on either side of the leather surface. Each drawer had a small brass fitting into which a label had been inserted to identify the contents. The labels revealed a strange new language – bobbin holders, dubbing needles, hackle pliers, whip-finishers. Sanderson, pipe in mouth, began to explain the workings of what he called his 'system'. The feather and furs needed to tie the flies were subdivided by species – pheasant, partridge, grouse, teal, hare, seal – and also in keeping with the different hues – dun, honey, honey dun, pale blue dun. The feathers had individual names according to where they grew on the bird – cape, flank, breast, belly and rump. 'My grading system takes account of everything,' he said. There was pride in his voice. 'I have them sorted in descending order from crest to tail.'

All of this was entirely unexpected and new to me, yet I felt a rush of recognition. As a child I had kept my toenail clippings and chickenpox scabs, collecting them in small matchboxes and labelling them before storing them in a corner of my bedroom in an elaborate arrangement of my own devising. I hated the idea of things that had once been part of me being discarded, washed away, or thrown in the bin. Everything had to be preserved, and in a careful, organised way. Clutter was unsettling, whereas sorting things into groups and special collections was truly exhilarating. As time went on, my hoard extended to eyelashes, hard skin from my feet, and detritus from my navel – this being carefully extracted, with the precision of a forensic scientist, by means of fine tweezers. As I surveyed Sanderson's magnificent desk – with its boxes and compartments, labels and drawers – the memory of all this surged back. After too much sun I would wait eagerly for my skin to peel, removing it in pieces as large and patterned as possible before pressing them flat in the pages of a photo album, my favourite specimen being in the shape of the map of Africa. At secondary school my harvest had even come to include blackheads, whiteheads, chest hairs and pubic hairs, these last sometimes rooting themselves, like pernicious weeds resisting removal, in the white linen sheets on my bed. I shrank now from the memory, yet looking back it was hard not to feel a certain sympathy with my younger self and that obsessive need to catalogue every last little piece of personal debris. In a curious way I marvelled at it still, much as I now marvelled at Sanderson's fine 'system'.

'Shall I show you?' he asked, selecting a fishing hook and locking it into the vice. First he wrapped fine golden silk round the shank of the hook to form the body of the fly. Then, as if in preparation for a solemn act, he laid out the materials, naming each one as he did so: yellow floss silk, black floss silk, an orange hackle taken from a cockerel, some well-marked mallard feathers, one from a jungle cock, another from a blue jay, two more from a golden pheasant and a black ostrich. This last was known as a *herl*, he said, a kind of barb whose fibres radiated not just from either side, which was usual, but from all round – 'which is rare and exquisite,' said Sanderson, his voice undulating softly. *Herl* was another of those words that I knew would cause me difficulty on account of its 'h' and 'r'. Fortunately I would have no need of it. Until a few minutes before I had not even imagined that a man could engage in this sort of activity.

'Have you ever cast a fly?' The question felt like a test of character.

'No, I wouldn't know how,' I said.

'I could show you if you were interested.'

'Yes, I'd like that.'

'Come with me next Saturday. I'll take you to my river.'

The invitation had a certain ring to it, as if membership of an exclusive club were being granted. Sanderson then began to select strips from the different coloured feathers to make the first wing of the fly. His fingers looked too big for such fine work. They should have been slender and nimble like a surgeon's, but instead they were thick and red and bloated, like a murderer's hands in the old Hollywood movies. And yet they moved deftly and expertly over the materials. First he peeled the downy barbs from the base of the feathers, placing the soft fuzz into a special box. Then, with a tenderness that must have come from years of application, he stroked the remaining fibres upwards between his thumb and index finger, coaxing them to interlock until they were joined together and the marriage was complete. For a few moments he looked masterful.

Dressing flies, as he called it, was a constant in his life. He'd done it since boyhood and he couldn't imagine ever not doing it. It was exciting and relaxing in equal measure. It could quieten a thumping heart, he said. He also regarded it as a kind of privilege to take part in an ancient art, something that fishermen had done for perhaps two thousand years. As he tied in the hackle fibres, clipping the tips so that they were flush with one another, he told me about the time in a library in Rome when he had seen an ancient manuscript dating from the third century AD in which the author described catching fish in the Astraeus, the river that connected the cities of Verroia and Salonika. The fisherman had evidently used a fly made of red wool and feathers taken from below the wattle of a cock. 'And when I read that, I felt a kind of atavistic thrill.' At this point he let go of his creation for a moment, removed the pipe from between his teeth and rested his hands on his knees – a man seemingly content in himself and in the world. 'When you think about it, nearly everything changes and you never know where you are, but the principles of this little beauty' – with the stem of his pipe he pointed to the fly in the vice – 'haven't changed at all.'

Machines had taken over everything else, he said – metalwork, shoemaking, carpentry, not to mention gadgets for making bread and peeling tatties. 'But a good fly will always be made by hand – it's such a personal undertaking. It could never be done by the cold dispassionate workings of a machine.' Sanderson was a different man from the previous evening. He had seemed then, in talking about himself, to be stuck fast in a particular script, but now in this other setting he was flying free, singing from a wonderful new libretto.

It could take anything up to an hour to tie a single fly, he said. The time was unimportant. He would gladly spend hours and hours at it, which he often did here in this very room. The box room, he called it – 'Which makes it sound of no consequence at all, but I don't mind in the least.' He said he wouldn't have wanted its importance to be known, or even guessed at. Most Edinburgh flats of a certain age had this kind of space, he explained, usually off the drawing-room, sometimes off the hall. In the past it would have accommodated all manner of coffers and trunks, portmanteaux, and probably hatboxes containing wide-brimmed bonnets of Chinese silk, festooned with flowers and feathers and ribbons. 'Sometimes,' he said, 'I like to picture elegant Edinburgh ladies of days now gone wearing these confections on top of their upswept chignons, and at a slight tilt, as was the fashion of the day.' He tilted his own head to demonstrate, and held the rim of an imaginary hat. Since fly-dressing made use of all kinds of feathers, furs, mohairs and silks, he liked to think that he was carrying on something of the spirit of the age. The hatpin was also a vital piece of equipment – 'Now virtually defunct as a ladies' fashion accessory, of course,' he added, 'though my own mother would never have left the house without one.' The other essentials were a pair of straight-blade scissors, bent-blade scissors, pliers and a file for pointing dull hooks. 'And a good strong vice of course.' He patted the vice as he said this, in the way one might pat the head of a clever child.

Certain procedures were impossible without two sets of pliers, he said. On and on he went, providing more and more detailed information. He sucked on his pipe earnestly and had a look of intense concentration. Some fly patterns required a body hackle with all the fibres lying on the top of the body only. The neatest way of achieving this was to attach a pair of pliers to each end of the feather, then suspend it, shiny side down, over the index finger of the left hand. The weight of the pliers made the two sides of the fibres stand up straight from the finger. You gave the pliers a tug and at the same time you stroked the fibres from left to right till they stayed together. Sanderson seemed to be in his element now, the teacher with his pupil.

I asked him how he had learned all this. 'My father taught me when I was a boy. The best thing by far he ever did for me.'

I continued to watch as he worked the fly, tying in the wings and trimming them with the scissors.

'And yours?' he said after a while.

'Mine?' I said. 'My what?'

'Your father. How did he end up in France?'

'Oh, the age-old reason,' I said. 'Love.'

I could feel the whisky beginning to take effect. Sanderson poured me another, and I settled back into the leather armchair and told him what I knew.

13

In the year that war broke out my father had been appointed to a fellowship in philosophy at Cambridge. He had done a first degree in Edinburgh and left Scotland to study for his doctorate in Cambridge, where he had known and been taught by Wittgenstein. He almost certainly had a promising career ahead of him – until the war intervened and everything was changed.

In 1940, shortly after marrying the daughter of the Master of Trinity College – he had met her during his postgraduate days – my father was called up to work for the Special Operations Executive. A year or two later, in the course of a secret mission in Normandy, his cover was blown and he was given refuge in the attic of a house belonging to a family who worked for the Maquis. He owed his life to the bravery of that family, a fact that undoubtedly played a part in his falling in love with Marianne, the daughter of the house, a spirited, cheerful young woman who crawled daily into the tiny attic with his food, every third morning or so bringing him a bowl of hot water and holding a mirror under the tiny skylight so that he could shave. She even carried up and down what she called *le pot de chambre*, an old bucket that served as a toilet. All their conversations were conducted in whispered French, which seemed to lend them a particular intensity and significance. My father lived for Marianne's visits; they were what kept him sane. When she went away he filled the hours that followed by anticipating her return, listening to the complex sounds that came from the house below. At the same time he also made himself think of his wife waiting at home. That was reality, he told himself, and everything else – the strange by-products of war – would pass. But his attempts at reality were enfeebled by Marianne's visits: reality lay in his arms, whispering hope and encouragement, giving him news of small victories in the Resistance and lifting his spirits. These moments began to shut out everything else. The puzzle was how they could take up so much space in his imagination. They became everything to him, his whole being it seemed. He could not believe they were transient, something snatched between other existences, his wartime service and the life he'd left behind at home.

After the hostilities, back in Cambridge, he tried to resume his previous life. But he could not settle. Everything had got mixed up in the war. The things that had once been fixed had become fatally disturbed. And so, at the age of thirty-two and in the name of love, he left his young wife and returned to France to be with Marianne, with whom he had exchanged feverish anguished letters in the intervening months. His wife's father, Master of the College, denounced him as a villain and a scoundrel – such a man would never work again in any university if he had anything to do with it. And he never did. Nor was it possible to make a living in Marianne's village in Normandy. By 1946 she herself was already spoken for – betrothed to a garage mechanic a few streets away, the son of old family friends and suitable in all the ways that my father was not. After a tempestuous few days during which the mechanic, supported by umpteen vehement members of both families, fought to keep his bride-to-be, my father and Marianne fled to Paris, where they hoped to be anonymous and set about trying to recreate what they had felt in the attic during the war. They were both in exile – from their families, from everything that was familiar – and they had only each other. 'But it didn't feel like an *only*,' my father once said to me. 'It felt as if what we had was perfect, complete in itself – each of us felt necessary to the other.' Love would be enough. It would see them through.

For many years, I knew none of this. Yet these simple events were not only the reason for my existence, but also for the unusual circumstances of my upbringing and much else that followed. It was hard, particularly as I grew older, to regard my mother as someone over whom men might quarrel. And I couldn't help wondering about the young woman back in England, the Master's daughter, and what became of her. I never felt able to ask my father for fear of causing him distress, or adding to the guilt I was sure he must have felt. 'We are not free when it comes to falling in love,' he told me one day towards the end of his life as we sat in a café in the Marais, 'and yet we perceive it to be one of the freest things that we do.' Was it kindness that he had fallen in love with? I asked. Was it possible to fall in love with kindness, or did there have to be more? Who knows, Eddie, he said, who knows? He lit a cigarette and inhaled deeply. 'No one really knows what binds people to one another.'

On the way back from the Sandersons' that evening, with the whisky warming my veins, I thought about the beginnings of friendship and the unlooked-for possibilities that beckoned. And how therapists are paid a lot of money to ask questions that new friends will ask for free.

14

My days began to settle into a rhythm: mornings spent at home transferring my notes to the computer and spending two or three hours on the translation, followed by afternoons in the National Library working on the manuscripts. Laptop computers were allowed in the library provided you obtained a special pass, but I decided against it. Lacking the confidence to break the mould, I still clung in those days to the old familiar ways, including the quaint belief that libraries should be places of peace and quiet, undisturbed by the click-clack of modern keyboards. Some people – those who had cut their teeth on a typewriter, I suspect – struck the keys far too hard, making the noise levels sometimes intolerable. So much so that once or twice I found myself entertaining murderous fantasies, toying with the idea of a quick strangulation or two with my white cotton gloves. I had grown far too used to working on my own.

Translating philosophy was also something of a departure for me. I was much more versed in literary fiction, in particular the sort of novel that is set in the emotional landscape of the British middle class. The hallmarks had become as familiar to me as my own skin – lots of interior monologue, introspection, problematic relationships and a whiff of fatalism. It's a compelling cocktail, and in the wrong hands it might easily lead to a terrible bleakness, but 'my' authors generally know how to balance things out with a good measure of comic absurdity, the true redeemer of this kind of fiction (and of reality too perhaps). In the year or two before going to Edinburgh my translation work had branched out in a different direction – a trilogy of novels, high-grade detective stories by an Oxford academic – which had proved to be quite lucrative. The books had become wildly popular in France, and since there was a small royalty built into my contract, I found for the first time in my life that I was earning more money than was needed to live.

Things could not have been more different when I first started out in the translation business, more than twenty years before, when I was obliged to accept whatever came my way simply to survive. This included everything from technical pieces on the nuclear industry in France to short news pieces for AFP. Translators (in France at least) are poorly paid – a fate they share with all but a few writers – and there were times when I came close to giving up. But since by then I had already tasted failure at other things, it seemed important to stick at it. Over time translation became more than a job for me. It began to feel like a calling.

By the time I reached the age of forty, just a year or two before coming to Edinburgh, I had fallen into the habit of looking back to what had gone before, not so much with regret, more with a critical eye. It was quite a shock to realise that my early years as a translator counted hardly at all, that I had been far too busy learning my trade to have been much good at it. But I recognised too that things had changed: at last I had reached the happy position of being able to pick and choose my books. In this sense at least I was my own man.

Translators are a lowly, benighted bunch – this much has become clear to me over the years. French publishers seem to regard them as a necessary evil, a means of getting a potentially valuable commodity into the bookshops. Of course publishers would much rather the book had been written in French in the first place, without having to spend the time and money waiting for a translation. Being forced to make this irksome investment, however, they then want the result to be so fluent and smooth as to give the illusion that it is not a translation at all but The Real Thing. As if writing were always fluent. To help with this illusion they often hide away the translator's name, somewhere on the prelim pages, a tiny intimation alongside the printer and binder. Book reviewers also tend to ignore translators – that's something else you learn to accept – though in fact my reputation had been steadily growing and I was beginning to get the occasional mention on the book pages. This is often a mixed blessing, since hardly any reviewers have the first idea of what they are talking about. In practice they fall back on one or two hollow adjectives –'able' or 'unobtrusive' usually – to describe something they have no means of evaluating. The irony is that reviewers happily discuss the style and the language of the book as if this had everything to do with the author and nothing to do with the translator. Just ignore the reviews, said the publisher, when I once vented all this. But I don't. My best compliment so far was to have been described as *un traducteur sensible* in an otherwise unremarkable review in *Le Figaro*. That's another thing that happens to translators: you get a disproportionate kick out of even the faintest praise.

My work definitely matched my temperament. It is a solitary business for the most part, and the solitary life agreed with me. Aloneness gets a bad name: people confuse it with loneliness, which is something else entirely. It was my father who persuaded me, both through example and sustained argument, that although we might spend much of our time with other people, essentially we live our lives alone. Of course we connect with others all the time – that's how it appears at any rate – with people on the train or in the street or at the shops, but these contacts are as nothing compared with the lifelong communion a man has with himself. Even so, too much solitude could be a terrible burden, he said. David Hume had certainly found it so, and solitude had undoubtedly played a part in his nervous breakdown. Shortly after this conversation I came across a French edition of Hume's *Treatise* in the bookshop, and it was there I discovered Hume's conviction that his life of study had placed him in a kind of solitary confinement that he found almost intolerable. It is central to Hume's doctrine that we are naturally sociable creatures, and that we languish if left on our own. Pleasure is heightened when it is related to others, and pain becomes less tolerable if it is suffered in isolation. *La parfaite solitude est peut-être la plus grande punition que nous puissions souffrir.* This struck me as an extravagant claim, perhaps because at the time I was still in thrall to Sartre and his famous dictum: *L'enfer c'est les autres*. The *worst* punishment, I repeated to my father afterwards. (I spent much of my life alone and hated the idea that it might be the worst thing.) Surely there are worse things than solitude? Perhaps not, said my father, for a man who has been driven to the very edge of madness by it. Yet being solitary, he added, evidently contained a fortunate paradox: 'It is when a man is alone that he best understands how he is hitched to the world.' And in many ways, he said, David Hume seemed to have lived out this paradox perfectly: at one time he felt *utterly abandon'd and disconsolate*, as he put it, because he was unable to mix properly with other people, and this had the effect of turning him in his own eyes into *some strange uncouth monster*; yet in later life he attributed the origin of his entire philosophy to what he called *the pleasure of solitary reflection*. As a matter of fact, my father said, it was Montaigne, not Hume, who seemed to have understood the paradox almost better than anyone. 'Montaigne saw that it was important for people to keep a space apart, somewhere away from the daily demands of life – what he called his *arrière boutique*. I suppose in English we would say *a room behind the shop*, though I must say it loses something in the translation.' We were standing in the bookshop when this conversation took place, and instinctively we both turned towards the back of the shop, as if to suggest there might exist such a room that had escaped our notice. We laughed at our own silliness, but afterwards I reflected that as a young man at that time there was nothing I could yet call my *arrière boutique*, and I couldn't help wondering when it might materialise and what form it might take.

Translation is one of those jobs that very few people know how to talk about. Either they are not interested enough to find out what's involved, or they think they know all there is to know and regard it as mortally boring. This means that you are almost never called upon to give an account of your work. On those rare occasions when I found myself in a social gathering, people didn't know what to say to me. 'Ah, a *translator*,' the emphasis intended to signify interest. 'Well, well,' they would say, trying to conceal their panic. I had got used to this reaction and it suited me perfectly. Talking to people was not something I was good at.

Compared with fiction, philosophical essays were very different, but David Hume's later prose style, as well as being polished and refined, is quite remarkable for its clarity and elegance. It felt like a privilege to translate him. Hume wanted all his life to make his philosophy more accessible, to connect with the common man, and to this end even his most difficult abstract ideas are made lucid by ordinary everyday examples, simply put and delivered at a manageable pace, as if he is conducting a friendly dialogue with you. It comes over as a very pure and beautiful form of the English language. The tone is urbane – the tone of intelligent conversation – and his concern is always with what it is to be human, what it is like to be a particular sort of person. He carries you along with him, using a remarkable emotional range – pathos, comedy, and immense compassion – all of which have the effect of persuading you that whatever he is writing about is quite simply the most interesting thing. It is intoxicating stuff.

Years before, when I first mentioned to my father my idea of working on Hume, he showed me a book containing a letter from Voltaire to Mme du Deffand. The subject of this letter was the failure of the famous Parisian man of letters l'abbé Le Blanc, some two hundred years before, to translate Hume into French – something Voltaire compared to the failure on the part of the French to defeat the English at sea. '*Nous traduisons les Anglais aussi mal que nous nous battons contre eux sur mer.*'

My father chuckled as he read this out to me. Though it might easily have had the opposite effect, this was his way of encouraging me. 'Anyway, don't worry, David Hume was a Scot,' he said. 'There's no need for *you* to try and defeat him – the Auld Alliance puts you both on the same side!'

As I worked on Hume's manuscript and got to know him better, that's just how it struck me: we were on the same side. There seemed to be a kinship between us, and soon I felt I had known him all my life. The task ahead would be a challenge, but one I was relishing. There was also a sense in which everything else felt like a preparation.

This last thought had been uppermost in my mind when I first approached the publisher with my idea. Éditions Scolaires, one of the oldest publishing houses in France, with an excellent reputation for academic textbooks and philosophical commentaries, had already published modern translations of Hume's best-known works: *A Treatise of Human Nature* and *An Enquiry Concerning Human Understanding*. This made me hopeful that they would be receptive to my proposal: an edition of selected essays, including Hume's short autobiographical work, *My Life*, written just before his death, plus two previously unpublished essays, held in manuscript in the National Library of Scotland. The plan was to have a short introduction, tracing Hume's importance in France, his strong attachment to French life and culture, his three years spent in Descartes' old college writing the *Treatise*, and so on. At the end of the main text I also wanted to include a short piece about the importance of David Hume in my own life. Of course I knew very well that a personal memoir had no business in a scholarly work, and I therefore decided to leave it out of my original proposal. As things turned out, however, it was this that made the difference between acceptance and rejection.

After my written submission to Éditions Scolaires, I was invited to the publishing house to discuss it further. An encouraging sign, so I thought, but my hopes were soon shattered. The publisher, a man called Mauvignier, was at pains to tell me just how many ideas for books landed on his desk in an average week. It was a matter of regret, he said, but there simply wasn't enough interest in David Hume to justify a translation of the essays. Mauvignier was scrupulously courteous, but he had the self-important air of a man who was prepared to impart nuggets of wisdom to lesser mortals, providing of course they knew their place and were grateful. He was clearly enjoying the power he wielded, and soon I had him down as a second-rate sadist. 'When it comes to essays,' he said, 'we have our very own Montaigne. That's just how it is – *c'est comme ça*. Why would we need David Hume?' He gave a shrug and held it fixed for a moment or two, just to rub in his point. With an attitude like that, I thought, it was a wonder he published anything at all – the yahoos were evidently still in our midst, right here in Paris. Though it seemed pointless I took a deep breath and tried to get him to see things differently: Hume was already held in high esteem in France, I said, and there were signs that his reputation was growing – in fact an excerpt from his *Treatise* had even formed part of a recent baccalauréat. He listened politely, but it was clear he wasn't persuaded. Then, just as rejection seemed to be filling all the available space, he said that I mustn't think he had anything against Hume. The fact was he had rather a soft spot for him. At this point he asked if by any chance I had ever visited Café Le Bon David on the Left Bank.

'Or maybe you're too young?'

I laughed and told him there had been no need to visit it because it had been my home for the whole of my childhood. I explained that my parents had owned the second-hand bookshop that had become Café Le Bon David.

'In fact I was actually born in the bookshop. My mother went into labour halfway up a ladder as she stacked volumes of Proust on the shelves. A makeshift bed was arranged on the floor and a doctor hastily summoned. So the story goes anyway.'

'Incredible!' he said. 'Why on earth didn't you mention this before?' He was animated now, eager for information. Sometimes people can change before your very eyes. 'Ah, so your father was the *libraire*. Amazing!' It turned out that Mauvignier's own father had taken him as a child to my parents' bookshop, and it had made a lasting impression. He had never forgotten how, like a magic trick, it was much larger on the inside than it seemed from the outside. And the books were everywhere: on shelves high up to the ceiling, in boxes on the floor and laid out in rows, spines up, on a large table in the courtyard at the back, where the smell of new-baked bread from the *boulangerie* next door wafted over the wall, and where men like his father gathered to smoke and drink coffee and talk about serious things. 'Café Le Bon David – well, it's part of our history. It's our cultural heritage, every bit as much as Les Deux Magots.'

I managed a smile. The comparison with the favourite haunt of Sartre and de Beauvoir was intended as a compliment, but those who frequented my father's place would have been insulted by it.

'Is your father still alive?'

'He died a couple of years ago. A heart attack. In the bookshop. He was stacking books on a high shelf, and they fell over him *in a shower*' – I used the English phrase.

Mauvignier looked blank.

'*Une grêle de livres fondit sur lui.* Like Leonard Bast in *Howard's End*.'

'Ah, yes. Of course.'

For several minutes Mauvignier fired questions at me, all the while expressing his amazement and enthusiasm. And then he folded his arms and sat back in his chair, undoubting now, like a man whose sole purpose in life was to instruct and enlighten. 'I think we may have the makings of a book after all,' he said. For the next half-hour or so we discussed the shape of the book, the length – 'maximum 250 pages' – and what would be required by way of an introduction. We were of the same mind now, old comrades.

In the end, however, Mauvignier drove a hard bargain. Because he judged the market for a book of philosophical essays to be highly specialised, he would pay me 'only as an author', as he put it – in other words not as a translator. I would be given a modest advance payment, half on signature, and half after the first thousand copies had been sold. This struck me as monstrously unfair, though not quite as monstrous as the refusal to pay me for the translation. When I queried it, he assured me that translations – he curled his lower lip round this word and pulled a bad-smell face – didn't sell very well, and in any case in these 'rather difficult times' it was quite a normal arrangement. He clapped his hands together in a take-it-or-leave-it gesture, indicating that this was the end of the matter. His manner grated painfully, and I had to keep reminding myself how much I wanted to have this book published, how important it would be as a kind of *hommage* to my father. With that in mind, I affected a grateful smile, swallowed hard and agreed to his terms.

15

After a week or so in the National Library I began to recognise familiar faces, most of them starved of daylight, their complexions suggesting long years spent in a bunker or a submarine. It was possible to believe that there was no blood beneath the skin, only soapsuds or – since this was Scotland – porridge oats. Every other day an elderly woman, her hair tied back in a hangman's noose, shared my desk. She wore a tweed jacket and skirt, and supported herself on lean heron legs that looked as if they might give way when she tottered up to the issuing counter. Her research was on the first missionaries in Africa – this much I gathered from her conversation with the coughing man – and her voice, which was beautiful, seemed to come straight from an old black-and-white film, her vowels exquisitely modulated like those of Celia Johnson in *Brief Encounter*. I could have listened to her all day. I wondered what sort of life she had lived – had *she* experienced passion, like her sound-alike Miss Johnson, and had it been requited? At the desk opposite mine there was another regular, a large and scrofulous man with poor personal hygiene, his bald pate as perfect and smooth as an unbroken egg. I pictured him in a lonely garret, eating out of tins and living with mice. And at the desk furthest from the door sat an older man with the look of White Russia about him. With bad teeth and breath smelling of raw onions, he was dressed in ill-fitting boots and a drab suit that seemed not to belong to him. On close inspection I decided he was a destitute Ukrainian, an ex-academic familiar with libraries but using them now as a source of warmth and shelter.

When not inventing tragic lives for my companions, I spent my time checking the original manuscripts of Hume's essays against the English edition I was translating from. There is no absolutely authoritative English edition, partly because Hume spent much of his life revising and altering the text of the essays – in fact there are seventeen editions in all. Hume also changed the order of his essays as they appeared in different editions throughout his life, withdrawing some pieces altogether or postponing the publication of others until after his death. I therefore made a key decision: in my translation the essays would be arranged chronologically, with Hume's own cuts and revisions, and in his own chosen order, thus reflecting his development as a writer and a thinker.

Once in a while I discovered a mistake, which made all the painstaking work worthwhile. For example, in his essay *Of Tragedy*, the phrase 'sweet sinning' appears in a sentence to do with what the Italians consider essential to all pleasure. These words, translated from the Italian phrase *dolce peccante*, are reproduced in all the modern editions, and come from the posthumous 1777 edition, which of course Hume himself, on account of being dead, was unable to check. On looking back to the original manuscript, I found that what Hume had actually written was *dolce piccante* – in other words, 'pleasantly sharp', and nothing to do with sinning at all, sweet or otherwise. After this sort of discovery I would leave the library walking on air, as if I had just solved the mystery of the world single-handed. In a tiny corner of my mind, I knew this behaviour to be ludicrous.

Even so, with each passing day there was a growing sense that this period of my life was quite perfect, and that even though it could surely grow and change and surprise, it could not be improved upon. Each morning before breakfast I would scramble up and over Salisbury Crags – a natural amphitheatre of solid rock – joyfully walking in the shadow of Hume, deepening the connection with each strong step, so I imagined. On my way home from the library I took to visiting the old cemetery on Calton Hill where Hume is buried. In this way each day was topped and tailed with a little ceremony of *hommage*. I loved the sense of binding, followed by unbinding, only to bind again.

According to the plaque by the gate the cemetery was opened in 1718 for the burial of tradesmen and merchants. The gravestones bear this out, with their concentration of traditional Scottish names – Alexander Henderson, Alexander Walker, John Middleton, John Reid. Along the southern edge of the cemetery there is a row of grand walk-in tombs, like miniature stone-built houses, without roofs. In the tomb of Jean Ormiston (died 1817, aged 52), spouse of William MacRedie (died 1831, aged 72), the wall at the back is not built up. In its place is an iron railing, and if you press your face to the bars you are rewarded with a wonderful prospect of Edinburgh – the Old Town, the tall thin painted buildings on the Royal Mile, Arthur's Seat, the new Scottish Parliament – and immediately below, the roofs of Waverley Station. When the wind is in the right direction the announcements of train departures and arrivals drift up to the cemetery and drop down among the graves. If only the dead could hear and see, it would be the perfect place to be buried – panoramic view together with a sense of the continuity of things. No wonder Hume had chosen this as his final resting place. In 1776, anticipating his death, he had bought a plot for burial. It was to be a simple affair, without fuss – *sans cérémonie*, as I wrote in my introduction to the essays. In his will he specified that a small monument 'at an expense not exceeding a hundred pounds' be built over his body, with a simple inscription giving only his name and the year of his birth and death. But in fact his monument is a rather grand affair, a large cylindrical neo-classical mausoleum with an elegant urn set in a niche above the doorway. It isn't at all a grave to suit such a modest man, yet I grew to love it. Most days I would push open the wrought-iron gate and stand inside, persuading myself that doing so invoked the presence of Hume. Sometimes I even spoke to him, reporting on my progress and the odd problem encountered. The aborigine believes that he can know the answer to any question three days after his mother's death. He simply has to stand at the foot of her grave and ask. I didn't hold with anything like that; for me, standing at Hume's grave was just a kind of pleasing ritual to mark the end of the working day. But somewhere at the back of my mind I suspected that even modest rituals might have a transformative power.

16

The next time I saw Sanderson was about ten days later, at the end of my first full week in Edinburgh. I had gone to George Square in the late afternoon to have a look round the philosophy class library, open only in term time and for just one hour each day – something that seemed both pitiful and scandalous in a university with such a strong philosophical tradition. The new academic year was just beginning, and the streets around George Square were filled with fresh-faced young students. By contrast the departmental library was gloriously empty. I stood in the middle of the room, a high-ceilinged space of generous proportions, and drank it all in – the tall wooden bookcases with their deeply filled shelves, centuries of learning in old leather bindings, scuffed with age and use. To be alone with hundreds of books is always humbling – exhilarating too: the idea of so many scholars, working for years, adding to the knowledge of mankind. Just thinking about it can make your head spin. My father used to say that wherever old books were gathered together, the souls of old writers also gathered. He would have been the first person in all other circumstances to dismiss the idea of a soul, but it didn't seem to bother him when applied to collections of books.

The clocks were chiming 5 o'clock as I left the building. Perhaps Sanderson would still be in the philosophy department just across the square. We were due to go on our first fishing expedition the following day and it would be sensible to check the arrangements – what I should wear, where to meet, and so on. I found his office on the third floor – it bore the nameplate DR H T M SANDERSON. I knocked on the door and waited for a moment or two. No answer, but just as I was leaving a faint rustling sound came from inside. I put my ear to the door and knocked again, louder this time.

'Go away! I'm busy! No more appointments today!'

'Sorry, it's me – Eddie. Nothing important. I was just passing by.'

I walked away, wincing with embarrassment, down the corridor towards the stairway. But before I could disappear completely the door opened and Sanderson called me back. 'Why didn't you say it was you?' he growled. Only his head was visible, the face red, the hair tousled. The rest of him was hidden behind the door, which he closed and locked as soon as he'd let me in. His appearance was intriguing: trouser legs rolled up above the knee and round his feet what appeared to be polythene bags, tied with string at the ankles. He hobbled over the carpet and sat down on the chair behind his desk. On the floor under the desk I noticed a container – an old plastic basin half-full of a greenish liquid. There was a smell I couldn't identify, sweet and grassy, like summer.

'I'm not a pretty sight,' said Sanderson, walking gingerly towards the chair by his desk. 'You see before you a man diseased. Leprous.'

And indeed, the parts of his body on display might have been afflicted by some Old Testament plague. The scaly patches I'd noticed on his hands when we first met extended the length of his arms. His knees, too, were covered in thick red skin, fiery like a volcano, with silvery kaleidoscopic eruptions on the surface. They were turned towards me now – morbid exhibits from a pathology lab. I thought at once of David Hume's dreadful scurvy spots and the mental turmoil that had led to them. It was hard not to stare, and I had to remind myself that beneath this dreadful exterior there lurked a sentient human being.

'What on earth is it?' I asked, hoping my voice indicated concern rather than repugnance.

'Oh, some ghastly skin thing. I've had it before, but never this bad.'

'Does it hurt?'

'Hurt? Not really. But it feels hot, and it itches like mad. And you shed your skin everywhere. Like a snake, but less tidily.' He pointed to the floor, which was covered in a kind of confetti. He explained that he had been soaking his feet in olive oil – 'the cheapest money can buy, but still not cheap' – to deal with the cracks that had opened up on his soles. The polythene bags were to seal in the moisture, he explained. Inside the oily bags, beyond the misty film, his feet looked small and vulnerable.

'I keep all the paraphernalia here,' he said. 'It's not the sort of thing I want to be messing about with at home. A man with pustules and plastic bags on his feet can hardly expect to keep his wife interested in him.' He gave a loud laugh, like a gun going off, and I felt a sudden surge of sympathy.

From the top drawer of his filing cabinet he took out a bottle of whisky. When I turned down the offer of a drink he poured himself a sizeable measure into a white polystyrene cup, took a large gulp, settled back in his chair and put his plastic-wrapped feet on the cluttered desk.

'What you told me about your father has stayed with me,' he said. He sounded wistful. 'Can't get him out of my head. I keep thinking about him, stuck in that French attic, day after day, hour after hour – all the time in the world to plan the rest of his life.'

'I'm not sure that's the way it happened,' I said. 'The way he described it – well, it was not anything as clear-cut as planning the rest of his life. Afterwards, yes, he understood that a decision must have been forming over a long period of time, but even when he got back to civilian life in England it was still vague and blurred. Nothing he could bring into focus.'

'Do you think your father ever came to regret his decision?' he asked. On his desk the bags at the end of his feet shifted around, discrete alien creatures.

'If he did, he never referred to it. Though it was something I myself occasionally wondered about. In many ways it must have seemed a costly decision. He lost a job he loved, then my mother – the reason for his decision – became unwell, and she remained so for much of their married life. And yet he appeared to find contentment.'

'Contentment, I can't help thinking, is one of the words people use when they are trying to avoid the H-word.'

'Happiness, you mean?' The mention of it made Sanderson recoil in fake alarm. 'I wasn't consciously avoiding it – though I agree it's a hard word to pin down. For my father it actually wasn't a taboo word. In fact, I remember him telling me not long before he died that one successful shot at happiness was enough to sustain a person for a lifetime.'

'And did you believe him? On the evidence of his own life, I mean.'

'Well, come to think of it, I suppose I did. In spite of obvious difficulties, he behaved as if continued happiness was at least possible. I think he also understood how near one comes to it, and yet how distant it often remains.' My next thought – though I didn't share it with Sanderson – was this: perhaps one reason my father had held himself together was precisely because he had moved away from the formal study of philosophy. It was enough that philosophy was integral to his later career as a bookseller, rather than an end in itself. It had not turned in on him or against him. He had not been prey to *the disease of the learnèd*.

Sanderson was staring straight ahead, like an Easter Island statue – strong chin, broad nose, sunken eyes. No wonder Carrie liked to paint him. To try and keep things going, I said it was possible that unhappy times, too, had their own value. They were not for nothing. But this particular conversation was already dead, and when he next spoke it was about himself.

It was a bad time of year for him, he said. He hated the start of a new academic session. 'There ought to be a feeling of renaissance to it – you know, all that fresh energy and the business of breathing new life into the place.' But there wasn't, he said. Not any more. He had felt it in the past, years ago, but now it felt like the cranking-up of old machinery, too rusty to function well. Earlier that day he had given his introductory talk to the students who had signed up for philosophy – and it had gone badly, very badly. He gave a loud sigh, in recollection. I found myself sighing too – an involuntary reaction, like yawning. At this point Sanderson opened the bottom drawer of his desk and removed what looked like an empty yoghurt pot. He got up, lifted his chair to the other side of the room and clambered onto it in his pitiful polythened feet. Once his ample frame was balanced, he placed the plastic pot over the smoke alarm. It fitted perfectly, as I had guessed it would, each of his movements having been quite precise and evidently part of a well-rehearsed routine. There was a pause while he lit his pipe, coaxing it into life with a run of rapid inhalations till the bowl glowed red and the smoke swirled. He turned to check the yoghurt pot high on the wall, as if to say: Don't let me down. For the next hour or two we sat there in his office, sweet-scented smoke filling the air, and the light fading outside. In that time Sanderson must have drunk a quarter-bottle of whisky, but it had no visible effect other than to make him more voluble.

I decided to risk asking him again about his forthcoming book. My father used to say that prompting a man to parade his erudition was the quickest way to gain his trust.

'Oh, there's nothing to tell really. It's a sort of guided tour to happiness. You know the sort of thing, a trawl through all the philosophical mudflats.'

In my mind I saw apartment blocks, built of dried mud.

'Mudflats?'

'You know, the coastal wetlands where the tide deposits mud and sand and all kinds of detritus from the sea bed. They're called *flats*.'

'Oh, I see,' I said, not sure if I did see.

'It's basically a trip round all the *isms* – hedonism, stoicism, scepticism, Epicureanism, and so on. Nothing particularly original about it. Except perhaps the conclusion that when it comes to happiness, philosophy is no bloody good to man or beast.'

He laughed again, another burst of gunfire. At heart he wasn't a philosopher at all, he said, staring into his polystyrene cup. 'That's the inescapable conclusion.' He had a sense of having betrayed his calling – 'You know, like a character from a Chekhov play. All those lost dreams. The impossibility of getting to Moscow, the destruction of a cherry orchard. Ha!'

'Didn't you set out to be a philosopher?'

'Actually, no. I just fell in with the wrong crowd.'

It was hard to know when he was being serious. Or how much of the apparent belligerence was part of an elaborate defence. I couldn't even be sure it was belligerence. It could just as easily have been a complicated modesty.

When I asked him what else he might have done, he considered the question for a moment before saying that for a time at school he had wanted to be a linguist. He had been fascinated by language, not just the grammar and the syntax, but the different sounds contained within it, as well as how language was acquired in the first place, and the powerful things that could be done with it.

'Language seemed to hold out the possibility of an ordered universe,' he said. 'Have you ever had that thought?'

'All the time,' I said.

'Then you will have discovered by now that it's just a beautiful trick: order and harmony are just an illusion. One that language helps us create. The world is actually random and chaotic.'

At the age of twelve, he said, he had started learning Latin, and that had been a revelation. On the first day each pupil had been given a book, *Kennedy's Revised Latin Primer*, and for him it had become a treasured possession. 'To know this book is to know a beautiful language – that's what our teacher said. Everything reduced to hundreds of tables – verbs, nouns, declensions, conjugations. It was just a question of learning the rules and memorising the exceptions. Wonderful stuff it was.' Looking back he saw it as a model of logical thought. He even wondered now if it was Latin that had set him on the path to philosophy. By working out the puzzle of the words and their relationship to one another, he sometimes liked to imagine that he was unravelling the mystery that was the universe.

'Of course, I was young then, and didn't quite see it in those terms. But looking back, I do think it was some sort of school-boy quest to understand the world.'

The trouble was, Latin was a dead language. With the stem of his pipe he brushed some dead skin from his arm onto the floor. 'No one was ever expected to speak it – it was purely a scholarly thing, an educational tool.' Gradually he had begun to feel the need for a foreign language that was alive, one that was spoken in the world by living people. He had thought that Spanish might fit the bill, even French or German, until – quite unexpectedly – a better solution presented itself. During the Sixties, when the Cold War showed no sign of thawing, it had become part of government educational policy to encourage the teaching of Russian in schools. Russian sounded exotic and dangerous, a double attraction.

'They needed people to understand the mind of the enemy,' he said, affecting a sinister voice and tapping his temple with his thick fingers.

And so he had learned Russian, continuing with it at university level. At that time philosophy was very much a second choice. He liked the fact that Russian had many of the charac-teristics of Latin –'It was as if I'd lost sixpence and found a shilling. All those declensions and cases and genders to get your teeth into.' At first he shone, and after a year or two he became just about good enough to be able to read some of the great nineteenth-century novelists. To his great and lasting regret, however, he had never reached the stage of being able to speak the language fluently. And if he had to single out a reason for this he would point the finger at the Russian verb. He had driven himself half-mad trying to master it, but to no avail. Since there were only three tenses – past, present and future – it ought to have been simple. A piece of cake, he said. But the Russians – Russkis, he called them – had invented something called *aspects*, designed to compensate for this shortage of tenses.

'Utterly baffling they were. Still are, I expect.'

He poured another shot of whisky into his cup.

'Quite pernicious in fact. And a hopeless substitute for the present continuous or the past perfect. You know, English-speaking people have no idea how lucky they are to be able to say *I am writing a letter* or *He has been considering his position*. I bet you'd like some of that in French. Such *useful* tenses. Too wonderful to be taken for granted.'

Sanderson's expression was one of comic surprise, as if he'd managed only now, and purely by chance, to identify the problem that had been blighting his life. But it failed to convince. There surely had to be more to his malaise than a youthful failure to master a foreign language. For a minute or two he stared into space, and when he next spoke it was once again on the subject of his introductory talk to the students.

'I should be used to it by now,' he said. 'It's the same thing year in year out – the necessary business of processing large numbers of students at the start of the autumn term – or *semester* as everyone now has to call it.' He likened it to tagging cattle before they went into the field – 'Not that I've ever done that, you understand.' The students always took a couple of minutes to settle down, he said – you noticed that sort of thing when you'd been doing it for years. Some of them would find a seat near the front, before thinking better of it. Then, with that artificial cool designed to conceal first-year nerves, they would take cover in the rows further back. It had been cold and wet that day, and the room was soon filled with the smell of damp clothing. Nearly everyone, he had noted, was wearing a fleece with cryptic words written on the front. The start of each academic year was such a catwalk for students, he said, everyone strutting and posing and displaying to one another. This year several of the young women seemed, improbably, to be wearing skirts over trousers. Though he was used to his wife's rather unorthodox dress style, these new fashions made him feel quaint, obsolete, out of touch. As he surveyed his audience, full of 'fresh faces not yet discouraged by life', he had played his usual game: trying to spot the sheep and goats among them. Through long experience he had learned to apply something akin to the principle of triage – 'you know, the sort of thing those brave men from the medical corps did in the war,' he said. 'Crawling over the bodies in the battlefield, assessing the urgency of medical need, making split-second decisions about who could be saved, passing over those who would die anyway.' For a moment he had even imagined himself in khaki and a tin hat, he said, flat on his belly, pulling himself along on his elbows among the wounded, closing the eyes of the dead, comforting the no-hopers, performing small acts of gentleness in the field of battle. Sanderson's eyes had a faraway look. 'Absurd, of course.' He drew on his pipe. 'Courage is not something I've ever possessed.'

Yet he pursued the comparison. Out of these hundred or so students, he said, the majority would be left to die where they fell. Some would do so in silence, even with dignity. Others would prolong the process, 'covering the syllabus, yes, but futilely and unbecomingly, emitting noises consistent with their inexorable decline'. At this point he made a low bellowing noise, like a birthing cow. He thought that American students in particular were often eager to live long after all hope should have been decently abandoned. 'They have a misplaced trust in the world, and even when the situation is dire, they give off a whiff of optimism, like the smell of fresh paint.' By way of an afterthought he said that he was fond of American students and felt something approaching tenderness for them.

I wondered to what extent the whisky was dictating these lines, and right on cue he reached for the bottle again. After pouring himself another he held it out towards me. 'Are you sure you won't?' he said. I told him I tended to drink alcohol only with food, adding – to avoid sounding censorious – that it was the same with most French people. 'And I tend to drink alcohol at every opportunity,' he quipped. 'You'll find this applies to most people in Scotland.' When I asked if perhaps he was drinking to ease the discomfort of his skin condition, he looked touchingly surprised, as if it were the strangest notion. 'That would imply a rationale for drinking,' he said, sidestepping neatly. 'But I'm not sure there is one in my case. Sometimes I drink just because I'm alive – *I drink therefore I am*, our Cartesian friends might say. And then I drink more to sober up. Which is an old custom in Russia. They even have a special word for it.' And with another sidestep he returned to his winding narrative of the day's events.

Surveying his fresh young audience, he said, he had suddenly been struck by how absurd it was to be in the business of teaching when he himself had learned so little. At which point his colleague, a man by the name of Gordon Macrae, had breezed in and asked with a grin if Sanderson was ready to be thrown to the lions. Macrae was head of department, 'a ludicrously young specimen', someone who had made a habit of taking up positions to further his career – 'a *faux bonhomme*, if ever there was one!' Sanderson couldn't stand him. He was a medieval beast of a man with an orange face, like a root vegetable, and with one of those moustaches men sported a hundred years ago. In fact he was 'a whole study in orange', his freckled skin merging with his tweed jacket to produce the semitones of an English autumn. His teeth were stained russet brown, and his hair – 'in keeping with his Celtic origins, but no less unfortunate for that' – was what people normally called *ginger*. Sanderson said that ginger was one of those cheating words, like moribund or stout, that didn't begin to convey the disagreeable thing they purported to describe. Carrot, or plain orange, would be nearer the mark. He had contemplated his younger colleague, as if for the first time, and realised that he knew scarcely anything about him. How was it possible, he wondered, to work in the same small department, to see someone day after day, to exchange greetings, and yet know nothing of the man?

The question was rhetorical. By this point in his story Sanderson seemed scarcely conscious of my presence. If I had slipped out of the room he would surely have continued talking. His gaze had floated off somewhere into the middle distance and the tight smile on his lips was fixed like a bayonet.

'What about your other colleagues?' I asked, thinking back to the strange group I had met after the Hume lecture.

'I don't really know them either,' he said. 'Not as people anyway. And they don't interest me much as philosophers. They're just daft laddies really. Too busy applying for grants and aggrandising themselves. You know the sort of thing – the wind in their own sails. The rest are like Macrae – managers. Though I must admit Macrae is good at getting the attention of the students. He has a natural authority about him.'

Sanderson had observed him closely that day. How did he manage it? Like many academics, he said, Macrae spoke haltingly, and portentously, as if his life experience had been so profound as to make it virtually untranslatable to ordinary mortals. 'And yet he was talking to them about timetables and course requirements. Amazing.'

When Macrae had finished, it was Sanderson's turn. There was the usual coughing and babble to accompany a break in the proceedings. Sanderson got to his feet and waited for quiet. He had begun by welcoming everyone to the Department of Philosophy, remembering, too late, the circular from the

Faculty Office advising that there would be no more *Departments*, only *Schools*. As usual the Executive had urged *compliance*, and he had just failed to comply. He found he had to settle himself, take a deep breath. At this point in the narrative I too took a deep breath, as though to stave off something bad. Sanderson said he had felt awkward in his body, strangely self-conscious. His voice, normally quite smooth when he was relaxed, struck him now as hoarse and strained. I could hear it reverberating, he said, as if something had plugged my ears and was forcing the sound inwards. He heard himself drone on and on, trying to clear the choke from his throat, the plugs from his ears, all the while outlining the different courses on offer – *modules* they were called now – as well as the number of essays required, not forgetting the policy in case of non-attendance at tutorials. As he spoke he had been assailed by a number of images that had nothing to do with the task in hand. He tried to pull himself back into the warm damp classroom, but the images kept coming, not always in sequence or focus, but persistent and continual. One was the face of a small boy, maybe seven or eight years old, anxious to please his parents, trying to understand house rules that were sometimes inscrutable. Another came from a different time, maybe ten years later, but still the same small boy, now a man in appearance, his innocence lost along with his desire to please, leaving home with a sense of joy and relief and the determination never to return. That image had given way to another, fresh in his mind from this morning, an unremarkable morning, attended by dull, predictable exchanges between himself and his wife. His voice ringing in his ears, he had imagined himself in the missionary position, bearing down heavily with enrolment procedures, heaving his way through the *module* requirements, and finally ejaculating the marking system. 'Though climactic, the marking system brought no relief,' he said, turning to look at me and discharging another blast of laughter. He was at full throttle now, unflagging, unstoppable. There was plainly an implacable need to go over the event, again and again, to bludgeon it into a tame thing that would no longer snarl and bite. He held his pipe so tight that his knuckles shone white amongst the suppurations. They looked liked small exotic fish with barbels and staring eyes.

He had felt exposed in front of his students as never before, he said. And all of a sudden he had grown conscious of his hands, problematic now like his voice. They were the same hands that he used to tie the most delicate trout fly, but suddenly they felt thick and heavy. I thought I must be having a stroke, he said. The movements he made with his hands had struck him as curiously unsynchronised, like a badly dubbed film. He could not be sure if this was a question of *seeming* rather than *being*, a confusion that had spread to different areas of his life just recently. He had tried putting his hands by his sides. They hung there limply for a while, but soon they started jerking and twitching from the wrist — 'just like a swimmer waiting to dive into the water before a race'. He tried hooking his thumbs over the waistband of his trousers, only to find himself worrying that the students would find his trousers *sad* or *uncool* or whatever word they used nowadays.

'My wife says that there's a certain kind of man who wears his trousers hopelessly high above the waist,' he said, his face pulling a sad-clown expression. 'And that men can't begin to imagine the level of despond this can engender in a woman.'

I smiled at the idea, and at the same time found myself checking my own trousers.

'Oh yes,' he continued, taking another swig. 'She can tell a lot about a man from his trousers, my wife. So she claims. She says they provide a guide to his character at least as dependable as any other ready reckoner.' Of course he had disputed that, but she maintained it was the result of many years of observation, and as a theory it had achieved the status of empirical fact. Empirical fact! Huh, he had scoffed, what the hell did she know about empirical fact? But quick as a flash she had come back at him:

Empirical fact is that which is based on experience, observed neutrally and dispassionately, and derived ultimately from the five senses. Oh really, and where had she learned that little nugget? As a matter of fact I learned it from *you*, she said. Sanderson sighed in recollection. That was the trouble with women, he said. They could build elaborate theories on the basis of negligible data, and just as you were beginning to think they were on shaky ground they would hit you with something irrefutable.

On and on he went. By the end I wasn't so much listening as taking shelter from the barrage. It amazed me that Sanderson could talk at such length about himself, without the least encouragement, and to someone he had met only a short time ago. Was the famed reticence of the British a myth? I remembered reading somewhere that people who were marooned could set themselves afloat again by telling stories. Perhaps this was what was happening with Sanderson. Talking at length was his means of survival.

'I'm a disappointed man, that's what I am,' he said. 'But at least you know where you are with disappointment, whereas with happiness, anything can happen.'

17

During our fishing trip the next day, Sanderson would confide
to me that in the early days of his marriage, he was convinced
that he had felt happiness – 'whatever anyone means by happiness'. We were packing up our gear on the coarse grass at the
edge of the loch, where the water was making a soft slapping
noise. By now the sun had gone, leaving behind dark blue shafts
across the sky. My day had been spent learning how to cast a fly
on the water, hour after hour of curling the line back behind the
head and dropping it lightly on the loch, with Sanderson at my
side, gently guiding and encouraging. It must have been a thank-
less task, but he gave no sign of it. Which endeared him to me
greatly, and made me think about the possibilities of friendship.
More than that, everything about the casting business – feeling
the weight of the line, finding the right balance, the rhythms and
repetitions, the arc in the air and the circle on the water – all
this seemed to have acted on the mood of the day and made it
benign. I seized my chance.

'Well, what do *you* mean by it?'

For a few moments he continued to sort his fly-box, arranging the flies in neat rows according to size and colour. After
which he said that it was hard to feel confident about using the

word, at least without some qualification or modification, and without sounding self-conscious or mocking. 'But since you press me, here's a concrete example.' And he asked me to imagine sitting on a crowded train from Edinburgh to London, with someone talking inanely and at volume in another part of the carriage. 'You know the type – a loudmouth touched only very lightly by education or imagination, absolutely nothing in his head worth saying, but determined to say it anyway. By the time you reach Newcastle you are ready to strangle him with your bare hands – anything to stop him yakking. And then – hallelujah – he gets off at York.' Sanderson clapped his hands together. 'Now *that* is happiness!'

I couldn't help feeling let down by this. I had expected more. He was trifling with me.

'Oh, but I'm not, Eddie,' he said. 'I'm deadly serious. If you've read your Montaigne you'll remember his saying that the greatest feeling of wellbeing in the whole of his life was when a kidney stone popped out of his penis.'

'*La belle lumière de santé* – that's what he calls it,' I said, as if quoting the original French might give me the upper hand. 'But surely that's not happiness. That's relief.'

'Relief certainly, except it's more than that. It's not just the physical release from pain – it's a transcendental thing. A lightness of being.'

'Well, people in France – and I tend to agree with them – think that Montaigne talked far too much about his urinary tract problems.' Even as I said it I knew it sounded stupid and childish.

'Surely you can do better than that, Eddie,' he smiled, giving me a gentle kick with his wellington as if to mark our friendship.

'Sorry,' I said, feeling slightly shamed. But I was actually glad, not sorry. Sanderson had extended an amiable boot in my direction and it felt good.

'So, what are you saying? That happiness – in the examples you give – couldn't have arisen if it hadn't been for the initial torment?'

'Precisely,' he said. 'Which is why I think that happiness often reveals itself as counterpoint. It is edged about with things that are opposite to it.'

He went on to say that the word itself had been hijacked. By the evangelicals – the happy-clappy brigade – and by those who traded in trite new-age psychobabble. Which made difficulties for the rest of us, he said.

'Even at the philosophical level, it's almost impossible not to end up with slogans. You know the sort of thing – John Stuart Mill's *If you have to ask yourself if you're happy, you're not*, or the Hedonists' mantra: *The more you aim at happiness, the less you get*. It all sounds so glib. They tell you how it's *done*, Eddie, but they don't tell you how to *do* it.' He laughed. 'If that doesn't sound too nonsensical.'

I reminded him that he still hadn't actually said what *he* meant by it. He snapped the fly-box shut, and for a moment I thought the subject might also be closed. But instead he turned to face me and, hesitating for a moment or two, as if there was some indecision about how to proceed, he said that what he believed was this: that there was such a thing as ordinary happiness – nothing too exalted or thrilling – and there was also something that could be called ordinary unhappiness – again nothing too extreme. No famine or flood or multiple tragedy. Within these parameters there was a scale, and at different points in our lives we were on different points of the scale. 'The trouble with all the *isms* in my book is that none takes proper account of human nature.'

Was it always subjective? I asked. Or could it be measured objectively? 'In so far as it's a feeling of wellbeing, a state of mind – call it what you will – it has to be subjective.' Could it be isolated? He doubted it. But yes, people had tried to measure it. Scientists had looked at factors that promote happiness – calibrating levels of serotonin, and the like. And governments were interested in their findings. There was even evidence to suggest that the happiest people were those with religious faith.

'And do you doubt that?'

'No, I don't doubt it. But where does it get us, Eddie? Belief in God is just another lifestyle choice, like jogging round the Meadows or going to Tenerife on holiday. It's only one possibility among many. It doesn't follow that religion is a necessary condition of happiness.' People talked a whole lot of rubbish about the meaning of life, he said, as if that were exclusive to religion. But meaning could be found in many things – tying the perfect fly, for example, giving a good lecture, or fixing a leaky tap perhaps. 'I, for example, couldn't ever bring myself to believe in God, not even if a gun were held to my head. But fortunately the religious frame of mind is not the only frame of mind. There are other less delusional states. Or maybe they are just other forms of delusion.'

'What do you mean by that?'

He hardly knew where to start, he said. The world was full of illusions and the way we interpreted them involved varying degrees of self-delusion. Religious belief was the most obvious one. Since earliest times people had had a propensity to believe in something. They wanted a purpose, a meaning that would render their lives significant rather than valueless – 'not the only two alternatives, though it often seems that way'. After food and water, he said, there was a search for meaning. But this meaning was endlessly shifting, and he gave the example of believers constantly oscillating between assertion of literal truth and metaphor, so that as soon as something was incapable of bearing the weight of significance placed on it by Christian theology – such as the resurrection – it suddenly became *symbolic*. And religion – all religions – existed in this realm of toing and froing.

'But isn't there such a thing as symbolic truth?' This was all I could think of, a way of staying in the conversation.

'Symbolic truth is just a kind of sophisticated equivocation, Eddie, of having it both ways.' He blew through his pipe. 'There is nothing that cannot be configured to fit with the belief,' he said. 'Believers interpret the world according to some divine plan, and whatever occurs in the world, however brutal and catastrophic, is accommodated within the plan, which is somehow considered noble and benevolent in the face of overwhelming evidence to the contrary. God is made to fill in the gap that man can't explain. Whatever happens, God has all the cards. The last word, and the last laugh.' He gave a loud cackle, competing with God.

'Doesn't free will come into it somewhere?'

It could have been an idiotic question, but Sanderson nodded his approval. 'You've put your finger right on it, Eddie,' he said. 'Free will is only ever mentioned when religious people want to point up the stupidity of man – never the cruelty of their benevolent God and his ugly divine plan.' The fact was that religion flourished on fear, and even now, in the twenty-first century, it was propagated compulsorily, 'like potatoes in the reign of Catherine the Great'. False narratives had power – 'it was ever thus' – and religion provided comfort, albeit a false comfort. 'Put it this way, Eddie, God is the ultimate imaginary friend,' he said.

'But don't we all have our own particular form of imaginary friends? It doesn't have to be God.' I was thinking of all the props that got me through my childhood years.

'Of course it doesn't, and that's the very point I'm trying to make. We all believe in something. It can be fate or chance or magic or some other wishy-washy unobservable – a metaphysical jumble sale from which a bargain might be plucked.' With his swollen hand he plucked an imaginary bargain from the air and brought it under his gaze. 'But it's all self-deceiving, will-o'-the-wisp stuff.'

Self-deception was a really interesting subject, he said. It even had a paradoxical look about it. Some people, philosophers among them, even argued that there was no such thing. After all, how could you set about misleading *yourself*? Surely you would know what you were up to, which would undermine the deception. And if you knew what you were doing, how was it possible to trick yourself into believing otherwise? But philosophers had always overestimated the rational side of human behaviour, he said. Self-deception might seem to require that the same person be both the deceiver and the deceived, and yet we all knew very well what was meant and understood by it. We were even quite lenient on it, precisely because it was regarded as one of those things that you couldn't quite help – an irrational minor-moral-flaw sort of transgression. 'This is where literature is more instructive than philosophy,' he said. 'Novels are full of unhappy people – not just because happiness is tricky to write about, but because there is a ton of unavoidable suffering in the world, and it is the job of writers to reflect that back to readers.' And if ever happiness *was* touched on, he said, it was always qualified or provisional, in exactly the way we knew it to be in life.

'Take *Anna Karenina*,' he said, animated now. 'Vronsky is happiest when he's on his way to see Anna, not when he's actually with her.' He paused to fill and light his pipe, disclosing between inhalations that he'd noticed something else: that those who were most deluded were often portrayed as the happiest. Happiness might even be a kind of madness. 'Maybe you've noticed that too? Think of Mr Dick in *David Copperfield*, for example. He's a gentle lunatic whose simple-mindedness enables him to know just what's needed in situations that paralyse all the other characters – those that spend their time thinking too much. And even though Mr Dick has the so-called trouble of King Charles in his head, his heart remains gentle and loving. And he's *happy*.'

'But you surely wouldn't want to change places with him?'

'I'm not so sure,' he said. 'I'm not so sure.' Sanderson had a touch of high definition about him now – the skin redder, the face fuller, the hair a little wilder. 'The unexamined life is much despised. According to Socrates, it is not worth living. But actually, the examined life can get you into all sorts of trouble.'

After which we packed everything into the car and made our

way back to Edinburgh. Later, in the pub where we had stopped off for a drink, I took him back to his starting point, when he'd mentioned that in the early days of marriage he had known happiness. He now had the air of a man trying to hold on to something before it finally slipped away. Looking back, he said, he was sure he could still pick it out – like a distant boat on the horizon. But something else had taken its place, the intensity of which was hard to account for. It certainly bore no relation to what he had once felt. But that was the trouble. He had become confused about feelings, which ones to trust, which to ignore – assuming you could ignore a feeling, though he was pretty sure you couldn't. For the most part he and his wife lived together like people under hypnosis, and their conversations were dead things. Now they didn't even use each other's names when they communicated. He had loved her name at the beginning – apart from being bright and cheerful, it had suited her. She herself disliked it greatly – she had never forgiven her parents for naming her, in a fit of enthusiasm for biblical virtues, *Caritas*. When she and Sanderson first met he had told her it was a beautiful name – and a million times better than Faith and Hope, the names that had cursed her sisters' lives. Besides, with its connotations of selfless love, *Caritas* fitted perfectly with his original sense of her. But this had been before everything 'thickened and coarsened', as he put it. And with the thickening his wife's name had come to sound ridiculous, a mockery almost. Nowadays he tried not to say it if he could help it. In fact, if a 'Carrie' slipped out accidentally he regarded it as an aesthetic lapse.

From an intelligent man this struck me as a stupid remark. It was Sanderson – not Carrie's name – that was ridiculous. And yet this was surely just another sign of his suffering – a minor ailment had become the focus of pain, a distraction from the underlying anguish.

It took away from his own name, he continued, perhaps sensing the need for explanation, yet becoming indignant in the process. How he hated that they were a 'rhyming couple' –

Harry & Carrie. And how strange that this doublet could once have sounded harmonious. Now it was merely laughable, 'like an irritating jingle or a has-been comedy act'. People in the pub were beginning to glance in our direction. It was time to go. It had been a long day at the loch, and though I hadn't caught anything, the smell of fish had mysteriously attached itself to my hands and clothes. I longed to get back and have a shower. But Sanderson was not yet ready to leave.

He said he couldn't remember when it had started. The doubt. The dismay. It was all a bit of a blur. His wife wasn't herself, hadn't been for a while. He couldn't say for how long. There had been the business with the boy, of course, but that was over now. And it certainly wasn't enough to account for everything. He now had no idea what was going on in her head. She avoided speaking to him if at all possible. Except when they clashed, which they did quite regularly. How had all this come about? The decline seemed not to be linear – more meandering and serpentine. No sooner had they confronted one difficult matter and put it to bed, than it mysteriously reappeared and had to be trudged through all over again. How did this happen? He wished he knew. In fact he could no longer recall the reasons for marrying in the first place, if indeed there were actual *reasons*. Perhaps his mind had been elsewhere and she, his wife, had done the marrying. Ha! – another pistol going off. Occasionally, he conceded, they would do something effortful and purposeful together, a conscious attempt to pull themselves out of the bog. Only last week, for example, they had bought a table at IKEA, a kind of nod in the direction of a normal life together – an IKEA table being both a frivolous and a more serious nod than a table from any other department store. *Frivolous* because of the ease with which you could drive up to the store along with hundreds of other people and just choose it, pay for it downstairs and take it away with you, there and then, instead of waiting a week or two for delivery – all of which led you to believe that what you were doing was absolutely normal and pleasurable, denoting domestic harmony, otherwise why would so many other couples be doing the same? But an IKEA table was also *serious* because you had to build it when you got home. You had to make sense of the diagram, try to be patient and reasonable, connect the picture and the instructions with the terrifying collection of parts strewn on the floor, and fit the right pieces together, male to female, screw to thread. A metaphor for domestic life in fact. Sanderson paused and sighed heavily – which gave me the first chance to ask:

'What was the business with the boy? What happened?'

'Oh, he went off the rails. Started imagining things. Hearing voices. The whole works. Happens a lot apparently.'

I couldn't help thinking that everything I had learned about Sanderson thus far must be connected to this larger story. This was just my sense – it was impossible to know for certain. You rarely see anything as it truly is – something else my father said to me not long before he died. We had met for lunch and I had been trying to get my father to talk about the war, a subject on which he was maddeningly reticent. I had wanted to know more about his missions in France, whether he had felt fear, how he had found the courage to keep going. Courage hadn't come into it, he said. It was just a question of obeying orders. When pressed, he stayed firm. It was something you didn't think of, he said. You just kept your head down and got on with the job. He told me to remember that the whole picture was seldom to be seen, far less understood. You saw only individual fragments, and you built up a picture from these fragments, filling in the gaps as you saw fit, always according to what you sensed, or had been told, rather than what you knew. The picture is never complete – it's always lopsided or distorted in some way. Like a child's drawing, the composition is usually out of proportion or foreshortened. It's the same with people, he said. 'What is known about any individual is finite, and what is not known is infinite.'

*

But this is jumping ahead with my story. Back in his office that day, amidst the smoke and the whisky fumes, Sanderson was still wound up, preoccupied with what had happened earlier. 'I've been giving introductory talks to philosophy students for longer than I care to remember,' he said. They had improved over the years – he liked to think so anyway. He had polished the jokes, cut out the fat. Now he could give them standing on his head. 'In fact, that's what I told them. I can do this standing on my head, I said. Perhaps you'd all prefer it that way. At least it would amuse you. Whereas in truth there is not a lot that amuses in my subject. Ah *truth*! There, I've said it. Truth!'

He was sitting opposite me on the other side of his desk, but at this point he got up and walked on painful feet to the window. He stood now with his back to me, addressing an imaginary audience. 'I suppose there are some of you here who think philosophy is to do with truth. Let me tell you, you are mistaken. Truth is an awkward bugger. Most of us go through life seeking it, looking for something we can call true. When we find it – *if* we find it – we feel more secure, and we repeat it to others, as much to affirm it to ourselves as anything else. But the truth is not necessarily valid. It's temporary, provisional. Accept one truth, and we deny another. The difficult business is admitting it. Others among you may think that philosophy will provide us with answers. Ha! You couldn't be more wrong. I'd love to be able to tell you that philosophy is a way of life, a manual for everyday experience – How Best To Live, and all that crap. But it's not. The most philosophy will teach you is how to identify the problem.'

When he was done he turned to face me once more, and was silent for a moment or two before explaining that at this point in his address to the students he had become aware of Macrae – 'old Carrot-Face' – looking askance at him and jotting something down in a notebook. This had served only to provoke Sanderson, who had warmed to his theme and abandoned all restraint. 'I gave it to them both barrels,' he said, eyes blazing now and taking another swig. 'I told them there's a lot of nonsense talked about philosophy these days, and a lot of cod philosophers giving philosophy a bad name.'

Cod philosophers? I pictured a shoal of thinking fish, engaged in Socratic dialogue.

You should not imagine, he had advised the students, that studying philosophy would help with the chaos of life. Nothing could help with that. 'In this benighted subject everything has to be deconstructed first before it can be responded to,' he said. 'And what's the use in that? My colleagues will no doubt lecture you on reason, and the supremacy of the rational life. But it's all a joke. We kid ourselves into thinking that we make purely rational choices. Reason is something we attach to the choice *after* the initial impulse or desire. And one thing you can be sure of: desire is anarchic, unpredictable. It strikes unbidden and overwhelms its victim. Literature will teach you that, and philosophy will not save you. Nor will philosophers. Like everyone else, we lead ridiculous lives.'

I found it hard to disagree with this last statement. Sanderson cut a pitiful figure, and with trousers rolled up, bags on his feet and skin peeling off, his appearance hovered between comedy and farce. There was also a touch of performance in his rant, something Thespian – Alice's influence perhaps? Back in Sanderson's narrative, however, this mention of ridiculous lives had evidently been too much for the head of department, who had leapt to his feet and announced abruptly that time was up. Details of all the courses on offer could be found in the leaflet at the back of the room, he told the students, and appointments could be made with individual staff members to discuss any questions arising.

What happened, he had asked Sanderson as soon as they were alone. What on earth happened? Macrae's face was red with anger, his freckles a shade or two darker.

'What happened? What *happened*?' Sanderson spat Macrae's question back at him – and now, in the retelling, he discharged a small slobber in my direction. 'As a philosopher, you should know that nothing can ever be said with any degree of precision to have *happened*. There's a quality of ambiguity about everything – different interpretations, different accounts. Make of it what you will, dear boy. You're the head of department. Make of it what you will. That's my advice.'

And for good measure he had added a *fuck you* before leaving.

I wondered why he was telling me all this. At that stage we scarcely knew one another. The following day we would experience the sort of fellowship that comes from two men spending the day fishing together, but for the time being there was very little to connect us. His professional conduct was really none of my business. Yet it had all come pouring out unbidden, as if he could not help spilling it. I was torn between awkwardness and a kind of ghoulish prurience – also a desire to help, overlaid by a stronger feeling that there was nothing to be done. He was plainly a man in crisis, unravelling before my eyes, and the odd thing was that I felt pulled in by it and detached from it at the same time. Detachment was something that came naturally to me. The other impulse was unusual – it embarrassed me. Sanderson himself evidently felt no embarrassment. In a curious way he seemed invigorated by his outpourings. He talked as if his life depended on the talking. And he required very little in return from me. At certain points he would ask: Do you see what I mean? But he didn't wait for an answer.

Were his troubles professional? Or purely domestic? I examined him for possible clues. His face, which must have been handsome once, was bloated and slightly flushed. Beneath the blotchy skin there were signs of a complex vascular system. He had become animated in the telling, swinging back on his chair, thumping the desk with his bandaged feet, cutting the air with pipe in one hand, whisky in the other. I thought of Kafka's beetle, on its back, legs flailing.

It seemed a good point to leave. I stood up to go. Sanderson, suddenly aware once again of my presence, turned to look at me. Blowing through his pipe, holding his thumb over the bowl, he said:

'Do you ever think about what you might have been, Eddie?' His voice was quieter now. 'I mean, if you hadn't gone into translating.'

Moving towards the safety of the door, I told him that I had once wanted to be a philosopher. The irony caused me to blush.

'Well, well,' he said. 'You had a narrow escape.'

'It was to do with my father. I suppose all boys at some point want to become their father.'

'I didn't.' He looked into his whisky. 'Sometimes I feel quite ashamed to think how much I didn't want to be my father.'

'Why not?'

'Why not?' he repeated, evidently surprised by the question. 'I'm not really sure. I hardly ever considered him as an individual. Someone in his own right. He was just there. To be argued with, to feel ashamed of.'

'Ashamed?'

'Ashamed. Huh, the irony!' – another explosive laugh. 'To think I'm now ashamed of being ashamed.'

Sanderson spoke no more about his father, but he wasn't quite ready to stop. He said he sometimes considered who else he might have been, what else he might have done. After a short silence, he said: 'A plumber. I think I would like to have been a plumber.' People were always pleased to see plumbers, he said. All over the world they were greeted with a mixture of gratitude and relief. No one was ever pleased in quite the same way to see a teacher of moral philosophy. In fact outside the protected environment of the university, Sanderson was embarrassed to admit to what he did for a living. If ever he went to the dentist or the barber, he kept quiet about it. 'Whereas no man need ever feel ashamed to say he is a plumber.'

It had taken him forty years to realise that a great deal of what was crucial in the world was not understood by academics. They thought they knew the important things. He had even thought so once himself. Nowadays he made only an occasional nodding gesture at an idea, but otherwise his thinking was moribund. It was all about pulling the right levers, flicking a few switches, like driving a crane. Meanwhile the admin people wanted him to think of students as clients. And the clients wanted answers that philosophy couldn't give. He should have stuck with Russian literature.

'Just think, Eddie, the pathos of it. I used to love my job. There was a connection between the teaching and the rest of life. It was hard to tell the dancer from the dance. The dancer *was* the dance, yet he was also *other than* the dance. At any rate I dared to think that I might have been quite good at it. I believed it made a difference. Others seemed to think so too. Until a year or two ago I was someone who had status, respect, self-esteem – what the trendy evolutionists call *mate value*. Now I sit here with my feet in oil, soaking them in the basin I use for gutting fish, and with my skin shed all over the carpet.'

He paused for a moment or two. Somewhere along the corridor the drone of a distant vacuum cleaner could be heard.

'One day you're a peacock,' he said, 'the next you're a feather duster. It's an old, old story.'

18

On the day of our fishing trip Sanderson picked me up on the Calton Hill road and we drove out on the A7 towards Selkirk. He had two favourite rivers – one north and one south of Edinburgh – but for my first experience of fishing we would go to a small loch, he said. It would be easier for me to learn the principles of casting without getting the line snagged on trees – a common hazard on the riverbank.

After about an hour we turned off the main road, continued up a rough track and walked over a stony path for the last few hundred metres. The land seemed to unfold in all directions, a variety of greens tumbling into one another. And in the distance a patchwork of stone dykes and fencing that marked the land as being owned and of value.

In his fishing gear – waders, waterproofs and flat cap – Sanderson appeared altogether healthier than the shuffling, ailing figure of the previous evening. Clothes cover up as well as cover. Only his hands showed the telltale signs of affliction. One or two of the sores were open and bleeding.

The loch was long and narrow, nestled in between gently rolling hills. Sanderson said you could get waves on this loch as if it were the Atlantic Ocean. But that day the wind was light, barely ruffling the skin of the water. For a few moments we stood at the edge, looking out over the loch, as if by prior arrangement, not speaking. After which Sanderson started to get everything ready, first removing his split-cane rod from a cloth bag and laying the three sections, delicate and beautiful, onto the ground, then rolling up the bag and placing it under a stone before setting down the reel and fly-box next to the rod. The whole procedure was carried out with sacramental solemnity. He then showed me how the rod was put together. At the end of each section there was a brass ring known as a *ferrule*, bound with scarlet thread called *whippings*. Sanderson fitted the ferrules, male to female, together – 'See how perfectly they fit,' he said, and to demonstrate the perfection he pulled strongly to get them apart again. On separation they gave an audible 'plop' – the sweetest sound you could ever hear, he said, grinning broadly. 'Beats a champagne cork any day.' Slowly, reverentially, he joined the sections, attaching the reel and threading the line through the metal-ringed eyes that were whipped at regular intervals along the length of the rod. 'Your fly is connected to the line by a leader,' he explained. 'And remember, the fly itself weighs hardly anything – it's just gossamer silk and feather on a small hook. This means that before you cast you have to pull the line off the reel and shoot it back and forwards.'

To learn how to cast, he said it was best for me to watch first and listen later. He chose a fly from his box, attached it expertly, and to my surprise he then removed a square of material about the size of a pocket handkerchief from his fishing bag, placed it on the ground, and weighted each corner with a few pebbles. He then walked away for twenty metres or so. 'The trick is to try and place your fly, get it in the centre,' he said, and with that he did a deft back-flick so that the line uncurled behind him, after which he flicked it forward – just a gentle movement of the wrist as in striking a glockenspiel – whereupon the line snaked in the air in a perfect parabola before straightening and falling soundlessly onto the handkerchief with the fly dead centre. This pinpoint accuracy was repeated again and again, and I felt completely captivated – as much by the sheer skill of it as by the quiet dignified demeanour of the man. 'The split cane holds the energy,' he said, 'and this energy translates the quick forward flick into a kind of serpentine elegance.' It had the rhythms of poetry, and he was the poet.

When he had finished on dry land he waded into the water, taking time to find firm footholds. At about ten metres out he started to cast, backwards and forwards, backwards and forwards, swinging his right arm to and fro, cutting the air with the loop of his line. He made it look simple and natural. I could happily have watched him all day long. It was like some magical performance, a circus act that made you hold your breath in admiration. He was a lion tamer with an extra long whip, supreme master of the ring.

When it was my turn he gave me his second rod to hold and stood behind me, his arm underneath my arm, his hand holding my wrist. Slowly he moved my arm up and back. I felt stiff and awkward at first, uncomfortable at being held by him. Relax, he said, bend your arm, find a rhythm, loosen your wrist. The secret of good casting was to start with the line straight. The fly would move with the line, he said, and the line would follow the tip of the rod. At some point during the forward thrust the rod should be brought to a halt, and at that point the line would project in the direction that the rod was taking before it was stopped. Think of it as flicking paint off the end of a brush, he said. The more abrupt the flick, the more the paint comes off and the further it goes. Not that distance was everything, he said, especially not at the beginning. Instead I should concentrate on getting a continuous movement through my casting arm, starting slowly and building up momentum, then stopping and watching the line go. It was a lot to remember and, not being a natural angler, I groaned inwardly as my first attempt curled behind my head in slow motion, ending up tangled in the long grass that skirted the loch. 'Don't worry,' he said. 'The first cast is like the first pancake. It doesn't count.'

Sanderson was a patient teacher, gentle and encouraging. His words were light and airy, not freighted with the gloom of the previous evening. In fact his whole disposition seemed to have been rearranged into something altogether more genial and at ease with itself. As if reading my thoughts, he patted me on the back and declared that all my efforts would one day be worthwhile – the greatest pleasure in all of life being to catch a trout on your own dry fly. 'It's the nearest thing to transcendence,' he said, 'provided you do it the right way – the hard way – and follow the rules.'

When we stopped to eat an hour or two later, however, his other side emerged once again. Carrie had packed a lunch for both of us. More rabbit food, he grunted, unpacking the bag. But he was wrong – there was crisp French bread as well as two kinds of cheese, olives and plums. We sat on a grassy bank, the sun casting a long shadow to the middle of the loch, and while we ate, I learned more than I cared to know about what Sanderson called the ruin of his marriage. Since we sat side by side, looking out on the black water, his words seemed not to be directed at me, but at some unseen distant witness, who might or might not have been listening; and perhaps because we were eating food prepared by Carrie, I had the idea that we were in some sense devouring her character, sinking our teeth into her being, swallowing her spirit. All of this felt treacherous. Sanderson's narrative was sinuous, exasperatingly so, and I longed to pin him down to dates, times, reasons, circumstances – but instead I let him tell it in his own way without interruption. This was when 'the boy' was first mentioned, in the context of Carrie's behaviour and her pursuit of fads such as meditation and breathing techniques. The narrative went off in various directions, some of them leading nowhere, but by the time we had finished eating, our fingers having stiffened with cold, a picture of the Sandersons' home life was beginning to emerge.

19

Carrie McLeod had turned up as a first-year student in Sanderson's moral philosophy class. He had noticed her straight away, he said, partly because her young neck was as long and smooth and graceful as a swan's, partly because she was quick to answer questions – though there was also a dreaminess about her, as if she were less than fully present in the room. She would sit on the window side of the classroom, her hand cupped under one elbow, the other hand cradling her chin. Sanderson thought her face had something of the quality of a medieval saint – eyes set wide apart, and the features soft yet powerful, containing the promise of healing and protection. Unlike the other students, she didn't seem to be part of a group. Sanderson had concluded that she was either too unusual to belong to a group, or that she generated envy and was therefore excluded. Although she did well in her term exams she left before completing her degree.

In those days Sanderson was dating a lawyer, Elsa King, a career woman in her early forties – the same age as Sanderson at the time. Elsa was an adviser to the university on legal matters and had a position on the university court. She and Sanderson had been together for about three years, not living together, but seeing each other regularly while making minimal demands on one another. She had been married before and it was clear she would not be taking that route again – which suited Sanderson perfectly. He was not seeking commitment, and he liked the fact that he was not responsible for her happiness, nor she for his. It pleased him that they didn't cause each other trouble or share anything much apart from their bodies. His university pension plan was described in the advertising literature as 'low-investment, high-return, variable-term, zero-maintenance', and this was how he had come to think of his relationship with Elsa. He was also encouraged by the fact that she was able to separate sex from love, something he had thought up till then only men could do. In his experience women usually wanted more, and in this regard Elsa was refreshingly different. Not quite perfect, however. He sometimes had the feeling that Elsa approached sex with a clipboard and pencil, ticking things off the list, giving marks out of ten: timing, positions, foreplay, imagination, and so on. This could be testing for a man, he said, inviting me to agree and causing me to blush. Moreover, during sex she made 'a great song and dance', leading him to assume she had reached undreamed-of heights. But immediately after climaxing she would speak in a normal voice about something completely banal – *Have you seen my nail clippers?* or *I must take the cat to the vet.* Which rather broke the spell for Sanderson and made him feel that he had failed to hold her attention.

One day, he had gone to the Signet Library on Parliament Square, where he knew Elsa was sitting for a portrait. The Law Society of Scotland had commissioned the top three graduates from Edinburgh College of Art to do portraits of a number of distinguished lawyers – of whom Elsa was one. Sanderson had arrived at the Signet Library, in the heart of Edinburgh's Old Town, a place of Georgian splendour, he said, once described by King George IV as 'the finest drawing room in Europe', and it was there, as he stood in the doorway of the lower library, that his life changed direction. At first he hadn't recognised the artist. She had her back to him, and it was her back he studied as it flexed and rolled, apparently in perfect harmony with her paintbrush. It was a beautiful sight – strong and vital and completely spellbinding, he said. Compared with the artist, who went about her business with such energy and flow – all this being evident from the back view – the subject of the portrait, Elsa, looked stiff and lifeless, all blood and vigour drained from her. Sanderson stood for a while, concealed from both of them, contemplating the scene and all that it implied.

He had not at first noticed the little boy, so small and still was he, perched on one of the ornate chairs on the back wall. But when the boy looked up from his book Sanderson caught the movement and was surprised. At this point he walked forward into the enormous room, thinking he had better reveal himself. The artist turned round, and he was astonished to see that it was Carrie McLeod, the quick bright student who had been only half-present in his classroom years before. Now she looked fully present in the world, confident in herself, connected to others. The effect on Sanderson was both sweet and sharp. As soon as she greeted him, in the hypnotically lilting Hebridean tones that he remembered from the time she first spoke in his philosophy class, he felt the tug of desire, the faint allure of sexual possibility. From that moment on his relationship with Elsa would deflate like a slow puncture.

The second shock was to discover that the boy – he was about two years old at the time – belonged to Carrie. A child must have a father, he thought, and a father would surely interfere with the idea that was already beginning to form in his imagination. But he quickly established – not too eagerly, he hoped – that Carrie was a single parent. The father, whoever he might be, was completely absent from the child's life as well as her own.

The next shock came later when he realised that he felt almost no regret in letting go of Elsa. And to think they had been so well suited. 'As I said, it was a perfect arrangement.' It was, of course, a common mistake to equate sex with love. Even so, he was surprised to learn that satisfying the first with Elsa had not elicited the second.

20

Some weeks later, in conversation with Carrie, I had reason to recall this part of Sanderson's monologue. In describing her own early response to Sanderson, Carrie would call it a *crush*, before revising it in the next moment to a *crushette*. 'It felt like a pang,' she said. 'Nothing you could call love. My father had just died and Harry filled the gap.'

Back at the side of the loch, however, Sanderson continued with his story. Before meeting Carrie, he said, he had never properly considered marriage as an option. In so far as he had thought about it at all, in the abstract, he had hoped that he wouldn't have to draw up a balance sheet. With luck, he would just *know*. And with Carrie he did know, though he couldn't help filling in the balance sheet anyway, if only for the pleasure of discovering that it was heavily weighted in favour of marriage. It seemed to be just what was required. She was vulnerable – he would protect her. She was the artist, chaotic and free-spirited – he was the thinker, ordered and disciplined. She was young, no more than a girl really, with a lot of growing up still to do – he was much older, with all the benefits experience can bring. Best of all, she already had a child – he therefore wouldn't need to provide one. With the big picture taken care of, the details would surely fall into place. They were married within the month.

Later in the pub Sanderson's mood had darkened. Jealousy was the last thing he had expected to feel, he said. Yet it came in torrents, and the shock of experiencing something he thought himself incapable of did nothing to stem the flow. 'I wanted her whole attention,' he said. But Carrie was completely caught up in the boy. It affected everything, including her judgement. She sacrificed herself for him selflessly and uncomplainingly, and he, Sanderson, was left with the scraps. Emotional leftovers, he called them, taking out his tobacco pouch. With the fingers of one hand he rubbed the flakes of tobacco into the palm of his other hand, breaking them down till they were loose enough to pack into the bowl of his pipe. 'I adjusted my expectations and told myself this was in the nature of marriage. But I knew it was a lie. It was in the nature of a particular sort of motherhood.'

His own mother had always maintained it was bad for children to be allowed to see that you loved them. It gave them ideas above their station, she said. Had Sanderson been a parent, this advice would have been followed to the letter, he said. Carrie, however, was 'profligate with love' – at least towards her child. She appeared not to be able to help herself.

'As the boy grew older, everything that people regard as good and miraculous about childhood was replaced by something less good, less miraculous. Innocence became wilfulness, wonder became rationality, playfulness became moodiness. By the time he was fifteen he was sullen and morose, lost to us. Well, lost to me anyway. His mother still had a way through to him.'

'And what happened to him?' I asked.

'He became delusional. At first I thought he was just acting up, but eventually he was admitted to a psychiatric unit and diagnosed as schizophrenic.'

'How long ago was this?'

Sanderson had to think before he answered.

'Nearly three years, I suppose. Seems longer.'

'What's his name?'

'His name?' he repeated, as if startled by the question. 'Alfie,' he said. 'He's called Alfie.'

For a while neither of us spoke. Then Sanderson broke the silence:

'You don't have children, do you?'

'No.'

'Take my advice, Eddie. Keep it that way. You can choose your partner in life, but you cannot choose your child.'

21

On our way back from the loch we were travelling along a narrow stretch of road. Sanderson was unusually quiet. In front of us was a huge lorry with lots of signage on the back, including a phone number inviting people to ring and comment on the quality of the lorry driver's driving. I turned this over in my head, wondering what sort of person would respond to such an invitation.

When at last Sanderson spoke, it was about Alice's art gallery. Sometimes he travelled like a crab, sideways, into a conversation.

'You should go there some time. It's worth a visit.'

Then, in a tone completely neutral, he suddenly said that Alice had given him up.

'Given you up? What do you mean?'

'I mean what I say. Given up being my lover. Given up having an affair. Given up fucking me. Given up *me*.'

A single piece of information, but hard to process all the same.

'Why?' The wrong question, but I could think of no other.

'What do you mean *why*?'

'Why has she given you up?'

'What sort of question is *that*? How should I know why she's given me up?'

'I'm sorry. I didn't know what else to say.'

'Don't be sorry. There's never any point in being sorry.'

A moment or two later he admitted he had wondered the same thing himself – why she had given him up. It had worked perfectly for more than ten years, he said, and posed no threat to either marriage. Alice and her husband got on very well, much better than most couples in fact.

'If their marriage were a painting, it would be all smooth brushstrokes in oil, lots of repetitive sweeps and nothing too violent or incongruous.'

Charles, Alice's husband, worked as an astronomer at the observatory, he said, while she ran the gallery. They were splendid hosts to their many friends. But Charles was gay, incorrigibly so, and though the two of them shared a bed at night, there was never any sex. They shared other things: the responsibilities of marriage, social engagements, friendships, the quiet rhythms of living in the same house.

'As I say, it was a wonderful arrangement,' said Sanderson. 'A model of its kind.'

'Do you love her?' I asked. He gave me a look as if my question had offended against common decency. Changing tack, I asked how they had met. How people came to be with one another was always interesting.

'Through my wife,' he said with an inscrutable snort. 'When she began to exhibit in Alice's gallery.'

I asked him if Carrie knew. Certainly not, he said. Then he cited Chekhov, 'who believed that every person lived his real, most interesting life under the cover of secrecy. I tend to agree. Don't you?' Besides, what his wife didn't know couldn't hurt her. 'Ignorance protects, reduces suffering.'

'What about honesty?'

'Honesty?' He repeated the word as if it were new to his lexicon and he had to try it out for size. 'Look, Eddie, take the advice of an older man. Honesty is one of these overrated virtues. When it comes to something like this you have a simple choice: to tell or not to tell. They're like different magnetic fields, and if you're not careful you end up being pulled taut between them. Best to keep quiet. Telling always runs the risk of wrecking lives.'

'And not telling – does that never wreck lives?'

He paused for a moment, taking his eyes off the road to give me a pitying look, before denouncing me for having read too many novels. He spoke as if he had a private source of knowledge, as if he didn't have to make do with what was available to ordinary mortals.

'People who take up honourable positions are often just serving their own self-image.'

I was stung, but said nothing. It was one of those put-downs that you can't answer without running the risk of seeming to act out what you're being accused of. My thoughts turned to poor Carrie and the pain this would surely cause her. Perhaps Sanderson was right: it was better she didn't know. And now that the affair was over, there would be no need for her ever to know.

It turned out that Alice had told him of her decision only a couple of days before, the day before the start of term. Which perhaps explained his outburst in front of the students and his prolonged agitation afterwards. She hadn't given a reason, except to say she thought it was 'time to move on'. Sanderson was scornful. Surely you can do better than that, he'd told her. *Move on?* It was as bad as the management-speak at the university. But she just smiled in a way that indicated there was no point in saying any more on the subject.

'Twelve years we were together.'

'It's a long time,' I said, wishing I could have offered a less banal response.

'And during those twelve years we had sex over four hundred times. Four hundred and thirty-one, to be precise.'

'You kept count?'

'I kept a log. In my desk, along with my fishing diary.'

'Why?' Again the question sounded feeble. But what I was really wondering was whether in the same circumstances I too might have kept a log. There was a fastidious side to Sanderson that intrigued and connected with me.

'Hard to say. I suppose it was some sort of record that I was alive. You know, in the world. Vital.' That was probably the point of most affairs, he said. Together with the feeling that everything becomes new again.

'I see.'

'You know, Eddie, one of the wonders of sexual behaviour is that a self-possessed, cool-headed, sophisticated woman, with bags of sangfroid and American propriety, can suddenly metamorphose into a shit-hot tigress with insatiable desires who begs to be fucked over and over, harder and harder.'

I tried to picture the scene: Alice and Sanderson – the slurp-click of interlocking parts. It wasn't possible.

'And you know something else? Four hundred times – that's not a lot. Not over twelve years anyway. That's the surprising thing. It sounds a lot. But it's less than once a week.'

He said that in the early years they had seen each other more often, but things had been tailing off for a year or two now. And scarcely anything at all since his skin flared up. He surely repelled her now. He repelled himself, after all.

'How did it start? Your affair, I mean.'

'I can't remember exactly. It was just one of these things.' He made a clicking noise with his tongue. 'Sometimes impulsive acts become permanent arrangements. The reason for starting gets long forgotten – maybe there never really was a reason – and the thing itself just carries on. A bit like marriage, come to think of it.'

He raised his head, as if to sniff the air or display a kind of chin-up stoicism – I wasn't sure which.

'I suppose I wanted something swift and convenient, without

the complications of commitment – you know, the always-ness of marriage.' Then: 'Does that shock you, Eddie?'

'I suppose lots of things shock me.'

'That doesn't of course mean that they are inherently shocking.'

'No, of course.'

'Anyway, I thought everyone knew all about this sort of thing in France.'

'I suppose it depends what you mean by "this sort of thing". Balzac, for instance, thought there could be no infidelity where there had been no love.'

Sanderson drummed his fingers on the steering wheel, as if deciding whether to take issue with Balzac. 'Well,' he said at last, 'one definition of an adulterer – the one I myself have come to favour – is a man who is in two ruts rather than one.'

I laughed. 'That sounds a bit like special pleading.'

'Well, another way of looking at it is that sins aren't what they used to be. They're just pleasures, transient like the rest of life.'

22

I was keen to get home. There had been enough talk for one day. Sanderson had other ideas, however. 'Let's have a quick drink to round things off,' and he pulled up at a pub in the Old Town.

'This is one of the few pubs that haven't been taken over by the gay boys,' he said as we took our seats in The Blue Thistle, a traditional bar with oak panelling on the ceiling, stained-glass windows and etched mirrors. Then a quick afterthought: 'You're not gay, are you?'

'No,' I said.

'Somehow I didn't think you were.'

Over his beer Sanderson launched himself into another vale of tears. I had to remind myself that this wasn't really a drama unfolding: whatever had happened to him had already happened. He was simply recounting past events – albeit the very recent past in the case of Alice's decision to end the affair. It transpired, however, that another blow to the spirit had taken place that very morning. Most of what his wife talked about nowadays made only a vague impression, he said, much of it being lost for ever and beyond recovery. He had once attended an inaugural lecture entitled *Memory – The Choice is Yours* in which the speaker, a confident dapper little man, explained about short-term and long-term memory, and suggested the reasons why certain things made it through the hippocampus. Of course he'd now forgotten most of the content of the lecture, but he remembered thinking at the time that the speaker had completely failed to demystify the business of memory. His own view was that we delete much of what happens in order to avoid chaos, but there were some things so painful that they could not be forgotten. The best you could do was to try to distort them, to make life tolerable. A case in point had occurred that very morning, when Sanderson had asked Carrie what she thought about when they made love.

'She paused, and I knew she was weighing up the merits of truth telling and lying. When at last she spoke, it was crushing. I knew immediately I wouldn't be able to erase it.'

'What did she say?'

'She said she thought of Somerfields.'

'Summer fields?' I imagined bright colours, fragrant grasses, meadow flowers.

'Yes, Somerfields – at the bottom of our road. As supermarkets go, it's not even high-grade.'

His mouth was suddenly soft and slack, like a spaniel's.

'How did we arrive at this point?' he asked. (*Does he mean us*, I wondered.) 'I mean, how did we get from there to here?' (*No, he doesn't mean us.*) 'That's what I'd like to know. We used to have what people call a healthy sex life. Now my wife takes refuge from the marital bed in a virtual supermarket – down one aisle, up the next, weaving through the fruit and veg, past the dairy products, the ready-made meals, the dog food and the goldfish pellets – all to escape the reality of being fucked by her husband.' During his rant he pushed an imaginary trolley, steering it recklessly round the corners of his spleen.

When he next spoke it was to say that the marriage was never going to be what he had hoped for, what they had both hoped for once. That day when he had spotted her at the Signet Library he had experienced a huge surge of pure joy. He did not know then that it would not come again in the same intensity or immediacy. 'But to end a marriage, you've got to want to get out, more than to stay put.' He did not know if he had reached that point. His head felt too addled to cope with the question. 'To be honest, what I want is for my wife to want me, to accept me as I am.'

'That's like Montaigne. He thought it was much worse to be accepted out of pity than to be rejected outright.'

Sanderson sniffed. 'Are you trying to make me feel better, Eddie? If so, you are failing.' But he smiled as he said it, and this lightened the gloom. We finished our drinks and got up to go.

'I suppose marriage is a question of sustained belief,' he said. We were out on the busy street now, life going on all around. 'A necessary but insufficient condition of its continuance.'

This was the philosopher talking.

On the way home that evening I contemplated the mystery of marriage. It was clear to me that yes, it formed some sort of basis for living. But it was equally clear that it involved pain and misery for one or other partner. Or rather both, for surely if one is miserable the other feels the same. How could it be otherwise? People talked about unconditional love between a man and a woman, but this love was quite outside my own experience, with or without conditions. And not for more than a mad moment had I ever imagined being able to sustain any kind of live-in relationship, never mind a marriage. I had unfitted myself long ago for anything other than solitary living. The messiness of what I understood to be normal life kept me from getting too close to anyone. Just to think of sharing a bathroom – all those creams and potions, the denture in the cabinet – could bring me out in a cold sweat. The very idea held a kind of terror. Which was why, I supposed, books had been my compensation. Books allowed you to think you were connecting with others – an important illusion when you lived by yourself.

At the same time I was not entirely fooled: books did not

equate to real experience. Sometimes I would test my nerve and try to imagine getting older and sliding into the worst kind of lonely existence: poor personal hygiene, meals out of packets, no one to talk to, private sorrows, the hell of reality TV, failing eyesight, rotting teeth, smelly socks, underpants clotted with dried semen. When all of this became overwhelming I would make an occasional foray in the direction of real experience: human warmth, intimacy, soft flesh.

From an early age I had loved cinema, not just the films but almost everything about the experience: the lights going down, the curtains drawing back, the magic of the big screen. Every two weeks or so I would visit my local arts theatre, which specialised in showing foreign films as well as cult movies, ancient classics and experimental cinema. Occasionally there would be a talk after the film, usually given by the director. Years ago, at one such event, Bernard Tavernier had spoken about *La Vie et Rien d'Autre*, his film portraying a man whose task it is to find the identities of unknown dead soldiers after the First World War, and who forms a relationship with a woman looking for her missing husband. During the question-and-answer session, someone sitting two or three rows behind me asked a question about the difficulty of balancing huge epic themes with stories that are much smaller and more intimate. I turned to look at the questioner and was surprised to recognise her as one of the copy editors at the publishing house that commissioned most of my translations. Afterwards I introduced myself and discovered that she still worked for the publishers, though no longer in-house. Her name was Amandine Pommelet. My mother's name had been Amandine, as a result of which I had learned at an early age that it meant *she who must be loved*. Whenever my mother was behaving badly, I would remind myself of this. I said it now under my breath: *Amandine*. That evening we had a drink and a meal together in a little restaurant near the cinema. At the next film session we met again, and this time I asked where she lived and if I might walk her home. It was late November and the streets were glassy like granite. It might have snowed that evening if it hadn't been too cold for snow.

'There's no easy way of saying this,' she said, biting her lip. '*Je ne vis pas seule.*'

'You have a boyfriend?' I was already processing the expected answer, arranging my reaction.

'No. It's not that. My sister lives with me. I look after her.'

It turned out that she provided care for her twin sister, brain-damaged after a road accident two years previously. Since when Amandine's own life had grown smaller: her husband had walked out, most of her friends had deserted her, and her job had been reduced to part-time. Once a month an agency provided respite care for a period of twenty-four hours. She lived for these days, planning them meticulously and using them with care. Sometimes she went to art galleries or treated herself to new clothes; at other times she would sit in a park, eating a sandwich and watching the world go by, just enjoying the fact that she could. Her pleasures had become uncomplicated, but the happiness they contained was no less. In fact her happiness, if anything, was sharper and sweeter now. On her one free evening each month she always made a point of going out, usually to the arts cinema. The rest of the time she was on call.

As liaisons go, so I came to think, this was more manageable than most. The brain-damaged sister put limits on it – for which I was grateful. She was a helpless reminder that each new delight contained the promise of suffering.

Every so often I would call round to Amandine's apartment with a bottle of wine. She watched a prodigious amount of television. It was always on in the background, always on the news channel. *C'est en marche pour ma soeur*, she would say. It was for her sister. But my own theory was that the news allowed her to feel part of the unfolding dramas of the world, a defence against the humdrum sameness of her own life.

Sometimes I would cook a simple meal for both of us while

she settled her sister down for the night. I would switch off the television, and over dinner Amandine would entertain me with stories from the novels she was working on, always careful to include her wry editorial critique: too many abstract nouns, not enough verbs, the importance of the semi-colon, the huge scaffolding that was required to hold up a novel. All of this I enjoyed.

Her sitting room was filled with soft materials and furnishings, carpets and cushions, everything very full and plumped up, no hard lines or angles anywhere. Though it wasn't my preferred style, I was drawn to it at first: this was something a woman could do for a man, something he might not do for himself. It felt rich and comfortable and enticing. Over time, however, it came to seem like a padded cell: you were safe in that you couldn't do yourself any harm, but it was a kind of prison just the same.

Once in a while, sunk in this female landscape, we would indulge in what I came to think of airily as a *sans-culottes* romp, followed by light gratification. (This was a phrase picked up from an English novel that seemed to specialise in the language of evasion, what the English call beating about the bush.) Though it pains me to admit it, my experience of sex was pitifully limited. In the manner of the amateur art critic, I knew hardly anything about it, yet I knew what I liked. And there were some discoveries along the way: that sex was a precarious route to self-knowledge; that it could remove the symptoms of feeling adrift without treating the underlying cause; and that it was probably better to keep things marginal, complementary. Just occasionally I would stay the night, though it was better if I didn't. The morning protocol would always serve to banish the mood of the previous evening. My relationship with Amandine was not without human warmth or tenderness, yet I always thought of it in the present tense. I believe she did too. She seemed to expect very little of us, just some mutual comfort perhaps. 'A little love is homeopathic,' she once said. 'In the same way as a little arsenic.' Her eyes clouded over. '*Le semblable est soigné par le semblable.*' Like cures like.

By the time I came to walk home after leaving Sanderson outside the pub, the day had darkened several shades. Everywhere lights were being switched on in apartments. Most city centres have become depopulated – everyone knows this – but it hasn't happened in Edinburgh. Through lighted windows I glimpsed scenes of domestic life, ordinary things just beyond reach – young children in pyjamas, families gathered round the kitchen table, an old woman playing the piano – and felt the lurch of something I could not give a name to.

23

Back at the cottage something wasn't quite right. Someone had been there in my absence. It came to me the moment I put my key in the lock and opened the door. It must have been the cleaner – this was my first thought. But it wasn't a Tuesday, and Mrs Bannerman, as she had said herself more than once, was a woman of strict routine. Just to be sure, I checked the lavatory, which always flushed a darker blue after her visit. But not today. In any case the house didn't look or smell as if it had been newly cleaned. It was much more vague than that, just a sense of something being different. Of someone having just been there, and now gone.

At the same time I didn't quite trust my own sense, mainly because after a short while I thought I recognised it as a kind of whisper from my childhood. Even now, I hardly know what name to give it. Intuition? Intimation? At any rate, whenever it settles upon me, it amounts to a suspicion that I am not quite alone. It is a feeling that lasted off and on throughout my early years, though it varied in intensity. I can't pinpoint exactly when it started, nor even whether it came before or after my mother told me about the fact and the fate of my siblings. It would return at odd moments during adolescence and into my student days, a mysterious glimmering from long ago, not haunting me exactly, but reminding me that everything has antecedents, that there is an infinite sequence of interconnected events, and that not everything can be properly understood.

The 'whisper', if that's the name for it, takes me back to my earliest memories. I should say straight away that I'm a little suspicious of childhood, the vast load it is asked to bear, as well as the significance placed on it. But there's no use pretending that you can escape its effects, just as there's no doubting that it provides the grain on the parchment that later is called your life. This is why people scour their early days for anything that foreshadows the adult specimens they have become. Not always a good idea, but it can't be helped.

Everyone has pet theories. One of mine is that three people connected by flesh and blood can live in the same house and not really know each other. This was undoubtedly the case with my parents and me. We occupied the same 100 square metres or so above the bookshop, but we all went about our business independently and were not fully present in each other's lives. My father's domain was the bookshop. You could tell that he felt most at home there, returning to the apartment only to eat and to sleep. In fact, after the bookshop extended to a café, where customers could sit and read over a cup of coffee and a croissant, he usually had lunch at work and ate only the evening meal at home. My parents were the sort who acted as if talking and eating were utterly separate activities, and it was a mistake to mix them. Ours was different from other households. Whenever I went home with my friend Jean-Claude, the kitchen at his house was alive with noisy chatter and bonhomie, even the odd argument, but our meals – though always preceded by a short grace, spoken by my mother – were eaten in silence, broken only by a complex series of nods and murmurs that would have meant nothing to anyone outside the family.

Another theory of mine is that children are instinctively aware of the deficiencies of their parents, but they forgive them effortlessly and often go to any lengths to cover them up. Is it love that makes them do this? Or dependence? Or is it a basic awareness that the task of children is to please their parents? Whatever the truth, when it comes to trying to describe your own childhood, words aren't quite adequate. So much is bound up with the senses, together with the strong images that come back to you in frozen frames throughout your life, even if you have no sense of what went before or what came after. You can't entirely erase these pictures, even if you want to; they keep coming, as slide transparencies pop out from a carousel, sometimes out of sequence, sometimes out of focus, combining to make a kind of jerky motion picture. And how the finished film gets spliced seems quite random – young children having little sense of time, still less of chronology,

As far back as I can remember I wanted to become my father. It had in part to do with everyone liking him, and also perhaps the fact that he kept something of himself hidden. I would watch him carefully, studying his habits – his straight back when he got to his feet, the purposeful stride when he walked, the rigmarole when he lit a cigarette. In time, so I told myself, I would do these too, in the same way. There was an air of mystery about my father, but also of solidity, like the heavy boxes that were stacked downstairs in the shop. His knowledge of old books and what they contained seemed quite miraculous; he seemed to know the answer to any question asked. Amongst the clientele he had quite a reputation. They looked up to him as they might have done a priest or a sage, delighting in testing his learning and scholarship. Sometimes his answers took on an element of performance, with the exaggerated movements associated with pantomime – scratching of the head, sudden flash of brilliance, a quick dash up the bookshop ladder followed by a triumphant *Voilà!* as he removed a book from the topmost shelf. This would sometimes be accompanied by applause or gasps of amazement, at which point I always felt proud. But occasionally there was something else mixed in with the pride, a sort of unease at the idea of my father providing a spectacle, like a performing chimp or dancing bear. In a book about India I had seen a sad picture of such a bear, whose 'dancing' came from being made to walk over hot coals while his keeper played an instrument called an ektar. I fancied there was something of my father in that bear.

As I got older I began to realise that the bookshop was also a place where people brought their troubles as well as their questions. There was solace to be had in books; escape too, from whatever it was they were escaping. The French have a reputation for being too intellectual for their own good, too Cartesian for comfort, gathering in cafés to talk gloomily about nihilism and existentialism. All that is no doubt true, but in my father's bookshop all those years ago, although there was no shortage of what might be called the misery of living (as distinct from the misery of thinking), there was no shortage of humanity either. In my eyes, my father stood at the very centre of this humanity. People took from him much more than the titles they purchased. And he gave willingly and discreetly. By seeming to focus exclusively on the books in question and what they contained, he had a way of tackling the undergrowth and weeding out troubles that would never have been disclosed to direct inquiry.

The first inkling that he was different from other men was when a friend from school said what a pity it was that my father was *un étranger*. I had no idea what he meant by it. '*Étranger? Ça veut dire quoi?*' My friend repeated the word and said that's what you called a person who wasn't French. He meant no harm by it, but I felt the sting all the same, as if my own skin had been pierced. Oddly, this immediately made me love my father all the more.

At home I tried to find out more, but it wasn't easy. Most of the time I just breathed in the secrets of the household. What they meant was not clear, but they clogged the airways anyway. My mother was reluctant to answer any questions about the past, and my father seemed to take his cue from her. Perhaps the trick would be to get him by himself. Sometimes he took me along to people's houses to collect boxes of books for the shop, and whenever he did I would ask him some more – just one or two questions, not so many as to make him irritated. Gradually it emerged that he had been born in a tiny village by the sea in another country called *la Grande Bretagne*, in the far northern part known as *l'Écosse*, that he had grown up speaking English, not French, but that he loved France so much he had come to live there. Later he told me that he had met my mother during the war, while on a secret mission in Normandy.

This was as much as I learned at the time – my imagination did the rest. For years I borrowed heavily from war films – mostly British films with French subtitles – the old black and white classics full of heroism and personal sacrifice. Images sprang from the screen – a soldier shot through the chest, men tunnelling their way out of a prison camp, submarines and tanks, guns and gas masks. Somehow these images became part of another story entirely, just as much of a construct as the films themselves. I found I could turn my father into anything at all – a fighter pilot, the sole survivor of an enemy attack, the code-breaker who saved a thousand lives. Suddenly it was easy to impress my friends at school. My father, well, he fought with the Free French, you know . . . he was a key part of the French Resistance . . . a true *maquisard*. In those days there was no end to my pride or the claims I made for him.

24

It wasn't until much later – on my thirteenth birthday to be precise – that I spoke English with my father for the first time. Up
to that point English had been a forbidden city, sealed off by my
mother, who wanted desperately for us to be 'a normal French
family'. Being normal was a fluid notion in our house, but when
it came to speaking our own language the rule was rigid.
According to my mother, if we mixed it with English we would
chip away at our identity until it ceased to exist – at this point
she would grab from the air an imaginary hammer and chisel
and proceed to make high-pitched, staccato noises with her
murderous tools. My parents discussed me high above my head,
as if words spoken up there were beyond the hearing of a child.

'The boy's mind is like a sponge (*comme une éponge*),' said my
father. 'Beautifully absorbent.'

'But he will become confused about his roots (*ses racines*),' my
mother insisted. From my father's tone and inclusion of the
word 'beautifully', I decided that having a mind like a sponge
was not necessarily a bad thing, however disturbing the image.
But the idea of having roots, which I associated with weeds and
things that were fixed in the ground, troubled me greatly. The
menace in my mother's voice, as well as the moral authority

implicit in it, was utterly convincing – further proof of her ability to see into the future. By then there was plenty of evidence that my mother possessed extraordinary powers. Her periodic caution on the necessity of speaking French and only French was simply another manifestation.

Of course I hadn't the first idea about *identity* or what it might signify, but this in no way reduced its potency as a concept. On account of my mother's vivid hammer-and-chisel routine I imagined it as a lump of stone big enough to be made into a statue, like the one of Balzac on the corner of boulevard Montparnasse, but ending up through neglect or indiscipline as no bigger than one of the ordinary cobblestones in our yard.

My mother's special powers were first revealed to me when I was playing one day with toy soldiers in the corridor outside my parents' bedroom. The door was ajar and, as I lay face down preparing my soldiers for battle, I could see my mother sitting at her kidney-shaped dressing table with the glass top. She had her back to me and was wearing her lovely sea-blue dress with the white flowers. Perhaps, I thought, she will put on her stockings, which I could see hanging from the back of the chair. I loved watching her do this: the clever way in which she would take first one stocking, then the other, collapsing them into a concertina shape before inserting her delicate feet, stretching each leg out as she did so. But what I saw this time was completely new. To my amazement she suddenly removed her hair and laid it in a heap on the table in front of her. What a brilliant trick! Better even than my father who could take off the tip of his middle finger and put it back again without spilling a drop of blood. I leapt to my feet, pushed open the door and called to her in delight: 'Show me how you do it! Show me how you do it!' She turned to look at me, and in that moment I saw that she was beautiful. It had something to do with the pale soft contours of her head, which I wanted to touch and caress and press up against my cheek. But she raised her hand to stop me, and with the other she lifted up her hair and put it back on her head, then held two fingers to her lips to show me it was a secret. Still now, whenever my mother appears in my dreams, she has that pale soft hairless head.

As for the English language, it became, like all forbidden cities, a place of huge attraction. In my mind it was full of treasures and riches and secrets just waiting to be discovered. Alone in my room I used to practise saying out loud my few English words, turning them over in my mouth like morsels of exotic food. Stop it at once, my mother would say if ever she discovered me doing this. 'Something terrible happens to the shape of your mouth,' she said. But for me it felt like moving to music, dancing on a sprung floor – the way we did at school sometimes.

When you are seven or eight you can scarcely imagine being thirteen. 'Why thirteen?' I would ask, but the answer was always the same: 'When you are thirteen, you will understand why.' A child hates this sort of answer. The explanation emerged only much later. At thirteen, I would be eligible for confirmation in my mother's church – something my father regarded with abhorrence. But in the end he did a deal: a meaningless ritual in exchange for the right to speak his native language to his own son.

There are terrible myths surrounding childhood, one being that children regard whatever happens to them as normal. As a former child, I take a different view. Children may *accept* what happens, more readily than a seasoned adult might, but that doesn't stop them questioning or wondering about things. It's only later that they are able to connect things up and make patterns of the past, by which time it's impossible to separate what they thought at the time from what they thought afterwards, and to know the difference between the two. In this way the past is fluid and fixed at the same time.

I mention all this because there's no point in believing (as I used to do) that you're immune from the effects of childhood; not least because in some sense you remain a child for the rest of your life.

Without anything being said openly, it became clear that my father wasn't party to the embargo on English. He didn't contradict my mother, but there was something in his manner that told me he didn't support her either. At such times of ambivalence he would remove his silver cigarette case from his inside pocket, turn it over once or twice in his hands, as if looking for something on its smooth surface. He would then open the case and take out a cigarette, flicking it like a baton between his fingers, before tapping it, first with one end then the other, on the silver case, which by now he had clicked shut with his other hand.

For years the day itself had been keenly anticipated, and fervently prepared for. I had even given it a name: *Le Jour Anglais*. These were the words I inscribed as a young boy on a small leather-bound notebook, into which I copied English phrases and passages from books. To begin with it wasn't important to know what the words meant. It was enough to collect them and admire them. The notebook quickly filled up, and soon I needed another, then another. On these later notebooks the cover inscription was *The English Day* – there was no point in having a French name on something that was quintessentially English. Each letter was painstakingly drawn in what I imagined was a bold Anglo-Saxon script.

Meanwhile I searched my parents' collection of books for anything in English. The bookshop was an extension of our living space and a kind of indoor playground for me. My parents didn't object and the customers, especially the regulars, were used to seeing me there. I would set up battlefields in different corners and place plastic aeroplanes at the top of stepladders. And when I flew my planes along the top shelves, I would inspect the spines of all the books for titles in English. I started with illustrated books, trying to match the words of the captions to the pictures. By the time I was old enough for English to be taught at school I was way ahead of everyone else.

Over the years I would examine my father carefully, trying to discover clues to his Englishness. This was perhaps a futile exercise, possibly even insulting, given that he had been born and raised in the Highlands of Scotland. At the time in question, however, I knew very little of his background. Like his native language, it was seldom referred to except to ban all talk of it, and as with most family secrets it was deficient in facts. My father was at the centre of my life, but half of him, the half that my mother had banned, was closed to me.

One day after school I ran upstairs to find my mother. I was bursting to tell her the news: Jean-Claude, my friend from school, had announced that a baby had been born during the night and – just wait, *Maman*, till you hear – Jean-Claude had invited me to his house to inspect his new brother. The baby was less than a day old – imagine that! He had not even opened his eyes properly. Please, *please* could I go? Perhaps in all the excitement I said that I wished I too had a baby brother at home – I don't remember. What I do remember, with piercing clarity, is the blue cotton handkerchief with an edge of lace that my mother pulled from her sleeve and put to her eyes, by then spilling tears. Until that moment I had not known that adults could cry.

What happened next is unclear, the memory blurred by the strangeness and puzzle of it all. From the drawer in her dresser my mother took out three small round jars, not unlike those on display in the window of our local pharmacy, made of thick glass and with a cork stopper in the top. Each little jar had a label with a name on it, though not the name of a medicine or ointment, but the name of a person. *Ce sont tes frères et ta soeur*, she said, and her tone of voice told me that this was no joke, not a trick like removing her hair, but something momentous and revelatory. For what seemed like an age, but in reality was perhaps just a few moments, I stared, uncomprehending, at the jars. *My brothers and sister.* They contained nothing that I thought could ever have been living creatures, never mind brothers and a sister, nor surely could they ever be in time to come. They contained only tiny lifeless things that looked a bit like forest mushrooms, dark and shrivelled, long past their best, the sort grown-ups warned you to leave alone.

'*Mes pauvres enfants chéris,*' she said – my poor dear children.

Afterwards I felt differently about going to see Jean-Claude's baby. The excitement had vanished, and strange emotions that there was no name for banged at the walls of my chest. I had no idea what to do with them, or how to stop them.

Proust said we could find everything in our memory, but it isn't true. The details surrounding some events, like this one, are all but obliterated, just heaps of shards, which, in your adult years, and if the need arises, you may place in some sort of mosaic and create a meaningful story. Even if I had wanted to get away from this story, to set it aside and ignore it, I could not have done so. For in some basic way, I am defined by it. It is part of what gives me my place in the world.

Back then, however, lost in the fog of childhood, I spent a lot of time wondering about my siblings and why they were kept in jars. Could they perhaps be waiting to be born? Had I too been kept in a jar at some stage? Was this how babies started out? But if so, why then was my mother sad? I'm not sure whether in fact I asked her any of this, or whether I just thought about it. When I mentioned it to my father, his face took on a strange expression, but all he would say was: *On ne reviendra pas là-dessus.* The matter was not to be spoken of again. *On n'en parlera plus.* After that, we colluded in our denial of it.

What I came to believe is that this turn of events may have triggered the feeling of not being alone; along with the idea that there were others who had come before me; that they were evidently contained in those small jars, suspended in a state of unbeing; and that I must try to avoid the same fate. Did it also mark the beginning of my own compulsive preservation of nail clippings and the like? I can't be sure. At this remove it's no longer possible to be sure of anything. You just dig up the past, the stuff under the topsoil, and force a meaning on it.

At long last it was my thirteenth birthday. I can still recall the sense of excitement as the day approached. For months beforehand I had wondered what momentous words my father and I would exchange for the first time in English. Sometimes I thought they would press in on the front of my brain and explode like fireworks. At other times I imagined them as a drumroll, weighty and dramatic like an address by President de Gaulle. Would it be fatherly advice to his son? Would he sit me down and reveal all that had thus far been hidden? Would he now talk to me of war and secret missions? These defining experiences, about which he had said so little, separated us. I longed to know everything, but all I had been given were morsels. And I knew that morsels were not enough to let me understand.

In the event it was all very matter-of-fact. 'Happy birthday, Eddie!' he said, putting his hands on my shoulders and squeezing them tight. 'You're practically grown up now.' Plain, ordinary English words, but to me they felt just right, and full of promise.

25

At some point it became clear that my mother was unwell. I began to notice that the regular customers in the bookshop used a particular tone when they mentioned her to my father. *How is your wife?* they would ask. *Ça va?* A normal question, but you could tell it wasn't a casual inquiry. They wanted to know if she was any better, and their expressions contained something that I thought might be pity. One day – it's hard to pinpoint exactly when – I asked my father what was wrong with my mother. I must have been at least thirteen because I remember asking him in English. But his reply when it came was in French, as if English might somehow be disloyal to the subject matter. He was silent for a moment or two. Then he cleared his throat. He said that she had not been herself for some years now, and it was unlikely she would get better. *Cancer?* I whispered the word, knowing it to be the worst thing. No, he said. *C'est la tête qui va pas.* It's her mind. And he put his arms around me and held me tight. From which I understood that the situation was serious and that we must pull together.

Some time before this exchange I had worked out that my mother wore a wig, but only much later did I learn from my father that her hair had fallen out in the course of a single night after losing the first baby. This event evidently framed everything else that followed. There were to be two more babies, both still-births, and several years apart, before I entered the world, wailing and squalling at the top of my lungs – the happiest sound, according to my father, that had ever been heard in the Logan household.

For a time after my birth my mother was caught up in the new dawns and fresh hopes that a young baby brings, but in truth the earlier grief had settled somewhere deep in her chest and would not lift. Over the years she became more and more congested with it. 'You see, Eddie,' my father explained, 'the new baby – that was you – went some way towards binding the wounds.' He paused, unsure about how to continue. 'But the wounds them-selves had not been cleaned.' He had believed that a new life would insulate her from further hurt, but he was mistaken. For the first few years, he said, her energies were taken up with taking care of her lovely little boy, keeping me out of harm's way, and coping with a general low-level anxiety. 'But underneath, the sad-ness gnawed away at her like a rat.' In time it became a monstrous malady, and gradually she lost her connection to the world.

We have no memory of infancy, but I did sometimes wonder if the same rat had gnawed away at me too, while I was too young to know it. Perhaps something from those early years had taken up residence in my own body – the thing that presented itself even now as an occasional tightness in the chest.

After my mother died, I learned more. By then my father felt licensed to speak about it. 'We should perhaps have learned together how to grieve,' he said one day, 'but we didn't.' And so they had gone separately down a long dark corridor, and my father had come out of it alone, while my mother remained there, caught in a wind tunnel of grief. 'It was almost as if she didn't want to be entirely healed,' he said. 'Part of her thought that if she relaxed too much, that if she stopped suffering and let down her guard, then you too might be snatched away. She felt she had to do penance, bargain with God. She had the idea she was being punished for falling in love, for breaking with her parents, for spurning the life they had planned for her. There was no point in telling her there was no God, no one to be bargained with.' He gave a sigh, stroking each of his fingers in turn, as if checking the thin bones for breakages.

'Before the business with the babies your mother and I understood all this very well. We used to find ourselves agreeing with Stendhal: you can be walking along the street, marvelling at the stars, and all of a sudden you get mown down by a horse and cab. That's how Stendhal thought of things, and that's just the way it is. During the war, we both knew this and accepted it. There's no earthly point in thinking you can guard against calamity. It's all utterly random.'

But instead of trusting Stendhal my mother had evidently gone about creating elaborate structures for how best to survive, so that all of us would be safe. To this end, she devised the rules we would live by – 'a vain attempt to conquer her fear,' said my father. He went on to recount how she assumed there must be trouble round every corner, sensing danger in even the most innocent activities. And although she was forever in touch with God she was unable to leave things entirely in God's hands, not even the big decisions. She had faith in the power of prayer, yet she also believed that once God had made up His mind no amount of prayer could shift a decision.

Listening to my father speak about such things brought one incident from childhood to mind. I had fallen down the last six steps of the staircase that led from our apartment to the bookshop. My head hit the stone floor with a crack but, although it hurt, there was no real damage. Yet in an instant my mother became hysterical, shaking me in her arms and demanding to know in quick succession the answer to all sorts of questions – name, age, address – as if arresting a suspect at the scene of a crime. My father tried to restrain her and calm her down but she broke away and threw herself on the floor, giving thanks to God for sparing her poor child.

Aside from God, said my father, there were the laws of nature to be reckoned with. And although these too could be credited to God, there was no knowing when a casual catastrophe might slip from His divine grasp. No disaster, however remote or unlikely, could be discounted. My mother extrapolated compulsively from terrible tales in the newspapers or on the radio. Famine, earthquake, serial murder – everything posed a threat. Out on the street it was even worse, for there you could *see* the danger. All dogs were rabid, all traffic deadly, all strangers psychopaths. In the end it affected the balance of her mind. Gradually she stopped working in the bookshop. Before long she hardly left the apartment. Sometimes she would find herself on the stairs, he said, not remembering if she was going up or down, or for what purpose.

All of this, written down cold on the white page, makes it seem a sorry tale, full of suffering. But to live through it was not like that at all, not the way it reads now when conveyed in these solid words. There was sadness in the shadows, a soft humming in the head, but it did not overwhelm. And eventually my mother was in many ways more endearing in her altered state than in her previous incarnation. Once you got over the pity of her not being someone you could call your mother and mean the usual thing by it, she was a dear person. She was also calmer than before, and though she never quite lost her anxiety, it seemed in her last years as if something tight had loosened in her.

26

In Edinburgh the shops open late on Thursdays, as do many of the museums and galleries. And so one Thursday after work I decided to take up Sanderson's suggestion and visit Alice's gallery in the New Town. It would be interesting to see Alice in her own milieu, and I was curious to view Carrie's paintings in a formal setting.

Darkness was falling as I parked my bike, but the space inside was so brightly lit as to give the illusion of daylight. The person sitting at the desk at the back of the gallery – not Alice but a wisp of a young man – leapt up enthusiastically to offer his services as soon as I opened the door. 'Just looking, thank you,' I said. At which point a voice floated down from the mezzanine level of the gallery, and there above my head was Alice, leaning over the filigreed balustrade like a Shakespearean heroine. 'Looking is absolutely the best thing to do,' she said, projecting her lines as if to a packed auditorium. 'You have to look and look and *look*, and the more you look the more pleasure you will get, the more the paintings come alive, the more you will see the colours and the rhythms and the beauty, the more your emotions will be nourished.' It was clear that she recognised me, but for several minutes she maintained a theatrical distance on the balcony, not greeting me by name; rather continuing her soliloquy on art in well-turned phrases spoken resonantly through thick red lipstick and perfect white teeth. When she paused I found myself making an involuntary theatrical gesture – half-bow, half-shrug – confessing that, alas, I knew practically nothing about painting. 'That can be a distinct advantage, Eddie,' she said, at last addressing me by name and stepping down the wrought-iron spiral staircase, heels clacking on the treads, to join me on the main level. I told her that Carrie had said something uncannily similar when we first met in her studio. 'Then it must be true,' she laughed.

My visit to Alice's gallery turned out to be memorable for two reasons – the first to do with Carrie's paintings, the second, less expectedly, to do with my own trade. But before there was any hint of this, the young wisp, seemingly in response to an invisible instruction, produced two glasses of chilled white wine. Alice immediately raised her glass and said: 'To translators everywhere!' – an inscrutable toast that became explicit only later. Meanwhile she linked her arm in mine and took me on a tour of the gallery, talking me through each painting as if I were a prospective buyer. There were several 'local' works – Edinburgh street scenes and the like, as well as grand vistas, one or two of which were already familiar to me. Alice commented on each painting, giving not just an overall appraisal or interpretation, but touching also on technical aspects like form and colour, line and tone. Most of this went over my head, though every so often when she mentioned the connection between the paintings and what she called 'the personal narrative', my full attention flooded back.

Carrie's work – three large canvases hanging at the back of the gallery – was left till the end, perhaps because Alice sensed that this was where my real interest lay. 'At her best,' said Alice, 'she has the power to lift the heart, as only a great artist can do.' Carrie was first and foremost a figurative painter, she explained, although there had been a move over the last year or two in the direction of perceptual art. 'Essentially she paints from experience, from the things in her day-to-day world. Of course, since the business with Alfie, her world has fractured. And this is evident in her more recent pieces, all of them shifting and unsettling.' In the three works on show Alice drew attention to Carrie's treatment of space, in particular emptiness – 'which sounds ridiculous, of course, for how can you paint emptiness?' But there was more to it than that, she said. Carrie was concerned with the sort of space where you would expect to see someone – it could be a room, a bed, a street – and it was this space that held the absence of a figure. By looking at the space you became conscious of the absence. 'Occasionally she introduces a figure – like in this one here,' she said, pointing to the middle canvas, 'but as you'll see, it's an attenuated, diminished figure. And it's the absence, the diminution that becomes the focus.' Alice said that each painting contained contradictions – light and dark, joy and sadness. 'It's a caress, but it's also a scream.' These words made me shudder. We stood in silence for a moment or two, side by side, looking at Carrie's paintings. Even the spaces in between the canvases seemed to me to be heavy with sorrow. Then, as if by way of reassurance, Alice turned to me and said: 'But loss, after all, is a natural thing. Like beauty.'

'Does loss count as beauty?' I said. 'Isn't it more like ugliness?'

'Of course,' she said, a little too speedily, as if it were self-evident. 'But art just looks at life, and life contains ugliness.' She made a clicking sound with her tongue. 'In fact, sometimes life is so ugly it's hard to get through the next five minutes.' She gave a throaty laugh, but I wondered if she spoke from experience, and if it had to do with Sanderson.

As I was on the point of leaving, Alice asked how my own work was going, and if the translation was progressing well. 'I have an odd interest in translation,' she said, sounding faintly embarrassed, as if she had confessed to a character fault. And with this she launched into another monologue, pacing back and forth on the wooden boards and pausing every now and then for dramatic effect. Her best friend from college days – 'a wonderful human being called Janet' – had married a Japanese businessman not long after graduation. Janet and her husband had gone to live in Kyoto, where they raised three children. Janet learned Japanese, her children were brought up bilingually, and in time she began to translate Japanese novels. Her first published translation was a short novel by a writer called Yuriko Mukoda, which had arrived in the post for Alice's birthday some years ago. 'It wasn't really my kind of thing,' said Alice. 'It was set in some fishing village in medieval times – and it was obvious from the cover that it involved real hardship and suffering. And I guess I'm not really into misery books' – she laughed at the very idea – 'but since it was a gift from a dear friend I decided to give it a go.' Alice described the novel as different from anything else she had read – she couldn't say exactly how it was different, except that it had to do with the style of the prose – 'very minimalist, quite distant and formal – very, you know, *foreign*'. She injected a little venom into the word *foreign*, remembering too late that it applied to me (and also to her, I couldn't help thinking). 'Don't get me wrong,' she said, rearranging her facial muscles into a benevolent aspect. 'It was just kind of *weird*. But also, you know, *interesting*. And I was even quite a fan by the end.'

I wondered where this was leading. As if reading my thoughts, she said: 'Now this is where it gets real kooky.' She explained that a year or two later she got an email from Janet with the shock news that her daughter had been knocked down by a car, had sustained a serious head injury and was in hospital in a coma. Over the next few months Janet emailed regular long bulletins to all her friends and family detailing her daughter's condition and progress – her gradual journey back from the dead, the moment she came out of the coma, her first motor responses, and so on. Alice had found the bulletins gripping.

They were meticulous and dramatic. In a strange way she had begun almost to look forward to the next one. And then one day, while reading the latest report, she had experienced a powerful sense of *déja vu* – these last two words an extended drawl: *day-jar-voo*. 'It was as if I'd read the whole thing before somewhere. And yet I knew that I couldn't have done, for this was a story unfolding in real time – it was my friend's daughter, not a character from a novel.' And then suddenly she realised what was so familiar. It was like reading the Japanese novel all over again. Not the story, not the situation, but the sound, the rhythms, the texture, the attention to detail – they were unmistakable. 'It was like being able to identify a painting from the brushstrokes.'

Alice said it was 'the weirdest thing'. It made her wonder how much of the Japanese novel had actually been Janet rather than the author. Or was it the other way round – that Janet had in some sense adopted the persona of her Japanese author without realising it?

'What do you make of that, Eddie?'

'I'm not sure.' I said, experiencing a slight sense of tumbling down a mine-shaft. 'I think in a translation there are mysterious forces at work.'

Walking back that night I felt the effects of the wine and lack of food. As soon as I reached the Calton Hill road I knew I would stop off at the cemetery before going home. Alice's story had unsettled me. It felt as if I had received an unwanted gift, a gift that could not be undelivered.

27

Sanderson had a point. Perhaps I had read too many novels. I had certainly read them in a particular way. As a translator you can't just rattle along, getting the gist, understanding enough to follow the narrative. It's much more intense than that. You have to look at all the words, every one of them, and how they are connected one to another. Afterwards you can feel exhausted, as if you have run a marathon. Even if you try to switch off, even if you are reading simply for pleasure, you can't help noticing certain things: the architecture of the book, the complexion, the stuff beneath the surface, the blood vessels, the veins – all the light and shade that the language casts on the page. The words are just the starting blocks.

It is an irony that I was first drawn to translating fiction because it seemed like the safe option. After my breakdown, this appeared to be what was needed. The rationale went something like this: fiction – that is to say stories that are made up – would be a kind of protection from reality. Of course, I soon made the unhappy discovery that this protection is limited. The characters and the plot are made up, yes, but all those feelings that underpin the narrative – love and loss, happiness and sadness – are exactly the same feelings that obtain in the world. And because you have to give each line such close attention – get under its skin, so to speak – you are even more exposed than the ordinary reader. I am sometimes struck by the unfairness of this, but that's just how it is. Nearly all of my experience of life – the highs and lows, the hopes and disappointments, the chaotic entanglements – everything that matters in fact – all of this has been mediated through the written word. With the result that novels have given me the sense – the illusion perhaps – of a connection with others, with the texture of real lives. This was how I had lived for nearly a quarter of a century and it had led to a contentment of sorts. Ah, *contentment* – that word again. Sanderson would have said I was avoiding the business of happiness. I'm not sure. With all its built-in expectations and burdens, happiness is a loaded word. Contentment on the other hand is more down-to-earth – as much perhaps as any man might decently ask of life. In Edinburgh, however, all this was under threat. It would have been easier to encounter Sanderson in a novel, to watch him come undone from a safe distance. But when you are used to connecting with people largely through novels, the real thing can come as quite a surprise.

Sanderson definitely counted as the real thing. And getting to know him was far from being a slow or gradual process. It was like learning a new language – not from a basic grammar or phrase book, but by the complete immersion method. As the days and weeks went by, it amazed me that, without the least encouragement, he could speak so openly about himself. It was hard to account for the suddenness, or the sheer incontinence of it, except to think of it as an unexpected interlude, the sort of intimacy that can occur on holiday between strangers, who unwind their lives to one another, confident that their meeting is a brief collision, hopelessly intense and indiscreet, but soon over and quickly forgotten. Sanderson had found someone he could talk to, without it mattering much, without having to think of the consequences, knowing that in a matter of months I would be gone from his life. It struck me that the same opportunity was of course open to me too, provided I cared to take it.

Though our conversations seemed at the time to range widely and freely, I would realise afterwards that the talk had mostly been about people and how they behaved towards one another. Aside from his own marriage, Sanderson regularly spoke about his parents, long dead, but vividly alive in his memory and his conscience. He said that he mourned his parents, not them exactly, more the idea of them, and how much better it might have been if only he had made an effort to appreciate them at the time. They had been good people. He could see that now.

'Perhaps ordinary goodness was easier in previous generations,' I said, thinking of my own father.

'What do you mean?'

'Well, people suffered all the same emotions – hurt, anger, guilt, shame – but they kept silent for the most part. They were stoical. It was how people behaved then.'

'Stoicism is hardly the same as goodness,' said Sanderson.

'It can have the feel of goodness about it.'

'Ah well, no one has ever accused me of goodness, that's for sure. But you, you're still young. There's still time for you.'

'I'm forty-five,' I said. 'Not so young.'

'But your mistakes are probably still ahead of you. Whereas I've made mine already. My future is all in the past.'

He pressed some tobacco into the bowl of his pipe, not perfunctorily, but in the manner of a man trying to suppress all that had blighted his life.

'When I lived at home, I lived in opposition to my father. I read books and felt myself superior. My father had no time for thinking. For him the *unexamined* life was the only life worth living – that's how it struck me at the time anyway.' Socrates had famously insisted on the examined life, said Sanderson, and in the end he died for it. 'But maybe my father was wiser than Socrates,' he smiled. 'He worked, he went fishing, and he tended his garden. Even the most ordinary life tells us everything we need to know about how to live. And yet it has taken me a lifetime to see it.' His father's work had been digging coal, he said. Underground, in the dark, with only a miner's lamp and a canary for company. Throughout his life he had avoided difficult topics. If ever one appeared on the horizon, he would start talking about his dahlias – a safe subject. 'He always said you couldn't go far wrong with dahlias.'

His father had also been a man who kept his head down – 'a peace-at-any-pricer', he said, a man who disappeared quietly into the garden at the first sign of strife. Sanderson now regarded him as a man of infinite courtesy and beautiful manners – 'nothing polished or false, but coming from a deep place'. In fact he had been the perfect embodiment of the ancient Greek *eudaimonia* – not happiness, as we now thought of it, but a concept much more akin to *living well*, being a good person. The best route to *eudaimonia* was by way of something called *ataraxia* – a state of being that might be expressed as imperturbability. Keeping calm, not getting into a flap. Philosophers down the centuries had argued about how best to achieve this state. Yet his own father, he now realised, had it all worked out. Why hadn't he seen it at the time, why hadn't he learned from him? Next to his father Sanderson said he felt himself feckless, weak, useless. Right now, what wouldn't he give for an hour in his company. He paused and cleared his throat.

Of course other boys' fathers had fought in the war, he went on, voice stronger now. One of them had had his leg shot off – a clear sign of heroism and bravery. But coal mining was a so-called reserved occupation, and Sanderson's father had not been called up. 'Which made him the butt of schoolboy taunts and ignorant mutterings.' Yet he had not seemed to mind. 'He himself had come from a long line of snubbers, so he understood snubbage better than anyone.'

Mining had not saved his life, however. 'Far from it. All that black coal dust must have worked its way in, and in the end he got lung disease.' He had been the kind of man who regarded illness as a deplorable character weakness, suffering terribly, but never complaining. 'He just tried his best to die without fuss. I visited him near the end. The doctor said he would not last the night, but my father would not have dreamt of dying in the presence of a visitor, especially his own son. He slipped away the next day, after I'd gone.'

On his mother Sanderson was more reticent, disclosing only that she had worn herself out thinking about other people, what to feed them, how best to care for them. It was duty that drove her, not love. 'She would never, not in a thousand years, have admitted to love.' Love was one of those things that could get you into a lot of trouble, particularly if you talked about it. Which she never did. Duty oppressed her, yet she was defined by it. After his father's death, when she had no one to think of but herself, she could discover no point or purpose to her life. Life stalled the day he died and she couldn't get it going again. She was cast adrift and died soon afterwards.

28

Towards the end of September it happened again. I had cycled home from the library, calling in as usual at the cemetery on the way back to pay my respects. Having just completed another essay, I had wanted to solemnise the occasion at Hume's grave. As soon as I got back to the cottage, however, it struck me that something was not quite right. I walked into the sitting room and switched on all the lamps. Everything looked the same. Nothing seemed to have been touched. And yet, though there was no supporting evidence, I couldn't shake off the feeling that someone had been there while I was out. Two days later, the same feeling returned. For a minute or two I just stood in the hall, listening, looking. But looking for what exactly? A few days after, when I discovered the door to the utility room had been left open, I knew beyond doubt that my suspicions were real. I was very particular about doors: they remained closed at all times unless I was in the room, in which case they were kept open. You get into habits – it comes from living alone.

In the utility room I turned the handle on the connecting door to the garage – still locked. I put my eye to the keyhole: darkness. Since all the cleaning equipment was kept in the utility room – vacuum cleaner, mop, rubber gloves – I told myself that it had to be Mrs Bannerman. It was a Tuesday, her regular cleaning day, but I had left the cottage after her, which meant that all the doors would have been closed. She must have left something behind and returned to pick it up. Simple. In this way I tried to put suspicion out of my mind, or at least prevent it from taking root and growing into something protean and unmanageable. Impossible, of course. On leaving next morning I propped up an envelope behind the door. If anyone came in through the door it would fall on the mat and just look as if the post hadn't been picked up. When I got back, the envelope, sure enough, had fallen onto the mat. But because the postman had delivered other letters that day, it was just possible that these had interfered with my simple trap.

Next day I decided to vary my routine, returning to the cottage in the middle of the afternoon. Nothing. I stepped outside again and stood for a minute, looking round the toy-town courtyard. None of the mews cottages had curtains, or if they did they were never closed. I did a panoramic sweep of the windows, looking for signs of life, finding none. In the far corner of the courtyard, on the opposite side from my own cottage, a dog lay sleeping on a doorstep, a lone living creature. Even so, I couldn't rid myself of the feeling that I was being watched. With a heightened awareness of my own movements, I locked up and cycled off towards the main road.

The following day after leaving for work I doubled back after a hundred metres or so, padlocked my bike to a lamppost and approached the mews courtyard from the other direction. Most of the garages in the terrace had been incorporated into the cottages, converted into studios or used simply as an extension of the downstairs living space. At least two of the garages, however, were used to house cars, and I had noticed that when the residents in question drove off to work in the morning the garage doors were left open. I had also observed through the empty spaces that each of these garages had a back entrance, which I guessed must lead onto the path that was visible from my upstairs window at the rear. A gate into a narrow passageway eventually took me to this path that ran on the other side of the mews. My heart was beating a little faster than usual, but I told myself that if anyone stopped and questioned me it would be easy to explain: Frenchman, slightly lost, new to the city, renting one of the cottages and trying to find its back entrance.

The first door was locked, so I moved three cottages to the left and tried the next door, which opened into an empty garage and the courtyard beyond. Once in the garden I exhaled my relief and took up a position that would not look suspicious if challenged – leaning against a copper beech tree towards the back of the garden, hands in pockets, as if waiting for someone. By tilting my head only slightly I could get a good view of my own front door. In the distance there was the muffled noise of city traffic. Otherwise the only sound was the faint rustle of the leaves that were beginning to loosen and fall from the trees. I waited, and waited, intensely aware of the slow passage of time, and also of the strange quality of the silence. I became convinced it was possible to hear the soft ping of thoughts ricocheting in my head, even the sound of my own stubble growing.

Suddenly within close range there was a recognisably human sound – a man blowing his nose loudly. I peered round the tree trunk and was amazed to see Sanderson, a few metres in front, facing away, his legs cut off by the shrubbery. How long had he been there? Could he have been there all night? He wore a shabby overcoat with the collar turned up, but his general shape and demeanour gave him away. He was behaving oddly, bobbing and weaving like a boxer, behind a large cotoneaster shrub. I watched him for a minute or two, long enough to establish that he too was watching the cottage. But *why*? What was he looking for? What was he doing there? I stood for a while, frozen to the spot, hardly daring to breathe, feeling at first unaccountably guilty, then a little resentful. This was *my* territory, after all. I had every right to be there. It was Sanderson who needed to explain himself. Why wasn't he at work? What on earth did he want? Perhaps he wanted to spy on me, track my movements. But *why*?

I tried to work out what to do. There was no way of getting back into the house, or even leaving the garden without revealing myself to Sanderson. A worm of panic wriggled in my gut. What to do? Should I show myself? Yes, I should. I would tackle him. Demand to know what he was doing. Yet I did nothing, and eventually a kind of paralysis set in, followed by a sense of the absurdity of two grown men, of uncertain purpose, hiding in a mews garden in the middle of Scotland's capital city. After a time I smelt tobacco smoke. Sanderson must have lit his pipe. Which irritated me terribly. The fact that he was lurking outside another man's home evidently did not embarrass him. A few moments later he even relieved himself against the cotoneaster – an amber trickle ran away from the roots to form a small puddle in a hollow just a metre or two from where I stood.

29

Dusk had fallen by the time Sanderson left the cover of the trees and made his way out of the courtyard. The day had left me feeling both restless and weary. I had nothing to show for it and no energy left to catch up on work. During a sleepless night I made up my mind to confront Sanderson. In the morning – it was a Friday morning at the end of September – I went straight to his office in the David Hume Tower, only to find a notice on the door redirecting students to another member of the philosophy department. At the secretary's office I was told that Sanderson had been signed off. In my mind's eye I saw suppurating sores. 'Ah, his skin,' I said, indignation quickly giving way to sympathy. The secretary pursed her lips. There was something odd in her manner. Awkwardness or embarrassment, it wasn't clear.

'Are you from the press?' she asked. She seemed nervous now.

'The press?'

'The media,' she said, pronouncing it *meeja*.

I told her I was a visiting fellow in the department, and that Sanderson was a colleague. She gave a flustered apology and said she had no more information.

When I called round at the Sandersons' flat, Carrie was

surprised to see me, so surprised that I thought at first I must have committed some terrible social faux pas. She started to say something, then appeared to check herself before telling me that she expected me to be hard at work. Your *routine*, she said, elongating the word, and reciting back to me what I'd told her previously about how my days were structured: mornings at home, afternoons in the library. Was she teasing, or mocking? Either was possible, and equally discomfiting. I had, just then, a sudden strong feeling, a disabling surge of something hard to recognise, seeming at first to be embarrassment but rearranging itself into an overpowering desire to understand her, to see into her heart. Beneath her artist's smock she wore baggy trousers with a colourful batik design. She folded her arms, cupping a hand round each elbow. There was awkwardness in the air, but whether it was hers or mine was hard to tell. She would ask me in for a coffee, she said, except that she was about to go out. No, no, I said, still in thrall to the strange feeling. I couldn't stay anyway. I had just wanted to drop in briefly on Sanderson – to check on the arrangements for fishing the next day. 'Harry? Oh, but he's at work. He's in the department by nine o'clock every day.' There was a nervousness in her manner. Or, if not nervousness, an affliction of some sort. I wondered if she was entirely well, but half suspected she was covering up for Sanderson, that he was actually hiding in his box room, tying a new fly and enjoying my discomfort. 'Harry has his routine too, you know,' she added, pleasantly enough, but evidently doubting that I had called round to see her husband. Which meant, in her mind, that I must have come to see her, and in the expectation that she would be alone. I left as quickly as possible.

30

Social interaction could be very problematic – I still had a lot to learn. After all, what I knew of the human character had been gleaned mainly from novels. But fiction did not teach a man how to live, or even what to say. You had to do that by yourself. It was the same with love. You could find it in the pages of most novels, but you couldn't always recognise it when you saw it off the page. Or if you did, you didn't know what to do with it.

I sometimes reflected that over the years I ought to have learned more from Antoine, who had all those qualities that the English have no words for – *panache*, *éclat*, *élan*. Antoine had remained my friend since university days, indeed the only person I could properly count as a friend, and whose life was so richly complicated as to be able to provide instruction for others. But his amorous adventures were more perplexing than enlightening. The two of us saw each other only sporadically – sometimes a whole year would pass between meetings – and usually at Antoine's instigation. He would ring me up and suggest a meal or a drink, often at short notice – a sure sign that he needed to speak about his latest entanglement. He was someone who felt truly alive only when embarking on a new love affair, which invariably rose out of the collapse of an old one. At the same time he cast himself as a victim, whose heightened sensibilities had exposed him to the pain as well as the pleasures of love.

'It's like an airborne infection,' he would say. 'You catch it like a disease, and there's nothing you can do against it.' And he would shrug his shoulders, as if to say: what was a man to do?

I had lost count of Antoine's marriages, near-marriages and liaisons – there seemed to be an insatiable need for new beginnings. He would begin each affair with fervour, usually seeking to make it permanent by marriage, there being no apparent limit to his optimism. Each time he was sure he had found a woman who would love him unconditionally and adore him (*love* and *adore* were separate verbs in his romantic lexicon). Conversations between us always followed the same pattern: Antoine would tell me about his latest amour, and in the telling would evoke the selfsame passion encountered at the birth of the previous amour, now in terminal decline. I saw it as a thirst for intensity: provided he was in the midst of a drama, he felt alive. Each new intimacy allowed him to reinvent himself, and this in turn gave purpose to his infidelity, until such time as the restlessness began again. It was a career in itself, a vocation you might say. The surprise was that he had any time left for work.

Since university he had been employed as a copywriter in a successful advertising agency, where people drank a lot of coffee and stayed late. Everyone who worked there was dedicated to creating a burning desire for some product or other. It was a heady atmosphere, the ideal mix – so I thought – for Antoine in his perpetual quest. I had a poor opinion of the advertising business. It was all a confidence trick: exaggerations, lies, false claims, all dressed up in fancy garments and silver-tongued slogans. Perhaps that was one reason Antoine behaved as he did. In his private life he couldn't help spinning the same kind of fantasies that were endemic in his professional life. *Nonsense*, he said when I aired my theory. Didn't I understand? There was no *need* to dress up his love, no need for hype. The reality was a marvel in itself.

After hearing about the most recent infidelity I would sometimes say: But what is the point, Antoine? It's obvious that if you search for the new all the time, the new becomes old and passé, and one day it has to be replaced, dictated by your own addiction to endless renewal. But it was never a serious question. My role – we both understood this – was to query and to cast doubt. Antoine expected nothing less, and it gave him the chance to persuade himself of the intensity of this new love, the perfection of it, its necessity to his future wellbeing – the sheer ineluctability of it. And if ever I demurred, he would give another shrug. It was so simple. Why couldn't I see it? Anyway everything had a way of working out. *Les choses s'arrangent, mais autrement.*

Though my objections were doomed, I sometimes asked him what was so unsuitable about his present wife that she had to be replaced by another.

'I can't explain,' he said, 'it's just the way it is.' He usually did try to explain, however, searching desperately for some suitable image or comparison to illustrate the nature of the difficulty. When at last he found one that pleased him he could sound like a lawyer or a politician, seemingly praising the thing he was about to destroy, using phrases such as *I'm sorry, but . . .*

'I'm sorry, but women are like those towels on aeroplanes,' he would say. 'They begin by being too hot to handle, then there's a brief period when they're just right and you feel all pampered and comforted, but before you know it they go cold and clammy and you can't wait to be rid of them.'

But shouldn't he give it time perhaps? This is the kind of thing I would say, steering a familiar path between tact and candour. Instead of inflicting all that pain and misery? Antoine would sweep this sort of remark aside, telling me that I'd missed the point. This was *love* and he had promised his *heart*. All this talk of love, I thought, and so little to warm the heart.

'It's not your heart that's engaged,' I once said to him, 'it's only your penis.'

'You must never place the word *only* in front of a *penis*,' he protested. 'At least not in front of *my* penis.'

He could be very solemn about sex. Which was endearing in its way. Denying the force of my new love is not an option, he always said. The enormity of the denial would make life quite impossible. What we do together, what we have together, is its own justification, he would say. It defines itself, and we in turn are defined by it. '*On fait l'amour, et l'amour nous fait.*' We make love and love makes us. This sort of talk sounded better in French – in English I knew it would seem a little ridiculous.

Antoine believed that sex, when it was new and fresh, was the closest it was possible to get to pure joy. He was transfigured by it. '*L'amour nous crée à nouveau.*' That was the way he spoke. It was like the wind before a storm, it swept over you like a flash flood, and between times it was like the warm sun after rain. Whenever he talked of physical love, you could count on an accompanying weather report. Or worse, something geological: earthquakes, volcanoes, tectonic plates shifting.

Sometimes he would even call on philosophers for support. 'Have you forgotten your Schopenhauer?' he asked me on one occasion, suddenly defensive. 'There is no point in abstract ideas, learning about theoretical concepts that are fixed by the language we choose to describe them. Real knowledge can be acquired only by direct experience. By *living* a bit.' *En vivant enfin*, he said. And then there was Socrates, who had pointed out the dangers of erotic attachment to one individual. 'According to Socrates this is no life at all for a free human being. He thought we should try to break free of the shackles, to liberate ourselves by having replaceable objects of love.'

Nonsense, I would say, knowing it was pointless. 'To state Socrates' position is already to set out what is wrong with it. You can't just go around freeing yourself from attachments, and it's stupid to try. There's perhaps a problem of the right attachment as opposed to the wrong attachment, but the problem is not in attachment itself.'

And so on, and so on. What remained unspoken between us was Antoine's supposition that I, relative to him, knew nothing of the unruly, chaotic ways in which most people lived. In fact I had scarcely lived at all. Which, since I knew next to nothing of love, was more or less correct. In some alternative, imagined world, things were not this way at all. As a younger man I had dreamed of one day having a wife and family, and living together in a home in which we would all flourish. But my experience had been more like that of the innocent bystander: if ever I got involved in anything, it was usually quite by chance. There had been no conscious decision to forgo sex – that was simply the way things had turned out. Not counting Amandine, that is. Who deserved to be counted. Though what was between us, Amandine and me, was not easy to fathom. It took place in some mysterious zone, and as seldom as decency allowed. There had been moments, yes, when it was possible to get completely caught up in the possession, in the giving and receiving, but in the quiet that followed, I knew I was on my own again. Without a doubt my few chance encounters, instructive though they had been, had confirmed that sex was not the proving ground for love. It was meant to be easy and uncomplicated, but that was a lie. It was actually difficult and mysterious. A mature endeavour. A test of imagination.

31

At the time of my visit to Edinburgh I had been well – that is to say free of further breakdowns – for over twenty years. As far back as my memory stretched, however, there had always been a certain dislocation from the world. Life was experienced through a sort of framing device that kept me apart from ordinary living. Mostly it was manageable, but from time to time the feeling would intensify and I would then be powerless in the face of it. My awkwardness in the company of others was anarchic. It had a mind of its own and could strike unbidden. It could even make my voice break or produce a burning in my eyes. The strategy for dealing with a severe attack was usually along the lines of the advice given in emergency situations like fires or flash floods – walk away as calmly as possible from the source of the flames or the water. Just occasionally, when it was not easy to account for a sudden worsening in what I thought of, in the manner of an invalid, as my *condition*, I would do the opposite and force myself towards the root of the thing. Confront the beast, get it by the neck and subdue it. At these times, I usually headed for the Gare du Nord, my nearest mainline station and well suited to my purpose.

How to define my purpose? At its simplest, it was to watch,

to listen and to learn. I was convinced that if only I observed others closely enough, it would be possible to imitate them, and in time it might even come naturally to me. It wasn't such a strange idea: even during those evenings spent with Antoine over a drink or two, some of his gestures would rub off – the Gallic shrug, his habit of looking away when he spoke, the way he bit his lip when he contemplated the enormity of the latest surge of passion.

Railway stations – rich breeding grounds for small intimacies and human drama – are ideal for watching and learning. The foyer of a concert hall or theatre just before the performance is also good. In these places you are allowed to stand and stare without being taken for some kind of dangerous maniac. Often the faces are blank and private; the trick is to fill in the blank, to make the private accessible. I would generally ignore those who were alone, unless they were obviously waiting for someone to arrive, in which case I would stick around for the special moment – the moment when eyes meet, faces light up and the human connection is made. Whether between friends, relatives or lovers, it is always worth waiting for. But most of the time my search would be concentrated on ready-made couples, those who arrived together, arms linked, tête-à-tête. I would try to get as near as possible, near enough to scrutinise the way they filled their moments with one another. All of this was absorbing.

I have never been confident about the world or what fits with it. This sounds like a kind of innocence perhaps, but unlike innocence it is not benign. It can wreak havoc in your life, placing you at a distance from things, separating you from ordinary experience, leaving you with the feeling that something is always disappearing round the corner before you can quite catch up. If ever I tried to remember as far back as it was possible to go, I felt sure there had always been something of this same sense, something that is experienced not quite as a loss, more as a lack.

When I was a child, my father used to tell me stories before

I went to sleep. The stories were in his head, not in books. Sometimes it seemed to me as if my father knew all the stories that had ever been told. They were not the usual bedtime offerings – fairy tales and the like – but tales from life, *histoires de la vie*, or more often philosophical puzzles that he made interesting and funny. I would go to sleep thinking of the paradox of Achilles and the tortoise, in which Achilles, although much faster, could never catch up with the tortoise; or of Tristram Shandy, who thought he could never finish his own biography because it had already taken him two years to write up two days. The problem I liked least, because it disturbed me most, was the paradox of the liar: if a liar says that he is lying, isn't he in fact telling the truth? Though my father smiled at my unease, he was gentle with me too, saying that I was right to worry: there was a universal fear of lying, and nearly everyone, even philosophers, would agree it was wrong. Mind you, they couldn't always agree on *why*. On the other hand, lying was just something that people did, simply because they were people. They're very good at it, he said, as if they've been born to it. And as if by way of compensation, he told me about the Houyhnhnms, the talking horses in *Gulliver's Travels* who had no actual word for lying – though they had their very own substitute expression: *dire la chose qui n'est pas* – to say the thing which is not. Gulliver adored the Houyhnhnms, said my father. He felt close to them and preferred the company of these curious horses to that of his fellow man. Except that there was a price to pay. Which was that Gulliver lived in a stable with herbs pushed up his nostrils because the stench of his fellow humans was more than he could bear. His wife became 'an odious animal' to him, and he found it impossible to be around her or their children. And the stench was not all: what was worse, much worse, was that Gulliver missed what might be called ordinary human goodness – things like love and passion and sympathy.

At other times my father told me bamboozling time travel tales, such as the one about the boy who went back in time to murder his grandparents, thus preventing his own birth. Or the famous thought experiment involving a cat that is simultaneously alive and dead in a sealed box. Even though my brain would sometimes hurt with the effort of unravelling the puzzle, these special times with my father meant everything to me. Sometimes I would feel so close to him that it was hard to breathe. He gave me the sense that together we knew things that were not available to other people.

One night he told me the story of David Hume and the Missing Shade of Blue. This was the first time my father had mentioned David Hume, but there was no doubting his admiration. He began by saying that Hume was both a great philosopher and a great man – *un des plus grands que ce monde ait jamais connu*. He had been born in Scotland but had lived in France as a young man, writing his best work in a small village about 100 kilometres south of Paris. French people took to him and came to love him, competing with one other to have him as a guest at their dinner tables. They called him *le bon David* – 'That's the reason I gave our bookshop that name,' he said, 'in honour of this wonderful man.' He went on to explain Hume's belief that all knowledge comes from the five senses, 'which is another way of saying that everything we know comes from our experience of the world'. We were sitting side by side on my bed, both of us leaning against the wall with our knees bent right up to our chests. 'For example, you can't know a fire is hot until you touch it, or until you feel the heat on your face. Seeing the fire is not enough.' According to Hume, this was how people acquired knowledge. He thought that nothing could exist in our minds, no idea either simple or complex, without it first being experienced by one or more of the senses. And yet – 'this is where it gets really interesting' – there was a marvellous exception to the rule. 'And it was Hume himself who thought of it,' said my father, eyes twinkling. At this point he leaned forward and rested his chin between his knees.

'Hume asks us to think about a man with normal vision who is quite used to seeing the full range of colours – except for one particular shade of blue.' This was not a stupid man, said my father, oh no. This was a wise man, who knew many things and had seen a lot, the sort of man who had looked upon the azure sky and the sapphire sea; who had also gazed in wonder upon cornflowers and the baby-blue eggs of a mallard duck. This same man had even sailed in the aquamarine Pacific ocean and encountered a blue angel fish. And amongst his most precious possessions was a box, imported from Afghanistan, made of lapis lazuli – the most intense blue that you could ever wish to see.

'And yet there was one shade of blue that this wise man had never set eyes on.'

My father paused. I held my breath.

'C'était la nuance inconnue de bleu!'

Hume, he said, was convinced that if all the other shades were laid out side by side, graded from darkest blue to lightest, and with a gap for the missing shade, it would be possible for this same man to fill in the blank. From his own imagination – without ever having seen it in life. *'Avec sa propre imagination!'*

Afterwards, when my father had left the room, I lay in bed and closed my eyes, trying to imagine a multitude of eggs and fish and cornflowers, laid out in rows, graded by colour. But I could see nothing except for a fuzzy mass, dark and blurred, with a slight grain – like the television screen when the transmission went wrong. Opening my eyes, I picked out the different colours from the patterned counterpane, trying to think about those that were not there in relation to those that were. But it was no good. My mind wouldn't work the way I needed it to.

In so far as a young boy can feel he has failed, I felt it then. And ever since, at odd times throughout my life, there had been that same sense followed by the same doubt: would I recognise the missing shade of blue? Would I ever be able to know something if I hadn't first experienced it?

32

After calling at the Sandersons' flat I picked up my bike and headed straight to Waverley, the mainline station in Edinburgh. The idea of work was impossible – I was feeling much too agitated. An hour or two at the railway station might settle me. After padlocking my bike to railings, I went down Waverley Steps, draughty as a wind tunnel, and made my way to the main waiting area, laid out like a street café with shops round the edge. For a minute or two I stood under the huge information board that displayed times of departures and arrivals. At the Gare du Nord in Paris I had done the same thing many times, pretending to be checking the details of a train, but in reality taking the chance to place myself, to get into the right frame of mind.

Here at Waverley there were fifty people or more in my peripheral vision, criss-crossing the concourse, heading for the ticket centre, the food stalls, or the wash facilities. There was the usual station hubbub: the ding-dong chimes of information announcements, the beep-beep of floor-sweeping vehicles making their way through groups of displaced persons, and everywhere the collective clamour of a population making and receiving mobile phone calls. Behind me a man was telling his companion: *she claimed to have one of her headaches, but I didn't believe her*, but whether in indignation or resignation it was hard to tell. Fridays are pleasingly busy days at all mainline stations. In this sort of crowd no one would notice me. I ordered a coffee and sat on a high stool at one of the raised tables from where there was a good view of the comings and goings. My eye is always drawn to those who are just hanging around, about to embark on a journey or waiting for someone to arrive. I have often observed that the waiting itself is a curious dead time, only partly in the present, but mostly elsewhere in some as yet undefined place. It's a time that has to be got through, and most people seem impatient for it to be over.

Every few seconds the huge glass doors that led to the railway platforms opened like stage curtains, unveiling vignettes of salutation and valediction. These doors had a hypnotic effect, calming too. Meetings and partings: this was perhaps what life mainly consisted in.

On the far side of what was called the travel centre, there were rows of seats, all of them occupied. When I could tear myself away from the doors, I did what I often do in public places: used my eyes as a camera lens, taking wide-angled pictures of the crowd before zooming in on a particular face, holding the shot long enough to look for clues to the life behind it and reinforcing my theory that everyone is escaping from something; a marriage, a family secret, a criminal past.

At first I thought I had imagined him, conjured him out of the shadows of my mind. But there was no mistaking the uncombed hair, the shabby overcoat, those iron features, cast in a foundry. He could have been one of the tramps from *Waiting for Godot*, a man who might struggle to remove his boots. He was sitting in a corner of the bar that opened out onto the concourse. So much for his routine, I thought. The coffee bar with its frills and canopies was perfectly placed to observe him without being noticed. What on earth was he doing at the station? It was just possible that he was waiting to meet someone off a train –

perhaps a visiting philosopher – though it seemed unlikely, especially after what the secretary had said. It was much more likely that he himself was about to travel, though apart from a briefcase he appeared to have no luggage. It became progressively clear that he was there to drink. During two hours he left his seat only twice, both times to order at the bar. Meanwhile I myself drank excessive amounts of coffee. I had come to the station in search of calm, but my head was now whirring.

All of a sudden he drained his glass and left the bar. He headed out of the station, slowly on his painful feet, but purposefully all the same, in the direction of Princes Street. It didn't occur to me to do anything other than follow him. Halfway up the Waverley Steps, he paused, holding on to the railing to catch his breath. I was close enough to see the festering sores on the back of his hands. Sick leave – it was the obvious explanation. He must have decided to keep it from Carrie.

At the top of the steps he turned right and crossed over North Bridge at the traffic lights. Dodging pedestrians and prams, I kept at a safe distance, determined not to lose sight of him in the crowd of shoppers, already wondering how I would later excuse this behaviour to myself. On the other side of the North Bridge he headed away from the city centre, up towards Calton Hill, in the direction of the mews cottages. At which point I decided to go back for my bike and follow him up the hill – that way it would look entirely innocent if he happened to spot me. I would simply be a man returning home, not a man acting suspiciously, following another man acting suspiciously. My other thought was this: how unjust to be experiencing guilt.

When Sanderson turned off the main road into the side street that led to my cottage, it seemed sensible to hang back for a while. That way he would have time to go about his business before being caught in the act – whatever act that might be. But when I cycled into the cobbled courtyard there was no sign of him. And yet he had to be around somewhere – there was only one route in and out. Was he already inside the cottage? Stay calm. All would be explained. After parking my bike against the cottage wall I dug into my pocket for the door key. Just then I glimpsed the court-yard garden reflected in the window pane, and for just a fleeting moment the unmistakable movement of a human shape was caught in the glass. Sanderson was lurking in the bushes again.

For a few seconds I froze, half expecting a machete to cleave my skull in two. In the preceding weeks he had impressed me as a man of complexity, a man in turmoil, but until that moment it had not occurred to me that he might also be a dangerous psy-chopath. Excitable, yes, and at times overwrought. But surely not fiendish. Yet why, if not with malign intent, did a man loiter outside the home of another man? Not for the first time I longed to be more confident in my assessment of others. The trick was to be able to join the dots. The dots themselves were of course interesting, but they were not enough.

With a shiver I entered the cottage as quickly as possible, clos-ing the door behind me with the weight of my whole body, leaning up against the door to prevent the world from somer-saulting, trying to gather my thoughts. Before any thought could form, however, something else bore in on me: the sense that I was not alone in the cottage. I checked each room in turn, like a detective, though one ignorant of what he was looking for. I touched the furniture and ran my hands along the walls, as if to make sure they were solid. Back in the hallway a faint whiff of something entered my nostrils – something subtly perfumed, an eastern scent like sandalwood or musk. My nose led me to the utility room. Nothing obvious. As before I put my eye to the keyhole of the door leading to the garage. But this time, instead of darkness, it was possible to make out on the other side of the door two oval shapes, white at the edges and black in the centre, glinting slightly. A pair of human eyes.

I flee from the cottage, not locking up, not looking back, my heart pumping in my throat, darting down Calton Hill, past the cemetery, round the back of the railway station, running all the way to Holyrood Park and Salisbury Crags, and beyond to the lung-busting slopes of Arthur's Seat where I fling myself on the grass and hold my head to stop it pounding. There is a dreadful urge to weep, and I have to concentrate hard to stop a single tear coming – for some reason this seems important. There is a whimpering sound that must be coming from me. I pick up a small stone and throw it as far as I can, then another, then another. The weak sun has given way to a mass of mulberry veins in the huge sky, a mixture of clouds and dark descending. In the park people are going about their normal lives – jogging, walking dogs, kicking balls – but I hardly see them. They are in another world, hugely distant. All I can see, still, are the eyes on the other side of the door – a troubling vision of something inexplicable at the heart of things.

Who knows how long I sat there or what I did to pass the time? Eventually the chill in my body took me back to myself. As I buttoned my shirt, still wet with sweat, I suddenly became aware of a movement in my line of sight, a little way off behind a clump of shrubs. In the half dark it was just possible to make out a couple sprawled on the grass. How lucky they were to have each other, to be lying in each other's arms on a Friday evening instead of shivering in a damp shirt – this was the thought that was forming in my addled head when all at once the man – he looked no older than a boy – leapt up and started shouting and gesticulating at me. '*Yewfuckinstarinatus-eh?*' he yelled. 'Fuck off, yewfuckinpervert!'

A terrible heat rose up on both sides of my neck as I reeled across the grass and away from the couple, holding up my hands as if under arrest or expecting to be shot in the back, the ground sloping away and cracking beneath me. I ran all the way to the cemetery where, by Hume's grave, I sat very still till darkness fell.

33

The following day, a Saturday, Sanderson picked me up as usual on the Calton Hill road. By now I had acquired my own waders, waterproofs and fishing bag – all second-hand from a charity shop. It felt almost natural to be putting my gear in the boot of Sanderson's car, as if I'd been born to country pursuits instead of life in a French city. Almost, but not quite. I knew it was merely a game, trying out something for size. I had learned long ago that much of life was like that: looking in on yourself playing a role, putting on other clothes.

Except for all the shadowing and counter-shadowing, Sanderson and I had not seen each other or spoken since the previous Saturday's fishing expedition. Sanderson must surely have seen me run from the cottage the previous day, but he made no mention of it, and nor did I.

'How was your week?' I asked, getting into the car. Best to act normally.

'Oh, nothing new. Nothing new. Just an endless recycling of the same old shit on the way to oblivion.'

'You must be pretty busy at work – now that term is under way.'

'Yes and no.' He exhaled noisily, the breath whistling through his stained teeth. 'I suppose it's a bit like being in a barrel of worms. Eerily quiet, but a lot happening.'

'How's Carrie?'

'Hard to say. Busy being Buddhist no doubt.'

'Do you mind that?'

'Mind? No, why should I mind? Everyone needs a hobby of some kind. I've got fishing.'

It was hard to read this mood. I was on the lookout for anything that might give a clue to his strange behaviour over the past few days. But his eyes were fixed on the road ahead and he sat straight-backed at the wheel, intent, like a man planning a military campaign. In profile he looked weary, older. There was blood on his face where he had cut himself shaving, and the remains of soap stuck to his ear. His skin was raw in places – red, angry, excreting patches that had spread to his scalp.

After a while, he said: 'You know, if you put a frog into a pan of cold water and turn up the heat, he will cook slowly and die slowly. If you plunge him into boiling water, he will jump straight out, scalded but alive. I used to be that second frog, but now when I think about my life, I identify with the first one.' It was then that he said that his wife was 'seeing someone', the phrase I misunderstood, thinking that Carrie must be consulting a doctor. Not a doctor, said Sanderson. 'Another man, that's who.' Nothing else was said till we reached the river. In silence we removed the tackle from the car and walked the now familiar path through the trees and the undergrowth down to the riverbank.

'Now, let's see what we can find to whet the appetite,' he said, referring to the appetite of the fish. Opening his fly-box, he revealed a magnificent kaleidoscope of perfectly tied nymphs and lures, wet flies and dry – all representing a number of food possibilities for the hungry fish, or even just the curious one. Each Saturday he revealed a little more about the varieties of fly patterns. Today he explained that they were divided into two main categories: the attractors and the deceivers. The attractors were designed to stimulate the predatory instinct and to invite an attack. The deceivers were meant to resemble natural food forms, the stuff on which fish depended for the whole of their lives, however long that might be. 'In practice the boundaries are somewhat indistinct, but I can't help thinking of the attractors as male, and the deceivers as female,' he said. 'The deceiving fly fools the fish into believing that it is being presented with its favourite food – just the sort of thing a woman would do.' He groaned as he pulled on his waders. From his position on the pebbled bank he looked up at me, as if to gauge my response. 'I suppose you think that's a bit unfair,' he said, not waiting for a response. 'But in fact the distinction works rather against the male of the species – attractors being made-up, artificial things that bear no relation to anything occurring in the natural world.' That's how he sees himself, I thought. A manufactured creature made up of disparate bits, not drawn from nature, vulnerable to attack.

'Deceivers on the other hand,' he went on, 'though bearing every resemblance to the real thing, are not at all what they seem.' This should have been a lesson to him, he said. He should have learned about life from fishing. 'But like the poor fish, I have been altogether too unsuspecting of the artificial. It's been my undoing.'

Wasn't it a mistake to extrapolate too eagerly from fish to man, I asked, aiming to lighten the atmosphere. But he was determinedly solemn. 'It doesn't have to be fish,' he said. 'Take deer, for example. The stags compete for the attention of hinds – everyone knows that – but what's not so well known is that while the stags with the biggest antlers are exhausting themselves in the rut, some of the females slink off to have sex with the less flaunty males.' This had been discovered by a man called John Maynard Smith, he said – 'He's the famous evolutionist in case you've never heard of him. Worth looking him up. Maynard Smith called these females *the sneaky fuckers*. And quite right too.'

I had come to love the river. The loch where I had first practised my casting was beautiful, but the river seemed a more vital thing. Sometimes it flowed so steadily and evenly that it was hard to detect any movement, unless you set it against something large and inanimate like the trees on the far embankment. But that October day, though there was hardly any wind, the water was everywhere broken and full of sound after heavy rainfall during the night, and in those places where the river narrowed and hurried over the rocks it boiled into an agitated spume. Sanderson waded out two or three metres to reach his usual pool. He always used a wading staff, a tall cane weighted with lead at one end, to help him keep his footing, the bottom of the river being lumpy and slippery. Wading is a dangerous game, he had said more than once. The pool was edged on one side by a mass of rock worn smooth over the millennia. The rock was less visible that day on account of the height of the water, which came over halfway up Sanderson's chest waders. With his long split-cane rod held high above his head, and his landing net hanging from the back of his belt, he might have been some eccentric explorer from ancient times, inching his way into the unknown, off to bag an exotic wild creature.

There were trees on both banks of the river, some mature beech, and occasional willows bending over gracefully to drink from the water, but mainly birch and rowan, the latter laden with scarlet berries. I walked upstream a little and settled down on a rock to watch Sanderson fish. He had talked about the beautiful harmony of the materials: the silk line, the varnished cane and the carefully dressed fly. And now I could see this harmony with my own eyes in the delicate movements of a lumbering man, who could send his line snaking across the water, unrolling at the tip of its arc to drop the fly on the surface – an act of prestidigitation, so it seemed, verging on the miraculous. During those moments on the rock I decided that whatever the complexities of this troubled man there was an exquisite integrity to this side of him: his patient teaching, his fly-tying skills, his simple enthusiasm – all of it benign and attractive.

After a while I wandered further upstream till there was a clearing in the trees. My casting was not yet good enough to avoid snagging on overhanging branches, and though Sanderson had shown me a simpler cast – the single Spey cast he called it – I was nowhere close to mastering it. It's a roll cast, the secret being its smoothness of action, with hands placed on either side of the reel, so that you get a good grip – the way you might hold a baseball bat, Sanderson said. But it was a gentle action, one that involved a sort of 'floating' of the line.

There was also quite a lot to learn about the places where a trout might lie in wait for a meal. According to Sanderson, fine fishing depended on fine observation, but I was not yet in a position to know precisely what I was observing, far less what it might imply. Yet this did not detract from my love of the river in all its variety: the shifts of current, eddies and swirls, bends and runs, the sparkling freshness on a bright day, its dark secretiveness when the weather was dull. From the moment I set eyes on the river I had delighted in it. And the delight was partly to do with my incomplete understanding of it, as well as the sense of possibility that it held out.

Once the fishing proper began the two of us would leave each other in peace. Which seemed the natural thing to do. Fishing is a solitary activity – this much was clear to me – and it requires immense concentration. Sanderson was fond of saying that nothing focused the mind so intently as casting your fly on a rising trout. He had advised me to fish with a nymph – 'it will suit your style' – designed to imitate the larva on the riverbed. Since larvae formed a large part of the trout's diet, there would be in theory at least a reasonable chance of catching something. He himself was a dry-fly purist, which is to say that his fly was intended to dance on the surface of the water, simulating the real thing. 'It's the difference between poetry and prose,' he said. The well-dressed fly, he said, must possess all the qualities necessary to behave naturally and realistically. This was achieved by choosing materials that would float well – the hackle from a cock, for example, and a lightweight hook. Whenever he arrived at the river he would shake the boughs of the trees and observe the insects that flew out. The result would determine his choice of fly for the day. After that it was a question of judgement and skill, together with stealth. If the trout rose to your fly and you missed your strike, you had to try and let it hover delicately on the surface of the water, lifting it off and then laying it on again a metre or so upstream. 'And it's surprising how often the little beggar will have another go at the fly.'

At the clearing I entered the water and prepared to cast in the way I had been taught. According to Sanderson it was best to begin with a short line and aim at a spot where the fly could happily land. You had to find a comfortable length of line and stick to it – that way you could fish easily and comfortably for hours. It was always a mistake to try and cast too far. Sanderson had weighted my nymph with lead wire along the shank of the hook before building the body. In this way the nymph would get down quickly to the riverbed, where much of the natural nymph's life was spent. One of the hardest skills was to place the fly in the desired position, before letting the current take it. This had to be practised endlessly. A fish must have no inkling that he is being fished for, Sanderson said. His advice now made me smile. Even the dimmest of fish would straight away have me down as a hapless novice.

For the next hour or two, my right foot slightly forward for balance, I made cast after cast, back and forth, back and forth, driving the line outward with the rod tip, making the movement down an imaginary line running straight from my right shoulder. The rhythmic repetitive movements seemed to relax the mind and bring about an unusual physical calm. Little by little, as I gained in confidence, the casts became more fluent until gradually the rod and line, right down to the fly, began to feel like an extension of my own body, part of me. One day perhaps I might make a fisherman after all.

From time to time my gaze turned downstream towards Sanderson, a distant figure up to his waist in the water. The colours were incipient autumnal, the greens having given way to russets and browns. More than once I thought I saw a bend in Sanderson's rod – a signal of success. The scene had the quality of a painting: a pastoral idyll from an earlier century, man at one with nature in an age of innocence.

34

At some point – afterwards it was not easy to recall the exact moment – I thought I heard the cry of a bird, full-throated and urgent, but muffled by the loud chatter of water running over the rocks. I looked up, expecting to see a bird warning its young, and only when the cry came again, this time not bird-like but human, did I look in the direction of Sanderson. Who was in trouble. He had evidently lost his balance and was waving his arms madly, like an acrobat trying to stay on a tightrope. I dropped everything and cut down the water's edge till I came alongside him. But when I ran into the river, the water immediately felt solid, and my legs heavy, as if they were trailing through wet cement. 'Stay there! I'm coming!' I shouted. But with each step there was huge suction on my boots as they sank into the greedy gravel. My waders soon filled with water, cold and sharp. By the look of them Sanderson's waders were also flooded. His legs were being pulled up to the surface – a sign that air was trapped inside. With one hand he was clinging to a large boulder – too smooth to allow a good grip – and with the other he held on to his rod. 'Let go of the rod!' I yelled. 'Let go of the rod!' But the noise of the water swallowed my words and with the next step or two the uneven floor of the river threw me off-balance, and down I went into the seething rush. With a great effort I managed to steady myself against a slab of rock and found my feet once more. He was almost within reach now, and it was clear what had to be done: get him upright again and lead him safely back to the riverbank. There was no doubting my own strength to do this; I even indulged in a brief heroic image – the gallant *chevalier* coming to the rescue of his friend, who would never thereafter have cause to doubt the strength of the bond between them. After breasting the undercurrent and regaining my balance, I grabbed his shoulders from behind and shouted instructions at him to leave go of both rod and rock. It was reversal of roles and for a moment there was a feeling akin to exhilaration. 'Don't worry. You're safe now!' But Sanderson gave no sign of being relieved to see me. Worse than that, instead of allowing himself to be rescued, he fought like a bear. It must be the fear, I thought. He thinks he is going to die. There was a look of dread on his face, and in his panic he lashed out, thrashing his arms and slapping the water, at one point grabbing me by the throat, making at the same time a fearful braying noise like a man in the last throes of death. Before I could exert full control Sanderson placed his huge hand under my chin, thrusting it back and dashing my head against a rock. After which – I have no idea for how long – all was black and silent, and there was just the faintest sense of everything winding down, like the picture on an old television screen, reducing to a tiny white dot at the centre. The next thing I registered was the chill of the water on my face and on top of me a terrible weight – the ample mass of Sanderson's body.

Physical danger stirs up ancient reflexes, bringing with it a particular rush to the head and to the heart, making seemingly hopeless situations tractable. This at any rate seemed to be the only explanation for the superhuman strength that all at once became available to me and allowed me to pull Sanderson from the dark throat of the river. Even so, I would long continue to marvel at the resources I had been able to call upon to get myself and a drowning man to the safety of dry land.

For a while we sat on the grassy bank, dazed and sodden. When the cold set in, we struggled back to the car, Sanderson leaning heavily on me, both of us stumbling and staggering through the long grass and stinging nettles. We could have been a couple of drunks making our way home on a Saturday night; except that there was no carousing or laughter, just the grunt of Sanderson's laboured breathing and the squelch of our rubber boots, making a noise like windscreen wipers on dry glass.

That night I dreamt I was being carried along by a fast-flowing current. On and on I went, swiftly through the turbulent water, narrowly missing boulders and dead animals and fallen trees that were all a blur on account of the speed of travel. There's no way out, there's no way out – this was the single thought that repeated itself as I was swept along. The roar of the water was deafening, yet I could hear a whisper in my head telling me to translate the water into French – this alone might save me. But though I searched desperately for the words, I couldn't find them and didn't even know them, and in any case my mother was standing on the far bank, shouting something to me in French that I couldn't understand, and waving above her hairless head a blue handkerchief that changed from light blue to dark and back again. And beside my mother, dancing around her and looking everywhere for the head to which they belonged, was a pair of staring eyes.

35

When we came to talk about what happened that day, Sanderson said that he'd lost his footing – he'd seen a fish rising beyond his fly and had tried to get his cast a little farther. The strength of the current took him by surprise, throwing him backwards. His waders began to take in water, at which point he had called for help. The explanation was straightforward, and there was no reason for me to doubt it or disbelieve it. Yet I did. Not at the time, nor on the journey back, nor even when at last I had removed my wet clothes, taken a hot shower and felt the relief of sinking back into the solitude of my own place. Nor still as I cleaned the wound on my skull and began to replay the drama in my mind, pondering the different possible outcomes. No, it would occur to me only later, quite unexpectedly, during our next strange exchange on the Saturday following. Although I had no previous experience of rescuing a man in trouble in the water, something suddenly bothered me about the incident. It was not so much that Sanderson had resisted help (though he had); more that he had deliberately exposed me to danger and shown violence towards me. And that this perhaps had been his intention all along.

*

In the meantime, however, I was preoccupied by something else: the mystery of the garage, and what – or whom – it contained. I reread Martin Blandford's note: '*The garage contains my own personal effects and is therefore locked.*' My eye lighted on another sentence: '*There is a spare set of keys at No 16 in case you lock yourself out . . .*'

That evening I rang the doorbell of No 16, introduced myself to the amiable woman who opened the door, explained that I was the tenant at Martin Blandford's place, and that I'd locked myself out. Within seconds the spare keys were in my hand. 'No hurry,' the woman smiled as I promised their swift return.

How easy are these small deceptions, and how fruitful. As I had hoped, there was an extra key on the ring – the key to the connecting door into the garage.

My mind was open to all possibilities, but even so the inside of the garage took me aback, and I was able to absorb it only slowly, in a pinch-me, dreamlike trance. The first impression was of a Bedouin tent: rugs on the walls and floors, colourful prayer flags suspended from each corner, and everywhere rich fabrics and layered textiles. It was unlit, except for borrowed light from the utility room, and there was no light switch, only sconces round the walls containing stout candles, a few of which I now lit, till shadows danced on the thickly woven wall hangings and the full splendour of the room began to unfold. Against the back wall there was a low-level chaise, draped in a kelim the colour of burnt sienna, and on top of the floor mats there were several earthenware pots, large patterned cushions, a couple of ornate brass lanterns with decorated glass, a low wooden table covered in mosaic mats with tea lights and incense sticks on top. The tones were warm and earthy, as if painted from a palette of eastern spices, giving a rich sumptuous impression quite at odds with the rest of the cottage. It had the feel of a Moroccan bazaar.

In front of the table there was a strange chair, high-backed and padded, but without legs – the sort of chair you might see in a

Japanese restaurant – and positioned to face the connecting door to the utility room. It slowly bore in on me that through the key-hole I had seen the eyes of whoever sat on this low chair. On a wooden footstool near the chaise there lay an open book, *Meditation for a Quiet Mind*, with pencil markings in the margin and, folded between its pages, a typed sheet of paper. By the light of one of the lamps I sat down to read it:

Dearest Carrie,

Here are some notes to keep with you while I am away. I have tried to describe the process as it happens for me, and how it can soothe when nothing else seems able to. It might help you to think of it as a kind of quiet surrender. Good luck

   With Love, Martin

When you sit for a while, facing a wall, there is nowhere to go but in. In actual fact it does not usually feel that you are going in: it feels as if the inside is coming out. At first, and perhaps for a long time, there is just a succession of thoughts, of feelings, of dreams, of ideas, of memories, everything coming with its own shade of emotion. In the arena of the mind, all these things succeed each other in a kind of dance, a conga of semi-consciousness: they dance for a while, and then are superseded by the next sequence.

   Sometimes they are painful: memories of loss rear up suddenly, startlingly, making you flinch. Sometimes they are out of control: fear or rage or grief gets hold of you and you charge along with it, unable to control it or resist it. It can seem to have a life of its own. Sometimes you don't want to get free of it, at other times you want nothing more than to get away. Even if it does go away, it can come back again and again.

In time, even when something is clinging to you like a crazed pit bull, it becomes possible to let go. For a long time this may not work. You can get locked in a grim embrace with it, your hand round its throat, holding it off. But still holding it. And what you then learn to do is not to hold it at all, not even to hold it at bay. You let it go in the sense of letting it be – letting it be there, in front of you, inside you. This can be frightening. By letting it be, as it is, it is just there, in all its awfulness. And there is no other way. You cannot be free of it if you strive to be free of it. You can only be free if you surrender. No more likes and dislikes: you accept what comes. You acknowledge it and let it be there.

In this way, over time, it loses its power. It doesn't necessarily disappear. It can still be there a year later, five years later, but instead of trying to throw it away, or to conquer it, which doesn't work, you continue to let it sit quietly in the palm of your open hand, in the space of your rib cage, just being itself.

It turns out that if you want to give something up, what is needed is not to want to give it up, but to let it be. No turning away, no suppressing, no resisting in horror. You accept it, all of it, just as it is. It becomes an endless practice of surrender, until you realise eventually what is going on, and you just return to the stillness, the quiet of the space in which all this is taking place. The stillness that runs through all movement, the moving stillness that flows through every quiet thing, and every loud one.

MB

For a while I stayed, quite still, on the chaise, trying to hold on to the familiar space around me that I had always known, the space that now seemed to be occupied by something I did not recognise. Eventually I placed the notes face up on the seat of the strange legless chair, took one last look at the room and blew out the candles and lamp. I walked back through the connecting door, leaving it closed but unlocked.

36

Now that it was clear that Carrie was the invisible presence in my cottage, a sense of relief, followed by a delicious calm, seeped through me. It was perhaps odd not to feel intruded upon or in some way invaded, but in truth my sense was closer to a ridiculous delight at living in a place in which Carrie had an interest. When I thought of her letting herself in at my front door and slinking through the utility room to the garage with all its rugs and cushions and kelims, I felt as if my life had miraculously acquired a different dimension. Except that there was, too, a dull pain in my chest for the dimly understood suffering of a woman of whom I knew next to nothing. (Of the man she shared her life with it sometimes felt as if I knew next to everything.) None of these thoughts was properly formed or even fully conscious. I had no urge to do anything. It was simply a matter of waiting.

Meanwhile I got on with the business of translating – a labour of love in the case of David Hume. He was a constant reminder that if you want to be a decent translator it is never enough to have learned the language, however well you have learned it. You also have to be in harmony with the author, turning and shaping his words into new words that will connect with a different set of readers, strangers to the original. A translator has to be scrupulous and dutiful, but not simply to the words – that sort of rigidity can kill a piece stone dead. The spirit counts for just as much. Dante believed that changing a work from one language to another destroyed all its sweetness, and while there is perhaps some truth in this, I still think it worth trying, unsparingly, to prove Dante wrong. To this end I always apply the 'sweetness test' when I read over my day's work. French translators have a certain reputation for making free with the text, and if ever they are accused of altering the sense of the original, they usually defend themselves along predictable lines: *Everything benefits from being a bit more Gallic – surely that's obvious, and in any case the text sounds less 'translated' this way.* I myself have no time for this sort of cavalier approach. It breaks the bond of trust between the writer and translator. And the French language, like every other, has to be open to other currents and connections. This is the way it thrives. The purity of a language is mythical – it's the surest way to atrophy.

With translation you are exposing yourself to other minds, other manners, other possibilities. This is the beauty of it. You are able to imagine worlds you haven't had the opportunity to see. And this applies to the reader as well as to the translator. There should be a feeling of trust when you give yourself to it. It might not always repay the trust, but when it does the rewards are huge.

With Hume's essays the endeavour included catching the lovely lustre of his insights as well as the stylistic pitch of his sentences. I felt grateful for the elegance of Hume's style, not least because elegance was something that readers looked for in a translation, and if it was absent the translator was always the prime suspect. I have never forgotten the backhanded compliment paid by a reviewer of one of my detective novels: 'elegant even in translation' – *même en traduction*. As if elegance was something that translators normally killed off, just for the hell of it. Or that if a fraction of the elegance survived, it was entirely accidental. For some reason there is a lack of generosity towards translators, though it's hard to know why this should be.

With the current undertaking part of me longed to be able to restore belief in translation. It sounded like a ridiculously lofty aim, but there was never any danger of getting grand ideas about myself: my daily work constantly cut me down to size. This was in the nature of it. Even so, at the back of my mind there was a faint hope that if only I could do it well enough my translation of Hume might one day become trusted. Valued even. The task was huge, but there were brief moments – usually when I had just polished off one of the essays – when I felt equal to it.

One of Hume's own stated aims had been to reconcile philosophy with what he called 'the common life', and he was therefore at pains in the essays to make his writing both useful and accessible. *I cannot but consider myself as a kind of resident or ambassador from the dominions of learning to those of conversation: and shall think it my constant duty to promote a constant correspondence betwixt these two states, which have so great a dependence on each other.* His earlier *Treatise of Human Nature*, in which he had placed such high hopes, had failed to connect with the people, falling *still-born from the press*, as he despairingly put it. Determined not to repeat the failure, he used words in his essays that belonged very much to the common language of the time. For this reason the essays could reasonably have been translated into some sort of equivalent workaday French – a standard modern translation – and this is no doubt what my publisher, the lowbrow Mauvignier, might have preferred. But I had decided against it at the outset. It seemed important not to lose the diversity and richness of Hume's vocabulary, and just as important, by using slightly archaic French words, to retain the elegance of his pen and give the true flavour of certain paradigms that were characteristic of the times in which Hume lived. I did not take liberties with the text; my aim was always to transmit meaning as accurately as possible without addition or subtraction. It was important to reflect Hume's style, not impose a style of my own. To this end I sometimes spent a whole day on a single word, wavering between determination to get it right and despair at doing it justice. Recently, for example, I had agonised over the word *commonwealth*, which had connotations in Hume's time of the political body, the state, the community and the republic, without strictly corresponding to any of them. *République* would not do: it was too general, too French, and it implied that commonwealth was a sort of republican regime. After a day's indecision I visited Hume's grave on my way home and spent a few minutes in whispered consultation – a strategy that invariably led to a happy resolution. I left the cemetery with a spring in my step, the problem already disappearing into the dusk. The decision once taken was obvious: *commonwealth* was irreplaceable. It had no equivalent in French. It would therefore have to be retained – along with a footnote.

I had come to English full of hope and anticipation, and this optimistic feeling had never quite left me. How satisfying it was to make a living at it, and a life out of it – especially one that was low-profile to the point of invisibility. In fanciful moments I imagined myself as a kind of human bridge between cultures – a self-aggrandising notion perhaps, but tempered by an earnest wish that people would cross the bridge without even noticing I was there.

Long ago, when I had first announced my decision to become a translator, my father had declared himself proud to have a son who would work with words. He believed that language was the thing that hitched us to the world. 'When you think about it,' he said, 'it's the connective tissue. The vital organs can't do without it.' But he sounded a note of caution too. It could also be a barrier, he said, an obscuring screen, and even when people were speaking the same language, meaningful communication didn't always happen. 'In fact, whenever it does, it's something of a miracle.'

Moments like this, containing a fatherly seal of approval, were carefully stored in the memory. And it wasn't only the words I remembered. As if watching a film, I could see my father in fine detail, every nod of his head, each movement of his hands, the distant look in his eyes.

In my wallet I carry a photograph of my father leaning up against the shelves in the bookshop, cigarette in hand. I love this photograph, mainly because it perfectly captures the life and the death. This was a man who often rose as dawn was breaking and went downstairs to sit amongst the books. And it was amongst books that his life had also come to an end. I often take out the photograph and run my hand over the surface, as if to feel the rough tweed of his jacket and remember the complex smells that collected in the old fabric – unfiltered Gitanes, dust, moth-balls.

On the day my father died we had planned to meet for break-fast. It seems likely that he suffered a heart attack in the early morning while stacking the high shelves. But when I arrived in the bookshop he was lying, not yet dead, on the floor, and in those first moments everything pointed to a break-in: steplad-der on its side, books strewn around, and blood coming from a gash on my father's head. I knelt beside him, holding his head, telling him it was me, I was there, it would be all right. He could not speak, but his last penetrating look seemed to say: Don't worry, this is what happens, my time has come, I'm showing you how to do it, so that you in your turn will know. In those last intense minutes before the paramedics arrived I spoke softly to him, soothing words in his mother tongue, remembering all the while those times when it had been otherwise and he had held me in his arms and comforted me. Now it did not seem to matter which of us was which. We were one and the same person.

Afterwards I had the task of sorting out the books in the shop.

For weeks it felt as if I were dismantling my father and the life he had lived. Packing each box was a small act of aggression, and when it was done, the room was bare, emptied of meaning. For a long time a dreadful sense of loss followed me around, always visible in the rear mirror. And even when it was no more than a wisp or two in the distance it never quite disappeared.

37

In the half-light of an early November evening we sat together in my cottage, expectation in the air: if I waited long enough, she would begin. She would tell me her secret – why she had been entering my house without permission – and she would say how sorry she was and how stupid and furtive she had been. And I would say, no, no, it doesn't matter at all, there's no harm done, and in any case we all do things that are strange, things we regret. It would all be beautifully simple and gracefully executed as in a Japanese tea ceremony.

Her note had been brief and to the point. I had found it the day before, propped up on the little table in the hall:

I'm so sorry. I owe you an explanation. I will call round tomorrow after work. C

In the curves and loops of her handwriting I saw the contours of her face. The wide-spaced eyes with their quizzical look floated in front of me, bobbing along in dreamy soft focus on the arc of each word. Even her handwriting was unsettling.

And now we sit facing one another in the thinly furnished sitting room, rendered even more ascetic in my mind by the thought of the richly festooned garage space on the other side of the wall. Each of us is holding a glass of chilled white wine. The room feels spare and cool, lit with a bright cold light as in an operating theatre. The bareness of my living quarters suddenly seems comfortless. Perversely, I long for a plump floor cushion or a wall hanging to soften it.

She is wearing a dark green sleeveless top. The colour sets off her pale skin, which, in the cool of the room, is raised in tiny bumps, like the surface of an orange. I notice the fine white hairs on her arms. Is she warm enough, I ask, leaping to my feet as if to harness some instant heat. She nods, shivering slightly and arching her back as she does so, till I can pick out the thin bones that converge in a groove running all the way down her spine. For a while she sits quite still, barely disturbing the air, a statue carved in marble. The atmosphere is intensely charged. Just by waiting, however, all will be explained. At last she speaks.

'It's not what you think,' she says.

Truly, I do not know what I am thinking.

'I expect it looks to you like a terrible marriage.'

'What makes you say that?'

'No need to be embarrassed. It's what any outsider would conclude.' She sounds defensive.

'I haven't really concluded anything.'

This much is true.

'When Harry taught me philosophy, all those years ago, he could be quite intimidating. Clever, confident, a little pompous perhaps, definitely keen to display his wares. When we met again a few years later, I saw him in a different light. He was not so sure of himself. In fact he was awkward.'

She pauses, as if taking time to recall his awkwardness.

'And I liked that. It made him vulnerable. I was vulnerable too.' The important men, she says, had disappeared from her life not long before – the father of her child, as well as her own father. Harry pursued her, and she had responded. Before she knew it she had a crush on him. 'A small crush at least. A *crushette*, you might say.' She smiles. 'In any case it felt like a pang. Nothing you could call love. My father had just died and Harry filled a gap. We've never really had a body-and-soul relationship.'

'A marriage of convenience then?' I surprise myself with this.

'Well, that's just a neat phrase – it doesn't really mean anything.' She gives a wry laugh. 'People have been marrying each other for centuries for all sorts of reasons, and certainly without understanding one another.'

'But surely there has to be something that attracts you in the first place? Even if it's only the possibility of something?'

'I suppose that's right. Though it's hard now to think what it was.' Again, she smiles, indulgently this time. 'He was a bit of a shambles when we met, a big baggy monster of a man – not that I minded. He wore old-man trousers, the sort that used to be called flannels – you know the kind of thing. Gussets, two inches too short, too high on the waistband, tight at the top of the leg before ballooning. And in his short-sleeved shirts, his arms looked weak and defenceless. But all of this invited pity and a desire to look after him. The difference in our ages also seemed to be a good thing. A younger man can go in all sorts of directions, but I thought that Harry had probably stopped developing. Which made me think I knew what I was getting.'

'And were you right to think that?'

'Yes, in a sense. My own parents had always made the best of things, out of some nebulous gratitude to God. Anything that happened was dictated by the will of the Almighty. So they believed. They endured whatever was thrown at them, always in a thanks-be-to-God sort of way.'

Growing up with that was often stifling, she says. Harry on the other hand usually made the worst of things. He could be relied upon to make every situation worse – or at least appear to be worse than it was. 'And in some strange way this was liberating.'

'Didn't love come into it?'

My assumptions are under assault.

'It's probably a bit of a gamble to place love at the centre of marriage. Don't you agree? And anyway I'd done that, with the father of my child. And look where that got me. Time is probably necessary for love to acquire any sort of meaning. Don't you think?'

I cannot think. I have been watching, as she speaks, the movements of her mouth. I might have told her that I have no experience of what she is talking about, that in many ways my life is merely my childhood extended, that I am still mourning my parents, that I have always been afraid of madness – both the kind you inherit and the kind you might call your own – that I have a neurotic addiction to routine, that I am bedevilled by irrational fears, and that I have never had the courage to change anything much. If I hadn't become the thing that I fear, I might have said all this.

'I'm not sure,' I say.

'Marriages break up when people don't give them time,' she says. 'That's what I think anyway. People imagine that other couples are living happier lives, that all is perfect in the house next door. Maybe it is of course. But it seems unlikely.' She closes her eyes for a moment, and I notice the paleness of her long lashes.

'The trouble is,' she continues, twisting the gold band on her finger, 'the moment you try to explain things like this – big things like marriage that involve two people with all their quirks and foibles – you start to lie. Either to yourself or to others. And before you know it you've built up a whole story that has no connection to the facts.'

At last I know what she means. I have been doing this all my life.

'The people I know who have left their husbands or wives – well, they do it on an impulse,' she says. 'And then they make the story fit the facts afterwards.' She is examining her hands as if they hold the key to everything she is saying. 'In most marriages, I suspect, it's neither one thing nor the other. You just rub along on parallel tracks, getting on or not getting on.' She looks up to check my response. Her eyes are deep pools of blue.

'But it is worth saying, worth repeating, that the man I married seems different from the man I see now. Now he lends himself to caricature, for his flaws are so evident and open to ridicule. And yet there used to be so much more to him – far more than the farcical figure you could forge from the flaws. Something happened when I wasn't looking.'

'What do you think that was?'

'Who knows?' she says, turning towards the window as if the answer might lie just outside. It is only in the last year or two that she has begun to notice. She has been so wrapped up in other things. 'I am beginning to think he may be depressed. Not just, you know, fed up with life, but actually ill. A sort of low-level clinical depression.'

'What makes you think that?'

All sorts of reasons, she says, but one in particular, the kind of thing you know only if you live with someone. His smell is different, she says, looking suddenly perplexed. She's read that depressed people give off a distinctive smell, one that can't be washed away. And he's too centred, she says, not *on* himself exactly, but *in* himself. It's a bad business, definitely it is, and he's cursed by it. When they first met he would have done anything to avoid making a scene. Because of his background. Not that his parents were stuck-up toffee-nosed people with pokers up their bums. They weren't. They were just no-fuss law-abiding people, terrified of drawing attention to themselves. 'And that sort of thing, well, I think it's imprinted before we know it.'

She speaks jumpily now, doubling back on herself, qualifying her last statement, questioning the next even before she utters it.

'Also, he has started measuring himself against others – hair loss, teeth loss, that sort of thing. He has a premonition of decay. Especially now he's been dumped by Alice.'

'You *knew* about that?'

In revealing, without meaning to, that I also know, I feel like a traitor.

'Don't worry, it was no big deal. I didn't really mind.' She sounds quite calm now. 'In fact, it was better for me while it lasted. It's much worse now.'

'What do you mean?'

She hesitates. She looks past me, not meeting my eyes. 'I shouldn't really be talking to you like this. I hardly know you,' she says. She draws herself up and turns towards me, giving me a long, considered look, as if I might be something on a plate in a restaurant – to be eaten or sent back to the kitchen. 'But it's because I hardly know you that I can. It's easier to talk to a stranger.'

A stranger, that's what I am. *Un étranger*, like my father before me.

'How can I put it?' she says.

The way she puts it is that this side of things with Harry has never really 'done it' for her. Never really held her attention. For years now it has been just a quick pit stop, she says.

'Nuts and bolts, you know. A sort of tidy-up, the fleshly equivalent of a short back and sides – if you get what I mean.' It was heat on the body, yes, but on the whole it had become a pale thing, like invalid food – nourishing enough but in a vanilla sort of way. No colour. She had felt quite relieved he was having fun elsewhere. It had taken the pressure off her.

She speaks in waves now, each one topped in foam. Her voice is a melody in my head.

'The wonder is that Alice put up with him as long as she did. The more desperate he's become, what with his skin erupting and everything, the more he feels he has to prove himself. Now anything physical feels like a head-on collision. He's like a prop-forward, shunting and heaving and scrumming his way on the pitch.'

I am experiencing mild panic. And a powerful urge to consult my dictionaries. Certain phrases can throw you off balance. You know the individual words, but joined together they mean nothing. Not for the first time I think that the limits of language are in some sense the limits of experience. While I contemplate pit stops and prop-forwards, Carrie changes tack.

'I also think he wonders if he can ever again be surprised by his students. Or by life,' she says.

'You mean he's been in the job too long?' I ask, back on surer ground.

'Something like that, I suppose. It's become a burden to him. I think it happens a lot in universities. And he's hard on himself. There was a time when he enjoyed what he was doing, when he believed in it, when he thought it could make a difference, when he admired his colleagues and liked his students. It was a process that they all went through together, and everyone learned from it. At some point he seemed to develop contempt for his colleagues. And for his subject. Philosophy suddenly lost its attraction. Now it's just pulling levers. Covering the ground and leaving no mark. That's what he says anyway, though sometimes I think he *enjoys* sounding hopeless.' She gives an indulgent laugh.

'At least he talks to you about it. Better than keeping it to himself.'

'Sometimes I'm not so sure.' She lowers her eyes again and stretches her lips tight. 'He's become disappointed in himself, and that translates into disappointment with the world, and with me. More and more he speaks to me in a particular voice as if he's talking to an imbecile. Which I suppose I have become in part.'

I have an urge to defend her, but check myself, asking her instead if she has read Sanderson's book on happiness.

'I've read the proofs, yes.' No real surprises, she says – basically it was an academic book that set out the arguments, the different approaches to happiness. But the epilogue was more revealing, offering some insight into the man, along the lines they had been talking about in fact – you could almost feel the disappointment on the page. 'Well, *I* can at any rate. But I can also see the humaneness there too.' Her voice is hypnotic, so lilting and full of song that it would be easy to miss what she is saying, so beguiling is the music in it. 'No question about it,' she says, holding out her glass for a refill, 'philosophy can seriously damage your health.'

'David Hume certainly thought so,' I say, standing over her now, pouring the wine and thinking how small and vulnerable she looks on the sofa. 'He was a brilliant scholar but too much philosophy led to a complete collapse. His physician called it *the disease of the learnèd.*'

'And what was the treatment?'

'To do everything more moderately, to walk every day, to stop work before he was *weary* – as he put it.'

'And did it work?'

'It did. He came to see that a happy life was made up of quite ordinary moments – in the company of friends, dining together, drinking together, being active, not thinking too much.'

It sounds simple, she says, but she has always believed that the things we crave – 'like happiness and love' – are quite elusive. Why is happiness so elusive, I ask, ignoring love, but feeling something akin to exhilaration now, no longer held hostage by reticence. She gives me a sideways look, not disapproving exactly – perhaps simply wise to the question-and-answer drift of the evening.

'Because it's not something to be thought about, it's something that just happens,' she says. 'I mean, if you were to ask what would make me happy at this moment, I'd settle for being alive in the world with no more than everyday worries. But if that were to happen, then happiness would probably be something else entirely.' She draws down the corners of her mouth with both hands, making a sad-clown face. 'People say: *I'd be happy with a nice cottage in the country*, or *Just give me a quiet life with a husband and two kids*. But once they've got that, it doesn't stop them hankering after the next thing.'

'Yes, but don't you think we make too much of happiness? It's become a sort of cult, a drug. Don't you agree? It makes us afraid of sadness – we push it away from us.'

'What do you mean?'

'Well, there almost seems to be a requirement that people be happy – it's a duty, and we have to attend to it all the time, pushing away anything negative, anything sad. For example, people don't really mourn any more, certainly not in France. It's gone out of fashion. We used to be very good at it, but now it's discouraged.'

'Maybe we don't have the same need to mourn,' she says.

'I certainly do,' I say, surprising both of us. 'I mourn my parents dreadfully. Practically everything I do is a form of mourning for them.' She is giving me a prolonged and penetrating look. 'Of course,' I say, 'this is not the sort of thing you go around admitting – admitting to yourself is enough.'

We start then to discuss how things of this kind differ in our two countries. In French the word for happiness is *bonheur*, I say – the old word for chance. And it was the same with many other languages – English too. The *happ* part was chance – like *happenstance*. But the modern word had lost all its association with chance. 'I suppose I think that's a pity.' *Joie* on the other hand – *joy* – that was a much more useful word than happiness. *Joie de vivre*, she says, in a funny Celtic inflection. 'Precisely,' I say, 'but the *joie* is the acceptance of life in its good *and* bad parts.'

The light from the lamp now seems too bright and cool for this conversation. I excuse myself for a moment and fetch some candles from the garage room. She watches me move around, making small adjustments. 'That's better,' she says once the lamp is off and the candles lit. When we are settled down in the new soft light I ask her to describe the Sanderson she met fifteen years before.

She begins to laugh. So many questions, she says, not seeming to mind in the least. He was always more Mr Rochester than Darcy, she says – saturnine, broody, a dark undertow of danger, but also dynamic and audacious. 'At the beginning, he could be appalling and hilarious at the same time. He used to tell stories at dinner parties about how we met – he always said it was my backside that he fell in love with, beautifully set off by the gilded splendour of the Signet Library – until everyone groaned because they had heard it so many times. But he had a sense of fun. In fact he could do a whole comedy act by himself – the funny guy and the straight guy rolled into one. His timing was spot on.'

In the early years too he had been sentimental in matters of love. This had been harder to deal with. Sometimes he would write little notes to her – billets-doux folded into neat little squares – and push them under the door of her studio. At other times he would leave cards lying around the flat for her to discover. *My dearest wife* they invariably began, which always made it sound to Carrie as if he had several.

'They usually continued with a message of self-chastisement, which seemed self-indulgent as well as insincere, such as *I know I must be a disappointment to you* or *I am so sorry to neglect you*, finishing up with some awkward endearment that limped off the page.'

On the days that Harry left these notes he would grin knowingly at her, seeming to confirm that they were more for his benefit than for hers, as she'd suspected all along. Besides, she was puzzled by their content. It never occurred to her to feel neglected, or to think that he was away too much. In fact, what she minded, if she minded anything, was quite the opposite: that he always seemed to be *there*, in the flat, appearing and reappearing at odd times, upsetting the natural rhythm of her working day.

'You haven't been married, have you?' The question sounds neither accusing nor pitying.

'No,' I say, feeling I have failed a test. 'But the subject interests me.' An embarrassed laugh. 'I am full of human curiosity about other states of being.' I want to play my part in this conversation, to share information and experience on an equal basis. This was surely how it was supposed to be: you listened to the other person's story and then you told yours – a mutual interaction, feeding and being fed, giving nourishment and getting it in return. Why was I so ill-equipped for it? I try to engage, but everything feels wrong. Even my thin responses – a sympathetic tilt of the head, a gentle hand movement – feel stagey and over-rehearsed, making them doubly awkward in a minor role such as mine.

'Does he still write these notes?' This is all I can manage.

'No, not in the same way,' she says, adding that he did however feel the need to solemnise all the significant moments in his life with letters. Lengthy undertakings usually, sometimes running to a dozen pages, always meticulously punctuated, and strewn with parentheses and allusions. 'Just as some people need to take photographs to mark the big events – as if without the camera nothing is quite believable – Harry tends to validate the high points and low points, especially the low points, with some sort of written discharge.'

For a minute or two she is silent, and in the guttering light she looks stricken. But in her wry comments about Sanderson's epistolary habits she doesn't *sound* stricken, and I begin to think that beneath the rather downbeat exterior there is a spirited, vivacious variant.

'I sometimes think that writing letters gives him more satisfaction than almost anything else. Apart from tying flies perhaps. My own theory is that for him they capture a moment in time that would otherwise vanish without trace. He likes to imagine the letters being received, being read and reread, slept on, dreamed of. All of this gives him so much pleasure – pure and unsullied because he alone controls it.'

She sits in profile now. I cannot see the look in her eyes, but I can sense her amusement.

'Some things you come to understand only when you are on the inside,' she says, serious once again. 'There are things you get used to, things that another person would find hard to believe and impossible to understand. When I was young I used to think that bad marriages could just be terminated, like nuisance phone calls. But it's not like that. People can behave very, very badly in a marriage, yet still be loved and cherished. Even in my previous relationship, which I thought would lead to marriage and happiness ever after, he buggered off and never looked back. Frightened, I suppose.'

A long pause. She lowers her eyes.

'You get used to one another – the presence at the breakfast table, the lump in the bed. Over time it matters more and more. Familiarity breeds more familiarity. That's the way our lives are made up. That, and the terrible things we do to one another.'

'And is familiarity enough?'

The question hangs in the air, waiting for an answer.

'Most of the time it is enough.'

She pulls herself up in a way that suggests these might be her last words on the subject. 'I suppose I have no right to be surprised,' she says. 'I mean, being married has never been a restful business. Harry was always maddening in the way he could find fault with the simplest of statements. To that extent I knew what I was taking on. But until a few years ago he was just like plenty of other people – a bit rumpled and out of shape, disappointed with the world, taking every opportunity to express his dissatisfaction with it . . . ' Her sentence stays unfinished, but it leaves its mark on the evening. Her eyes travel all round the room before meeting my own. 'No, I suppose what changed for me was my ability to cope with him. That and what life threw at me.'

38

The story of what life had thrown at her was shot through with love and pity. Harry was quite right, she said. The love a mother felt for her child blocked out everything. She had not wanted to be pregnant, but as soon as the baby was born she was completely enraptured. The baby was placed on her soft damp body, and what she felt when she first saw him had stayed with her always. Nothing since had been as intense or as important. He was a funny creature at the start, she said, like a little elf – a wise face, thin red legs and downy black hair all over his back. It was love at first sight. She had called him Alfie, a name that meant wise counsel of the elf. He had been a model baby – no baby ever smiled or rolled over or sat up or took his first steps quite as perfectly as Alfie had done. He had grown into a sensitive, gentle child, acutely aware of his surroundings and the feelings of others. They had become so close, she and Alfie – quite inseparable. There had been a tacit understanding that Harry would never be a father to him. She had not minded. In fact she secretly wanted Alfie to herself and might almost have found it hard to share him. And she knew Harry could never have loved him as she did. It wasn't just that he didn't have a natural fondness for children – he just wasn't physically *connected* to Alfie. The bond was with her. She remembered lots of happy years, filled with a sort of blithe spirit. It was a golden time, she said. But in due course nature played its cruel trick. First came the joy, then came the hammer blow to remove it. The joy had lasted well into his teenage years – that was something she felt grateful for – with little warning of what was to come. The first sign of anything being wrong was when Alfie began to withdraw into himself. He stayed in his room more and more, missing meals, not washing. That's what teenagers *do*, Harry had said. Then came the strange behaviour. Harry said it was bad behaviour, and what could you expect. But it was not bad, it was merely strange and unpredictable. Alfie began to hear voices, receive signs. It seemed positive at the beginning, not pathological – the associations were interesting and intense, bordering on the brilliant. But the voices crowded in, the signs were everywhere – in the cracks on the pavement, the leaves on the trees, cloud formations. He had read about the network of vaults and underground chambers in the city of Edinburgh, convincing himself that they contained evil forces out to get him. He began to speak in the voice of a prophet, warning them of impending disaster. Their only chance of being saved was to listen to him, take heed – this is what he kept saying. He alone could receive the signals. He pretended to be brave and strong, but it was all whistling in the dark. All the while he was afraid, and in time the fear pushed out everything else. He began to rearrange the furniture in the house, to wear lots of jerseys one on top of the other. He stuffed plastic bags up the water taps. Anything to keep the forces at bay, and the fear. People were watching him, he said, with cameras and microphones. They could get at him down the chimneys, or through the telephone wires. The messages multiplied. He became convinced that they were planted in his ear canals, in the fillings in his teeth, in his hair follicles. He begged to have his ears syringed, his teeth extracted, his head shaved. At which point she had taken him to a doctor, then a psychiatrist. She felt ashamed now of her middle-class confidence – it must be a ghastly misunderstanding, she told herself, it would soon be cleared up. When they saw Alfie, they would know. They would see how much he was loved and cared for, and they would laugh and say he was just a brilliant boy with a vivid imagination, nothing to worry about. But they didn't say this. They used words like delusional and paranoid and rapid onset. They would have to admit him to hospital, assess him properly, treat him with drugs. From the start Alfie hated hospital. His room was full of Nigerians, out to get him, so he said. An attack was imminent. It would be a gas attack, it would come through the light fittings, through the shower head. It won't be for long, she told him, not knowing it was a lie. This is a hospital – they will help you here, make you better. But they didn't make him better. They gave him drugs that he didn't take, or worse, pretended to take. In his own mind he wasn't ill – it was all a conspiracy. She visited him every day, returning home to weep. She hated leaving him there. It felt like a betrayal. And the hospital staff all had reassuring voices with jaunty, breezy, nice-nurse manners that made her scream inside. Even when Alfie made a bid for freedom – something he did many times in the beginning – they said: don't worry, this is what they *do*, this is *normal*. But it wasn't normal, it was unspeakably dreadful, imagining your son ill and frightened and on the run, not knowing whether he would turn up alive or dead, hearing the missing-persons officer describe him as dangerous, when the greatest danger was to himself. Soon she could do nothing but weep. In those early months she could not even paint. Harry said Alfie was a succubus, draining life from the host, his family. Friends stopped talking about their own children, and if ever they did it was a lapse that they quickly covered up. When you had this sort of trouble in your life, she said, you frightened people off. Even your friends thought they would be contaminated in some way, that their own children would catch it. So they steered clear. People did not want suffering in their living rooms, not even when it was their friend's suffering. They sympathised in whatever way they could, but they couldn't let this bad thing into their own lives. So they extrapolated for a minute or two, as much as their sensibilities allowed. Then bang! – the door was shut. The requirement – here she echoed what I had said earlier – was for happiness, positive thoughts. Anything negative had to be kept at bay. Only Alice had not minded, and that was because she did not have children and because she was sleeping with Harry. Whenever you spoke to other parents about your damaged child, Carrie said, you heard your voice take on a strange tone, as if you were a professional carer and needed to keep control, instead of a frantic mum out of your head with worry about your darling son. And this tone, this self-restraint – this was something that you did for *them*, so that *they* would not feel awkward. Several people – including Harry – seemed to think that Alfie had brought it upon himself, that he'd had it coming. Or worse, that *she* had somehow brought it upon him, by loving him, by spoiling him. And now that he had been pronounced ill, she was colluding in his illness. There was no end to people's ghastly theories and imaginings. Gradually she had felt everything unravelling. She didn't know how to live her life, even how to sit still. She began to wander the streets, trying to walk off the pain, searching for signs of it in other people. There must be a community of sufferers, she told herself, travelling about incognito. She couldn't stop weeping. And Harry, who hated her weeping, couldn't stop drinking. Her mother declared that she had brought it on herself, that God was punishing her. She should have done God's bidding all those years ago and married the boy's father. Harry called her mother dangerous and reactionary – he had of course fired off one of his letters – only to be told that suffering was spiritually instructive, that it would introduce the living Christ into her daughter's life.

In the end it was Martin Blandford who had stopped her from going mad. The Hindus, she said, believe that when you are in need of a teacher, a teacher will appear. And one had appeared in the form of Martin, who had taught her to accept the pain, not to feed it, not to deny it, but to open herself to it until it was just there, in the sense that other things were just there. They would sit together for hours, she and Martin, in silence, holding the stillness. He himself had lost someone – years ago the man he loved had taken his own life. Of all people he understood what it was to feel desperate, and he knew how to help her. Soon Martin's garage room became her place of safety. He had given her a key so that she could come and go as she pleased. When he left on study leave, she kept the key.

When she has talked herself out, there is silence, which eventually I break by saying how sorry I am, that it is one of the saddest stories I have ever heard. 'It isn't really a story,' she says. 'It has no narrative integrity.' She tugs at the comb in her hair, sliding it up and down repeatedly. 'It is all askew, like a child's painting. It's a blur, a dense fog, lit only by moments of sweet poignancy.' Then she removes the comb, and her hair comes down over her face, like a safety curtain. 'It's as if there is a permanently open wound,' she says. Which makes me think of my mother's wounds all those years ago – bound and dressed but impossible to clean.

'And how is Alfie now?' It seems the right question.

'It's good of you to ask,' she says, her voice catching. 'No one does any more. Not even Harry. He's afraid to ask, you see, afraid of all the emotion.' I feel a sudden hot welling under my eyelids. 'He's always reminding me that he makes his living out of reason.' She drifts for a while down this road, and at the end she takes a deep breath. 'I'm slightly hesitant about saying this out loud, but Alfie is actually beginning to make progress. He's on new medication, and for the first time in three years it's looking hopeful.'

As she stands on the doorstep ready to leave, I ask if Sanderson knows she comes to meditate in the garage room. No, she says, he doesn't know. And she is not going to tell him. He would not understand. It is on my lips to tell her that he is hanging around outside the cottage, but I think better of it. She has been through enough for one evening.

That night I went to sleep thinking about Carrie's life, the suffering involved, and all the love that had gone into Alfie, from the moment of his birth. What had happened to it? Where was it now? I also thought about all the unused love that I, who had never had a child, must contain. There should be surplus love, love to spare. Where on earth was it? My mind also turned to Martin Blandford and the kindness of a man I had never met but in whose house I was staying – in whose bed I was actually lying. He had helped Carrie so much, in ways that Sanderson hadn't done and couldn't do. No wonder Sanderson was jealous. And yet he must surely know that Martin was gay? It had come as no surprise to me when Carrie mentioned it earlier in the evening, though I had felt some vertiginous emotion that was almost certainly relief. Admitting this to myself was my last conscious thought that night.

39

I have always worked on the principle that a translator is a guest in somebody else's house, and as such has to behave well. Since Hume's house was a welcoming sort of place, good behaviour came easily. However, translation also makes you aware of your own limitations, partly because it can only ever be a version, it can never be perfect. Even when the job is done, it can never be regarded as finished. A translator's work is therefore in some sense provisional, a quality that in my own life has floated of its own accord into other areas, setting up little satellite chambers of uncertainty. I believe that this caution, this discretion, is the besetting sin of most translators, when what is actually needed is what Danton prescribed to save France during the Revolution: *de l'audace, encore de l'audace, toujours de l'audace.*

I had recently started working on Hume's long essay *Of the Sceptic*, in which Hume set about excoriating 'the decisions of philosophers upon all subjects', describing their reasoning as an 'infirmity' – this I translated as *une maladie* – especially where it concerned 'human life and the methods of attaining happiness'. All of which brought Sanderson to mind. According to Hume, philosophers suffered from a narrowness of understanding; they were largely indifferent to the desires and pursuits of others, being completely taken up with their own inclinations. Hume did not exempt himself from this. After his attack of the disease of the learnèd he had felt a separation from his fellow man that he spent the rest of his life trying to reach across. He never married, and although he enjoyed the company of women he remained shy and reserved throughout his life. One of the problems he encountered was how to practise philosophy and still stay sane. His way of coping was to dine at as many tables as possible, to take exercise, and to play backgammon at every opportunity. And also, in the phrase beloved of my father: *Be a philosopher, but amid all your philosophy be still a man.* The problem Hume recognised was that philosophers, the *soi-disant* wise men, did not actually have the first idea of how to behave. Just as Sanderson had said in fact – *all pretty much up themselves.* Towards the end of the essay Hume touched on human frailties. One sentence in particular impressed itself on my consciousness: *If a man be liable to a vice or imperfection, it may often happen that a good quality, which he possesses along with it, will render him more miserable, than if he were completely vicious.*

These words were still circulating in my head when I next went fishing with Sanderson. It seemed at least possible that Hume's observation applied to Sanderson. He was such a striking mixture of good and bad, broken and unbroken, like a coin stamped on either side with incompatible values. Everything Carrie had said the other evening, even her criticisms, were laced with sympathy and affection. In her mind, so it seemed, he was a victim of the despair that sometimes attends clever men, locked in a solipsistic hell of his own devising. But a good and lovable man all the same.

We were back at the river, the place of such drama just a week before. The river was altogether more subdued, a tame thing compared to last time, but Sanderson himself seemed agitated. He looked weary, older. He smelled of alcohol. His eyes were milky and clouded, like those of a fish long dead. As I pulled on waders and started preparing my rod, he stayed sitting on the riverbank as if the day had stalled and couldn't be got going again.

He had been unusually silent in the car, holding tight to the steering wheel as if it were a security blanket. But now he launched into a long monologue, which he maintained with a degree of detail and precision that would have rivalled those of any policeman reconstructing a crime scene. He spoke calmly, with a certain stiffness round the mouth, and in the bland tones – slightly impersonal and robotic – of those who deal on a daily basis with the general public. His eyes were fixed on the grass in front of him.

It had happened some weeks ago, he began. On the day in question, he had been returning home after work. The light had been good that day but darkness was beginning to wrap itself round the city. As usual he stopped at the street corner and looked both ways – straight on towards his flat and back from where he had just come. This, he explained, was a sort of ritual to allow him to leave the life he led at the university and to think himself into his life at home. He wondered briefly what it might feel like for a man to look forward to going home, the consolations of family living, the antidote to a hard day at the office. As he approached the flat he was just able to make out the shape of a figure sitting on the steps in front of the entrance. He had seen this man once or twice in recent times, slumped against the low wall on the pavement outside the tenement block, an ageless, dishevelled heap, clutching a bottle in his fingerless gloves. Now the man had moved closer, and his sheets of cardboard suggested that the doorway to Sanderson's flat might have become a more permanent dwelling-place. September in Scotland was the time when down-and-outs, like migrating birds, had to begin thinking about their winter quarters. This had been the thought in his head as he stepped over the man to put his key in the lock, muttering some awkward greeting as he did so. He didn't have a strategy for dealing with the homeless, he said, or those who beg in the streets – not one that he could feel happy about at any rate, or one that showed any sense of common decency.

He turned to face me just then. There were dark semicircles beneath his eyes, and the lower rims of his eyelids were red and raw, like freshly slaughtered meat. 'It's an odd thing – maybe you've noticed. People who drink too much get fat and paunchy like me, but the real boozers, the winos on the street, they're as thin as rakes.' This, like everything else, was spoken without expression, in a mechanically generated answering-machine voice. He turned away once more, his face an empty room.

The main door to the building was on a spring, he said, and he usually left it to shut by itself. This time, however, he stood for a few moments until it had closed tight, catching in his nostrils as he waited the rank smell of this newest settler in the neighbourhood. As he climbed the four flights of the stone staircase, he continued to think about the homeless man and his own casual cruelty towards him. The moment he opened the door to the flat, he inhaled another fragrance, a sweetish mixture of lavender and pine, which told him his wife was in the bath. 'She likes bath essence,' he said, pulling a face at me, as if this were a moral failing. 'It's one of the many differences between us.' When he entered the bathroom he had found her submerged up to her neck in froth. It was a sight that always gladdened his heart, he said, not just because she cut a rather comic figure – a wet and pinkish face at the end of a mass of bubbles where her body should have been – but also because there was something newborn and innocent about her when she lay in the bath, making it possible, just for a moment or two, to believe that everything was well. He had even felt his heart lift with the familiar tug of fresh hope.

At this point in his winding narrative there was a long pause. He leaned his heavy frame on one elbow and gazed out over the river. He looked bloated and uncomfortable in his own body. His belly sprawled in front, almost a thing apart. With his free hand, the fingers of which were swollen and weeping, he patted it now, as if it were a sleeping dog, curled up into him. Then, with the same hand that had patted the dog, he delved into his fishing bag and removed a tiny jar, placing it carefully on the ground between us. Slowly he drew his hand away from it. It might have been a small explosive device, set to go off at any moment.

I considered the possibilities. One was that all the significant moments in my life were destined to involve a jar of some kind. I stared at it, as if staring would help it explain itself. Everything was beginning to levitate slightly, and in my head there was the sound of breaking glass. I was scrabbling about in that tiny space between illusion and reality, trying to make sense of what was happening.

'Exhibit A,' said Sanderson at last. 'I removed it from the bath.'

'The bath?'

'Yes, it was floating in the water, after my wife got out, after the bubbles had gone.'

'Floating in the water?'

'I scooped it up in a tooth mug.'

'A tooth mug?'

'Then I put it in one of my old maggot jars.'

'Maggot jars?'

It was inane to repeat everything. I knew that.

'Do you know what it is?'

'No.'

'Think about it.'

'I am thinking.'

My mind was a blank. Was this how men talked with one another? I felt too close to Sanderson – literally, in the sense that there was not enough space between us for me to feel comfortable. I had the same confined feeling that came when I sat in the front row of a cinema. It was too near the action, too intimate. It brought on a feeling of nausea. I longed for the safety of the back stalls.

'It's another man's spunk. That's what it is.'

'Spunk?'

'*Spunk*, Eddie. *Spunk.*'

'Are you sure?'

For my part I was sure of nothing. As far as I knew, spunk meant courage.

'Quite sure.'

'How long have you had it?' Was this the right question? I had no idea.

The answer was fired like a rocket.

'Since you entered our lives. Since you came to dinner. Since you brought my wife flowers. Since I followed her to your house. Since I saw her let herself in with her own key.'

Afterwards everything fell into place, and nothing did. It was hard to get my mental bearings – I was on the wrong side of something. The business of making new friends had not seemed possible until I met Sanderson, and I had dared to think that he felt a measure of the same, that we'd seen the possibility in each other. Had I got everything wrong? Was nothing as I'd imagined it to be? He was a self-declared jealous man, but it had not occurred to me that I might occupy any part of his wild suspicions. I sat on the riverbank, the blood thumping in my head.

Meanwhile Sanderson was off doing what he loved best – casting his dry fly on the water. After delivering his *coup de théâtre* he had simply picked up the offending jar, put it back in his fishing bag, got to his feet slowly and made his way to the river as if nothing had happened. I tried to remember how it was before Sanderson, before all of this. I even played a game with myself: imagining that I'd never met him at all, that he was just a character in a novel. But it was no good. I watched him now, up to his chest in the water, flicking his olive silk line back and forth, its loop slicing the air. If he stumbles now, I thought, I won't move a solitary muscle to save him.

40

It was the kind of event that alters the course of a friendship, a single occurrence from which, when you come to look back, everything else seems to follow. Sanderson's apology came eventually, but half-heartedly and spoken downwards, at the ground. He said he had been brought low by jealousy, the idea that Carrie was *playing away*. 'You can build something out of anything, I suppose.' He looked vulnerable, a man tragically wronged, yet hostile with it, still able to land a punch. And yes, he was perfectly aware of his own hypocrisy, he said, raising his eyes from the ground now to look me in the face, so there was absolutely no need for me to mention it. 'I wasn't going to,' I said, smarting at the unfairness of having to defend myself. 'Though it does occur to me that you may be having some sort of crisis. Perhaps you should . . . ' I searched for the phrase, '*see someone*'. But the battlements were all in place again. 'Crisis? *Crisis?* I'm with my old friend Chekhov on this one, Eddie. Any idiot can face a crisis. It's the day-to-day living that wears you out.'

I had thought of telling Carrie about all this, but something made me hesitate: perhaps it was the possibility that instead of being outraged on my behalf (as I would have hoped) she might find some weird way of excusing Sanderson's behaviour. It wasn't worth the risk. And in any case we were getting on so well. The news on Alfie continued to be positive, and suddenly there seemed to be more light than dark in her life. There was a new sparkle in her eyes, and I didn't want any specks of dust to dim them. She had taken to popping in for a drink and a chat in the early evening after meditating. I had adjusted my cold lighting to something softer and warmer, and had brought in a few cushions from the garage room. It was so much better now that everything was out in the open – not quite everything of course – and her visits rounded off my days perfectly. I began to feel a separation between work and everything else the day had to offer, and this was quite new. Conversation with Carrie became an easy thing, natural and enriching, so much so that I had come to think of our times together as somehow essential and significant, not just interludes snatched between other existences. Perhaps we should have told Sanderson about the garage room, but the right moment never seemed to come.

Carrie and I were talking one evening about our respective jobs and how they shaped us as people. 'I sometimes think translators are at one remove from life,' I said, pouring us both another glass of good French wine. 'There's something provisional about them. They know they are not the originators. Not the prime movers. And that can seep into their own lives. Which makes them rather private individuals. It's hard to generalise, of course.'

'How many translators do you actually know?'

'To be honest, hardly any,' I said, laughing at myself.

'I suspected as much,' she said, clapping her hands in evident delight.

'But in my imagination they are mostly middle-aged men in old overcoats still living with their mothers. If you passed them in the street you would not notice them.'

The conversation had started with me saying it was rather

hard to talk about translation – on the whole people didn't know how to describe it or explain it. Carrie said she felt something of the same about painting. She didn't like trying to describe what she did and how she did it, much preferring the process to remain mysterious, even to herself. 'I always think it makes the art sound deceitful,' she said, 'and the artist a charlatan. The important thing is to paint.'

It was important for the painter, of course, but what about other people, I wondered. Wasn't it valuable to help people like me appreciate and understand art?

'I'm not sure. I think it's more important for you to look. To look and to feel. Not to be told what to think. A work of art should open up the emotions. There's a lot of pretentious rubbish talked about painting – often by the painters themselves. They talk about *meaning*, because everyone always wants to know what something *means*. But in fact, you make marks on the canvas and you don't know what they mean. In a sense they don't mean anything, but something comes of them. It's an unfathomable business.'

'Translation is a mysterious business too,' I said, savouring this exchange, wanting to slow it down and make it last for hours. 'You find yourself looking for metaphors, as if translation can't quite be itself and nothing else. Which is odd perhaps, since it does not need to serve any purpose but its own.'

'Is that such a bad thing?' she asked. 'Don't we all use metaphors to describe what we do?'

'Yes, I suppose so. It's not that metaphors are bad – that's not what I meant. But they are always *instead of* the actual thing. And so translation is nearly always talked about in terms of something else. People – those who translate, I mean – are always comparing it to other things. For example, they might say it's like taking a living thing from its native land and transplanting it in another. Or dismantling a house, brick by brick, and rebuilding it on another site – it's recognisably the same house, but strange and new in important ways. Differently decorated perhaps. Others have compared translation to a musical or theatrical performance, with the translator as conductor or stage director, working with the original score or script, but adapting it for a different audience. You get the idea – you find yourself offering another metaphor to add to the metaphors.'

Had I said too much? It was so unusual to be giving an account of myself, to be venturing outside my own head.

'Go on,' she said. 'I'm interested. Tell me, when you're translating a novel, do you have to try and become the novelist, as it were?'

'It's not so much becoming the novelist as finding the novelist's voice. You shadow the novelist, live vicariously. First and foremost you are a reader, the closest reader the book will ever have. And your translation is your reading of the author, your rendering of the voice.'

I had an urge to move around, to break the intensity. I got up and walked over to the table where the wine bottle stood. 'I mean, I myself could never be a writer. To be a writer you have to have something to say. The translator's job is to find a way of saying what the writer has already said.'

This sounded very different from painting and drawing, she said, where you began always with a blank canvas. She tilted her head to one side and the evening light caught a corner of her cheek.

'Actually, in one sense a translator also begins with a blank canvas – or at least a blank sheet of paper.' I held out the wine bottle to her glass. 'It's true you always have something to go on, something that's been created already – the original work. But that's just your starting point. You then have to create something else from it.'

She wanted to know precisely how I went about it. Were there any rules, dos and don'ts? She'd removed her shoes now and tucked her slender feet up under her cotton dress.

'Well, first you read, and then you write. Exactly the opposite of what the author does.'

Then perhaps it wasn't so far removed from painting after all, she said. In the sense that painting was an intense form of seeing: first you had to look, and only then could you interpret what you saw. 'But surely translation must be more fixed than that,' she said. 'Less free in what you can and can't say?'

'Yes and no.' Translation wasn't really a fixed thing, I explained. There was no direct equivalence between languages – it wasn't just that they had different structures and grammars – they also had different fault lines, different textures. People sometimes described translating as a mimetic process, but that was misleading. There were always new discoveries – things you didn't have in your own language. And when you translated you put the language under pressure. It was a question of seeing what it would bear.

'It isn't just copying what you see on the page. It's more like reproducing and recreating. Of course, you have to give a sense of the original, and it has to be as close as possible, but in order to be close to the meaning of the text in front of you, sometimes you have to move quite a way from it. And it's surprising where the pursuit of the right word or sentence can lead.'

'Do you ever worry that you are betraying the book? Betraying the author?'

I had never had this kind of conversation with anyone. It was so rare for people to take an interest. And yet I felt sure this was how it was meant to be.

It was something you thought about, I said, something that was always at the back of your mind, but you tried not to let it get in the way. Translators had a responsibility – to the author, yes, but also to the readers in the new language. The way the words were arranged on the page, the cadences, the rhythms – all of this was at stake. In the translator's hands a book could become something else entirely, something far less than in the original. But if this happened you just had to accept it. And also the fact that you would make mistakes – it was in the nature of the job and it was impossible not to, no matter how hard you tried.

'Maybe that would be a good way of approaching life – accepting our mistakes,' she said.

'You know, it's strange,' I said. 'The French word for mistake is *erreur*, like *error* in English, but when it's a mistake in language, we say *faute* – like the English *fault*. In other words, getting the language wrong carries overtones of sin and guilt in our country.'

'Have you always lived alone?' she asked.

So sudden, this change of subject. Just by living alone, you could invite pity.

'I've forgotten what it's like to live by myself,' she continued. 'The nearest I get to it is meditation. It's a blessed state.'

So, it wasn't pity.

'My father always maintained that a man should first learn to live by himself,' I said. 'Until then he would be adrift in the world.'

'What did he mean by that?'

'Good question,' I laughed. 'I haven't the faintest idea. I sometimes think it must have been hard for him to live with my mother. But I imagine he meant something else by it – something to do with the inner self, what we call *le moi profond*. That is always lived alone.'

As she got up and prepared to leave, I inquired about Sanderson.

'Harry and I are a little more separate each day. So it seems. He's so much turned in on himself. It's not healthy.' Her expression was somewhere between regret and rebuke, not yet sure of itself. She slipped on her shoes, adjusted her dress and tied a scarf round her shoulders. Her movements were like a series of elegant brushstrokes. 'I'm quite worried about him. He's behaving oddly. As if he's coming undone. I'm thinking of going to see the Dean about him. Explain that he's not well.'

'Don't do it,' I said. The words came out sharper and more urgent than I'd intended. 'Don't do it,' I said more quietly. 'I think it might be better to let things take their course.'

41

I awoke to a strange noise, a dull repeated thudding that played into the rhythms of my dream. I staggered downstairs, dopey from sleep, blinking in the light. Carrie was on the doorstep, a pale apparition. Behind her the black trees loomed like mountains. She gave herself a shake like a small drenched animal. Her eyes glinted in her head, glassy and pellucid – what the French call *chatoyant*. My first thought was: could meditation be so urgent? My second: why hadn't she used her key? Next thought: in my flannelette pyjamas and old man slippers I must look to her like hope laid waste.

Meditation didn't come into it. She had been up all night. Sanderson had been drinking, his mood dark and hostile. He had been pacing the room, she said, a caged beast, fulminating at the world. My God, I said, had he threatened her, harmed her? No, no, nothing like that. It was something worse, much worse.

Nothing could be worse, I thought.

'Harry's been suspended,' she said. 'From the university.'

'Suspended? Why?'

'Pending investigations.'

'Investigations?' Here I was, repeating everything again.

'There are allegations. *Inappropriate behaviour* — that's what they call it. Towards a female student.'

I made tea, said what I could. Have a seat. Give me your coat. Try not to worry. The words did not come easily now. They were strung together clumsily. I was not used to women, their ways. Her hair was damp and clung to the back of her neck. I could see the pulse beating in her throat. Emotions were such untidy things. Human behaviour was a chaotic, imperfect, messy business. My bare spare house felt cluttered.

42

There were at least three versions of events, two of which I heard at first hand. Sanderson's version struck me as incontinent, and ultimately pathetic. It was filled with otiose spacers like *somehow*s and *sort of*s, each readily understandable in isolation, but cumulatively damning. And in spite of its prolixity it had the feel of a preamble, something to be got out of the way before the real thing could be faced. At the time it was told to me, I had barely recovered from the business with the maggot jar and the supposedly damning evidence it contained. This had the effect of pulling me between different magnetic fields: pity and fury. Fury at having been falsely – ludicrously – accused by a man I had thought of as my friend. Pity because Sanderson seemed to be bent on self-destruction. Pity was worse than fury because it took the feet from under you. In different circumstances I might have thought such a man unpitiable, but I could see that his behaviour contained something heartbreaking at the core. Like an actor in a tragic drama he had ceased to see himself; no more could he save himself, or be saved.

Sanderson's account went something like this:

He appraises the student before him. *Appraises* – he likes that word, perhaps because of its inbuilt bias towards praise, which it supposedly has yet to make up its mind about. She is having problems with her essay, she says. Plato? He doesn't need to ask. He knows very well it is Plato. Yes, Plato, she says. *The Trial of Socrates*. Ah, Socrates, he says. He wants to be the way he was when he first started teaching. Sort of confident and slightly aloof. She is American, as so many students are nowadays. Her voice is thick Midwest cream, pure stretch-vowels like white limousines. He thinks she could be an heiress, daughter of an oil magnate. She has the soft pampered hands of a girl who has never in her life washed the dishes. He looks at them now, fine fingers folded into one another. His own fingers look like battered cricket stumps. He is feeling all spent, he needs a drink, his skin is crawling. He has reached the age when he knows he is no longer young, and others know it too. What can I do for you, Miss Suzello? Tutors mostly use first names now, but her first name is Chelsea, and he somehow doesn't think he can cope with Chelsea. In any case he prefers the old style. The old style is all washed up – he knows that. Now the aim is for chumminess, everyone on the same footing, coequals in everything – except in the small business of learning. What seems to be the problem? he asks her. He could be a doctor, inquiring about symptoms. His own symptoms – the pain of suppurating pustules, his need of a drink and a smoke, maybe even a nice comfort fuck – are getting in the way. But when did he last have the last of those, except in his imagination? He can't remember. Sometimes he thinks about Alice with her gentle curves and glistening flesh. Ridiculous, of course. Like so much else Alice is part of the past. His thoughts have little to do with his actual memories of her. They merely form a pleasant sort of daydream, a small gratification that he directs and controls. The images are always a bit abstract at the start, but long before he wills it, they grow more precise. He does nothing to keep them at bay. To begin with it is enough to think of her sitting quietly on the edge of the bed, smiling at him, not coquettishly, but with a poise that he knows contains the whisper of sexual possibility. He loves this image and summons it again and again. After a while, when he knows it intimately, he begins to animate it so that Alice moves, jerkily, as in the separate frames of a motion picture. He can make her cross and uncross her legs so that her skirt rides up and down the tops of her thighs. He can make her remove her clothes, in a particular sequence, which he alone controls. The undressing is slow and modest in its way, nothing brash or sordid. He can feel the warmth of her body, lightly moistened, and he can hear the short little gasps that state her desire. All of this is predicated on the certainty, fantastic though he knows it to be, that Alice welcomes him, wants him, is ready for him, needs him. As she once did. Sometimes the images turn more imperative, more urgent, like a story waiting to be told. He gives himself freely to their elaboration. He feels no guilt; rather fear that if he tries to stop the images, he might not be able to summon them again. None of this, he reminds himself, has anything to do with Miss Suzello. Who is looking at him now. Expectantly. Waiting for wisdom. He has just given a lecture on the categorical imperative. Most philosophy, the kind he teaches, is abstract. But not the categorical imperative – a concept providing rational principles of action, in the light of which one's own selfish hopes and desires may be examined and assessed. The categorical imperative gives overriding reasons for behaving in a moral way. Indeed. And the certainty of what one *ought* to do is at the very heart of morality. All of this he knows. I've read Plato on Socrates, says Miss Suzello, and I still, like, have no idea why Socrates chose, like, not to save himself. She lifts her heavy lids to reveal eyes as black as coal and unfathomably deep. I mean, why would anyone, like, *do* that? Choose to *die* when you could, like, stay *alive*? Her sentences have the rising inflection of young people everywhere. Which normally irritates him beyond anything, but in Miss Suzello he finds it charming. He thinks he might tell her that a true philosopher is cheerful in the face of death, and none more so than Socrates, who knew that the essence of philosophy was learning how to die. But Miss Suzello is so absurdly young and vital that talk of death will sound ludicrous. Her notebook is open, waiting for instant enlightenment to flood its pages. Her white cotton shirt is open too, at the neck. There are five buttons, he notes, the last hidden beneath her waistband. Her frame looks as lean and firm as a boy's, except for the gentle rise and fall of her chest. Her lips are clearly defined, no lipstick, just a faint gloss. Her youth, her alertness, her optimism – all of these tear at his heart. She is still looking at him, eager for answers. He knows it is a game, a sort of courtly dance, in which each must do the right steps. For a moment he considers asking her about her own life, if she is happy. Are you *happy*? he says, startling himself. In your life, I mean. My *essay*, she says, on another rising inflection. He feels a gap open up between him and the world. Are you OK, Dr Sanderson? she asks. After what seems like an interminable passage of time – during which he has recognised, apparently for the first time, that as each moment of his life passes, it is gone and will never come again – he hears himself say no, no, no, by which time he is beyond the point of no return, the point in question being Miss Suzello's lap, in which he has somehow managed to bury himself and begun to sob. Even then he has the illusion that he has cradled his face in his own hands. He realises only later, through a watery mist, where he has slumped. He is not a man given to weeping, and if you'd asked him beforehand he would have said perhaps that he'd forgotten how to weep, if indeed he had ever known. But the tears, once they come, flow abundantly. His recollection was that the young American woman did not push him away – this became important later – but whether because she was frozen in horror or paralysed by disgust (both possibilities he later conceded) would never become clear. As he wipes his salt tears on her skirt, he notices a small hole in the material, spreading out in all directions like the points of a compass. This is the last time that day when ordinariness intervenes. The rest is chaotic and dreamlike.

*

'Couldn't you have stopped yourself?' I asked when at last he had stopped talking. It was not meant as a reproach. I was thinking of the time, long ago, when I went berserk in that philosophy class. I was curious to know whether or not his actions were willed. Or if they had seemed to be beyond his control – a sign of his fragile hold on the world. But he did not answer. Montaigne thought that the fundamental fact about the human condition was that people are fallible. Rousseau accused him of being disingenuous, on the grounds that while Montaigne portrayed himself with defects, he gave himself only lovable ones. No one could have accused Sanderson of having only lovable defects. And yet he was far from being what the French call *une véritable ordure*.

The American student's version, which quickly did the rounds at the university, was more succinct. Her recollection was that Dr Sanderson, behaving strangely and smelling strongly of alcohol, had suddenly fallen on her, weeping and wailing. When she asked him what was wrong, he said (she claimed to have perfect recall of this and wrote his precise words in a statement): 'My wife doesn't want sex with me any more. She can't bear me to touch her. She thinks of pushing her trolley round the supermarket when we're doing it. Meanwhile I mark essays for a living. The essays are bollocks and the living is a load of cunt.' In the statement she gave to the university authorities she also claimed that Dr Sanderson, in her presence, had frequently touched his genitals. (Later, when Sanderson was asked to comment on this specific point, he had been defiant: 'The genitals – as you call them – are designed to swing free at ambient temperature. I thought clever people like you might have known that. They are not meant to be cooped up in polyester pants. They need constant adjustment.')

It was Carrie's strange version of events, however, that I heard first. After telling me about the suspension, she said that it had all been a terrible misunderstanding. The inappropriate behaviour, so-called, was a fiction. A student was having difficulty with her essay and had come to ask Harry for help. Harry had not been in a good state that day: he was in low spirits, his skin was worse than ever, and the beginning of term had not got off to a good start. 'Also, Alice had just given him the heave,' she said. 'Not that he mentioned that when he told me, but I worked it out from the dates.' She paused between sentences, as if gathering her strength. 'The student could see that he wasn't well. She was concerned about him, asked him if he was all right . . . ' When she paused again, I felt my scalp contract – her unease was contagious – '. . . and at that point Harry was, well, unhinged by kindness.'

'What does it mean? *Unhinged by kindness?*'

'I don't really know what it means,' she said. 'But I can't think how else to describe it.'

She said that Harry had grown used to expecting the worst of people, herself included – it was a kind of protection – but when this young American girl reached out to him and showed compassion, he had lost control and wept in her arms.

Carrie's account had a curious appeal, but it failed to convince. Sanderson had put a spell on her. Whilst her rationalisation of events was admirably loyal, there was something desperate about it, like the plea of a defence lawyer, asking that good character be taken into consideration as mitigation of the crime. 'This girl, she *unmanned* him, you see. That's how he put it.' And now for some reason the girl had decided to lodge a complaint. And the university authorities had decided to take it seriously – 'They have no option, of course. They're afraid they'll be sued, you see. Americans always involve the lawyers.' But that didn't mean there was any *substance* to the charges, she said. 'It was an act of folly and self-indulgence, perhaps, but it was entirely innocent.' Clever people sometimes did stupid things – surely I could see that? – Harry was no exception. 'He's just . . . ' she hesitated, '. . . endearingly hopeless.'

It seemed likely that this was the way married people spoke when the marriage was troubled. That was my best guess. In times of trouble the bonds would tighten, threatening all judgement and composure. Why else would an intelligent woman leave her cool head behind and protest her husband's innocence in this way? These thoughts felt treacherous. I was becoming a hostile witness.

43

It turned out that senior university staff – the 'guardians of public decency', Sanderson called them – had given him just an hour to clear his desk: this in their watchful presence. The Head of Human Resources, a 'mouse-like creature with little pointy teeth', introduced herself. Sanderson had repeated her title back to her with barely concealed disdain. 'Head of Human Resources, eh? Stick around, and maybe you'll be Head of Human Remains next. That'll be a nice promotion for you.' The mouse was impassive, impermeable to irony. 'I hear what you say,' she said, before going on to explain that it was a *precautionary* suspension, pending investigation into the allegations made. She proceeded to read out a printed text from an A4 sheet of paper. Her facial movements bore no obvious relation to the words. In accordance with the university's disciplinary procedure the suspension would be subject to a thirty-day review. In the meantime Sanderson should refrain from entering university premises. Nor should he have contact with any university employee, student, contractor or supplier. *Contractor or supplier*, Sanderson had yelped in disbelief. *Are you mad?* Was he now considered to be a danger to contractors and suppliers? he asked. If that was the case he really hoped they had all been warned. Just in case he fiddled with their JCBs, or their polystyrene cups. I hear what you say, the mouse woman had said again.

'Human Resources, you see,' he said, scowling at me. We were sitting in the gloom of the box room. In the vice on his desk there was a half-dressed fly, a beautiful specimen with a striped body and wings in exotic colours. The air was filled with whisky and tobacco fumes, plus something astringent that I later identified as petroleum jelly. Sanderson was bare-chested, his skin scarlet and blistered – the result, he had explained casually, of an overlong treatment of ultraviolet radiation at the hospital.

'The name tells you all you need to know. In any other context, resources would refer to *property* or *possessions* – something to be exploited at any rate. That's why they have to put "human" in front of it – to let you know they mean *people*.'

The HR woman, he explained, pouring himself another whisky, was accompanied by 'her little band of helpers', who had looked at him coldly, judging him already. He overheard a whispered exchange about *attitudinal problems*. 'I might have been a piece of evidence in a criminal investigation, something to be placed in a plastic bag and produced in court.'

Plastic bag? I nearly said. Why not a jar? Sanderson's disgruntlement was catching.

Like duly authorised bailiffs they had begun systematically to impound his property. *Why doesn't everyone here just calm the fuck down*, Sanderson had shouted. To no effect, for they set about removing his computer, along with quantities of olive oil, polythene bags, rubber bands and a plastic basin.

'I told them they were wasting their time, that it was just paraphernalia for cracked feet – not for some bestial orgy. But they just looked at me as if they feared contamination.'

I turned all this over in my mind. At the edge of Sanderson's mouth there was a gob of congealed saliva, a pitiful sign of his decline. I turned my gaze from him to the resplendent fly and back again. *A man who spends his time tying flies can't be a bad man.* It was not the first time this thought had entered my mind.

'Is there anything incriminating on your computer, would you say?'

'Eddie, these idiots could find something incriminating in Plato's *Republic* if they had a mind to.'

For a minute or two he ranted against his colleagues, no longer his colleagues now, moral policemen with no intelligence. 'Philosophers? More like a bunch of daft laddies!' Each outburst had a scornful, embattled edge to it. He raged against the world. And yet it was plain to see that the boundaries of Sanderson's world were shrinking. In between outbursts he fell silent, but only for as long as it takes a screaming child to draw breath for another bawl. The university had once been a place of flair and imagination, he said, but now it was an ant colony — a life-form, yes, but not intelligent in the normal sense of the word, just a whole lot of creatures, eating and defecating, going through the motions to perpetuate the colony. Philosophy had once been to do with how life was to be lived, illuminating something larger than itself. Now it had become detached from humankind. There was a mad look in his eyes. Whatever holds a person together had gone. He stared into space like a prophet of doom brooding over a world gone wrong. It all felt too theatrical for the ordinary landscape of a box room in Edinburgh's New Town. With his bare red chest and baleful face he might have been Anthony Quinn playing Crazy Horse in *Custer's Last Stand*. Any moment now he would start clubbing and scalping everything around him.

When he calmed down he admitted that what he called 'questionable material' would almost certainly be found on his computer. On the web he had done searches for, among other things, 'women's bodily fluids', as well as 'sperm detector' and 'female secretions'.

'But *why*?' The moment I asked this I felt alarmed at the prospect of being told.

'I needed to check out the blob. The blob in the bath. I thought I knew what it was, but I needed to be sure.'

By surfing the web he had found a product that was just what was required. It was called Matecheck, an American invention that was available by mail order. He hadn't wanted to risk 'something dodgy' arriving in the post at home, so he had tracked down the only stockist in the capital, a twenty-four-hour pharmacy on the Royal Mile.

'I went there late one night, under cover of darkness. I thought it would be deserted, but it was busier than the pub. All human life was there – addicts, prostitutes, insomniacs, all the creatures of the night.'

I said: 'This Matecheck, how does it work?' This is grim, I thought.

'Huh, you wouldn't believe it! It's like voodoo, a sorcerer's trick. You take a tiny piece of card, a bit like litmus paper, and it detects an enzyme found in semen. This enzyme evidently hangs around for ages, so the test continues to work long after any sexual encounter. That's the beauty of it! There are invisible traces in a woman's underwear, or on the back of her skirt – whatever she wears after sex.'

'Even after it goes through the wash?'

'You're sharp, Eddie, I'll give you that. Not just a pretty face. No wonder you were my prime suspect.' And he gave me a crooked smile, which seemed to say it was all in the past and we were friends again. 'Alas, this was the precise difficulty I encountered.' He paused, as if to summon the difficulty, not to say the terrible disappointment it contained. According to the instructions, which he had studied with great care, if the paper turned purple five minutes later, it was a positive result. Bingo. The trouble rested in the small print, which stated that once the test sample had been washed or dry-cleaned, *detection was not guaranteed*. 'Completely useless!' he said. 'That blob had been soaking in the bath for God knows how long before I got to it. But long enough to drown every last effing enzyme, that's for sure.' By then, however, he had been 'on a bit of a mission', and not wanting to waste the other nine testers in the kit, he had raked about in his wife's lingerie drawer, searching for incriminating garments. 'Of course they were all *clean*,' he said, attaching to the word a loathsome intonation. No damning purple. No colour at all. He had felt cheated, let down. He had spent a fortune on the detection kit, and there was no proof that it even worked.

'And so I tested my own trousers,' he said. 'The ones I'm wearing.' He smacked the palms of his hands on the worn corduroy. 'They haven't been washed in years.'

'And what happened?' So grim, all this.

'Turned purple straight away! Didn't even take the full five minutes.'

There was a stupendous vulgarity about all this, as well as a piercing hopelessness. And not the vaguest sense of anything mattering on a human level. It filled the air, impossible not to breathe it in and become infected by it. I felt like a butler, seeing the dirty underclothes, and I came away in some sense sullied, as if there was something nasty under my fingernails.

44

I am not one of those people who attach great importance to the synchronicity of events. Things either happen together, or they happen separately. Later, however, I would come to believe that had it not been for the coincidence of certain things, the calamity that ensued might have been avoided. When I looked back, everything, every small detail, seemed to acquire a heightened significance.

Sanderson's book, *Happiness: A Philosophical Guide*, was due to be published in the middle of November. 'A non-event, Eddie,' said Sanderson confidently a day or two before publication. 'You are almost certainly engaged in something worthwhile, but my book is guaranteed to put people to sleep.' At best, he said, it might, after a year or two, get a short review in some obscure philosophy journal. But more probably it would just gather dust on a shelf in a university library somewhere.

His prediction turned out to be quite wrong. A day or two after his book came out scientists from the University of California claimed to have discovered a 'happiness gene', and suddenly every news outlet on both sides of the Atlantic was talking about happiness, as if it were an entirely new phenomenon.

Could it be true that happiness was inherited? Did it come down to your ancestry rather than external circumstances? Was it possible that it was all predetermined? Those responsible for setting the international news agenda quickly decided that happiness was *the* news item, and editors everywhere were eager to find different ways of presenting the story.

Since Sanderson's immediate state of mind precluded awareness of what was going on in the world, the invitation to appear on breakfast television took him by complete surprise. He was contacted out of the blue, he said, by 'some bright young researcher', eager to have 'a philosophical angle' on a discussion about the amazing new discovery of the happiness gene. Which was how he came to be sitting in a studio in Edinburgh early one morning being interviewed on *Good Morning Britain* by a breezy couple sitting on a pastel-coloured sofa in London. The clean-cut male presenter was smiling inanely and holding up a copy of Sanderson's book for the cameras.

'So, Dr Sanderson, is happiness still the preserve of philosophical study,' asked the female presenter, whose cheerfulness was also so intense as to be suspect, 'or does it just come down to whether your own parents were happy?'

Sanderson looked as if he'd just woken up from a long sleep that had removed him from the world. His eyes were rheumy and troubled, and across his face there were sores like craters, imperfectly plugged by the make-up artist. He looked startled by the question, and his head swivelled, as if to find the place where the voice was coming from.

'Well, it depends of course what is meant by happiness,' he said. 'People talk very loosely about happiness, but there's no such thing really.' He sounded tentative, unsure of himself.

'No such thing?' It was the turn of the smiling man. 'Yet you've written a whole book on happiness, have you not, Dr Sanderson?' He beamed a set of perfect white teeth.

'Ah yes, but I didn't exactly choose to. It was not a question of free will, you understand. And incidentally, one of the things that lead to a life that would be characterised – albeit pointlessly – as unhappy is when your choices are limited by the intervention of others.'

'Yes, well, going back to our subject this morning, what exactly *is* this thing called happiness, would you say? Philosophically speaking, that is.' The smiling man looked unaccountably pleased with himself.

Sanderson spoke with the diffidence of someone who expected life to treat him badly. Aristotle, he said, had taught that the ideal life was the life of *eudaimonia* – a word that was usually translated as happiness. But this was in no way related to the modern illusory sense of the word. It had to do with living a life in accordance with reason, with virtue, with duty – none of which had particular relevance nowadays. While it was perfectly true that ever since Aristotle, philosophers had believed *eudaimonia* to be the highest human good and had set about studying ways in which it might be attained, this had nothing to with what was commonly called *happiness*, which was essentially a subjective state, a personal assessment of the quality of one's life, more often than not related to sensory pleasure and instant gratification.

'Ah, but,' interrupted the cheerful female presenter, glancing at her briefing notes, 'is it better to be a pig satisfied or Socrates dissatisfied?' She had the look of a woman who was not acquainted with either Socrates or with pigs.

'Oh, that old chestnut,' said Sanderson. 'The happy pig or the unhappy Socrates. Well, if we're playing that game, better by far to be a happy Socrates, I would say. The trouble is, no one has ever proposed a sensible way of measuring happiness – by which of course people generally mean *pleasure*. You can't quantify the pleasure derived from watching football or reading poetry. There is no hierarchy. You can't weigh it. People like different things. Some people like to go fishing. Others like to sit in silence and stare at a wall. It's as simple as that. You can't index it.'

'Ah but surely you *can*.' It was the smiley man again, this time with a gotya gleam in his eye. 'Governments are in the process of doing just that. According to the Home Secretary our government is devising a Happiness Index *as we speak*.'

'But that's the sort of mad thing that governments *do*,' said Sanderson. 'They already tell us what to eat, where not to smoke, how many units of alcohol must not be exceeded. Future governments will probably tell us how to love, how to behave when we're in it, what to do when it ends.'

The cheerful woman began to look a little nervous. 'Well, what would you say to Leo Tolstoy,' she effused, 'who thought that all happy families were the same, but that each unhappy family was unhappy in its own way? Wasn't Leo Tolstoy, like yourself, also a bit of a philosopher?'

Sanderson snorted and said that Tolstoy was merely being epigrammatic. All happy families did not in fact resemble one another. Each happy family, if there was such a thing, had been fortunate enough to find its own way through the impediments to happiness, through the miserable swamp that was the family. Unhappy families were usually unhappy for near-identical reasons, all of which had to do with the travails of being a family.

At which point both presenters, still smiling, thanked Dr Sanderson in unison and brought the interview to an abrupt end.

I had watched the television interview with a mixture of admiration and concern as Sanderson refused to say what was expected of him. But I was willing him to do well, and the over-riding feeling was one of a strange sort of pride. Here was a man who was teetering on the brink, whose skin was peeling off his body, who had been suspended from his job, who was paranoid with suspicion about his wife and had become loathsome to himself. For such a man to have functioned at all in those circumstances was impressive. You did well, I said to him afterwards. Oh, it's just colluding in a pointless charade, came the reply. 'When you publicise your book, you dabble in the dark arts. That girl didn't know her arse from her elbow.'

The dark arts multiplied. The breakfast television interview was quickly followed by an article in the *New York Times*, filed by the paper's London correspondent, who had been much taken by Sanderson and what she described as 'his innocent concern with truth' and 'his refreshingly pellucid style'. The *New York Times* article produced an immediate reaction – who was this Brit who dared to pronounce on happiness? Was he priest or prophet?

Before long Sanderson was showered with invitations to appear on the major television networks in America, and this in turn increased interest in him at home. He continued to avoid all the normal crowd-pleasing devices, yet this had the perverse effect of increasing his popularity. The more he cautioned against happiness, the more people clamoured to hear him denounce it. In the space of a week he became the focus of a media frenzy. Meanwhile American politicians took to the microphones to remind their transatlantic neighbours that the pursuit of happiness was one of the inalienable rights drafted by Jefferson and the founding fathers into the Declaration of Independence. Maybe so, said Sanderson, but pursuit of happiness had merely translated into the pursuit of consumer goods – and men and women surely had not died for the right to unbounded cupidity. And actually, happiness was not really the point. It was a far more complicated story.

Sanderson's spell of fame reached new heights when he appeared on the BBC's flagship current affairs programme, with a satellite link to an American senator in Washington. The interviewer, a youngish woman with an elegant swan-like neck, had a look of permanent surprise. Her hair swished back and forth like a curtain and she regarded Sanderson with a kind of wide-eyed wonder as if to say: Look! A philosopher! Let's see what tricks he can perform. The camera zoomed in on his features. He had the beginnings of a beard, like peach fur. Evidently his skin could no longer tolerate a razor. The interviewer began by suggesting to the senator that the debate had moved on from genetics to the broader question of whether the pursuit of happiness was in reality a sensible ambition. The senator was defensive, but he worked hard at sounding reasonable, employing a number of uh-huhs and okays, as if he were being patient with a small child. He then launched into gee-whiz folksy talk, a stream of kindas and gottas and gonnas. The right to pursue happiness, he said, was built into the American founding document. Like life and liberty, it was part of the American ideal. And so it would remain. Simple as that.

At which point Sanderson argued that happiness, as it was commonly understood, would almost never be found where it was actively pursued. It would only ever be a fortunate side-effect, not something that could be engineered or calculated. More importantly, not only was it pointless to pursue happiness, it would at best be morally equivocal, at worst downright immoral. This was because the pursuit of one's own happiness nearly always entailed harm to others. Logically, in order to be happy we would have to remove whatever it was that made us unhappy – poverty, for example, or sexual frustration, to name just two. If these were the particular obstacles to our happiness it didn't take much imagination to think of the variety of ill that could be done in the removal of the obstacles, or indeed the number of people that could be shafted in the process – quite *literally* shafted, he added, with a watery smile.

The senator, clearly shaken by this assault on an inalienable right, now shifted the argument in the direction of religion, reaching for the tried and tested words that would get him out of trouble: the founding fathers believed that the right to pursue happiness was God-given, and to this day that was a strongly held belief in the United States.

'It's true,' said Sanderson, into his stride now, 'that Americans have a natural appetite for belief.' I was surprised to hear him pronounce the indefinite article as *ay* – *ay* natural appetite. 'They believe the literal truth of many things that are dismissed out of hand in my own country. Critical scrutiny is not highly developed over there – millions of Americans believe, for example, that at one time or another they have been abducted by aliens. And in my own country we have a prime minister whose ghastly decisions are – so he *believes* – sanctioned by the Almighty. Belief is not always *ay* positive or *ay* reasonable thing.'

The senator interrupted Sanderson to remind him that the Christian idea of happiness was very much concerned with love of one's neighbour. It wasn't simply about being 'out for what you can get' – which was a depressing indictment on human behaviour. Americans sincerely believed that a daily diet of God and good works would lead ultimately to *everlasting* happiness as promised by Jesus Christ.

'Actually the Christian idea of happiness, as I understand it, is very much concerned with your own soul. It involves a personal quest for a state of grace, whatever is meant by that. This may involve good works along the way, or it could in the past have involved a few crusades. Nowadays it's more likely to be a bunch of Jesus freaks waving their arms in the air and banging tambourines, though it could of course mean a monastic secluded life, praying for the souls of others. Whatever the case, it generally involves suffering – the more lice in your shirt the better.' Which was only one of the odd things about religion, he said. After all why would anyone seek pain if ordinary pleasure offered itself? But that was another matter. However people interpreted God's plan it would just be another form of human construct. And that certainly didn't render it valid, or even sensible. People believed in things not because they were true, but because it made them feel better to believe. Think of Tony Blair's distressingly flawed mantra: *the right thing to do*. As if that conviction had done anything to reduce the catastrophic consequences for the world, he said. And as for belief in life after death and everlasting happiness, this was something that had been shown to be culturally determined. 'For example, when the Chinese have near-death experiences and report back on what they have "seen", it includes being confronted by every tiny creature whose life has been sacrificed in order for them to live, together with the figure of a judge meting out retribution for these misdemeanours. Whereas in my society, and doubtless in yours too, there are usually reports of a white light and out-stretched hands welcoming us "home", invariably into the arms of Jesus.'

On and on he went, taking bold steps now, not stumbling. The senator was visibly felled. Each entry wound had been tiny, but the overall effect was deadly. It amazed me that there was no contempt in Sanderson's manner, no arrogance. He still looked vulnerable, uneasy under the studio lights, but his approach came over as amused perplexity, as if there really was no case to answer.

Over the next week or two his star continued to rise and he became an unlikely celebrity. He was acclaimed in print and on the airwaves as someone who looked as if he might have had a difficult life, yet whose vision of the world had remained impressively accommodating and reasonable. His book, which by any known predictive means ought to have languished in obscurity, was catapulted into the bestseller lists, partly on account of the ferocity of its critics. 'It's done better than *Lust*,' said Sanderson's publisher when he rang, his tone somewhere between exultation and incredulity. Meanwhile the university was inundated with so many media inquiries that a statement had to be issued to the effect that Dr Sanderson was a first-rate academic, justly recognised by the School of Philosophy for his pioneering research. Since he was currently on leave of absence, however, the press office would not be in a position to set up any interviews until further notice.

'Ironic,' I said to him, meaning the suspension and the timing of it.

'Irony is the humour of the defeated,' he said. 'That's why we're so good at it.'

45

On the last Friday in November a private view of Carrie's latest work was held at Alice's gallery. I had of course been to exhibitions before, but there was something new and thrilling about being invited to a private view. I also felt a little nervous. Art was mysterious, and I was unsure of how to talk sensibly about it. I spent a longer time than usual getting ready, considering carefully what to wear, deciding in the end on a grey silk shirt with no tie.

The atmosphere was celebratory like a party, suffused with hearty greetings and loud laughter. Everything came across as a little exaggerated, but real nonetheless. Alice, looking radiant in a red diaphanous dress, hailed me like an old friend. I moved towards her obediently, whereupon she introduced me to her husband Charles, an attractive man with lovely soft hands, gleaming fingernails and exquisite manners. I immediately experienced a kind of panic brought on by being privy to the details of Sanderson's affair with this man's wife. Especially since Charles and Alice struck me as the perfect hosts, the perfect couple in fact – handsome, charming, and setting each other off beautifully, not just in their physical appearance, but also in their manner and manners with each other. Charles was gently solicitous towards Alice, bending down to catch what she was saying, touching her repeatedly and being refined in an old-fashioned way. They seemed so exquisitely matched that I found it impossible to believe that they were not in fact lovers. Appearances are misleading, I decided, and there is no accounting for sexual preference. I was also struck by the degree to which Charles seemed to elevate Alice's charms. When we first met in the Sandersons' flat, and later when I called in at the gallery, she had seemed theatrical and affected; yet with her husband she came over as a real person, rendered whole and possessed of a certain purpose. She still had stage presence – on this occasion the large exhibition space was her theatre – but her performance seemed more natural, as if she had ceased to be an actor and had instead entered fully into the character.

Paintings – these paintings at any rate – seemed to me both less ambiguous and more ambiguous than the written word. I moved slowly from one to the other, thinking of all the energy and emotion that had gone into the making of them. The exhibition was entitled *Displacement*, and it was clear, even to an untrained eye, that the twelve pieces were all thematically linked. Each of the large canvases showed a figure, always on the margins, never centre stage. The figure had a strong presence, but it was – as Alice had hinted – the sort of presence that implied an absence: invariably the back view, lightly contoured, face turned away, looking out towards the edge of the painting, as if on the point of leaving the world. The huge space around the figure was strangely powerful. It was also – this was just my sense – slightly threatening. The colours in the centre were light, growing darker towards the edges. There was no doubt in my mind that the artist's sadness had leaked into the canvas, spreading all over it and through it. In two or three of the pictures there was another figure, a slighter, shimmering, wavering image, which I took to be a version of Carrie – a guardian angel hovering in the background. No, said Carrie some time afterwards when I commented on the second figure. It was probably some sort of benign spirit, she said, but as spare and useless as a shadow. Then why was it there? I asked. Who knows? she said. Things bubble away beneath the surface, and sometimes they boil up and spill over onto the canvas. Painting was just a way of connecting with the world, being alive in it, and in some sense also keeping the world at bay. Something travelled from the inside to the outside, and it could creep out of the back of your mind as well as the front, she said. It seemed to come from the same seed, but each time the germination was slightly different. She supposed there must be some sort of interplay between the painting and the life, but it was poorly understood – there was no certainty about it. 'It's like your translation – at best provisional.'

'Yes, but why are you so downbeat about it, so hard on yourself?'

'I'm not,' she said swiftly, as if there had been some dreadful mistake. She fixed me in her gaze. 'That's how *you* see it, not how I see it. And you're projecting what you see on to me.'

I looked round the gallery at the assembled crowd. Just before Christmas was a good time to have an exhibition, Alice had said. People were upbeat and in the mood for buying. And sure enough, several of the paintings already had red dots next to them. Later, when I asked Carrie if she had mixed feelings about letting them go, she thought for a while before answering. Then: 'I suppose it's a bit like having a child go out into the world – a mixture of joy and heartache.'

Though the art world, like the academic world, was reputed to be riven with envy, I could see no evidence of it in those gathered in the gallery. There must have been a hundred people or so, all of them apparently engaged in animated conversation. The whole room seemed to be alive with unfeigned merriness and bonhomie. I imagined these people going back to their own homes, a room or a flat somewhere, closing the door behind them and setting about their other lives, inventing and reinventing themselves with ease. Watching and listening, I felt the painfully familiar undertow that separated me from the crowd. This old feeling took up residence in my mouth, where it became a bitter taste, not shiftable by the wine and canapés that were doing the rounds on little silver platters. It was something that had happened before, mostly when it was borne in on me that I was for ever outside someone else's story, and that no one was inside mine. From this thought it was but a short leap to imagining myself in one of Carrie's huge canvases, another sad lonely figure loitering on the edge.

Suddenly Sanderson was at my side, blinking in the strong light. His clothes were crumpled and dirty – the livery of a desperate life. He could easily have joined the beggar in the cardboard box outside his own apartment. With his scruffy appearance, weeping sores, patchy facial hair and fingernails rimmed with dirt, he made Alice's husband look like a Greek god. The gallery lights gave him a sickly look, which set off the rest of his morbid appearance – bloodshot eyes, ruptured skin, dirty teeth, armpits darkened by sweat. He sniffed and said: 'Welcome to the art world, Eddie,' and I caught a whiff of his sour breath. Horrific. Was his inner putrefaction now seeping out through the pores of his skin and the cavity of his mouth? Carrie had mentioned the smell of depression, but surely no depression could account for this advanced stage of rankness. Whiffs of gas from a rotting bundle – how had he come to this? It had to be a recent development – otherwise how could anyone have survived being intimate with him?

Despite the familiar sense of dislocation, I was reluctant to leave the gallery and its party atmosphere. This was because I detected another feeling – a slight suggestion of getting away from my everyday self, from all the things that hemmed me in and fixed me to the same old spot. Outside Sanderson was in the doorway trying to light his pipe. 'Do you fancy a bite to eat, Eddie?' he stuttered between puffs. 'Shall we wait for the distinguished artist?' When Carrie came out, her face flushed with the evening's excitement, she smiled at both of us and linked arms, gripping both of us tight as she half-walked, half-danced along the pavement. Her hair was tucked into a crimson beret, and a silk scarf rippled round her neck. For a moment I thought of her as Jeanne Moreau in *Jules et Jim*, captivating the two men with her spirit and caprice. And then I remembered that in Truffaut's film it did not last, nor did it end well.

46

The following morning, the last in November, I went back to the river with Sanderson. The trout season was effectively over now, but there were still grayling to be fished for. During the winter months it was easier to catch grayling with a nymph, he said, getting it deep in the water where they did most of their feeding. Even so, he would stick to his dry fly. 'Nymphing is for wimps,' he snorted, attaching a weighted nymph to my leader. I pretended not to know the meaning of wimp, and when he explained I told him there was no equivalent in French. 'It must be a British thing,' I smiled, childishly pleased with myself.

It was a bright day, sharp with cold and promise, but Sanderson's mood was dark. He explained that on the way to pick up the car he had bumped into the departmental secretary in the street. She was a well-meaning woman, he said, with a natural empathy, probably on account of having suffered a lot. 'Her husband is a terrible boozer who drinks most of the money that should go on the children, and yet somehow she has managed not to let it get her down.' She had asked him how he was and said how sorry she was that things were difficult for him. 'Which was fine,' said Sanderson, 'until she advised me that it might help to get in touch with my feelings.' Only the fact that she was a nice person, he said, had prevented him from bashing her brains out. Even now as he recounted their exchange, he imagined pinning her up against a wall, looking her straight in the eye and saying: *Get in touch with my feelings? And what makes you think I can avoid being in touch with my feelings? Christalmighty, do you know what I would give to get OUT OF TOUCH with my feelings?* The parting shot of the well-meaning woman had been that he mustn't blame himself. *(Oh really? Why ever not?)* He had forced a smile and waved goodbye.

As we walked on the path to the river I said what I had planned to say: 'Carrie told me all about Alfie. Last night at the gallery. It must be hard to bear.' The words hung limply in the damp air.

'Hmm, a bad business,' Sanderson said, 'a bad business.' But instead of enlarging on the bad business he launched into a general attack on the folly of having children. All that fear, he said, all that worry. A child was too much at the centre of its mother's life. And parents in general were far too *involved* with their children. 'It was better in the Edwardian age, when parents – fathers certainly – were remote from their children, and still respected.' I didn't know what to make of this. Was it fear? Was it genuine antipathy? It sounded like a cold heart. Which made me think of Rousseau – a *tartuffe* who dared to pontificate on man's sensibility and natural goodness, while having the five children he fathered by his mistress consigned to *Enfants-Trouvés*, a foundling hospital in Paris. Just as it always distressed me to think of Hume – a genuinely good man – having a connection with Rousseau, I did not want to believe that Sanderson might share Rousseau's heartlessness. Instead, I held on to something Carrie had told me during our long talk: 'Harry's cynicism is an act. It stops him from going mad. It's the way he copes. A way of alleviating his dissatisfaction with himself.'

'In the case of the boy,' Sanderson continued, avoiding Alfie's name, the trouble had started straight away. 'I always resented being talked to *through* him – which is what my wife did in the beginning.' He couldn't bear all that ritualised baby talk. And the baby talk never quite disappears, he said. It just takes a different form. 'Children wreak havoc in the lives of adults, and the adults put up with it. It's one of the great mysteries of the world.'

'But this is how life continues,' I said, feebly – 'we were all children once.'

'And that's one of the poorest arguments in favour of children – the idea of creating miniature versions of yourself. I'm not talking here about the dangers of replicating a bad childhood, not in the Romanian orphanage sense of bad, but the idea of seeing all the normal hurts of your own childhood enlarged and vivified through your offspring . . . well, it's a grotesque idea.' What was actually grotesque, I thought, was Sanderson's frame of mind, his attitude. Every day there seemed to be more slippage, less self-restraint.

'In the Chinese calendar I am apparently a rabbit,' he said, in what seemed, but turned out not to be, a sudden change in direction. 'Which is evidently the happiest sign of the Zodiac – but ever since discovering this as a young man I have been terrified of producing other little rabbits and all their piles of shit.'

As we set up our rods, I moved the conversation on to what I hoped was safer ground: Sanderson's book and his new celebrity status. It was such a feather in his cap, I said. He must surely be delighted with the way things had turned out. 'I am certainly delighted *for* you.' He scoffed and made the usual self-effacing noises, but suddenly demurral seemed to stick in his throat, and for a few brief moments I thought I detected pleasure and maybe even pride – rare chinks of colour in the ghastly naysaying. His scowl vanished and as he puffed on his pipe he could have been a man quite at ease with himself and his lot. But just as suddenly he reverted and was having none of it. Philosophers were by and large impostors. 'I should know – I've been one all my life.' He followed this remark with his trademark laugh – a round of gunfire. And they were certainly not free of prejudice, he said, as they were sometimes thought to be. In fact they were plagued by it. They were generally a bunch of snivelling wimps, sitting in heated offices, cloistered from the outside world, polishing their petty rivalries and delusions of grandeur, breathing clean air, with no diseases named after them.

'There's *the disease of the learnèd*, don't forget,' I said when he reached the end of his rant. But he was not in the mood to be teased. 'That's just it, Eddie,' he said, quiet now. 'We're not learnèd. Not any more.'

As for appearing on television, he continued, that was a double curse: it inspired loathing in others, at the same time as deepening the loathing you felt for yourself. 'People are intimidated by a philosopher – they assume your brain charges along on fast circuits, and that you deal in truth.' But this was so far from being the case it was laughable. The truth used to be transmitted by oracles and sybils, he said, it was veiled in mystery and imbued with authority. Before that, in the primitive world, the truth was equivalent to people's strongest feelings. And now something similar was happening again. Truth had been blown apart, into shards of competing theories, each one claiming equal validity, usually for no other reason than that it was strongly held. It really had no independent value, separate from those who believed it. 'The truth is a thick grey colour, too murky for illumination.'

'Are you saying we can never call something true?'

'We can. And we do. But truth is a relative concept, Eddie, invariably dependent on the language in which it is expressed. Words don't have meaning in isolation. And there is no guarantee that the language in which we formulate truth matches the world in which we live. Truth doesn't correspond to something *out there*.' He pointed his fishing rod skywards, flexing it gently as if to indicate the location of *out there*.

'I've sometimes thought that novels contain truth – not

anything that would hold up philosophically perhaps.' Did it matter, what I said? Like the departmental secretary I meant well, but meaning well seemed hard for Sanderson to bear.

'The truth of novels, like the truth of life, is at best provisional,' he said. 'To say that something is true in a novel may be no more than to say that the emotion it evokes strikes a chord in the reader. It doesn't have to relate to something in the world beyond the story.' His tone was utterly neutral, betraying no feeling. He had put his rod down now and was fumbling in his pockets for his pipe and tobacco.

'You know, the Russians have a word – *vera*. It is the certain belief that something is true, that it can be acted upon and lived out. We don't have that.'

Towards the end of the afternoon we packed up our stuff and returned to the car. I did not yet know it, but we would not fish together again. When we got back to Edinburgh the weak winter sun lay low behind the tenement buildings, sending pale fingers of light into the roadway. People went in and out of the shops, walked hand in hand in the streets, pushed babies in prams. Other lives were continuing as normal.

'Let's have a quick drink, to mark the end of the fishing season,' he said. How did he occupy his weekends, I asked as we took our seats in the bar, when there was no fishing? 'There are always flies to be tied,' he said wearily, looking down at his hands as if they were not his own hands but those of some strange alien creature. 'There's no end to the flies you can tie.' With his index finger he traced round and round the rim of his glass. Had there been any communication from the university, I wondered. No, there had not, he snarled, and the thirty days were nearly up. 'Mind you,' he said, eyes brightening, 'it will take them more than thirty days to travel the length and breadth of their egos.' He hasn't quite given up, I thought – there is still a certain spark, still fun to be had, albeit the one-last-cigarette-before-the-guillotine sort. There was one small piece of good news, he said. He had heard on the grapevine that his accuser, Miss Suzello, would not be bringing separate charges, that she would be content with an internal inquiry. 'Which is an improvement, I suppose. But only inasmuch as the Salem witch hunts were an improvement on the Spanish inquisition.' He smiled as he said this, but it was a Norman Bates *Psycho* kind of smile, the smile of a maniac. 'But to be honest, I don't think I mind any more. Being suspended, I mean. At first I thought it was . . . well . . . the end of me, the end of everything. I was looking over the edge, into the abyss.' Now he felt more like old blind Gloucester – convinced that he had been led to the edge of the cliff and about to die, only to find that it was just a small step down.

'They've done me a favour actually. I've become a third-party participant in my own affairs, only partly myself, mostly a stranger. I should get out while I can, while I still have a soul. Whatever a soul might be.' We sat in silence for a while. Sanderson played with a beer mat, turning it round and round as if looking for clues. He did not seem fully present in his own life.

'You know, Eddie, I sometimes wonder how different life might have been.' He sounded quite matter-of-fact now. 'Do you ever do that? Sometimes I find myself thinking: what if I'd grown up in a household full of books?'

'Well, I did grow up with books. I spent the whole of my childhood in a bookshop. And my father always maintained that to work with books was to live in the light. But it doesn't solve everything.'

'No, but I suspect literature can solve more things than philosophy. Philosophy is good at asking the questions, but literature gets us closer to the answers. It might even save your life – in a way that philosophy never could.'

'What do you mean – *save your life?*'

'Oh, it's just a manner of speaking. I was actually thinking about the things that help and the things that hurt, and the connection between them – what Henry James calls *the bliss and the bale*. You don't get this in philosophy, you get it in novels. In poetry even more perhaps. There is a deep place inside us that poetry can connect with.'

He closed his eyes for a moment. A milky purple translucence lay over the eyelids. The trouble was, he continued, eyes open now, that when you got to his age you couldn't help looking back. And in his own case it was over a past littered with lost opportunities, roads not taken.

But that could apply to nearly everyone, I said. 'It certainly applies to me.' Surely the way to cope was to try and shape the past in a way that removed its sting. And I told him about my friend Antoine, who had so shaped his story that it might have been a piece of finely hewn sculpture. 'It seems to help him to live with the trail of wreckage he has left behind,' I said.

'It's too late for that with me,' he said. 'You turn your back for a moment, and it's all over. And what does your life amount to? Nothing at all.'

'You're very hard on yourself,' I said, knowing it would make no difference what I said.

'You're wrong, Eddie. We can love ourselves only if we are lovable in the eyes of others.'

'What about Carrie? Anyone can see that she loves you.' I had come a long way. This sort of remark, in my previous existence, would have been much too personal, too close to saying the unsayable. I might have said even more had Sanderson not started to speak again, this time hawing and hesitating, fumbling for his words, then stumbling over them. Just as one sentence seemed to be forming, it would pack its bags and break camp, leaving behind the merest trace of having been there at all.

Eventually he said, quietly, thinly: 'Love and pity are not the same.' Surely I could see that? 'Carrie pities me. And pity is a killer.' He nodded his head, agreeing with himself. I held him in my gaze, taking in the wreck of his appearance and trying to square it with the rows of neatly labelled drawers in the box room and his exquisitely dressed flies. Then, as if reading my mind: 'I mean, just look at me!' Wittgenstein believed that the human body was the best picture of a man's soul, he said. 'What a picture! What a soul!' There followed another torrent of despairing talk and self-inflicted wounds – he had lost the art of living, the art of thinking, he was a slug wending its way at ground level, depositing slime – after which he said I mustn't take him too seriously – 'I get carried away' – before making a sudden sharp turn into the problem of free will, seeming to take up where we had left off on our very first fishing trip.

'Throughout our lives we think we have *free will*' – he drew out these two monosyllables to a heartbreaking length – 'but this is thrown open to doubt by the way patterns repeat themselves endlessly. I'm not suggesting it's all predetermined, but there is actually very little in the way of unexpectedness. The idea that what is happening to us is unique – well, it's just a trick. And it's a trick that we all fall for.'

I was in over my head, but almost for the first time I thought we had a sense of one another. This despite the colossal gulf between my own neat little life and his chaotic turmoil. 'Is that such a bad thing?' I said. 'After all, Hume understood three hundred years ago that there was no free will. That freedom was an illusion. That free will would require a mind. Not just a collection of impressions, mental perceptions.'

'Ah the sceptic's mantra,' he said, managing a smile that implied its opposite. 'Free will is no more than our ignorance of cause and effect, and cause and effect is an illusion, so free will is an illusion. There. Simple really.' Sometimes he was like a Magus figure, playful yet disturbing. At other times, like now, he was brooding and full of misery. He used misery like a drug, marvelling at his own addiction.

Maybe the problem was to do with looking back, I suggested. Of course, I said, I knew only too well that it was impossible not to look back, but there was no point in it. You just encountered an endless series of antecedents to current events, and in no time at all they too would join the queue and become antecedents in themselves.

'Well, whichever way you look at it, you don't have the freedom you think you have,' he sighed. 'What you say to yourself that you are going to do has already largely been decided. It just gets turned into narrative form, to maintain the illusion that you're in charge.'

Truth to tell, he said, he had had enough. Enough of the university, enough of teaching, enough of everything. He was suffering from what the Russians called *toska* – nothing to do with the Puccini opera, he said. It was T-O-S-K-A, with the stress on the second syllable – tahskáh. 'There is no single word in English that expresses all the different shades of *toska*,' he said. 'I suppose French comes a bit closer with its *malaise* and *ennui*. But *toska* is more than that. It is a kind of sweeping anguish, a nostalgia for something only dimly understood, with no specific cause – at least none that you can identify. A yearning for what you don't have, as well as what you did have that is gone. And all the time you have the feeling that the story unfolding is really about something else – like a parable – except you have no idea what it can be.'

For most of his life he'd had the feeling of wanting to solve something, without knowing quite what. Once or twice he'd thought he was getting close, but just as the thing, whatever it was, seemed to be within reach, it had disappeared round the corner. It was a feeling that had informed his dreams as much as his waking life. Randomness was largely what determined the future. Along with chance and absurdity – 'its close cousins'. Just as you thought you had things sewn up, they would be lurking up ahead in the bushes. 'It's so hard to get beyond your own story. You just keep on, doing the same thing day after day. Why do we do it? Because it is the thing to do.' He looked at me, as if expecting contradiction. You got to a certain point in your life, he said, and you noticed it was impossible to change. 'I need to do something while there's still time.'

And then suddenly he had to go, my goodness look at the time, he would be late. I did not think to ask what it was he would be late for.

47

The ring of the telephone was like glass shattering. It broke the night in two, and its jagged edges stuck out, waiting to snag me. The fog in my brain told me it must be Mrs Bannerman to tell me she couldn't come in that day. The cleaner had become a convenient explanation for everything. But it was never the cleaner.

'Harry hasn't come back. I'm worried.' Carrie sounded distraught. She was not in control of her voice.

'When did you last see him?'

'Yesterday morning, at breakfast.'

'And was he OK?'

'Yes. I think so. He had an appointment at the hospital. Ultraviolet treatment. I called the hospital. He didn't show up.'

'And nothing since?'

'No, I thought he must have gone to the pub, stayed there all day. I've been waiting ever since.'

'Give it a little while. I'm sure there's a simple explanation.'

It was the middle of the night, but I decided to go downstairs. There would be no more sleep. On a whim I opened the door, half expecting Sanderson to be on the doorstep or lurking in the bushes. But there was only a chill mist, swirling in the lamplight.

The stillness was palpable, as if the whole city held its breath. I shivered and went inside, picturing Carrie all alone, longing for her Harry to return.

That day, a Tuesday, I could barely focus on my work. My brain was addled from lack of sleep, and I kept thinking of Carrie, sitting by the telephone, waiting for news. Stick to your routine, I told myself. And so I clambered over Salisbury Crags, imagining David Hume doing the same thing when he was troubled. After which I read over the previous day's notes as usual, typing them into the computer, and making the necessary adjustments and refinements as I went along. But my mind kept turning to Sanderson.

Mrs Bannerman was moving about downstairs. It was always hard to concentrate when she was in the house. In due course, right on cue, she appeared at the door of my study. 'I'll just give your carpet a quick hoover – you won't even know I'm here.' She always said this. She flicked her duster along the bookshelves, barely making contact. She didn't see much point in books – she'd told me this at the beginning. You could find everything you needed to know just by living, she'd said. Sanderson's book lay on my desk – pristine in its shiny new dustcover and completely dust-free. Mrs Bannerman flicked her duster at it anyway, curling her lip at the bold letters of its title. 'Huh. As if we were put on this earth to be *happy*!' she said. 'He should maybe try working for his living.' Mrs Bannerman was not endowed with the gift of clarity, but her views were seldom in doubt. I made polite noises and fled from the cottage. I would head for the library, earlier than usual. It was a break in my routine, but what did it matter? When I got to the bottom of Calton Hill, however, I found myself turning in the direction of the Sandersons' flat, past all the streets with regal names – George Street, Hanover Street, Frederick Street, Queen Street.

Carrie let me in and immediately hugged me, not as a woman might embrace, but too tight, like a frightened child. Oh, Eddie, she said. I was afraid she must have heard something terrible. Was there news, I asked. No, nothing. She was pale and her voice trembled. I didn't know what to do when women wept. I had not known all those years ago with my mother, and I did not know now. Yet I had a profound urge to comfort her. There could be all sorts of explanations, I said, not necessarily sinister. Had she checked to see if he'd taken the car? It wasn't in the usual place, she said, but that didn't mean anything. We drank coffee, and more coffee, trying to ward off the worst imaginings. She sat at the kitchen table, folding and unfolding a small piece of paper. There could be all sorts of explanations, I repeated. People sometimes stepped out of their own lives, for example. It was a known psychological condition. *La fugue dissociative* it was called in French. 'It happens suddenly, when someone can't face his life and he runs away from it, reappearing a week or two later – maybe a month or two, longer sometimes.' How did I know about this, she asked. Had it happened to me? No, no, I shook my head. I had come across it in a book about the First World War. People witnessed such horrific things that they sometimes just fled from their own lives. It was a kind of disappearance, just not in the usual sense. Back then no one had understood it – in fact they called it the malingerers' illness, dismissing it as cowardice. Some were even shot for it. But what horrific thing, she wanted to know, could Harry have witnessed? The veins stood out on her head. Oh, it needn't be something witnessed, I said, regretting having embarked on this train. There could be different triggers, I told her. All sorts of things – I was sure of that.

'And you think one of these things could have happened to Harry?'

'I don't know.' It was cruel to give her hope. Later, when it was time to leave, I said: 'If you don't hear from him soon, perhaps you should call the police.'

48

When I got back to the cottage in the early evening, there were two shocks. The first was the blank screen on my computer. In flight from Mrs Bannerman and the vacuum cleaner I had left the computer in sleep mode – I was quite sure of this. But there was now no reassuring little green light and the power was off at the socket. I phoned Mrs Bannerman, knowing there was no point. Just wondering why you switched off my computer, I said, not wanting to sound too harsh. It is an awkward relationship, cleaning and being cleaned for. She *always* made a point of switching off the lights when she left, she said. That's the way she'd been brought up – 'You'll be surprised at the money it saves you,' she chirped. I spent hours trying to get the computer to start, but nothing worked. I had copies of most of the essays, but there were three on the computer, recently worked on, none of them backed up.

The second shock had arrived in the post and was lying on the mat, hidden amongst all the pre-Christmas junk mail. It was an A4 envelope, with my name and address in bold black pen, and inside a typed sheet with a picture postcard clipped to the top of it. The image was a close-up of a fly, long-tailed and dark toned, with the caption: *Thunder and Lightning – Traditional Scottish Salmon Fly*. On the back Sanderson had written:

Dear Eddie,

Please be good enough to deliver the enclosed letter to the university.

Yours aye,

Harry

To Whom It May Concern*

Every resignation letter should have an epigraph, don't you agree? Mine appears below. Make of it what you will. Feel free to adopt it as part of your mission statement.

> SOCRATES: I will illustrate my meaning, Theodorus, by the jest which the clever witty Thracian handmaid is said to have made about Thales, when he fell into a well as he was looking up at the stars. She said, that he was so eager to know what was going on in heaven, that he could not see what was before his feet. This is a jest which is equally applicable to all philosophers. For the philosopher is wholly unacquainted with his next-door neighbour; he is ignorant, not only of what he is doing, but he hardly knows whether he is a man or an animal; he is searching into the essence of man, and busy in enquiring what belongs to such a nature to do or suffer different from any other – I think that you understand me, Theodorus?
> Plato, *Theaetetus*

Like Pascal, if I had had more time I would have written a shorter letter. But when it comes to resignations, brevity isn't everything. My communication will arrive via the tourist route only because I am constrained by the conditions of my suspension, one of which forbids me from contacting any member of the university. This will therefore be delivered to you by a third party – an exemplar of the Auld Alliance, a man I am happy to count as my friend, and someone sufficiently acquainted with David Hume to be unintimidated by those twin sentries, righteousness and hubris, stationed at the gateway of your own egos to protect your mortal mediocrity.

A passing word on my suspension. What was my crime exactly? A sober judge might say my only crime was weeping without due care and attention. Hardly a capital offence. Unless I am to be punished for the lacrimae rerum. And if that is the case, what about dear old Heraclitus, our very own 'weeping philosopher'? He was revered for his wisdom and sensibility, albeit in pre-Socratic times. Maybe nowadays he too would have his computer removed. Alas, it would appear from your line of inquiry that I stand accused of some sort of dreadful molestation, evidenced by an overwrought girl and the discovery of questionable apparatus (olive oil, rubber bands and plastic bags forchrissake!), now doubtless feeding the lurid fancies of my erstwhile colleagues. Well just for the record, I did not lay a swollen suppurating finger on that American girl. This is not a Clintonesque denial (though perhaps Miss Suzello is a close cousin of Miss Lewinsky, and they share a fevered imagination?). Smoking without inhaling and all that. For the avoidance of doubt, I have always inhaled at the least opportunity, just not with Miss Suzello. But in this instance, my only offence was to cry. Which evidently alarmed Miss Suzello. Ironic really. My dear wife has always held it against me that (on the whole) I do not cry. This is something women do, I believe – complain about the lack of crying in their menfolk. 'Why is it bad not to cry?' I have sometimes protested. 'Maybe *you* cry too much. Is crying too much not bad also?' Now that I have cried, look where it has got me – relieved of my duties, and my fate in the hands of a gathering of lost souls. How I wish I could be a writer like Chekhov, to transform this mortal banality into something worth recording.

The greatest illusion, however, is to think that one is indispensable, that if one disappeared tomorrow it would make the slightest difference. But if I have learned anything in this life, it is – as my dear old dad used to say – that we all piss in the same pot. I leave, therefore, without illusion and without regret.

And fear not, I have a plan. I have decided, at last, to do something useful with my life. From now on my brain will be used to solve the problems of U-bends and S-bends. My mission will be Manichean: to stop floods and to get the water flowing again. My place of work will not be an overheated office, but under sinks, in basements and in lofts. I have long had an ambition to be a plumber, and it's hard to think of a more important job. No one really needs a philosopher, but we all need a plumber at some point in our lives. And that point is invariably challenging: when the pipes burst, when the cistern overflows, when the drains block – all curiously potent symbols of a troubled life, la condition humaine. And so, dear colleagues, whenever you can't find your stopcocks, or your toilets back up, I trust you will think of me.

Finally, to those in my department – they will know who they are – who cling perversely to faith in God, let me leave you with the words of Woody Allen: How can you believe when you can't even get a plumber on a Sunday?

Harry Sanderson [signed]

*I love that phrase, don't you? To Whom It May Concern. It sounds so proper and formal, as if everything is being done by the book, with impeccable restraint. And to whom is so diplomatic – it doesn't single anyone out – and the may so tentative, inviting the reaction: Me? No, it doesn't concern ME. And then there's concern, an ambiguous word if ever there was one, allowing the possibility that the contents that follow may simply be pertinent without being troubling.

49

In times of dread, time itself seems to slow. The waiting was a torment, the hour-after-hourness of it. But soon, as suddenly as Sanderson had disappeared, a body answering his description was discovered. The police search had concentrated on his favourite fishing haunts south of Edinburgh, but it was in the River Tay, fifty miles north of the city, that they found him floating. My God, Carrie said. I said it too. My God. We could not get beyond this senseless repetition.

For the next several days and nights nothing mattered much. Carrie described herself as an assortment of unconnected parts. If she moved too quickly they would all separate and end up in a chaotic heap. Her brain sent out instructions, and only much later, so it seemed, did her body obey them. There was no alignment between the mental and physical, she said. She proceeded slowly, slept fitfully, and held her body tight to stop it falling apart. Half-formed thoughts flitted into her head, and as she tried to hold them, they would suddenly collapse like the changing patterns of a kaleidoscope. During this time she spent hours in the garage room, meditating like mad, as if her life depended on it. A week or so passed. Then one morning, something cleared, and the contents of her head felt looser. This, she said, was not something she willed; it just happened. There followed a kind of composure, after which she felt she could perform simple tasks. But each time Harry entered her mind he was lying dead on a trolley in the morgue. Try as she might, she couldn't remove the image or improve it.

I was with Carrie when they told her. They didn't use these words, of course. They didn't say: *Your husband is dead.* Instead, they said something quite formal and as far removed from the actual meaning as the situation allowed. They cradled their police caps under their arms, and their sombre faces told two things: that they must have found Sanderson, and that he would not be coming back.

Police differ from country to country – this is my impression. In France a policeman is a superior kind of thug – a criminal in uniform. In Edinburgh they are gentler, not yet deadened by what they have seen and done.

The kitchen seemed too small to contain two uniforms. The policewoman approached Carrie and asked if there was somewhere they could all sit down, but Carrie had already ceased to have normal responses. Instead she moved away from the uniforms and stood with her back to the warm stove, her hands turned inwards, gripping the railing, as if to harness whatever it was that connected her to the world. The kettle on the hob was coming to the boil, mocking the circumstances with its busy tune. Something was happening to the room: it felt darker, the air thicker. The police officers rubbed the rim of their caps.

'Mrs Sanderson.' The policeman cleared his throat. So, he would be the one to break the news. Men were supposedly the ones with gravitas, suited to solemnity. The female officer would be there to comfort – traditionally a woman's talent. Despite all the gender blurring of the last half-century, conventional roles were alive and well, here in urban Scotland certainly.

'At 2.30 pm today a body was discovered on the north bank of the Tay,' the policeman began, reading from his notebook.

I noted the passive tense. If you removed the agent of discovery, was that supposed to dull the pain? If you made the verb passive, not active, did that lessen the hammer blow? Were tenses a feature of police training? Would there be a subjunctive, to deal with what was at this stage only possible rather than actual?

'The body showed signs of having been immersed in water. We have reason to believe the deceased to be your husband.'

There was something fascinating about the way people conveyed their meaning, or hid it – the way facts were expressed minimally or wrapped in prolix phrases. Later Carrie would say to me that *the deceased* and *reason to believe* belonged to police dramas on television. They had no business being spoken in her kitchen, pretending to be able to bear the enormity of the message they conveyed.

The kettle continued to sing. As time seemed to slow I observed some small particles of water condensing on the tiles behind, trickling down the channels between the rows. The grout between the tiles was quite grey now. Had it once been white? Greying grout between the tiles: this prosaic observation marked the last moment of normality in that day. Everything else, in some small or large way, intimated the sorrow that was to come.

50

There were so many questions, each one leading off on its own puzzling trail. Why had he gone north, why was it the River Tay – which as far as Carrie knew he had never fished? His favourite rod with its brass rings and scarlet whippings had also been recovered. Everything pointed to a planned fishing trip. There was even one of his beautiful salmon flies attached – though at the beginning of December a salmon fly made no sense. Perhaps he lost his footing, I said, wondering if his wading staff had been found along with his rod. But why had he told no one – this she asked over and over – why had he not left a note? Perhaps the letter of resignation was a form of note, I said. Neither of us mentioned suicide, but it was in the background, occasionally slithering into focus when Carrie said things like: 'I didn't think he was *the type*.' And in an irony that Sanderson himself might have appreciated, the essay I was translating during those dreadful days was Hume's *On Suicide*, in which he argues that *no man ever threw away life while it was worth keeping*. We might even think of it, he writes, as *our duty to ourselves – notre devoir envers nous-même*, providing happiness and well-being can no longer be achieved. I considered mentioning this to Carrie by way of comfort, but decided against it. In time she began to question the point in trying to understand what exactly had happened, or why. It was not as if the discovery of the precise sequence of events would make it more bearable, she said. By putting events into a chosen order, she thought, you simply formalised the horror of what had happened. You're right, I said, desperate to go along with her, perhaps it was a mistake to try and see a situation too clearly. Yes, she said, people seemed to suffer more when they understood things too deeply. If you looked at life slightly askance, you might be spared some of its harshness. 'Reality kills, obliqueness saves.' That was the notion she clung to, and everything that followed was in some way a distillation of it.

We were picked up in an unmarked police car – 'I thought you wouldn't be so keen on the Panda,' said one of the police officers breezily – and driven the fifty miles to Dundee. Carrie's cheek was pressed to the car window all the way. Later she would tell me that she had concentrated on keeping dark thoughts at bay by giving a name to everything she saw from the window, like someone learning a language. Along the waterfront there was a train taking the wide curve of the railway bridge across the water. It was a long train, which traced a near-perfect arc as it prepared for its approach to the station. The river that had taken Sanderson glistened benignly in the sunshine as it merged with the sea.

The mortuary was part of a sprawling hospital, a monument to modern planning to the northwest of the city. The huge complex was dug into a gentle slope, a large Legoland village looking over the river valley into the heart of Perthshire. The approaches were all paving stones and concrete, nothing to calm the soul or relieve the eye.

As we came near to the entrance, there was an assorted group outside the doors, not a welcoming party but a squad of smokers, set apart by their habit. They stood in various attitudes, an unlikely fellowship – old men, skinheads, amputees in wheelchairs, pregnant women – inhaling deeply, tracing patterns on the ground with discarded butts and spent matches.

Tacked on to the main entrance was a high porch-like construction made of glass and steel. The automatic doors opened and closed every few seconds, but the air inside was hot and sour. Beyond the porch was a large area not unlike the central concourse in an airport – and just as busy. Half the people were going somewhere, the other half were sitting around with nowhere to go. There were clothes shops and flower shops and cafés. Outside the newsagents a billboard read: BODY RECOVERED FROM TAY. I tried to concentrate on the surroundings. There were no curves, I noticed, only straight lines and cruciform columns which divided the huge expanse into nave and transepts. I wondered if the architects had wanted to hint at a church, to help soothe the private dramas played out here.

As we turned off down a corridor, as lonely and deserted as an empty stage, we began the long walk, the two policemen slightly ahead, turning round to check on Carrie every few paces, holding open each set of fire doors that punctuated the corridor at regular intervals. We proceeded in silence. The only sound was the click-click of Carrie's lace-up boots on the grey lino tiles. Not talking seemed the only possible defence against what was happening.

Each of us was constrained by the protocol of the occasion, though in my own case I had no idea of what it might possibly entail. For the policemen I imagined it must be part of the job they performed, just as much as directing traffic or dealing with stolen property. For me it was an absurd duty, a consequence of being connected with a man who had evidently drowned in a river. But also a strange kind of privilege to be with Carrie at such a time. The police officer who broke the news had asked her for the name of someone who could make a formal identification of the body. In certain circumstances, he explained, a second person was required by the procurator fiscal to carry out this duty. 'It has to be someone who has knowledge of the deceased,' he said precisely, as if reciting from a rulebook. What a strange expression, Carrie said to me afterwards, as though you could have knowledge of a person in the way you might of a fact. It had taken her a few moments to realise that the policeman meant someone who *knew* Harry. And then she said: 'Oh, Eddie. Edgar would be best,' motioning towards me. 'Edgar?' repeated the policeman. He had his notebook out and pencil at the ready. 'And does Edgar have knowledge of Dr Sanderson?'

We came to a door marked Reception Area. The police officers stood on either side of the door and motioned to us to go inside. The room was about the size of a dentist's waiting room, windowless, with several low armchairs arranged round a glass coffee table with tubular legs. The ceiling was low and in the corner was a door with the letters WC in imitation gold. It reminded me painfully of my room in the psychiatric unit all those years ago. It seemed that lack of beauty was a requirement in these places.

We all sat down, as if by prior arrangement. I sensed that there was a kindness in the air, that the policemen would be gentle, as much as the situation allowed. Just by looking at them you could tell they had been here many times. Afterwards Carrie said that the thought that her pain was not new, that it had been lived through and suffered before, made it even harder to bear. It ought to have been a solace, she said, but for some reason she wanted this experience to be unique, to be hers and no one else's.

'Mrs Sanderson,' the police officer began. 'We are very aware of how difficult this must be for you.' My throat tightened. 'We need a positive identification of the body we have recovered, and we hope that you and Mr Logan will be able to provide us with the positive identification we need.' The policeman's cheeks were hollow, as if he had sucked on a bitter fruit.

'In a few moments I'll ask you both to stand by the window from where you can view the body.' He nodded towards the far side of the room where there was a glass panel – strange to call it a window – cut into the wall at eye level. It was about one metre long and oblong-shaped with a thick curtain behind the glass. On the other side there would be an attendant who would remove the sheet from the body when Carrie was ready. There wasn't enough time for all the words to acquire meaning. This is too terrible, I thought, this can't be happening.

'Are you ready, Mrs Sanderson? Take your time.'

We stood in a row in front of the glass, the policemen flanking Carrie. I could see our absurd reflections in the glass. The policeman's large hand reached forward to press a button on the wall. There was a low buzz and the curtain began to open.

There is a time when you imagine other outcomes are possible. This was my thought as the curtain opened. It is only a brief moment, but it is hugely significant and can seem like an eternity. You sense the inevitable, yet you try to resist it with all your strength.

Through the glass, on a steel trolley, Sanderson lay dead. There was no doubting that he was dead. Even if we had not been told, we would have known. His body was noticeably bloated, his complexion darker in death than in life, as if he had absorbed the black mud of the river. The skin on his chest looked cold and macerated, like a goose prepared for the oven, and the backs of his hands were blanched and swollen. The places where his skin was broken by sores had the appearance of gunshot wounds. Yet the horror was strangely fleeting – how could this be? – and I found myself absorbing the detail as if I might later be tested on it. Nostrils of unequal width, fingernails peeled back, eyes like Quasimodo's, one dipped lower than the other. As for what I thought I ought to *feel*, there was almost nothing. In so far as I experienced sadness, I experienced it only vicariously, through Carrie. Most keenly when she reached out instinctively to touch her dead husband, and found the glass wouldn't let her. Afterwards she would complain that his hair was too smooth, that someone must have oiled it and combed it the wrong way. Why did they have to do that?

'Do you recognise the body, Mrs Sanderson?'

'It's Harry,' she said, clamping her tongue between her teeth.

'You're quite sure?'

'Quite sure.'

How quickly is the extraordinary absorbed and assimilated, and what violence it does in becoming ordinary: Sanderson, lying on a trolley, waiting to be shoved back into the fridge. People spoke about dignity in death. Whatever that meant, it did not mean lying on a slab under a burgundy sheet.

In the immediate aftermath, everything was blurred for Carrie – so she later reported. There was frenetic activity – phone calls, visitors, the exhausting practicalities of death, all the shock and disbelief. But the activity seemed to be elsewhere, out of reach. She herself felt like an invalid, or a small child, too young, too infirm to make decisions. Meanwhile everything was covered in a sort of sepia fog through which she waded, half stumbling, crumpled by the sheer density of it. Would she like some tea? Was she warm enough? What about a walk? No answers were required. The questions merely expressed the needs of those who asked them.

After those early days were over Carrie said she could not have reconstructed them. How many had there been? Two or three, nine or ten – she had no idea. People subscribed energetically to the imperative: Life Must Go On. But it was a strange life, seen through the fog. Her sisters arrived with their husbands, looking awkward and pious. They handed over flowers in cellophane and exchanged horrified glances. And left again. Her mother turned up briefly and spoke about the power of prayer. Others came and went and promised to come again. They talked to fill the silence, gabbling because they could not stop themselves, charging the atmosphere with that special pity, deep and tinged with guilt, reserved for someone else's bereavement. The phone rang its head off, but Carrie didn't answer it.

Neighbours brought pots of soup and large cakes. So much food, said Carrie. Other callers fussed over small practical tasks, making coffee, folding napkins, digging out crumbs from the toaster, wiping surfaces that were perfectly clean. Whatever they were feeling was turned into vigour and good works. I began to wonder if it was only when someone was dead that things were made this clean. Carrie herself scarcely noticed. When she talked about these days after they were over she said that the good kind people had barely registered. She had seen their shiny faces through frosted glass, heard their voices in the distance, and longed for Harry to be at home and not on a trolley in the morgue.

Meanwhile, in the odd moments that were not taken up with Sanderson's death, I contemplated the disaster of the lost essays.

51

Two days after the visit to the mortuary Carrie turned up at my place. Not to meditate, but to howl like a banshee. That day she had found crumpled pieces of paper in the bin in Sanderson's box room – half-started letters to Alfie mainly, and two to her, barely begun, one addressing her as *My own dear love* and containing a single line from a poem by Douglas Dunn: *Look to the living, love them, and hold on*; the other with the scored-out words *I have looked for love in all the wrong places*. 'But this is the most poignant,' she said, passing me a crinkly page covered in thick stubby handwriting: *Dear Alfie, I should have taught you how to fish, or to tie flies. It would have been good to pass all this on, in the way my father did to me. But I didn't. And I regret that now. Perhaps there's still time. With . . .*

After discovering the letters she had telephoned the hospital and asked for the morgue. She needed to see Harry again. 'To whom would you like to speak to, madam?' – the switchboard operator had been over-trained. The person in charge, Carrie replied. 'There is no one in charge, madam.' Was this egalitarianism or anarchy? Carrie told the operator that anyone would do. 'I'll give you the secretary, madam.' The operator had sounded pleased with herself. Perhaps her whole day consisted in small triumphs and disasters, Carrie said. After identifying herself to the secretary, Carrie asked when she could bury her husband. That was a matter for the procurator fiscal, said the secretary, not the hospital. The body could be released for burial only when the procurator fiscal was satisfied that all the correct procedures had been carried out. But what did this mean exactly, Carrie had asked. The secretary told her that an autopsy report establishing the cause of death had to be submitted by the pathologist in written form to the procurator fiscal. Hadn't the police explained all that? Carrie could not remember what the police had or had not explained. Pathologist? Procurator fiscal? It was all part of the fog. 'I don't understand the procedures,' she said, thinking how unfair it was to be made to feel pathetic. 'The procurator fiscal requires all uncertified deaths to be reported to him, including a death in suspicious circumstances.' The secretary spoke slowly and calmly, like a hypnotist putting a patient under. Suspicious circumstances? What did that mean? Carrie was struggling to get beyond the *fact* of Harry's death, quite terrible enough without having to deal with circumstances. Trying to stay calm, she told the secretary she would like to see her husband again, she hadn't seen him for three days, she couldn't bear to think of him lying under that burgundy sheet, being stored in a drawer, it was so barbaric, and she wanted to be with him, not just looking at him through glass, like staring into a fish tank. It had all come out more shrill than she had intended, but she could do nothing against it. 'I completely understand, Mrs Sanderson.' The voice was suspended somewhere between embarrassment and sympathy. 'If you wish to view the body, you will have to contact the police. We are not in a position to authorise it.' At that point Carrie had screamed down the phone: 'I don't wish to view *the body*. I want to see my husband, for Christ's sake!'

Some hours later a police officer, identifying himself as Sergeant Wallace, phoned to confirm that the hospital authorities had acted correctly. She had not expected otherwise. It would be best, he suggested, if he came to the house with WPC Andrews and went over everything again.

'I don't need you to come here,' said Carrie. 'I just want to see my husband again.'

'We actually advise against that in these circumstances.'

'What circumstances?'

'Following a post-mortem examination. The circumstances following a post-mortem. Experience tells us that it is usually better if the family of the deceased remembers the loved one as he was in life, in happier circumstances.'

When Carried tearfully poured all this out to me she said she couldn't stand hearing talk of *the loved one*, and there were altogether too many *circumstances*. She hated being at the mercy of them, and of Sergeant Wallace. In real life, she thought, as distinct from this grotesque parody she was caught up in, he would be a man of such fantastic dullness that she would almost certainly feel ill after even moderate exposure. As it was she had to hang on his every word, so hungry for information, even crumbs would do. You haven't lost your spirit, I told her, risking a smile. And I gave her a hug, awkwardly.

'I just want to see him, Eddie. Not through glass. I want to touch him. They're going to arrange it for tomorrow. Will you come with me again?'

We arrived at the hospital for a second time and began the long trek to the morgue. This time we went past the door marked Reception Area and stopped outside a door further along the corridor. There was a bulb made of thick amber glass above the door and a notice: DO NOT ENTER IF LIGHT IS ON. The light was not on, but Sergeant Wallace gave three sharp knocks and put his ear to the door as if waiting for some coded message to be tapped back. After a few moments the door was opened by an amiable man in a white coat and matching wellington boots. A man who likes his job, I thought. We were ushered into a small room and given white coats and plastic galoshes to put over our shoes. It was all quite surreal. In our fancy dress we went through another door leading to a large room, the one we had seen from behind the glass a day or two before. It smelled of chemicals and refrigeration. 'Let me know when you're ready,' said the amiable man. He stood by the trolley, preparing to turn down the burgundy sheet. 'Take your time.' After a few moments Carrie nodded to indicate that the cover could be removed. In her sorrow she looked beautiful. She said nothing, nothing at all. She was intensely calm. When it was time to leave, she bent over and kissed Sanderson's forehead.

Afterwards we went back to my Calton Mews cottage. Carrie spent nearly an hour in the garage room before reappearing, looking as if a weight had been lifted. Over a glass of wine she said that when she kissed Harry's forehead, cold and hard as granite, she had come to realise why a dead body was called the remains. She had always thought it a strange description, she said, faintly distasteful, hinting at leftovers on a dinner plate or sweepings from the shop floor. But in an instant she had seen, starkly, that the remains were just that. What *remained* after life had gone – the physical leavings of a life. Everything about him indicated outside intervention. 'Did you notice?' – his clothes had been removed, he had been shaved, ineptly, and his hair was still all wrong. He was in the hands of strangers. Harry, the living, breathing Harry, was gone, beyond reach. All the life and breath gone from him. He was also beyond love, she said, beyond reason, beyond laughter, beyond pain, beyond any feeling. 'He's completely, utterly dead,' she whispered, 'and not just dead today, but the next day and every day after that, and for all possible days.' How could the reality of that be described?

'Perhaps it can't,' I said.

'This is where we need your metaphors,' she said, sounding suddenly exhausted. 'To translate the actuality of death.'

*

I made some simple food and we talked late into the evening. I told her I thought it was actually a good thing, a salutary thing – to be faced with the physicality of death. 'By and large we've moved away from this. Which is a pity.' What did I mean, she asked. I thought it was too soon to say more on the subject, but she pressed me. 'Well, I just think we're too keen to make death remote, to cover it up and hide it away, to be silent on the subject. In every other age, death was more immediate. It was brought into the living room. That doesn't happen any more.'

'I'm not sure I could handle death in the living room,' she said, looking round the room where we sat as if expecting to see a corpse appear.

'It was just a manner of speaking,' I said. 'I suppose what I'm getting at is that we are now so at odds with the nature of things. And death is very much in the nature of things. We don't – like Hamlet at the graveside – hold a skull in our hands. We don't smell our dead or light the fire that burns them.'

'But would you really want to do that?'

'Probably not,' I said. 'But there's a price to pay for not doing it.'

'Which is?'

'An inability to deal with death as part of life. When the Neanderthal widow sat next to the rotting corpse of her mate, sooner or later her nose would tell her she would have to do something. Probably sooner. She would have to dig a hole and shove him in. Or push him over a cliff. Or leave him on the hill for the birds to peck.' Carrie looked slightly horrified. What are you saying? she asked. 'Only that I think you're handling this dreadful business in the best possible way,' I said. 'I saw both of my parents as corpses, and in a curious way I believe this has helped me. It's important to bear witness.'

52

After my mother died she was laid out on a trestle table in the *chambre d'amis*, the spare bedroom, a room that was never in reality put to the purpose of its name. There had been no friends and no one had ever come to stay. As I stood by my mother, lying in her simple coffin, it was as if the spare room had finally found its point. That evening, when dusk fell, I left the apartment and wandered aimlessly around the *quartier latin*. Returning home several hours later, I saw that the bookshop was lit up. From the opposite side of the street I observed my father, walking sentry-like up and down the length of the shop, pausing from time to time to trail his hand against the spines of books. This simple gesture seemed to contain everything my father normally kept hidden. I took it as a sign that in spite of lost hopes he was a not a broken man. Nor was he a man who had ever stopped loving his wife. In those few moments, watching him framed in the window, I was overcome with tenderness towards him.

For much of my childhood my mother had been wrapped in a cocoon of unwellness that was hard to enter. But children take love wherever they can find it – that is what I came to believe – and I managed to find love also in my mother, albeit in homeopathic dilution. Over time she gradually gave up speaking. She was no longer dependent on words, having moved beyond them. I marvelled at her silence, her self-containedness. When first I had learned of my mother's illness, I watched her carefully for signs of decline. Standing outside her room, I would listen for the sound of her breathing, and when I left for school in the mornings I took to putting her blue handkerchief in my bag – my childlike way of keeping her safe. If I looked after the handkerchief and kept it clean, fate would be cheated and she would stay alive. For several years she continued to suffer from a catastrophising imagination, the curse that meant she had to stay perpetually vigilant. In later life, however, a calm seemed to settle on her. At the same time, some of the light went out of her eyes and she shrank into herself. She no longer went to the bookshop. Mostly she sat alone, unspeaking, limbs taut, her head tilted oddly, as if her whole body could turn only on the axis of whatever it was that afflicted her. We must do what we can, said my father, to help make her whole again.

The following year, in the early days of spring, he made a small garden for her in the courtyard at the back of the bookshop. First he arranged for a delivery of rich black soil. Then he bought seeds and cuttings and a number of large earthenware pots. With immense patience, talking to her all the while, he showed her how to sow the seeds and pot the young plants into containers. Day after day he did this, and gradually she appeared to be comforted, as a child might be, by the repetition of it. Soon she began to sow seeds by herself and plant out the young flowers into the soil. The garden became her domain. It seemed to harness her fear and protect her from its worst effects. She was not exactly made whole again, but it was possible to believe that a kind of contentment was emerging. Not *bonheur* or *joie*, but *contentement*.

In time she acquired more pots and seed boxes. She grew aromatic herbs and scented roses, climbers and trailers. Eventually the courtyard was ablaze with colour and filled with sweet perfumes, each individual plant seeming to be an agent of pleasure for her. Regular customers at the bookshop made a point of visiting her and complimenting her success. When I came back from school she was always to be found in the garden – and not just sitting as she had done in her room, but busily doing something. She flinched sometimes when I spoke to her, like a frightened bird, making herself small, trying not to be seen. I liked to think it was less to do with her being afraid, and more because she was absorbed in her own world. Sometimes she would look at me, as if trying to remember if we had met, and if so where on earth could it have been. Do I know you? she would say. *Je vous connais?* Which made me hope that she was perhaps protected from the sort of suffering that comes from knowledge of the world. At other times, when she became aware of my presence, she would smile and I would know then she recognised me and was pleased to see me. Have you come to see my garden, *mon bébé*? She never said my name now, always *mon bébé*. Which made me think of the babies she'd lost and the plants she'd adopted, and whether they were connected. As she slipped farther and farther into herself, her world became horticultural. Plants and flowers were what mattered.

One day, not long before her death, she whispered to me: 'Sometimes I can feel myself dying, you know. I have to try and stop myself before it's too late. Once you start dying, it can be difficult to stop.' Her voice was thin and small, and her head shook from side to side like one of those dolls that hang in the back of cars. She stretched out her hands, palms upwards, as though giving in to mysterious forces at work. 'Do your plants ever die?' I asked her then, on an impulse, not meaning anything by it, just saying it for something to say. Yes, they did die, she said, but they couldn't help it. It was the love that killed them. The *love*? I repeated. This is my mother, I told myself. In a deep sense we were strangers to one another. 'Can you keep a secret, *mon bébé*?' As she beckoned me closer she told me that her plants could keep secrets. I bent down, close enough to feel her breath on my cheek. '*L'amour, c'est pas ce qu'on croit,*' she said – love is not what it seems. 'Other things, which are not love, live close by. A slight shift sideways can destroy everything.'

53

In the aftermath of Sanderson's death, Carrie came nearly every day to my place, spending an hour or so each time in the garage room. The connecting door was no longer kept locked, or even closed. She came and went freely. The trick with meditation, she said, was to know the darkness, to accept it, and with it the light. This time between us seemed to have its own special value, its own rhythms. Stay in the moment, I told myself. Don't let it pass. More than once during this time I thought how lucky, how undeserving, Sanderson had been to have shared his life with Carrie. And how disloyal it was to think this way.

For Carrie everything was both clouded and clarified by death. 'When you think about it,' she said one evening, sitting at the kitchen table, pressing flowers from the funeral into a book, 'love and death are the principal concerns in most people's lives. However you look at it, this is one of the verities.' She regularly went over the same ground, reliving particular scenes and conversations, getting nowhere. Of course, it was entirely possible for love and death to be quite separate things, she said, to enjoy a mere nodding acquaintance with each other during a normal lifespan. But it was more common for them to mingle, the one brushing against the other. 'A bit like ears of corn in the wind.' The worst was when they collided, she said, hemming you in, leaving you no time to prepare, no means of escape. This was how she had felt when they told her Harry was dead.

I myself tried not to talk about Sanderson. There was no need. Even in death he was always there in the room.

54

Meanwhile there was the dispiriting business of retranslating the lost essays. I had taken my computer to the service department at the university, but they could do nothing. The hard disk, they said, had suffered a 'heart attack' – they could not say why. The advice was to send my computer back to France. It was just possible that the supplier might have a component to 'jump-start' the disk. But they were not hopeful.

I bought a new laptop.

There was some irony in the fact that one of the lost essays was entitled *The Stoic*, in which Hume expressed the stark view that happiness was possible only through honest and hard work. In the second of the lost essays, *Of the Dignity of Human Nature*, Hume argued that people inclined towards morality if they held an optimistic view of human nature, not a pessimistic one. But it was the third, *Of the Delicacy of Taste and Passion*, that seemed to apply most tellingly to the immediate situation. According to Hume it was delicacy of passion that made people sensitive to life's joys and sorrows, while delicacy of taste made them sensitive to art.

As I worked on them for the second time I found it troubling that the translation did not come any more easily or quickly than it had the first time. I reconstructed what I could from my notes, but it was a slow, painful business. During this period I visited the cemetery more than usual, hoping to settle an unquiet mind. But the cemetery had become a meeting place for gay men, and more than once, at the gate of Hume's mausoleum, I found myself being propositioned.

55

The problem of Christmas loomed. Carrie said she felt oppressed by it. As far as she was able she tried to ignore it, avoiding the fairy lights and the Santa music, all the enforced jollity. It was a time to be got through, she said.

We spent part of Christmas day together, but it was a subdued affair. In the morning she had visited Alfie in the psychiatric unit, where she had been taken off guard by a special Christmas service. The bleakness occasioned by what she called *all that sweet Jesus nonsense* hung around her all day. It was something she would normally have gone out of her way to avoid, but this was a hospital at Christmas, and the options were understandably limited. The service had been sparsely attended – just a few family members and a handful of staff and patients, including Alfie, who had been 'allowed out' for Christmas Day. Though whether this was preferable to a locked cell, Carrie said bitterly, was highly questionable. Still, the lack of congregation had given the chaplain the chance to say: 'Where two or three people are gathered together, there I am in the midst of them.' Carrie laughed as she told me this, but it was a hollow laugh. I poured her a glass of wine, hoping to cheer her. The chaplain had all the usual faults of his vocation, she said, but he was a decent enough man and she did give him full marks for trying. She raised her glass theatrically: *The Christmas message is a message of hope*, she proclaimed, her voice studiedly clerical with weird undulations. I expect he was just doing his job, I said, hoping to put the subject to rest. But she was not quite done. During the sermon the chaplain had interpreted everything – every good thing, every bad thing, *every* damned thing – as a sign of God's plan. 'He was seeing signs *everywhere*,' she said, 'just like the inmates.' And yet he was free to leave the building afterwards, while they had to return to their rooms for treatment. What also distressed her was the fact that religion flourished on fear, and a psychiatric unit was an environment where fear was endemic. Not just the crazy fear of the patients – all the space invaders and the messianic messages – but the chill fear of their families, she said. I thought then of my mother's fear and her own crazed efforts to please God. People turned to religion in times of distress, Carrie said. They clutched at straws, desperate for answers – 'And what happens? They're fed pap.' What was *pap*? I asked. 'Oh, you know, baby food. Soft mush, stuff that's easy to swallow.' One of the things that had most attracted her to Harry, she said with a sudden gearshift, was his *unbelief*. 'Nothing, no amount of personal angst or distress would ever have shaken that.'

Sanderson was everywhere, as surely as if he'd returned from the dead. Every conversation came back to him. Sometimes I could see his bloated body floating before my eyes – which made me think of Ionesco's dreadful story about a bloated corpse growing continually in the next room until it fills the entire space.

56

Towards the end of January, when Edinburgh was in the grip of winter, Carrie told me she needed to get away. Winter in the city could be such a grey time. What she craved was colour. Would I come away with her? She didn't yet feel able to go away by herself. She would show me her island, off the west coast, the place she called home. February was a kinder month, full of the promise of spring. By then the days were beginning to stretch, and I would be able to sense the cloak of winter being lifted, she said. But what about work, I said, despising my self-control – there were only a few weeks left to me, I explained. Sometimes when we mean to say yes, we say no. What would have been wrong with telling her the truth: that I was thrilled to be asked? If I lost this chance it would be my own stupid fault.

But my chance was not lost. It could be a *working* holiday, she said. She would take her paints, I would take my books.

Some days later she called round again, this time flushed and in high spirits. The doctors had said that Alfie was definitely improving, that he was well enough to spend some time away from the unit – under supervision. She would love to take him to the island, she said. It was such a safe place, not threatening to him like the city. Would that be all right? Did I mind? This time I did not hesitate.

It took nearly a day to get to Carrie's island – several hours by road, a long ferry crossing, followed by a short ferry crossing, then another hour or so along narrow roads, with the silken sea visible at every point. We covered the last part of our journey on a rough track. The last time I had travelled in this car had been with Sanderson on the way to the river. It still smelled of pipe tobacco. No one mentioned him, but I felt sure each of us carried a sense of him. Alfie sat in the back, not saying much, looking out of the window, occasionally tracing patterns on the glass with his fingers. I had been nervous of meeting him, but I took to him straight away. I had imagined him subdued and withdrawn, dulled by the medication he needed to keep a hold on life. But he was alert, open to the world, intensely alive and interested in everything. His face was ever mobile and yet inscrutable, a lovely mystery waiting to unravel. There seemed to be no hard edges to him, and he still had his elfin looks – diminutive, a shock of auburn hair, bright green eyes and a kind of magical charm. 'His illness has changed him,' Carrie had told me before we set off, 'but many things about him have stayed the same. He's still sensitive and affectionate. And he's lost nothing of his humanity.'

By the time we arrived at the cottage, darkness had set in. In this part of the world night was as black as night could be, blacker than anything I had ever known. We pushed open the front door and a bell at the top of the jamb rang out, a delicate sound like a cow bell.

I woke next morning to the smell of coffee. Which signified another human being. Of course. The feeling that I was not alone spread through me like a narcotic. Before breakfast I went outside. The light was just breaking in the east, but already it was sending giant streaks across the sea – livelier than the previous day, its waves now tipped with white. The water was only a few metres from the cottage. I could hear it surging and drawing on the sand. As the light got stronger it was possible to make out two or three islands in the near distance, and beyond them, far away, the notched outline of the mainland, where we had boarded the first ferry. As I breathed in the air, purer than any air I had breathed before, Carrie appeared at my side with a mug of coffee. 'What do you think?' she said, taking my arm. 'Isn't it wonderful?'

'Breathtaking,' I said.

'Breathtaking and breathgiving – both at once.' She looked radiant. The light on her face was unearthly, beamed in from another planet.

The cottage had belonged to her grandfather. It was an old restored 'blackhouse' – the typical Outer Hebridean dwelling until well into the twentieth century, she explained. Families had lived in blackhouses with their livestock – animals at one end, people at the other, with the floor on a tilt so that all the dung, liquid and solid, remained in the lower end. 'You are sleeping in the lower end,' she said, laughing and throwing her head back, the way she'd done in her studio the first time we'd talked together. She told me that in her grandfather's time there had been no windows and no chimney in the cottage. Even so a peat fire had burned constantly in the middle of the room, with the smoke rising naturally through the thatch. 'It must have been a hard life,' I said, scarcely able to imagine the grimness of what she described. Perhaps so, she said, but it seemed also to have been a good life, for the blackhouses had been based on sound holistic living. The peat and the animal urine had acted as a natural antidote to lung disease and other illnesses. 'When chimneys were installed and animals removed, all in the name of civilisation,' she said, 'there were immediate outbreaks of tuberculosis and the like.' The local people had also begun to lose their skills and their knowledge – 'just like the Kalahari bushmen when all the modernising do-gooders turned up'.

Even with windows and no animals, the cottage was quite cramped. There were just two rooms: the 'animal room' – the small space where I worked and slept – and the 'everything room', for cooking and eating and sitting by the fire. In the everything room there was also a recess set high into the thick outside wall – this was Carrie's bunk, and although it looked too narrow, it had been where both her grandparents slept. Adjacent to the house there was a timber shed, anchored to the ground by four large stakes, and with windows on two sides looking to the north and east. My island studio, said Carrie. This was where she worked for the first half of the day. In the evenings it was given over to Alfie – 'that way he can be alone if he wants, without feeling he has to join in the whole time,' she said. The studio also had a bunk in the rafters. This had been Alfie's bed as a child, and he seemed genuinely pleased to be reunited with it.

During the first few days I was astonished by the sheer amount of weather. I had never experienced so much of it, certainly not in such quick succession, nor in a way that made me feel part of the huge elemental sweep. In Paris it was possible to live without noticing the weather, apart from the stifling heat in the metro in summer. Here none of it lasted for long, except perhaps the wind. I learned to keep looking to the vast western sky to see what was in store. Sometimes the rain battered the windows like handfuls of rice, but the clouds would suddenly fold back to disclose a huge sun. Even without sun there was always a radiant quality to the light, as there was with the sea colour – sometimes blue, other times a luminous green. The islands in the distance seemed mysteriously to come and go, peeping shyly through the mist or rising dramatically out of the seabed, one minute framed in strong clear light, the next disappearing behind a veil of soft rain.

Much of the time we sat in our own silence, broken only by the cry of the seabirds dipping and diving. 'You can hear yourself living here,' said Carrie, and I knew what she meant. Alfie spent his days collecting things from the beach, sometimes arranging them on the sand in striking collages. When the tide came in he would stand and watch his creation being taken back to the sea. Don't you mind? I asked him. No, he said, he found it exciting. For my own part I spent a lot of time looking at the rocks and the waves, trying to fix the spirit of this special place like a print on my memory.

One day while out on a walk the three of us got caught in a storm. The sky went suddenly dark and the wind whipped up the sand. Don't worry, Carrie said, it's only a squall. *Squall?* The way I pronounced this new word made her and Alfie laugh, and they started to run ahead, mother and son hand in hand, with me chasing, pretending to be offended. We ran all the way to the cottage, trying to beat the rain, which caught us on the home straight, blowing horizontally, coursing across our faces, leaking into our sleeves. By the time we arrived back we were madly whooping and yelling at the elements as we fell through the door in a heap, drenched in rain and laughter.

In the mornings Carrie painted in the shed as if she were possessed. Not by demons, but by good Hebridean spirits. Meanwhile in the animal room, I sat at my computer by the window, watching her. She had her back to me, flexing and rolling in the same attitude that I imagined had captivated Sanderson all those years ago in the Signet Library. Watching Carrie painting seemed to help with my own work. My routine had been all but abandoned and there were many distractions, and yet I was gliding through the essays. I even had the feeling that I had never worked so well. Each time I looked up and saw her at work by her easel, good thoughts bore in on me and I felt a deep contentment – *joie*, even. It occurred to me then that as a translator, or as an artist, it was possible to lead a quiet and honourable existence. There was no cheating involved, no double-crossing. No one was harmed in the process. Your integrity was all wrapped up in the words or in the brushstrokes.

It was strange to be in Carrie's Hebridean hideaway, with Alfie and without Sanderson – it was all so different and new, and yet it felt just as if it was meant to be. It was even stranger being part of a household, helping with domestic tasks, lighting fires, disposing of the rubbish, cooking dinner – in short, being with other people more fully than ever before. I was surprised to find myself coping – even a streak of toothpaste stuck to the basin had not troubled me. Carrie and I had become a couple, in a way. A pretend couple at least – if only because of an absence. All this I knew and understood. I wondered if she, who was used to absence, felt something of the same. Had Sanderson become just another person missing from her life? Another attenuated figure in her paintings?

In the afternoons we walked on the beach, picking up drift-wood, examining shells, looking in rock pools, all of my senses under wonderful assault. With the wind and the movement of the waves I sometimes felt myself pitching dizzily backwards, delighting in the sensation. One day I gathered a handful of tiny shells, shiny and delicate like porcelain, all folded in on them-selves but translucent all the same. Close your eyes and hold out your hands, I said, placing my treasure carefully in Carrie's out-stretched palms, wanting to be giving her something, everything. 'Cowries!' she said. 'Luck and prosperity!' Till now I had not realised it was possible to get such a thrill from all this. I was a stranger on this island, but it embraced me, pulled me in, atavis-tically, as if the island itself was stored somewhere in my genes. Above all I felt an ordinary connectedness to another human being, another way of life. Or rather, a *reconnecting* – to things I had forgotten, or never known. Or perhaps even to things that were already in me, passed down to me by my father, who had been part of this place. How could I have thought that only cities offered the possibility of living? 'The rest of the world doesn't take much notice of this island,' Carrie said on one of our walks. But that didn't matter – it was home to her. Nowhere else felt as intense. 'When I am here, it's as if there is no space between me and it.' The place had entered her as a child, she said, and it would be with her always. When you were by the sea, she said, everything, including your own life, was washed fresh twice a day. 'Even the sun and wind become part of you.'

The nearest shop, which had only basic provisions, was over a mile away, and we took it in turns to fetch supplies. At first I went along the main track, the way we had come by car. But Carrie showed me a short cut, not a path exactly, just a faint indentation in the *machair*, the soft dune grass blasted by the wet and the wind. 'This is called a *desire line*,' she said. 'Ah, another borrowing from *la belle France*,' I teased, adding with pretend swagger that when it came to desire the French were world experts. 'And *chemin du désir* sounds *much* better, don't you think?' It was in the shop that I first heard Gaelic spoken – so lovely and songful that I felt quite transported by it. Back at the cottage I came across the Lord's prayer in Gaelic framed on the wall. Our Father, Which art in heaven; Hallowed be thy name – *Ar n-athair a tha air nèamh: gu naomhaichear d'ainm*. These words looked hard for such a soft tongue.

In the evenings Alfie would lay out the day's findings from his devoted beachcombing. Watching him sorting shells and pebbles and driftwood into elaborate groupings, I recognised some of my younger self in him. When you grow up, for a time you forget who you once were, but whatever is strong in childhood never quite disappears. It can go underground for a while, but it's always there, lying in wait. Meanwhile Carrie and I would talk long into the night, mostly about her work and mine. We seemed to like finding common ground between us. It was best somehow to creep up on a translation, I said, as if you hadn't seen it before, as if it was being written for the first time. And she said that this was something she also tried to do with a painting, especially here on the island. 'I try to capture the energy of the place, without locking it in – that comes later,' she said. 'The paint itself reacts in different ways, bleeding and weathering into the canvas, and you make use of that until you reach a point when you know it's all coming together.' As she said this, she held her face to the light, and I thought at that moment that in knowing her I might become a better person, and that if this happened it would be on account of her.

At other times I told her about my favourite authors, surprising her one time by claiming that a good novel was like a small miracle. She gave me a quizzical look, as if to check whether I was serious. *Miracle?* she said. Only figuratively, I said, in that fiction allowed us to live lives other than our own. 'Provided it's well written, you're carried along, waiting for everything to unfold – even if you know in advance what's going to happen.' And every so often, I said, something emerged from a novel that could only be called truth – there was no other name for it. 'Which has a paradoxical ring to it, since of course fiction is made up, full of lies.' The best writing had particular rhythms, a particular music, I said, and this was often the single most difficult thing to convey in the translation. 'And often you can sense the sadness in the rhythms, but somehow it's not depressing. In fact it's uplifting in a curious way.' For a while Carrie said nothing, and I wondered if she felt as I did that something of the same applied to the three of us, there and then – an undercurrent of sadness, yes, but a sense too of everyone becoming whole again. As if reading my thoughts she motioned towards the shed where Alfie was busy sorting his beach pickings. 'I have a recurrent fantasy that this place can make him well. Not cure him of course – that *would* be a miracle. He won't ever be completely cured. But this is a healing environment.' During those magical weeks this notion took root in both of us and grew into a solid conviction. As it happened, one of the essays I was translating at that time was *Of Miracles*, in which Hume argues powerfully that the standard of evidence required to believe in miracles is very high, simply because they are against the laws of nature. *A wise man proportions his beliefs according to the evidence.* Yet my own 'evidence' was laid out before me. From my window I sometimes watched mother and son walking on the shore, the sun dancing on their faces, the wind in their hair. Occasionally Carrie would throw her head back in delight, or prod and push Alfie as if she were teasing him about something only the two of them could know. I savoured these moments, wishing I could slow them down and make them last for hours. It struck me then that loving a child must surely be one of the best expressions of what it is to love. I remembered that Sanderson had told me of the sour slick of jealousy he felt, but for me there was no trace of that – just a tenderness I had not known was possible till then. I also had a kind of heart-burning, a longing to be part of it all. I couldn't help wondering if I could be part of their lives, if Carrie and I together might give Alfie what he needed to flourish. And if in turn this might be a completion of myself. My heart felt full at the thought, but I didn't say the words out loud, for they couldn't yet be said. The future was set aside. Everything was of the moment.

Though the cottage was small, we were all respectful of each other's space. Which probably had to do with our familiar cell-like existences – Carrie in her studio, me at my desk, Alfie in his hospital room. We were all good at being alone, and for me the distance between us, like everything else, became exquisite.

There was a radiant directness to Alfie. 'Do *you* think I'm mad?' he asked me one day. He was sitting on the sand, throwing pebbles into a rock pool. Sometimes he came across as sharp and broken, like shards of glass wrapped carefully in newspaper.

'Does it matter what I think, Alfie?'

'It does to me,' he said.

'Well,' I paused, groping my way towards honesty but afraid of where it might take me, 'I was mad once. At about your age, in fact. I spent some time in a psychiatric unit – a bit like yours, I suppose.'

'Did you hear voices?'

'I thought I did. But it was just my own. That was scary too.'

One evening as we sat in the candlelight by the fire Carrie told me that she had not known what to expect of her painting during this time on the island. She had thought the change of scene – the clarity of the landscape and seascape, to say nothing of the light – all of this would have taken her in a new direction. But in essence there was very little that was different. This had surprised her. Everything had changed, but nothing had changed, she said. Her lilting voice washed all over me. One way and another, she said, her painting was still all about loss. 'The four men I have loved in my life have all gone.' I was briefly startled to hear she had loved as many as four men – and for a crazy moment I thought that I must be one of them and had to stop myself saying: *Don't worry, I'm here! I haven't gone!* But just then she began to list them: 'My father. The father of my son. My son. And now my husband.' She paused between each beloved, giving them equal weight. 'Two of them dead,' she sighed, 'and the two who are alive not really present in the world.' On the mantle over the fire, a candle sputtered and went out.

'I don't agree,' I said. 'Alfie is exceptionally present in the world.'

57

The thing that developed between us was so natural and benign that at first I did not know what to call it. Could it be love? My father had once said that love could look a lot like other things that were not love. Also, perhaps on account of my friend Antoine's behaviour, I had expected love to be anarchic, chaotic. But this was a gentle, tender thing – something soft and new, like a delicate plant unfolding. I did not want to think about it too much, for fear of spoiling it, frightening it away. In the meantime I saw it as a validation of something I had long wanted to believe: that there could exist between a man and a woman something beautiful and tender, unattended by needs and presumptions, the sort of encounter that could nonetheless reach beyond ordinary experience. It's so hard to get beyond your own story – this was one of the last things Sanderson had said to me. Whatever he had meant by it, I had the feeling that my own story was just beginning.

I went on translating, setting down line after line, like beautiful equations. David Hume was my constant companion, and through Hume I got nearer to my father. Running parallel to Hume's essays was an ongoing essay in my own head – a work in progress, though barely started, with sub-verbal twists and half-formed clauses, an essay that nonetheless was taking shape and had the possibility of reconfiguring the world and mending my relationship with it.

In the shaving mirror I saw my father look back at me. What do you think of me now? I asked the likeness. The mirror was dull and steamed up, so it was more like a sepia photograph in the process of development. My father had taken risks in his life, but what risk had I ever taken?

The nameless thing began to grow, filling all the available space. Whatever was happening was completely unstoppably itself. There were times when I thought it could not be contained, that it was in danger of submerging me or choking me. During those next days, and for a long time afterwards, I thought that my life might have begun only with her. I tried to concentrate on the impossibility of what was happening. But happiness kept breaking through. Not happiness in the sense that Sanderson had dismissed, but a sort of quiet joy. And each new dawn brought with it new promise.

All the while Sanderson was vivid in his absence. Everywhere I saw his hair sleeked back, his puckered skin. Even the hairy crabs' legs, washed up on the beach, reminded me of the wiry tufts sprouting from Sanderson's ears. The dead shift about, much as the living do.

The last full day on the island came round. The day was still and clear, the salt-wet winds of the previous days completely gone, the sun lying on the water like beaten gold. The rain had washed all the dust from the air, leaving quite breathtaking clarity, with thick enamelled frost all the way down to the shoreline. Even the distant islands looked as if they had been newly etched in the vitreous northern light. Further round the point, the waves rushed up the cliff face. And everywhere the sky reached all the way down to the rocks, filling in the gaps with long fingers of blue. I scrambled up the steep path till I reached the highest point. I wanted to take it all into myself – the huge sky, its dominating presence; and the immense sea, the reason for everything here. I had never known such magical days. How strange that this remote place had allowed me to feel part of the world. Everything had played into it – even the cold I could feel in my marrow.

From my high perch, the cottage down on the shore looked like a doll's house. I could see Carrie moving around outside, a Lilliputian version of herself, in a silent film. Was it love that I felt? I had been waiting for love all my life, so I believed. It was the missing shade of blue, an idea stretched beyond its limits. It would take only a moment *not* to fall in love, I thought, holding the moment briefly in my hand, before it slipped through my cold fingers and leaked away into the white sand.

58

Back in the fifth arrondissement it was hard to grasp that this was home. Everything was cast in an unfamiliar light. A short flight to Paris, and now the taxi was moving slowly through the chestnut and plane trees. I tried to submit to the metaphysics of familiarity – the wide boulevards, the *bouquinistes*, the penniless chic, the little *ruelles* as we drew nearer – but my rear-view mirror was filled with white sand and Carrie and the wind in her hair. On the ancient stairs up to my apartment, I thought of one of those wood beetles that you might hear on the solid beams above you on the ceiling. You didn't become fully conscious of it till it dropped dead on the floor in front of you.

Waiting for me in the hallway was a package – the lost data from my stricken computer. I steadied my hand before inserting the floppy disk into the new laptop, and slowly I began to read the old translations of the lost essays. They were so unlike the new versions that they might have been done by a different translator, a different person. Which, in a sense, was the case. Later I would carry out a detailed comparison, work out what to do – with the essays and with everything else. In the meantime I tidied my apartment, putting back all the things the way they had been before a stranger touched them.

Acknowledgements

I would like to thank the French academic Gilles Robel, who from the beginning supported the idea at the centre of this novel with enthusiasm and practical advice. He is the real-life translator of David Hume's essays (Presses Universitaires de France, 2001), but there is no similarity, actual or intended, between him and my fictional narrator. I am indebted to Andrée Erdal and Hazel Duncan for correcting my French, Dr Douglas Fowlie for advice on psychiatric matters and Nick Erdal for passing on his expertise in fishing and fly-tying. Grateful thanks also to my wonderful agent Jenny Brown, to my inspired editor Richard Beswick and, of course, to the man at home.